THE HOWLING STONES

BY ALAN DEAN FOSTER

Published by Ballantine Books:

The Black Hole
Cachalot
Dark Star
The Metrognome and Other Stories
Midworld
Nor Crystal Tears
Sentenced to Prism
Splinter of the Mind's Eye
Star Trek® Logs One–Ten
Voyage to the City of the Dead
. . . Who Needs Enemies?
With Friends Like These . . .

THE ICERIGGER TRILOGY:
Icerigger
Mission to Moulokin
The Deluge Drivers

THE ADVENTURES OF FLINX OF THE COMMONWEALTH:
For Love of Mother-Not

The Tar-Aiym-Krang
Orphan Star
The End of the Matter
Bloodhype
Flinx in Flux
Mid-Flinx

THE DAMNED
Book One: A Call to Arms
Book Two: The False Mirror
Book Three: The Spoils of War

THE HOWLING STONES

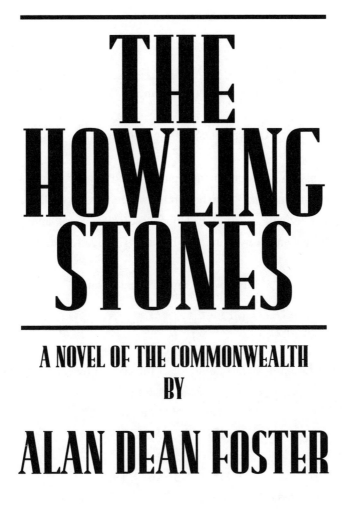

A NOVEL OF THE COMMONWEALTH
BY

ALAN DEAN FOSTER

BALLANTINE BOOKS · NEW YORK

A Del Rey® Book
Published by Ballantine Books

Copyright © 1997 by Thranx, Inc.

http://www.randomhouse.com

Library of Congress Catalogue-in-Publication Data
Foster, Alan Dean, 1946–
The howling stones : a novel of the commonwealth / by Alan
Dean Foster.
p.   cm.
ISBN 0-345-38375-3
I. Title.
PS3556.0756H69   1997
813'.54—dc21   96-47368
                                           CIP

Manufactured in the United States of America

First Edition: January 1997

10   9   8   7   6   5   4   3   2   1

CHAPTER
1

People tended to overlook Pulickel Tomochelor in a crowd.

It was something he'd grown used to. He'd always been overlooked: in academia, in sports, at social gatherings. Only a few unusually perceptive instructors had taken note of his singular abilities. These he'd paid close attention to, and by cleaving to them, he had been correspondingly raised up.

His accomplishments were never spectacular but always solid, satisfying without standing out. He was, in short, that most valued of all commodities in both business and government: the reliable employee without a personal agenda.

And yet there was enough there, determination compensating for lack of brilliance, for him to be called upon more than once to deal with problems that others could not solve. Where they could not succeed, Pulickel Tomochelor invariably produced results. From this he took, as was his manner, a quiet instead of boisterous satisfaction. Not for him a plethora of medals or awards, not for him applause during multiple personal appearances or the rapt attention of the media. A commendation in his official record was recognition enough. Nor did he disdain the occasional bonus.

There had been a woman once, too, to offer praise and support. She had moved on, leaving behind a confusion of memories leavened with vague dissatisfaction. Domesticity was the sole task at which he had failed; the only matter left inconclusive in his life. It rankled and left him unfulfilled inside. As with the responsibility, the fault was not entirely his, but it ate at him nonetheless. He stored it in a far recess of his mind and moved on, concentrating on his work and his career, which by all accounts were far more successful than any selective component of his personal life.

Keeping busy was part of it. His schedule allowed little time in which to develop a social life, much less raise a family, and the nature of his work mitigated against long-term relationships. It was hard enough to sustain intimacy when one was sent to different parts of the same world and well-nigh impossible when constantly on the move from world to world.

Other men and women managed to establish and maintain long-term unions, but they usually worked together. Pulickel preferred to operate alone, with his thoughts his sole companion. Or so he frequently strove to persuade himself. While the sociology of other beings opened for him like ripening fruit, the actions and reactions of representatives of the opposite gender of his own species remained as impenetrable as the core of a neutron star, and often weighed on him equally as heavy.

There was a lurch as the shuttle skewed sideways and the pilot's voice sounded apologetically over the cabin speaker. A couple of passengers grumbled. Senisran being a frontier world, there weren't many of them. Save for a few barely developed diplomatic communities and a smattering of isolated scientific outposts linked by satellite relay, the world expanding in the viewport off to his left was populated solely by a substantial but scattered native population. The locals raised no objections to the relay system because they couldn't see it and didn't know it was there anyway, their knowledge of astronomy being limited to that which could be observed by the naked seni eye.

Pulickel shifted in his seat as much as the landing harness would allow. He was shorter than the Commonwealth average, slim but well built, his olive-hued skin reflective of his ethnic heritage. His features were small, fine even, and distinctly nonthreatening. Similar in appearance to the superb wood carvings his Javanese ancestors had turned out in quantity, he revealed his inner humanity only when he smiled, his teeth a slash of perfect white like an ivory inlay set among paduk wood. He did not turn the eyes of attractive women, but neither did they find him displeasing to look upon. His desert-dry personality generally took care of any initial interest, filtered through speech that was always proper, polite, and reflective of an advanced education.

His eyes were small, black, and active, his hair black, long, and combed straight back. Pressed as if in preparation for a formal dinner, his field shorts and short-sleeved shirt collapsed in a jumble of angles against the less disciplined curves of his body. An experienced traveler, he'd brought one case only. It rested snug in back, in the cargo bay, and if properly looked after contained everything he would need no matter the length of his stay.

He spared yet another glance for the attractive middle-aged woman seated on the aisle two rows in front of him. It was always difficult when they were taller than you, he reflected, and many were. Unfortunately, he did not possess the drive necessary to overcome his perceived handicap. As a result, he had not spoken to her since boarding, and doubtless would not speak to her when they disembarked. Experience had shown him that attractive single women preferred their men tall, muscular, slightly uglified, and dangerous. He was none of those things.

With a sigh he turned to the port and studied the atmosphere through which the shuttle was dropping rapidly. One day he'd find someone, he told himself. One day when he had time to look and his work didn't interfere. Meanwhile he would have to content himself with the accolades of superiors and colleagues, which he received in ample quantity.

The sky outside darkened and Pulickel thought immediately of inclement weather. Again the shuttle bounced and for a second time the pilot was apologizing.

"Sorry. We just ran past a flock of cemacerotic gliders. At least, that's what I'm told they were. Minor evasive maneuvers were in order. We're descending and now they're slightly above us and to port. Those of you on that side may still be able to see them."

Everyone on the left side of the shuttle leaned up against their respective ports. Among the thick clouds overhead could be seen rapidly vanishing flaps of vast membranous wings. Pulickel recalled his weeks of studyprep on Senisran and its natives, flora, and fauna. The cemacerotic gliders were enormous aerial fliers who lived by skimming the surface of Senisran's seas for plankton-size life-forms, straining them through gigantic beaks that were lined with a substance not unlike the baleen of a whale. Living in small colonies on the peaks and crags of the highest islands, they were inoffensive, harmless creatures—unless one happened to run into you. Such accomplished soarers were they that some biologists suspected they often circumnavigated the globe without ever touching land.

Recently discovered Senisran was an ocean planet, not unlike the long-settled and well-known Cachalot. In lieu of any continental landmasses, the globe-girdling seas were spotted with thousands upon thousands of islands: some isolated, some clustered tightly together, most strung out like the strands of broken necklaces in hundreds of individual archipelagoes. A few were sizable but none especially impressive, the largest being about half the size of Earth's Madagascar. All save the northern- and southernmost were hot, though the humidity varied with location and latitude. There were no polar ice caps on Senisran.

On these innumerable island groupings dwelt the native population, organized into hundreds of different tribes, clans, associations, and alliances, each with its own government, social system, religion, and morality. It was this riot of cultural diversity that made formal contact between offworlders and locals a difficult and time-consuming proposition. Not only was a planetary government nonexistent, the aboriginal seni had yet to conceive of the idea of nation-states. In some cases, on small isolated islands, visitors making contact were reduced to signing treaties with the representatives of individual extended families, whereupon they would have to begin negotiations all over again with the inhabitants of the next island.

As if things weren't complicated enough, Senisran had been discovered simultaneously by the Commonwealth *and* the AAnn Empire. The result was that both sides had representatives on the planet, each attempting to secure covenants of friendship and alliance with as many of the native governments as possible. On a number of island clusters, contact teams operated in direct competition with one another. It was a frustrating, time-consuming process made all the more difficult by the sense of competition that existed between contact teams.

Local arrangements complicated matters even further. Humanx and AAnn representatives sometimes found themselves expected to go to war with neighboring islanders as soon as they formalized a treaty with a set of new friends, who, it subsequently developed, had formal alliances with three other island groups, but not the one just over the horizon. Or ancient family quarrels entered into the negotiating process. There was nothing straightforward about any of it.

Which was one reason why Pulickel had been sent for.

Neither the Commonwealth nor the Empire would take up arms on behalf of any native. That was strictly against the rules of contact agreed upon by both sides. They could only stand by and watch helplessly as treaties settled through arduous and difficult negotiation frequently came apart under the strain of local conflict, whereupon all would have to be completely renegotiated from scratch. It was a diplomatic nightmare, none of which would have had any ramifications beyond those tribes immediately involved save for two things: Senisran was strategically located in a region claimed both by the Commonwealth and the Empire, and it offered an assortment of valuable commodities actually worth transporting through spaceplus. It was valuable both from a politico-military and commercial standpoint.

Certainly the natives were willing to cement formal contracts and to open trade, he mused as the shuttle began its final approach. According to all the reports he'd perused, only a few island groups were openly hostile to outside contact. Since these more hostile natives expressed an equal dislike for humans, thranx, and AAnn, they could for now be passed over. They, too, would come around once they saw the advantages that accrued to their neighbors through contact with more technologically advanced off-world civilizations.

With Senisran boasting a planetwide insufficiency of flat, dry land, the shuttle set down on unsinkable pontoons, momentarily disappearing within a traveling fountain of its own making. As the craft slowed, Pulickel considered how best to acquire an assortment of the remarkable native handicrafts for which the seni were rapidly becoming known. He'd promised at least a dozen colleagues back home a representative sample each. Original art was one commodity that technology had yet to supplant and was therefore an item highly amenable to interstellar trade.

It being an ancient truism that commerce treads hard on the heels of exploration, many of the great Commonwealth trading houses already had representatives at work on Senisran. Dozens of others pressed the appropriate government departments for access credentials, eager to trade with the locals for their exquisite wood, shell, and bone carvings, necklaces, and sculpture. It seemed as if every island group had it own distinctive style, each more striking and beautiful than the next. The acquisitive AAnn were no less enthusiastic. Such trade was carefully regulated, lest the seni procure technology too advanced for their society to absorb.

In addition to an astonishing range of handicrafts, Senisran also offered an expanding selection of unique comestibles. The well-off of Earth, New Riviera, and other sophisticated worlds were and had always been willing to pay outrageous prices for new tastes, new sensations. Any dozen half-competent companies could introduce new electronic gadgets onto the market, but a new fruit or vegetable was infinitely more valuable.

It was endlessly frustrating to the backlog of commercial interests to have to wait for official contact to be established with each island or island group, but it was the responsibility of Commonwealth authority to see to it that trade and interchange proceeded smoothly and without acrimony. Commerce was not allowed to proceed until a point scout had established formal relations with the group of natives in question. First-person first-contact was a delicate and sensitive undertaking that called for highly trained individuals with plenty of experience.

Individuals like Pulickel Tomochelor.

He was a specialist's specialist, whose talents were in demand throughout the frontier. As there was only one of him, his time had to be rationed. He had devoted his career to unraveling seemingly insoluble conundrums. As a consequence of his success, it was going on ten years since he'd been given anything resembling an easy assignment. He didn't mind. It made his personal sense of satisfaction all the greater.

He smiled to himself as the shuttle turned to port and entered the harbor at Ophhlia, the principal Humanx base on Senisran. In exchange for its use, the increasingly sophisticated locals received a hefty monthly fee. A ridge of high mountains ran from east to west along the midline of the sizable island, protecting the harbor and its thriving facilities from the daily cloudbursts that blew up out of the south.

Personally, Pulickel always sympathized with the confusion that was common to undecided native groups, who were by far in the majority. Beset by endless requests and frequently contradictory promises from two different sides and species, whom were they to believe: human or AAnn? From the native viewpoint, who held the real power and offered the most benefits? With whom should they ally themselves? In such critical negotiations, the skill of each side's on-site negotiator was paramount.

Where Pulickel shone was in his ability to understand alien cultures and an alien point of view. He might never reach the exalted rank of Counselor, but in another ten years or so he could see himself in charge of the entire xenology department, passing judgment on the reports of others and handing out assignments from a spacious office high atop the Science Tower in Denpasar. Solving the problem for which he'd been sent to Senisran would serve to carry him a few steps farther toward that goal.

The distant whistle from the shuttle's engines faded as it coasted to a stop inside the enclosed, climate-controlled landing dock. Though they were now in a sealed environment, the climate processors could only mute the heat and humidity, not eliminate them entirely. Suitable comments were exchanged among the passengers as they disembarked. Pulickel kept silent, measuring the conditions against what he'd been led to expect.

Through the transparent tube that encased the walkway, disembarking passengers could see the shuttle floating behind them on brilliantly clear water. Beyond the polarized, diffusing material, tropical sunlight illuminated the jumble of low-rise buildings that comprised orderly Ophhlia. It flashed green off the mountaintops beyond. Even within the disembarkation lounge, the pervading smell was of damp green growing things: the musk of fresh soil. Inside, the treated, mechanically massaged atmosphere was cool but heavy.

He gave a mental shrug. He'd spent time on more than a dozen alien worlds, some hotter, some colder, a few where the atmosphere would kill anyone who tried to breathe it. Compared to the average, the air of Senisran felt like home. After the long journey out from Earth, he was eager to leave the shallow trappings of imported civilization behind and get out into the field. He looked forward to it much as another man might look forward to a date.

"Tomochelor?" A rough-looking, stocky, heavily bearded individual broke from the small crowd to block Pulickel's path. He wore a duty uniform of green shorts, shirt, and sandals. Insignia decorated his sleeves and shoulders. "Eric Train. On behalf of the department, welcome to Senisran." He extended a hand and flagged Pulickel's up and down. "No hand luggage?"

"No. I just have the one case."

"That'll be waiting for you in the baggage area." He turned and Pulickel fell in step alongside him. "I've seen your schedule. You have a couple of days here in town before you have to head out to the site. I'd be glad to show you around."

"I'd enjoy that." Actually, Pulickel wasn't sure that he would, but he'd learned early on in his career that when traveling, no amount of research, no matter how thorough, could substitute for the knowledge of someone local. While Train was exposing him to the few simple pleasures Ophhlia had to offer, Pulickel would patiently pump him for more practical information.

"How was your flight?"

"Like any KK-drive journey. Pleasant enough. Quiet and busy. I had plenty of time to study and to work with the language synapse. It's a long way from Earth." They left the busy main atrium and turned down a side corridor. "I must say that based on everything I've read I don't quite see why my presence is so actively required."

Train put a comradely arm around the other man's shoulders, a gesture that Pulickel disliked but had grown used to. "Let's just say that Parramat's a special problem that needs a specialist's attention." The newly arrived xenologist knew as much but politely allowed Train the pleasure of explication.

The terminal was busier than Pulickel expected. Though Senisran was a far-off, recently discovered world, Ophhlia was a busy place. Things were happening here.

"After the initial contacts," Train was saying, "the xenology department was able to put together a few basic contact templates. With minor variations for individual island groupings these have worked pretty well—until Parramat."

"So all the reports say." Pulickel commented only to show that he was paying attention.

"But these Parramati, they're different." Train was shaking his head dolefully. "Not physically, of course. As far as appearance, physical ability, and intelligence, they're no different from any of the other seni. By the way, except for the overtly warlike tribes, the natives are nice folks—for semihumanoid aboriginal aliens. And even the most aggressive tribes are usually ready to sit down and have a chat or share a meal before they paddle off to bash somebody else's heads in.

"Generally speaking, we're getting along well with them. Staying a few jumps ahead of the AAnn. You know the lizards: they tend to be kind of impatient, whereas the seni are a species that likes to take its time. It reflects the nature of their environment. That's not to say that if we weren't here that every one of them wouldn't readily align themselves with the AAnn."

Pulickel nodded. The AAnn were always in a hurry, expecting a yes-or-no answer to a question the first time it was asked. Establishing formal relations with new species often required a good deal more patience. This the AAnn had learned, but their natural instincts still had a tendency to frustrate their own efforts in that area. As a result, the Commonwealth had forged ahead in its efforts to secure alliances with Senisran's scattered and highly individualistic tribes. Struggling to catch up, the Empire had poured considerable resources into its local efforts. In territories where the locals remained uncommitted, such as the Parramat Archipelago, they were just as active as the representatives of the Commonwealth.

The Parramati had shown themselves to be wary of the offers from both sides, as was to be expected. Like primitive sentients anywhere, they didn't want to make the mistake of allying themselves with a weaker party. So they listened patiently to the presentations of both visitors, human and AAnn alike, and asked questions, and debated among themselves, and put off making any kind of final decision. Pulickel was being brought in to hurry things along.

"You know, of course, why we're making a greater effort than usual to bring the Parramati quickly into the Commonwealth fold." Train preceded Pulickel through a security door.

The slight newcomer nodded. The efforts to which his host was referring had less to do with the welfare of the inhabitants of the Parramat Archipelago than with what lay beneath their several dozen islands. Specifically, an unknown number of rare earth deposits of exceptional commercial value, from niobium and yttrium to obscure minerals with names even Pulickel couldn't pronounce.

Train was patting him on the shoulder. "You know, I envy you, going out to Parramat. Resolve this one and you'll really make a name for yourself."

"I have a name," Pulickel replied quietly. He wanted to shrug the other man's arm off his shoulders but restrained himself. False conviviality always made him queasy. He hated attending parties, even parties of two.

Instead of being offended by his guest's rejoinder, Train's grin expanded. "All right, so this'll help you enhance it. Obviously, I don't have to tell you how important the assignment is." He lowered his voice and his bushy eyebrows did acrobatics. "There's also the matter of your local support, someone who's already on site. I could tell you how many local xenologists clamored for this duty just because of that, but I don't want to intimidate you when you've just arrived." He chuckled. "Last poor schmuck I had to send out on contact duty ended up with an old thranx for company. That'd be okay for a few months, but for a year . . ." He let the implication trail away, then added, "Your position will be . . . different."

Pulickel made himself smile at his host. "Do not worry about me. I don't intimidate easily. What's the problem? Is the support individual in question particularly disagreeable?"

Train gave him a funny look. "You'll see."

"I find I'm able to get along with just about any personality type. It's a necessary skill when one is working for long periods of time in comparative isolation. I'm sure this individual and I will come to an accommodation. Could we pick up my case now, please? I'm anxious to see if everything's arrived in one piece."

Train was still grinning. "It should be waiting for us at Transport."

Pulickel debated whether to press his guide for additional details about his field support but decided he'd find out soon enough. As he'd told Train, he wasn't concerned. Young, old, male, female, thranx, or human, he'd worked with them all, often under far more difficult conditions. It came naturally to him. He was such a non-threatening personality that even initially hostile colleagues ended up adopting a protective attitude toward their new colleague. While he wasn't exactly a barrel of laughs, it was hard to pick a fight with someone who always attended strictly to business. The result was a mutually productive working environment, which was what the xenologist always strove for no matter where he was assigned.

Train's underlying urgency was no surprise. Pulickel had read the relevant reports, every one of them. Commonwealth commercial interests wanted the vacillating situation on Parramat resolved so they could move in and exploit the exceptional ore deposits that lay beneath the archipelago as soon as possible—in an environmentally and socially sensitive manner, of course. It was emphasized that the Commonwealth and not the AAnn should be the ones to do this.

Though he thoroughly understood the situation, Pulickel had no intention of hurrying his work. He would take his time and do his job properly. Not that he expected it to prove especially troublesome. A couple of months at most, he'd decided when he'd finished the last of the field reports. A couple of months and the commercial interests in Ophhlia would have their treaty of agreement and he would be on his way back to Earth, awash in accolades and official commendations. It had always been thus. Mentally he was already readying himself for his next assignment.

Meanwhile he expected as well as hoped to enjoy his stay on Senisran. New worlds and new alien cultures were endlessly fascinating. While certain patterns held true across the cosmos, every sentient species was different and presented its own unique problems to those charged with establishing formal contact. It would be interesting not only to meet the Parramati but to see how their culture differed from that of their fellow seni. Certainly he would acquire enough material for one or two formal papers, which when published would only add to his growing reputation.

The compact transport vehicle was waiting just outside the terminal, and his travel case, intact and unbreached, had been stowed securely in the rear storage compartment. Using a remote key, Train opened the single door and followed him inside. Cool, dehumidified air blew from several vents.

"I'm looking forward to showing you around." Train nudged his guest in the ribs. "Ophhlia ain't fancy, but with all the money that's pouring in here we've managed a few amusements."

"I can imagine," Pulickel responded amiably. He was more than familiar with the kinds of "amusements" common to newly contacted worlds—which was why he couldn't wait to be on his way.

CHAPTER

2

Though he'd believed himself fully prepared, the journey from Ophhlia to Parramat still took longer than he'd expected. He knew he shouldn't have been surprised. Distances on Senisran were substantial, and Parramat was located several thousand kilometers from Ophhlia.

As the low-altitude transport jet screamed through cloud-flecked sky, he watched the landscape change beneath him. Given the inherent limitations of Senisrani terrain, the panorama varied considerably. There were low islands and high islands, islands with marked volcanic craters and islands with heavily eroded ridges and peaks. He saw islands with deserts and islets so cloaked in green growth that no bare earth was visible. There were blindingly white atolls and blue holes, sandbars aligned like folds of pale skin beneath shallow turquoise waters, tiny islets strung like pearls on a necklace, and isolated exposed seamounts devoid of life. All were corpuscles aswim in blue blood. The largest took no more than a couple of minutes to overfly.

It was impossible to count them all, and indeed, ongoing surveys added dozens of new landmasses to the Senisran total every week. By no means were all inhabited, or even visited by the natives, but even the most inconsequential found its way onto the list. Geo-Survey was very thorough.

The AAnn were compiling their own overview. Chraara, their main base, was fortuitously located on the opposite side of the planet from Ophhlia, on a low, sandy island only an AAnn would find attractive. From there contact parties fanned out, attempting to secure the friendship of manifold native societies. Occasionally they found themselves competing with human scouts for local affections. At such times a frosty politeness was established and maintained. It was all very formal, very restrained, and deadly serious. Beneath the diplomatic etiquette lay a brutal competition for influence with the locals.

In the race to conclude treaties, neither side had any natural advantages. The seni were perfectly happy to listen to the supplications of both. As to local conditions, the AAnn handled the heat better while humans enjoyed a greater tolerance for the high humidity. Physiologically, the thranx were better suited to Senisrani conditions than either human or AAnn, but their dislike of open water rendered them unenthusiastic when it came to accepting assignments on an island world, and the semihumanoid natives found them unpleasant to look upon. So it fell upon humans and AAnn to compete in the face-to-face negotiations.

"There it is." Even as he pointed, the pilot banked to starboard and descended to give his passenger a better view. "Parramat."

Pulickel had been on many similar craft, but while seasickness held no worries for him, aerial maneuvers always left him feeling slightly queasy. He would be relieved when they were down.

The mass of islands and islets rising from the azure sea was in no way remarkable. As near as Pulickel could tell, it differed only slightly from the thousands of similar islands they had overflown on the long flight out from Ophhlia.

The pilot proceeded to circumnavigate the entire archipelago, pointing out the thirty-six main islands and the occasional important minor group that had been dismissed by Survey with a collective name. Pulickel did his best to pay attention. To the north lay the archipelago of Ririroarak, to the west Mosiniatan, to the south Bebat, and to the east the close-packed island groups of Komapau, Seriseri, and Apla. Other clusters lay farther afield. All were inhabited, but thus far only Ririroarak and Seriseri had been visited by representatives of the Commonwealth. The Department of Xenology had many demands on its time and resources. Senisran received its fair share of attention, but no more.

"You know that the AAnn have a station here, too." As the pilot maintained their descent, Pulickel did his best to match the view outside with the survey map of Parramat he'd committed to memory. The two lined up adequately in his mind, except that the reality was far more beautiful than the recordings he'd been given to study.

"I've seen the prospectus," he informed his guide. "It doesn't matter. Their base is on an island in the far north of the group. I don't expect their presence to affect my work."

The pilot grunted softly. "Hope not. I reckon trying to make sense of one island culture after another is hard enough without the lizards making things more difficult than they already are. Personally, the less I have to do with them, the better I like it." In response to a nudge on a switch, there was a whine from the belly of the craft as her landing pontoons deployed.

"They're not lizards." As the g-forces on him increased modestly, Pulickel shifted uneasily in his harness. "They're far more closely related to the extinct order *dinosauria*, being warm-blooded and possessing distinctive characteristics of their own. The resemblance to terrestrial lizards is purely superficial."

"Yeah, right." His attempt at casual camaraderie thus rebuffed, the pilot's voice returned to neutral. "Hang on. Might be a little bumpy setting down. The lagoon's ten kilometers wide and the water inside is flat calm, but afternoon winds can be tricky."

Pulickel went silent, wondering if the pilot was being honest or if he was simply tired of trying to make friends with his stuffy passenger. Not that it mattered one way or the other. They wouldn't be seeing one another again for some time, if ever.

Banking sharply, they made one overfly of the landing site to check local conditions. Pulickel's view filled with water in a dozen amazing shades of blue and green, all enclosed within a huge lagoon ringed with low islets composed of largely uncolonized sand. Although a fair proportion of the material was a familiar white, in many places it was a startlingly bright red or yellow. This reflected its origin in aqueous alien growths that, while analogous in form and lifestyle to communal Terran corals, contained a high proportion of silicon as opposed to the more common calcium. The result was sand that was not only differently and more brightly colored but extraordinarily reflective, and reefs whose component structures tended to be sharp and angular rather than soft and rounded.

A single sharp bounce and they were down. Garrulous the pilot might be, but he knew his business. Backjets roared, fighting to reduce the ship's speed and making conversation impossible. Ahead of the slowing craft, several dozen silvery, nearly transparent fleratii exploded from the surface of the lagoon, fluttered fluted fins, and dispersed toward the eastern horizon. From a distance they suggested a fistful of fairy dust scattered upon the sea.

Pulickel knew that Senisran's single world-girdling ocean boasted creatures that in variety and numbers put those of Earth to shame. Not all were as beautiful as the fleratii, whose glistening transparent skins scattered rainbows in their wake. There were thousands of forms glimpsed but as yet undescribed, and millions more to be discovered. The preparatory materials he had studied so assiduously prior to arrival had acquainted him with only a minimum of the most notable examples. What stood out foremost in his mind about Senisran's ocean life was that unlike on Earth and Cachalot, here invertebrate life-forms were dominant. One could fish but would do better with a basket than a hook.

As they slowed, the pilot aimed for a small, sandy cay located inside the lagoon. A second craft was already drawn up on the picture-perfect beach, its silvery-gray exterior at odds with the reddish-white surface on which it rested. Green crowns burst from the tops of three gently curving, blue-black boled trees. Their stiff, starlike crests provided the only shade on the little islet.

Beneath the largest of these hearty growths, Pulickel noted as the pilot cut the engine and they coasted into the shallows, was some kind of fold-up lounge. On the lounge lay a figure, which due to their angle of approach seemed to be mostly legs. The pilot chuckled.

"Your field support."

Mentally organizing his neatly packed gear, the xenologist turned to him. "Something funny about that?"

"Funny? Naw, nothing funny about that." And he chuckled again. "I guess there's worse fates than being stuck on an island for months on end with only Fawn Seaforth for company."

"Why? Does she have a reputation for inhospitableness?"

The pilot pursed his lips before replying. "I expect you'll find out, since you're the first person who's been assigned here to do more than temporary construction or delivery work." Both men lurched slightly forward as the ship's pontoons grounded on smooth sand.

"Yes, I suppose I will. I'm not worried, you know. No matter how obstinate or difficult they are at first, I've always been able to ingratiate myself with whomever I've been assigned to work with." For some reason this prompted the pilot to chortle even louder.

"Let's go." Grinning at some private thought, he wiped at one eye. "I'll unload that precious case of yours."

As the cockpit canopy slid back into the body of the transport, the landing ramp automatically deployed, coming to rest on a patch of dry, red sand that glittered like powdered rubies. Pulickel preceded the pilot, who was busy removing his passenger's travel case from the cargo hold.

As the xenologist marched down the ramp and into the heat, the figure reclining on the lounge raised up to get a better look at him. A hand waved in greeting. He ignored it, his first concern being for his kit.

He helped the pilot position the heavy plastic box on the sand. It contained everything of a personal and professional nature that he expected to need for the next six months. If anything had arrived damaged, it would take at least that long to replace it.

The one thing he wasn't concerned about was clothing. You didn't need much on Senisran. Though he'd been outside the air-conditioned cockpit for only a few minutes, he was already beginning to sweat. After weeks on a climate-controlled KK-drive ship in space-plus, it would take him awhile to get acclimated anew to tropical surroundings. As soon as they arrived at Parramat station he intended to shed as much of his attire as possible.

From a small pool in the sand he splashed a little water on his face. Warm on contact, it cooled him as it evaporated. What slipped into his mouth, while not drinkable, was mild to the taste, Senisran's world ocean having a lower salt content than those of Earth. There were no continents here to erode and replenish the seas with rivers of dissolved minerals.

Once the travel case was placed to Pulickel's satisfaction, the pilot looked longingly toward the lounge and its single occupant, who showed no inclination to leave her shady spot and come to greet them. Obviously disappointed, he bade his ex-passenger farewell and good luck before returning to his craft.

Pulickel stood just above the water's edge and watched as the stubby transport's engine whined back to life. Backing out of the shallows, the compact craft pivoted until it was facing southward. The jets roared, water rooster-tailed, and in a moment it was lifting clear of the glassy surface, climbing steadily into a cloudless sky. It circled once over the islet and, like a fleeing dragonfly, vanished into the distance.

Pulickel stared at the place where it had disappeared until he could no longer hear the fading rumble. As his eyes dropped, a dozen shafts of dark blue erupted from the water some thirty meters out in the lagoon. Averaging two meters in length, they looked like Olympic javelins equipped with multiple exhaust pipes. They were followed by something that resembled a flattened disk of barbed wire. It landed just short of where the javelins had reentered the water. In this hopscotching fashion, prey and predator made their way across the lagoon.

Only when all was quiet again did he kneel to inspect the lower half of his case. It was wet, but only on the outside. The unit was air- as well as watertight.

Straightening, he turned his attention to the three trees and the lounge beneath. Since his support seemed less than eager to make his acquaintance, he started up the gentle slope to introduce himself. She ought to come down to meet him, he thought. This wasn't the best way to begin a long-term working relationship. Mindful of his self-assured boast to the pilot, he resolved not to make an issue of this minor breach of protocol. At least, not right away.

He halted beneath the shade of the first tree and studied the portable flex-lounge. Fashioned of an aerogel composite, it looked as if its occupant was lying on an illusion. As his eyes adjusted, he saw that she was something of an illusion herself. Having worked with hundreds of specialists and contact personnel on a dozen alien worlds, he was prepared for almost anything.

He was not prepared for Fawn Seaforth.

But then, no one ever was.

Putting aside the chill-cup she'd been holding, she swung her legs off the side of the lounge and rose to greet him, hand extended. As she turned from the sun, her wraparound eyeshades lightened from dark to neutral so that he could see her eyes. They were bright blue.

"Hi! I'm Fawn Seaforth. And unless Dispatch has fouled up again, you're Pulickel Tomochelor."

He swallowed. "Pleasure to meet you, Seaforth. You—you're out of uniform."

She laughed, a wonderful, melodious sound that the breeze caught and cast out over the lagoon, as if she were trolling for poets. For an instant, the air in the immediate vicinity was as full of life as the sea below.

"Actually, as you can see, I'm just about out of everything." She spread her arms wide to reveal what he could already see: that the bathing costume she was wearing would fit comfortably in any pocket of his shorts.

"When I'm by myself, which is all of the time except when I'm making a supply pickup, I rarely wear anything. It's just too damn hot. Of course, I wouldn't think of wearing anything remotely like this in Ophhlia, but this isn't Ophhlia. This is Parramat. The natives, naturally, could care less." She paused, waiting for a response. When none was forthcoming, she added, "Don't worry. I'm not going to drive the skimmer like this. I have a wraparound."

"That's good." He knew he was staring, but he couldn't help himself. Doubtless she was used to it, and too polite to point it out. But what else was he to do? A full head taller than himself, well over the ancient six feet in height, she was a physical amalgam of Hera, several vit heroines, and the female bull dancers of ancient Crete. Her face reminded him of the famous bust of Nefertiti in the Berlin Museum archive. In addition to the sapphire blue eyes, she had shoulder-length blond hair wrapped in four tails. Her skin was the color of new-forged bronze. She was utterly and completely overpowering.

No wonder the pilot had been amused. Where "local support" was concerned, his unknowing passenger had been displaying ignorance on a global scale.

It wasn't Pulickel's fault. No one had informed him, no one had warned him that he was going to be working with a goddess. What was someone like Seaforth doing running a xenological contact station in the wilds of a frontier world, even as comparatively benign a frontier world as Senisran? Socioanthropology being what it was, he expected he would find out.

It would be exceedingly rude to ask her, having just been introduced. Meanwhile he would treat her exactly as he would any other colleague, except that he would have to watch where he let his eyes linger rather more than was usual. No doubt she was used to that, as well.

She laughed again. "Well, I'm glad 'that's good.' Bet you're tired. We're a long way from Ophhlia." Stepping past him, she headed for his travel case. "What do I call you? Senior officer on site, Pulickel, Mr. Tomochelor, or just Pu, as in Winnie the?"

Following her, he discovered, was no less distracting than talking with her face to face. He made an effort. "Pulickel will do fine, since we'll be working together for the foreseeable future." He glanced to his left. "I'm sure there's plenty of room for my stuff in your skimmer."

"You travel light." Her tone was approving, which shouldn't have mattered to him but inexplicably did.

"Experience. The controls for the built-in hoist are located in a recess on the other end."

"Glad to hear it. I'm not in a lifting mood." She held out the chill-cup as they reached the case. "Want a sip?"

He eyed the protruding siphon. Mindful of her admonition to relax, he tried to make himself sound less officious. "What's in it?"

"Fructosoid specimen number one twenty-six. Suaswana in the local lingo. There are about a thousand regional varieties of fruit and juice, some with conflicting names depending on the maturity or location of the relevant tree or bush. I'm still cataloging." She thrust the container at him.

He shrugged internally. So long as it was cold and wet . . .

The frosty liquid detonated against his palate, blasting out reminiscences of lime, pomegranate, and something almost intolerably sweet. Another exotic trade item, he thought as he passed the cup back. No wonder the big trading houses were salivating over development permits for Senisran.

"Very nice," he admitted readily.

She downed a swallow. "There's plenty more, some of it even better. You'll taste for yourself. Come on."

Using the case's integral hoist, they maneuvered his gear up and into the open cargo bay of the skimmer. It had no canopy, only an adjustable windscreen forward.

"Don't use the top much," she replied in response to his query. "It's back in the shed. I can reattach it when necessary." Vaulting up into the open cockpit, she turned and reached down. "Need a hand?"

Shaking his head, he put both hands on the gunwale and pulled himself up and in. Nodding approvingly, she slipped a dirty, stained mechanic's shirt on over her suit, settled into the pilot's seat, and flicked contact pads. Humming with restrained power, the skimmer lifted off, leveled itself, and hovered a meter above the crimson sands.

He eyed his precious case. "What about clampdowns?"

She looked back over her shoulder and shook her head. "Shouldn't need 'em. It's heavy enough that it won't blow out. You, on the other hand, might want to hang onto something." She indicated the seat next to her own.

Moving forward, he gripped an available handbar and braced himself. "I've been sitting down most of the way from Earth and all the way from Ophhlia. I'll stand, if you don't mind."

"Just hang on. Over open water this baby can fly."

With a rising whine they rose to a height of three meters. Seaforth pivoted the craft until they were facing the lagoon and gunned the engine. Sand flew and Pulickel nearly stumbled as the skimmer shot out over the water, accelerating rapidly. Beneath their shadow the placid surface of the lagoon rippled slightly.

Seeing him squinting into the wind, she helpfully raised the transparent windscreen to a height sufficient to shield his face. The gesture went unremarked upon and she shrugged inwardly. *Prim sort of chap,* she thought. If that was the way he wanted it, it was fine with her. Deity knew there was plenty to be done.

She was mistaking his indecision for stiffness. An attractive woman he could have dealt with, but Fawn Seaforth was as much beyond attractive as a diamond was beyond coal. She was representative of the type one saw on the vit, a human being who existed only in virtual reality and not in real life. Yet there she was, sitting in the pilot's seat not an arm's length from where he stood and doing her best to relax him by making small talk. At which he was failing miserably.

He was only being realistic. He was not the sort, physically or personality-wise, who appealed to goddesses. It was a law of nature. Better that she see him as a tool sent to facilitate her work. His worst fear was that she would prove even friendlier than she seemed. In that case he was terrified he would freeze completely.

This is ridiculous, he told himself firmly. She was a contact xenologist, just like himself only with less experience and a shorter résumé. If he was going to let her mere appearance—though there was little mere about it—bother him, he wasn't going to get any serious work done and his journey all this way would be accounted a failure. In his whole career he'd never had a failure, and he wasn't about to start now. Exhorting himself thus made him feel better.

The wind was brisk and cooling against his face as they crossed over the reef. Glancing down as they made the transition, he saw a waterscape alive with jewels. Once beyond the protective barrier, she angled north and pushed the skimmer's speed up another notch.

The reigning silence was becoming painful. "Interesting hairstyle," he ventured lamely. "What's that you've woven into the braids?"

She glanced over at him. "Kiswaa and socolo fibers. The plants are natural gold concentrators. As opposed to food, gardening Parramati grow them for decorative purposes like this, though they have no hair."

He blinked. "Gardening?"

"Wait till you see a Parramati garden. They're genuine works of art. Growing food is almost secondary to appearance."

"I look forward to seeing in person everything I've only had the opportunity to study." He turned to face back into the wind.

They'd long since left the huge atoll behind and were speeding along above open water. Islands sizable and small were visible in all directions, but Seaforth maintained their northerly heading, changing course only to avoid those islets that protruded a meter or more above the water. In the open passages between landmasses, strong ocean swells occasionally reached for the speeding skimmer, but none dampened its underside. High, chiseled, and overwhelmed by green, a cluster of larger islands loomed ahead.

"I didn't expect full field uniform, but do you always meet the supply shuttle from Ophhlia that way?"

Seaforth glanced down at herself. "Something wrong with the way I'm dressed?"

"I didn't say that. I just wondered."

"Sure you did." She kept her gaze forward and her attention on their course.

He struggled to recover. "It's just that it's been my experience that indifference to casual detail leads to sloppy work."

"Does it, now?"

He gave up. "If you're going to respond to everything I say with another question, we're going to have trouble communicating."

"You mean we're not already?" Her gaze narrowed. "Tell you what, Pulickel. Wait till you've been here for a few weeks. Then talk to me about protocol, okay?"

"Fair enough." He returned his attention to the view forward, blinking repeatedly. The tropical sun reflecting off the water was harsh against his pupils, and his eyeshades were still packed inside his travel case.

She was silent for several minutes, then sighed and reached into a side storage compartment. The goggles she handed him were similar to his own.

He accepted them gratefully. "I have several pair, but they're packed away. I didn't expect so long a ride from the pickup point to base."

"So they didn't tell you everything back on Earth."

"There wasn't much time. Normally I'm given more advance notice. I had to complete basic preparatory studies on the journey out from Earth."

"Yeah, well, everyone's in a hurry to get the situation here resolved."

He nodded knowingly. "The mineral rights."

"Among other things." She swerved to avoid a coral pinnacle that rose high above the water. "Smell that air, Pulickel! Everything's unspoiled here. Fresh, unpolluted, natural."

He eyed her thoughtfully. "Is that why you're here? I'd think someone like yourself would miss the excitement of a developed world, or at least the comforts of Ophhlia."

She turned to him so quickly that he started. "Someone like me? For a guy I met less than an hour ago, you presume a lot." Her darkened eyescreens prevented him from seeing her eyes. "For a supposed specialist with a fancy reputation, you show a disappointing tendency to fall back on unsupported assumptions."

He hastened to make amends. "I'm sorry. Let's start over, okay? I'm Pulickel Tomochelor. It's nice to meet you."

"Pardon me if I don't shake hands. I've got to steer this air skate." But she smiled, and he was relieved.

"It's not that I dislike parties and civilization," she went on, "but you can get used to peace and quiet. Even," she added coolly, "someone like me." After a moment she added, "Leastwise, it's peaceful and quiet most of the time."

"Trouble with the locals?"

"More frustration than trouble. You'll see." Reaching down, she pulled the hem of her overshirt out in front of her and eyed the stains. "I guess you're right. This *could* use a wash. Especially now that I have company."

If she was waiting for him to demur, she'd have a long wait. It was unfortunate if his attitude put her off, but he felt it necessary to establish from the start who was in charge and whose work philosophy was to prevail. She might be the one with on-site experience, but within the Department he easily ranked her. Convincing her to do some personal laundry was a relatively painless way of reminding her of their respective positions. Once she accepted that, their working relationship would improve.

Maybe she enjoyed going native, or playing beachcomber, or whatever it was that had happened to affect her attitude, but relaxation and indifference weren't going to solve the problems at hand. She might be in love with Parramat, but all he wanted was to fix what he'd been sent out to fix, receive his commendation, and get out. Goddess or no, he wasn't about to let her stand in the way of that goal.

About then she took a deep breath and stretched, causing him to temporarily forget everything related to his admirable work ethic.

Ten minutes on found them weaving between the larger, heavily vegetated islands. The southernmost reaches of the Parramat archipelago, Fawn informed him. Thereafter they were never out of sight of high peaks and their cosseting clouds. The sheer sides of many of the islands and the heavy waves breaking on their fringing reefs showed why she had traveled to the sandy cay in the lagoon to pick him up. There was no protected touchdown site here for the aerial transport.

One especially striking crag was several hundred meters high, a jungled spire rising sheer from the ocean floor. Flocks of unidentifiable flying things roosted in its hollows and ledges. Showing no inclination to reduce their speed, Seaforth guided the skimmer skillfully past.

As they entered an area of open water between two smaller islands, he found out why the spectacular beauty through which they were traveling needed to be taken with a grain of sea salt.

Something beeped on the instrument panel. Moving faster than he'd yet seen, Seaforth sat up straight and began checking her readouts.

"What . . . ?"

Before he could finish the query, she slammed the steering guide hard aport and yelled out, "Hang on!" Water rooster-tailed to starboard, an artificial geyser.

Following which she shouted something so unexpectedly obscene that he found himself rocked from two quarters. If nothing else, it permanently killed the goddess image he'd assigned to her.

"Damn! There's a whole school of the slimy bastards. They've come in from the deep ocean. Passing between islands." The skimmer lurched heavily to starboard as she threw it in the opposite direction.

"A whole school of what?" Making sure of his grip on the hang bar, he turned and leaned over the side to have a look at the sea.

"Hey, are you crazy? Don't do that!" A hand reached out and grabbed the waistband of his shorts, yanking him backward.

As he stumbled awkwardly in her grasp, a narrow stream of water shot skyward, passing through the space where he'd been leaning over the side. The fountain glittered in the bright sunshine, intense enough to suggest the presence of something more than just water.

Trying to maintain his dignity, he stumbled as he spun out of her grip. "What the devil do you think you're doing?"

"Saving your ignorant life, Tomochelor." She flung the steering guide hard over and he nearly fell down. Her gaze was focused on the instrument panel as well as the water ahead. "When passing over something dangerous, you don't lean over for a closer look at it."

He steadied himself as the skimmer twisted beneath him. He was more upset at the ease with which she'd pulled him away from the side than the manner in which she'd addressed him.

"An explanation might help. I didn't see anything dangerous." Without approaching the edge, he glanced cautiously over the side. As far as he could see, the water was undisturbed by anything out of the ordinary. "For that matter, I still don't see anything dangerous."

"If you're a predator, that's the idea." She glanced back over a shoulder. "We're clear of them now. I counted more than a dozen of the squishy monstrosities when they were on the screen."

Leaning against the front console, he crossed his arms and eyed her tensely. "I'm still waiting for an explanation. And I don't recognize 'squishy monstrosities' as an applicable taxonomic classification."

"They were *apapanus*."

He frowned. "I don't recall that name from any of the lists of local fauna."

"They're not in the catalog yet. Remember, Bioscan is accepting a dozen new species a week here. An apapanu is a big, fat, ugly pseudocephalopod. It likes to sit just under the surface in shallow water. In ambush."

"Ambush?"

"It ejects a stream of water under pressure. Many of the local oceanic life-forms propel themselves by squirting water through tubes on the sides of their bodies or at the tips of fins—from just about anywhere you can imagine. A few use similar high-pressure jets for predation."

He rubbed at his forehead. "What's the intent? To drown intended victims?"

"Are you familiar with the Terran archer fish?" Pulickel shook his head. "It lies in wait just beneath the surface of ponds and rivers and shoots a thin stream of water at insects poised on overhanging branches and leaves. Knocks them off into the water and eats them. The apapanu does something similar, utilizing a much higher volume. What distinguishes it is that it doesn't shoot just water." She put her feet up on the instrument panel.

"When it's not feeding, it nibbles on particularly tough quasi-corals. Instead of digesting, it passes this ground-up detritus into a special sac located behind its cranial ejection spigot. The solid material consists primarily of indigestible silicates. What it's firing at its prey is a stream of water under extremely high pressure that contains a high proportion of sharp-edged silicaceous aggregate. Think of it as a water cannon packed with ground glass.

"When you were leaning over the side, you were in danger of catching more than a faceful of seawater. An apapanu the size of the ones we passed over could have sheared your head off." One sandaled foot nimbly adjusted a minor instrument.

"Once when I was out fishing for eleuu, a flock of uluritei

flashed right past the front of the skimmer. They're low-level gliders that fish the surface waters."

"Like fleratii," he commented.

She nodded approvingly. "Yes, like fleratii, only much smaller. Wing-span of less than three meters. Anyway, one of them had just snapped something out of the water when an apapanu brought it down. Blew a hole clean through it. Apapanus have excellent diffraction-compensatory vision and can see anything above the surface while lurking beneath it." She eyed him meaningfully. "Could've cut your visit here real short. So to speak."

"It won't happen again," he assured her stiffly. "I suppose I should thank you."

"Why not? I adore novelties." There was silence for a long moment. "Well?"

"Well what?" His attention was on the large, high island directly ahead. Absently he added, "Thank you for saving my face."

"As opposed to saving face?" Her smile, never absent for very long, returned. "Don't take it to heart. You just got here. I didn't expect to run into any trouble between the landing cay and Torrelau myself."

"How do the locals avoid such creatures?"

"As best they can. When they don't someone usually dies." Her tone was flat. "The design of their outriggers is unique and they can turn quickly. The Parramati are skilled at avoiding the dangers of the sea, but they're not omnipotent. Sometimes the predators are faster."

He nodded slowly. "How do they cope?"

"High birthrate. And magic."

His eyebrows rose. "I beg your pardon?"

She lowered her voice, trying to make herself sound as mysterious as possible. "Magic."

He smiled thinly, doing his best to go along with what was

obviously a joke. "Do they employ any particular divinations? Or perhaps special powders and incantations?"

She didn't miss a beat. "Absolutely. Superficially, it sounds a lot like the magicks of Aluwela, Tesiratupa, Curusisim, and a hundred other island groups. The only difference is, here it works."

"Not all the time, according to what you've just told me."

"Parramati magic isn't absolute. It just seems to improve the odds."

He shrugged. "Chants and incantations are inherently superficial, but native herbs and powders can have powerful physiological effects. Something they might sprinkle on the water to numb the nervous systems of dangerous predators, for example. I could give you a hundred possible explanations for what you think you've seen, many from personal experience."

She leaned forward slightly, peering through the windscreen. "Pretty soon you'll have the chance to judge for yourself. We're almost there. That's Torrelau dead ahead."

CHAPTER

3

Seaforth swung the skimmer around a wave-swept point of rocks and into an exquisite natural harbor. Walls of green closed in on both sides. The fjordlike inlet would easily have accommodated a large cargo boat, but it was deserted save for their comparatively tiny craft. The cries of alien fauna rose from the surrounding forest.

"I understand," he said absently as he studied the dense foliage, "that the Parramati show little interest in contemporary technology. Whereas elsewhere on Senisran, the natives have taken to trading for simple Commonwealth manufactures with enthusiasm."

She nodded. "Not here they haven't. They say it goes against their *kusum*. Also, they think magic is better. Of course, they don't really use magic. Everything they do, everything that happens in Parramat has a logical and rational exegesis. I just haven't had time enough to study it. I've been too busy trying to get them to make treaty with the Commonwealth." She smiled up at him. "I'm expecting you to explain it all to me."

"I'll do my best," he replied without a hint of guile. "But as you say, a treaty is paramount. The section in my study guide on Parramati customs was slim. I expect you to warn me where not to step, what not to say, and how not to act."

"Don't worry, Pulickel. I'll take good care of you."

He tensed, but she didn't reach over to pat him on the head. Intellectual condescension he could handle, but not the physical kind. Especially not from an attractive woman. If that was irrational, so be it.

The skimmer slowed as they approached a narrow stretch of yellow-white beach at the head of the inlet. Beyond the sand he could see where jungle had been cleared away, leaving a wide path through the forest. Something in shades of blue equipped with multiple legs scurried piglike across the clearing and into the trees.

She drove the skimmer off the water and up onto the beach, rising to clear a large berm that was anchored in place by a peculiar, corkscrewing green-red vine. Purple fruiting bodies burst from conelike structures that emerged at random from each shiny coil. Without being obvious, he paid careful attention to everything she did. Unbeknownst to her, one of his ancillary tasks in accepting the Parramat assignment was to render and report a formal job evaluation on one Fawn Seaforth.

It was early, but so far his opinion was equivocal. Not that he was grading out at the top of his form since his arrival, either. How could he have known about the apapanus? Senisran was rich in unknown and undescribed inimical species. He was confident only in what he knew. He decided that her lapses in protocol could be overlooked in view of the fact that she'd saved his life—and might well do so again.

Of one thing he was already certain. This assignment could go one of many ways—but "by the book" wasn't going to be one of them.

Well, he'd improvised before. Adaptability was the hallmark of the truly successful.

A hundred meters from the water's edge, the skimmer hangar came into view. It was a large, unlovely, wholly functional structure: a roof, three walls, and a sliding barrier. Fawn pulled inside, cut the engine, and monitored instrumentation as their vehicle settled onto its mounting pad.

"The station's just up ahead." She jumped over the side. "Pass down your case and we'll walk the rest of the way."

Using the integrated hoist to control the heavy baggage, they walked the remaining meters along a narrower path that ran in a straight line through the trees. Pulickel was enveloped by the rich, musky aroma of growing things. Alien odors assaulted his nostrils. The majority, though not all, of them were pleasant.

Ideally, a contact station should blend harmoniously with its alien environment without challenging the position or preeminence of native structures or religious icons. This was not a problem on Torrelau since the nearest Parramati village was located several kilometers distant, over an intervening ridge.

It *was* important that the installation reflect the technological superiority of its builders without being overawing. The idea was to impress without terrifying. Nor could it be too elaborate or expensive; not with a world like Senisran requiring dozens of such installations. It should also be relatively quick and easy to assemble.

Therefore it wasn't surprising that Seaforth's habitation was of a design Pulickel recognized. It looked like a fat wheel mounted on an axle that had been shoved into the ground, with the body of the wheel parallel to the earth. Ascent to the main body of the station, whose rim was ringed with windows and observation ports, was via a lift located in the supporting axle. In the event of power failure, a spiral stairway encircled the elevator shaft.

With the wheel-shaped body of the station ten meters above the ground, it offered occupants safety as well as a pleasant view of the encroaching forest. The main work areas faced the exquisite, narrow bay, muting instead of encouraging hard work. A circular defensive perimeter consisting of charged posts that would deal unpleasantly with any living thing that attempted to pass between them ensured a safe outside working zone beneath the overhang of the station itself.

With its prominent reds and blues, the surrounding jungle was more colorful than its relentlessly green Terran counterparts. Pulickel recognized variations of the star-crowned trees beneath which Fawn had awaited the arrival of the transport. Among the other botanical standouts was a medium-size bush armed with scythelike spines. It looked like a refugee from some desert clime but was obviously happy to be growing deep within the forest. Flowers flared in abundance and in odd places.

Beneath the shady wheel of the station and within the defense perimeter was a junkyard of empty packing crates, storage containers, and unidentifiable debris. It stained the ground just as grease and soil marred Seaforth's overshirt. Its presence was strictly against general regulations and guidelines for the maintenance and operation of such an outpost. All nonrecyclable trash was supposed to be properly disposed of or neatly packaged for removal at some future date.

As they drew near, half a dozen small scavengers of unknown type burst from the mess and scattered into the trees. He could hear them banging through the underbrush. Several had neither feathers nor scales and appeared to be little more than fleshy blobs on legs.

He found himself gesturing. "It would appear that the station's defense system is not turned on."

She nodded slowly. "So it would appear."

"That is a violation of regulations." He gestured at the flagrant pile. "What do you call that disgusting mess?"

"Convenient. The Parramati get a kick out of poking through it. They use some of the smaller discarded packaging to store water or carry pickings. Impermeable plastic leftovers are highly regarded here."

"Letting natives scavenge a station's trash is counter to proper procedure." He eyed her disapprovingly.

She paid no attention. "I don't think letting them have a few scraps is going to disrupt their cultural equilibrium. The Parramati are a pretty stable society. Besides, I've found that trash can make you a lot of friends." She waved casually at their surroundings. "Welcome to Torrelau. It means 'the land' in Parramati."

"I know." The local dialect was one thing he *had* mastered during his studies. An accomplished linguist and a natural mimic, he believed firmly that you couldn't really convince an alien of anything unless you could speak to it in its own language. Whether they required chatting, whistling, clicking, harsh glottal stops, or signs, he'd been able to master them all. In fact, it was much easier for him to converse with aliens than with his own kind. Take the speech of frigid Tran-ky-ky, where he'd been stationed for a while. Rigid in inflection and boasting a highly formal grammar, it had been easy for him to master. Neither fluid, conversational seni or the local Parramati dialect had posed a problem for him.

Something induced him to look sharply to his left. "I get the feeling we're being watched."

"We are. They'll introduce themselves in due time. The Parramati aren't fearful, but they're cautious. You're new to them. Not that you're the second human they've ever seen. There was the crew that erected the station, though they never had any contact with the locals. Among other features, they're fascinated by our individual size variations. Mature seni are all pretty much the same height."

How tactful of you to mention the subject, he thought, then realized she probably meant nothing by it. He was far too sensitive on the subject.

Something that looked like a purple boa constrictor with feathery external gills running half the length of its body emerged from the trash pile and slithered out of their path as they approached the support cylinder. An irrational feeling, perhaps, but Pulickel felt more secure once they stood beneath the circular shadow of the station's bulk.

Fawn had to yell at the door several times before it would open. Whether the delay was due to an internal fault or poor maintenance he couldn't tell. She grinned apologetically back at him. It would not be so amusing, he thought, if something was chasing them. He wondered what else needed fixing.

"Been meaning to work on that," she told him as the door finally slid aside. At least, he mused, it did not make a grinding noise as it did so.

"Station upkeep is the responsibility of those working on site," he reminded her, "irrespective of specialty."

"Hey, I do what I can. The climate here is rough on electronics. My priority is the treaty, not janitorial work."

Not wishing to start another argument, he withheld the comment that was teetering on his lips and followed her into the lift. It was just big enough to accommodate the two of them and Pulickel's self-hoisting travel case. The door closed smoothly behind them.

The interior of the station was a revelation, but not the kind that inspires. Clothes were scattered about both the living and work areas. A few hung from the ceiling. Empty food containers clung to furniture like giant, brightly colored fungal spores. The tiny carcasses of dead arthropods spotted the softfloor. Fashioned of native fibers, a hammock hung suspended in the portal that separated the main living area from kitchen and sleeping quarters. Several water bottles in various stages of consumption occupied unlikely—and in at least one instance, unsanitary—locations within the room.

Lining the sweeping windows that ran around the station's circumference was a small jungle of native plants. Each chosen for its beauty or uniqueness, they flourished in improvised pots that were as much a product of Fawn Seaforth's imagination as they were of her resourcefulness. Empty food containers, cut-down power-cell packs, cleaning and maintenance tubes: all had been ingeniously pressed into service. Alien perfume and color filled the room.

Pulickel found himself drawn to what looked like a longitudinally sliced water carrier potted with miniature black roses. It was beautiful to look at, but the streamers and leaves and tendrils blocked windows and dirtied the floor. A thick mass of aerial roots threatened to overwhelm an atmospheric monitoring panel. Fawn noted the direction of his gaze.

"Have to trim that back." She bent to smell of something blue and gold. "What do you think of my collection? I cleaned the place up especially for you."

"Just for me? You shouldn't have."

"Yeah, I know, but I did anyway."

"Seaforth . . ." he began sternly.

"Come on: it's Fawn. We're going to be working together too long for last names. Especially last names as long as yours."

"All right, Fawn." With a sweeping gesture he encompassed the room and what he could see of rooms beyond. "How can you live and work in this squalor?"

"Squalor?" She made a face. "There's no squalor here, Pulickel. Just comfort. Don't you like flowers?"

"I love flowers, and houseplants, but I don't relish the idea of sharing my living quarters with alien species. Especially new ones whose properties and characteristics haven't been thoroughly cataloged."

"Relax." She moved to another plant. "I put each one through a rigorous quarantine and check before I bring it into the station. Make sure that they're all free of parasites and hangers-on. I even check pollen and spores for possible serious contamination. Sure there's dangerous flora on Senisran, but these here are all harmless to both human and thranx."

Carefully avoiding the debris that made passage difficult, he worked his way across to the outer wall and its bank of indigenous foliage. "I can understand a small collection, but these are taking over. They could get into equipment, clog filters, no telling what."

She spread her arms and performed a slow pirouette. "Honestly, Pulickel. Do I look in any way unhealthy to you?"

In point of fact, she looked healthier than any human being he'd ever seen in his life, but that wasn't the point. There were procedures that had to be followed, strictures that needed to be observed.

It suddenly occurred to him that he was more than a little tired. "Could you just show me my room, please? We can discuss all this later."

"Sure. I know you must be exhausted."

"I'm not exhausted," he replied irritably as she unhooked the hammock that was blocking the doorway.

"Sorry. This was the best place I could find to put it up. There's a lovely view of the inlet from here. You can lie here at night, open the windows, and watch the moons come up."

His eyes widened. "Open the windows? You mean, you consciously and willingly violate the atmospheric integrity of the station?"

"Frequently. I like the feeling of freedom."

"I'm sure that the native species that fly in and out at such times do, too."

"You are a worrier, aren't you? If it'll make you feel safer, I'll arm the external defenses. As for the open windows, I happen to like fresh air. When it gets too hot and humid inside, I close everything up again. Nothing really dangerous ever intrudes. In the morning, I go around and add to the station's collection of small flying arthropods."

He twitched at the thought of something small, alien, and buggy landing on his face while he slept. "I'll keep my quarters sealed, if you don't mind."

She shrugged. "Suit yourself. Makes me claustrophobic."

Thankfully, she hadn't even bothered to inspect either of the two unused sleeping areas. The standard room was typical in nearly every aspect, its familiarity a great comfort to the weary and troubled xenologist. It was a little musty from disuse, but everything was where and as it should be, and there were no extraneous decorations of either Senisran's or Seaforth's making. He reveled in its reassuring sterility.

He hastened to shut the door behind him to keep out any small uninvited locals that might be crawling about. "It looks fine. Let's get my case."

"After you, my honored guest." As her left hand swept out in a gesture of invitation, she executed a mock bow. He forced himself to smile at the harmless, mild sarcasm. The bow took his mind off her words anyway.

He spent the remainder of the day unpacking and putting up his equipment and personal gear. Several times he paused to ensure that the door was still tightly sealed against intrusion by anything larger than a human hair. He also carried out a personal inspection and cleaning of the room's overhead air filters. The curving window offered a view only of surrounding forest, but he was pleased with it nonetheless. Claustrophobic, indeed! Rather than closed-in, the room gave him a feeling of security.

As he put away the last of his gear he wondered why he couldn't have been sent to Miramilu. The largest and most important of the island groupings thus far contacted by Commonwealth representatives, it lay only three hundred kilometers from Ophhlia. Conscious of their status, its citizens had held off allying themselves with either humans or AAnn, sensibly evaluating the offers of assistance that both sides regularly presented to its chiefs. Already they were utilizing simple Commonwealth and Empire technologies to improve their everyday lives, advantages gained without committing themselves to either side. The Miramiluans were playing it smart instead of stubborn.

The station there consisted not of a single prefab structure unceremoniously planted into the ground but of a growing complex that in size and sophistication threatened to rival Ophhlia itself in importance. In such surroundings he knew he could make an immediate difference. The research that would result would be important and prominently featured in *The Journal of Xenological Contact*.

Instead, they'd sent him here. Because, it had been explained to him, Parramat was more of a trouble spot, more of an insoluble problem. Less insightful xenologists could be counted on to deal with Miramilu's more comprehensible recalcitrance. Despite one mild protest, he'd been sent where they needed him most—not where he'd wanted to go.

Well, it wouldn't take him long to compile a report on Fawn Seaforth. That part of his work here was already well on its way to completion.

His own personal computing facilities integrated seamlessly with those of the base. He was greatly relieved to see that save for a few minor glitches, that portion of the station was operating properly. As a test, he ran through a few basic setup programs, talking softly to the vorec and making sure the more powerful station unit responded readily to his stock inquiries. By the time he was finished, it was growing dark outside. The onset of alien evening arrived on sky streamers tinged with pink and gold.

His door chimed, using the musical quote from Brian's "Jolly Miller" that he had programmed into it.

"I'll be out in a minute," he told the door. He didn't want Fawn Seaforth in his room any more than was necessary. She might bring passengers along with her. Visitors from outside. He intended to preserve the sanctity of his quarters for as long as was practicable.

Setting the room on "constant clean" and his personal facilities on standby, he stepped out to join her, closing the door behind him as quickly as possible. They passed through the general living area and into the small dining facility. The same curving windows offered a view of rapidly darkening forest. Moments later, powerful lights on the rim of the station came to life, illuminating the vegetation and startling the early risers among the forest's nocturnal fauna. Unrecognizable creatures with large, glowing eyes vanished swiftly into the concealing treetops.

"Very little work's been done on Senisran's night life." Fawn was busying herself with the food processor. She had traded in her nonexistent swimsuit and dirty overshirt for clean shorts and blouse. A part of Pulickel was pleased, while the rest was gravely disappointed. This mental disagreement represented an internal conflict he would have to somehow resolve, he told himself.

"There's so much to study and catalog during daylight hours," she continued, "that none of the resident biologists on Senisran have had much time to devote to studies of life after dark."

He took a seat at the small oval table. "Anything dangerous around here?"

"You saw the revavuaa? The purple snakelike creature that slid from cover when we were approaching the lift shaft? That's got a real bad bite, but it's not exclusively nocturnal. As for the local diurnal life-forms, I've put together a small but necessary list of critters to watch out for. You can download the relevants into your files anytime."

"You let it hang around the station?"

"That's where it wanted to hang around. It may be poisonous, but it's not aggressive. You saw it slither off when we approached. I can't be shooting everything that comes poking through, and there's not enough power to run a full defensive screen around the clock. Besides which, the screen is a pain in the butt. It wasn't on when we arrived because I get tired of having to continually turn it on and off. Regulations or no regulations." She removed several plates and bowls from the processor and set them on the table.

"Don't expect me to wait on you like this every night. It's just that it's your first day and I know you're tired."

He studied the platters hungrily. "I'm perfectly willing to do my share of the domestics. These aren't native foods, I hope?"

She grinned. "I wouldn't hit you with that on your first day here. No, tonight we're having good old imported reconstitutibles. Local cuisine can wait, though I promise you, besides the fruits and vegetables there are some wonderful things the Parramati pull out of the ocean. In particular, there are some soft-shelled burrowing pseudo-mollusks that taste heavenly when they've been steamed and basted in butter."

"I look forward to it." He started helping himself from the assembled plates. "Could I just have some water?"

"Sure." Reentering the processing area, she returned moments later with a self-chilling pitcher and sat down opposite him.

"I'll try whatever you think I might like," he promised her as they ate. "The local foods certainly haven't done you any harm."

She smiled. "Why, Tomochelor, thank you for the compliment."

"I didn't mean—" He stopped, flustered, considered beginning again, and gave it up in favor of chewing his food. "I'll try them a little bit at a time, until my system becomes used to the local tastes and consistencies."

"That's the way I did it." She ate actively from her own plate, but with care.

He thought about complimenting her on her change of clothing, decided that anything he might say could be misconstrued, and determined that where she was concerned, it would be safer to avoid the topic of attire entirely. When they did speak, he forced himself always to meet her eyes. When there was silence, he struggled to look anywhere but at the rest of her. Clearly, being stationed on Torrelau was going to involve challenges for which he had not been able to prepare himself in the usual manner.

The dinner was excellent, the familiar reconstituted foods reassuring as well as nourishing. Near the end, he broke his own resolve and tried a sample of each of the three native fruit juices she had placed on the table. All were superb. He wondered if she gathered the fruits herself or traded with the natives for them. He could see her climbing the local trees, crawling out on limbs, her incredible legs twisting and dangling . . .

Resolutely he returned his attention to the meal. Tree climbing was not in his job description. Mildly amazed, he watched her pack away an astonishing amount of food.

"If you have work to do, don't worry about keeping me up," she told him in response to a question he hadn't planned to ask. "I sleep like a rock here and the soundproofing between partitions is excellent. Plus, there's a vacant room between yours and mine. Whatever you're doing, I won't hear you."

"I'm pretty quiet, though I do like to play music rather loudly on occasion. Contemporary inventions."

"Really? Have you heard the latest from Chikareska or Mattuzh?" Before he could reply she rushed on. "I can download via relay from Ophhlia, but they're not exactly up on what's new there either."

"I don't know Mattuzh that well," he replied, "but Chikareska is a favorite of mine. "Do you know the *Blue Collage*?"

"You've heard the *Blue Collage*?" Her excitement was palpable. "I've heard *about* it, but I can't get the philistines in charge of imports to shell out the necessary royalty."

Having unintentionally struck a topic of mutual nonprofessional interest, they engaged in an animated discussion of music imaging, both human and thranx. It made the rest of the evening pass very smoothly.

CHAPTER

4

When he awoke the following morning and stumbled tiredly into the dining area, there was someone waiting for him, and it wasn't Fawn Seaforth. Reddish orange in color, responsive localized chromophores flashed wavy light blue lines down its side. Dark red pupils centered in tiny, bright pink eyes stared sharply at him. The long proboscis resembled a collapsed balloon.

When he interrupted it, it was skittering across the dining table on comically short legs covered with fine brown fur, using the strange mouth part to suck up loose crumbs and food fragments from the night before. Turning to face him, it inflated its proboscis to half its body size and emitted a very human-sounding raspberry of impressive dimensions. This noise proved so unexpectedly farcical that Pulickel's initial apprehensions instantly evaporated.

"That's a floob," Fawn declared from behind him.

This morning she wore full tropic field gear. Loose-fitting and casual, it managed the difficult task of diminishing her figure. He found himself grateful for the visual respite. In addition to the knee-length shorts and regulation multipocketed shirt, she wore appropriate headgear. The face screen was flipped up and back, its visor powered down but ready for instant use.

She gestured at the table. "It shows up every morning, after I've turned off the defensive screen. Comes in through a window and cleans the place up."

He blinked. "Cleans it up?"

"In addition to table scraps, it gets all the local arthropods that I and the station cleanser miss." She whistled at it and the fuzzy floob squeaked a response. Approaching the table, she wiggled several fingers in its direction.

Inflating to several times its body size, the floob used its proboscis like a jet exhaust to rocket backward off the table, across the room, and through the open rim window through which it had entered. It was able to see where it was going because, to Pulickel's astonishment, its eyes had crawled up its spine and onto its back. It soared over the clearing and into the trees beyond, leaving him to eye the dining table distastefully.

"You've made sure, of course, that this charming regular visitor doesn't carry any kind of parasites or communicable diseases?"

"As a matter of fact, I haven't." She proceeded to make a show of scratching her sides and arms.

"Very funny," he commented dryly, less than amused.

She lowered her hands. "You don't really approve of me, do you?"

He didn't meet her gaze. "It isn't you so much, Fawn," he replied, neither confirming nor denying her accusation. "We just have a different outlook on certain procedural matters."

"I hope you have a better opinion of my work. You haven't seen any of that yet, except for my picking you up, bringing you here, and saving your life along the way." She sighed resignedly. "If it really means that much to you, I'll make an effort to clean the place up, even though we're really out of sight, out of mind here."

"I would greatly appreciate it, and I will do more than my share to help."

"Agreed. You hungry?"

He eyed the table uncomfortably. "No thank you. I rarely eat in the morning. What I would like is to get started."

"Just arrived and already you're anxious to leave."

He nodded. "Just because I've done a lot of fieldwork doesn't mean I particularly enjoy it."

"I'll bet you don't like having to rely on others, either." She disappeared into a back storeroom and returned moments later with a thin belt. Hanging from the belt was a qwik holster holding a compact needler. Extra power cells occupied the other side of the belt, balancing out the modest weight of the weapon.

"I think this one'll fit you." She tried to hand him the belt and gun.

He demurred. "Why give me this? Except for what's in the already outdated study file, I wouldn't know what to pet and what to shoot."

"I'll take care of the flora and fauna. This is in case we run into any AAnn. Their base is only thirty minutes away by fast skimmer. I haven't had any serious run-ins with them, but other outposts have. When they think they can get away with it, they're not above taking potshots at the competition, especially when it's isolated and alone out in the local woods."

"Meaning us?" Reluctantly he accepted the belt and began strapping it on.

"Meaning you, anyway. I've been so quiet here for so long I'm not sure they regard me as much in the way of competition. That suits me just fine. I've had a couple of chats with their local chief of operations, an oily type named Essasu. Everything very formal and polite. But if I didn't keep rigorous, recoverable recordings of my movements, I'm sure he'd cheerfully have one of his underlings slap an explosive shell into my spine the first time I wasn't looking. Traveling armed lets him know that I'm neither naive nor helpless. I'm a firm believer in discouraging temptation right from the start."

The needler was virtually unnoticeable on his hip. "Competition for the hearts and minds of the natives is supposed to be on a friendly basis."

She made a rude noise. "Sure it is. And the AAnn are happy-go-lucky comedians who'll gather 'round at every opportunity just to tell you the latest jokes from Blassusar." She patted the weapon that rode high and wide on her left hip. "That's why I'm always careful to carry my critic with me.

"Plus, there's always the chance that a *gribiwith* or a *cochco* vine will take a leap at you when I'm not in a position to help. Think of your needler as a prophylaxis." She nodded in the direction of their living quarters. "Any other gear you want to bring? I have my recorder with me."

He shook his head. "Not on the first visit. I need to acclimate myself first."

She nodded and turned in the direction of the central elevator shaft. Once he had joined her, she thumbed the single switch and the cylindrical conveyor started down. It squealed and whined outrageously, suggesting that it, too, had been the subject of less than assiduous maintenance.

"Why didn't they site the skimmer shed closer to the station and connect it with a sealed walkway?" he wondered aloud.

She shrugged. "Probably cheaper this way. I don't mind. I like being outside. Later I'll show you my favorite swimming hole. It's a deep pool fed by a five-meter-high waterfall. Smooth rocks on the bottom, clean sand around the edges. I'd call it Eden, if I were inclined to name things. When I'm bored or just hot I'll walk in to it on the little trail I've cut, take everything off, and just float or lie on the fronting beach."

Pulickel manfully turned his thoughts from the image thus conjured up. "The natives leave you alone at all times?"

She nodded. "They have plenty to do and as you know from your prep, the nearest village is a ways from here. I very rarely see them unless I go looking for them. They never bother the station."

The lift bottomed out with a grinding sound. When after a suitable pause the door refused to open, Fawn kicked it into compliance. She smiled apologetically.

"Damn thing's supposed to be permanently lubricated, but you know what a tropical climate can do to even the best machinery."

"Which is why," he observed as they stepped out of the shaft into the oppressive heat and humidity, "even supposedly permanently lubricated doors and glides need to be checked as part of a weekly routine."

"I agree," she confessed readily. "And now that you're here and I'm not expected to do everything myself, you can make that your responsibility, Pulickel. I'm sure you're *much* better at it than I would be."

They made their way toward the skimmer shed, the magnificent bay glistening in the morning sun as if it had been coated with powdered diamond.

"I think I'll be able to communicate without any trouble." At her mild urging he avoided a plant with thorny leaves that was growing over the edge of the path. "For alien vocalizations, the languages of Senisran are fairly simple, and the Parramati dialect seems to present no unique difficulties."

"Glad all those recordings I made proved useful. Of course, I could've been carrying out routine station maintenance instead." Entering the shed, she ran a quick check of skimmer integrity and functions, paying particular attention to the fore intakes, before climbing aboard. Apparently there were some things she was willing to spend the time to maintain.

Following her on board, he settled himself for the second time into the seat next to the pilot's chair. This morning's journey would be less eventful than yesterday's, he hoped.

"Where are we headed?"

She spoke without looking up as she efficiently checked readouts and instrumentation. "Northwest coast. The skimmer's only practical for overwater travel. Rest of the island is too rugged. You'll have plenty of opportunity to walk the trail to the main village, but this'll get us there in a couple of minutes." On a rising whine, the sturdy craft rose a meter into the air and backed out of the shed.

"The locals like to see me arrive by skimmer. They already know how to walk."

"How do they react?" he asked. "Are they awed, curious, indifferent, what?"

"Straightforwardly accepting, mostly. It didn't take them long to get used to it. They call it the boat that flies on air, which is pretty direct. I think the absence of outriggers surprises them more than anything else."

He settled himself back into the seat. "I'm looking forward to meeting the local chief, this being the dominant island in the archipelago." He smiled. "I'm sure the AAnn weren't happy about the Commonwealth setting up a station here first."

She shrugged. "They seem to be perfectly happy on Mallatyah. That's the second-largest inhabited island in the group. They're doing a good job of extending their influence from there."

Pulickel was mildly alarmed. "I've been wondering what kind

of progress they've been making. How are you doing with the Torrelauans?"

"As well, or as bad. It's hard to tell. As you know from your preparations, the Parramati aren't like any other society on Senisran." The skimmer crossed the beach and entered the bay. "They're special. Special unique or special frustrating, take your pick."

Wind began to ruffle his hair. "I'm sure as soon as I get to know the chief, we'll make some serious headway."

She adjusted several controls, preferring manual to vorec operation. The engine whined responsively and the skimmer accelerated. He frowned at her.

"What're you laughing at?"

She stopped chuckling. "If you wanted to speak to the chief on any other island group, there wouldn't be a problem. But you can't do that on Parramat."

"Why not?"

"Because the Parramati are different. As you'll find out. It's why I've stayed here, by myself. See, there *are* things that interest me besides lounging around, cultivating native flowers, and sampling the local foodstuffs."

"I didn't mean to imply otherwise," he muttered.

"Of course. Nobody ever *means* to." She boosted the skimmer another meter above the water.

Well out on the bay, the wind was now howling around them. He really would have preferred an enclosed, climate-controlled cockpit, but decided to hold off making the suggestion. Instead, he studied his surroundings intently. How the wind blew her burnished gold hair out behind her, how the sculpted profile of her face stood out pale against the green walls of the fjord—not forgetting to make mental notes on the surrounding terrain as well, of course.

"What's so special about the Parramati, besides their reluctance to formalize relationships with outsiders?"

Reaching the end of the bay, she turned west, following the coast. Beneath the skimmer's thrusters, the smooth waters of the encircling lagoon flashed by. Silicaceous pseudocorals shoved bumps and blades and nodules toward the surface.

"Everything. Their society is unique on Senisran. They're friendly, polite, but defiant."

"What are they defying? Everything is subject to negotiation. It's not like we're trying to impose our will on them."

"But we are. However benignly, we're imposing contemporary culture on them, be it in the form of a formal treaty of mutual cooperation, trade goods, weapons, politics, even comments and suggestions about art. The AAnn are doing the same. The Parramati reject nearly all of it. It's not part of their kusum, you see."

Pulickel blinked as the skimmer rocked slightly. "Their what?"

"The term is a phonetic coincidence, though it means much more than just custom. It signifies a way of life that goes beyond the superficial. It's a way of looking at the entire cosmos. They're afraid that if they ally themselves formally with either us or the AAnn, it will go against kusum and they'll lose their way."

"For a supposedly primitive people, that's a relatively enlightened outlook." He smiled thinly. "Of course, it never works. You can't reject and ignore advanced technology once it's been offered to you. If not the elders, then the youth of primitive species who are less steeped in tradition are always willing to try exciting new things. Historical xenology proves it over and over. Any group that attempts to exclude high tech soon finds that its less diffident neighbors have leapfrogged beyond them in terms of wealth, education, and the ability to wage war."

"I know that." She leaned back and let the autopilot guide the skimmer. "I've tried explaining it to them. They just humor me and insist that as long as they stick to their kusum, they'll be all right."

"Very admirable. Noble, even. But misguided. Stubbornness never works. Sooner or later on every inhabited world, those who advance assume control over or come to dominate those who do not. The natives of Ophhlia have already advanced a full classification by accepting and embracing the Commonwealth presence there."

"The Parramati wouldn't be impressed. You could offer them untold wealth. They'd consider it politely, discuss it at length, and if the determination was that it went against kusum, reject it outright no matter how many lives it would better. That's why I've had such a hard time getting them to accept gifts." The skimmer automatically eased around a small, sandy islet from which a flock of bright red gliders exploded into the sky like the outpouring of a burst crimson piñata.

"Like all the rest of it, the gift-giving rituals of their kusum are very elaborate. If I were to offer them something like a small, portable entertainment center, they'd have nothing equivalent with which to reciprocate and therefore, according to kusum, they couldn't accept it. About all they'll exchange readily are foodstuffs. There's a soft drink concentrate from New Riviera that they're particularly fond of. Swapping drinks doesn't make for an instant treaty, but it's a start. One of the few I've been able to make."

"So that's how you get your fruits and juices. Exotic tastes are always a good way to ingratiate oneself with natives, provided body chemistries are compatible, of course."

"It isn't the taste. The drink is carbonated, and the bubbles tickle their sensitive palates. They like the sensation." Leaning forward, she resumed manual control and turned the skimmer toward shore. "There's something really important to be discovered here, Pulickel. Something that extends beyond treaties and trade agreements and adding to the general bulk of xenological knowledge. I'm just not sure what it is yet."

"Pretty hard to verify something in the laboratory when you don't even know what it is you're looking for," he commented.

"Maybe you'll have better luck." She shook her head, chasing blond strands from her face. "A new approach, intuition—you obviously have a lot of experience."

"It would help if I knew what you were looking for."

"I agree. All I can say is that it's all tied up with what makes Parramat society so different from that of any of the other island groups and the Parramati different from the rest of the seni. They're not evasive so much as they are obtuse."

"Is obtuseness a component of kusum, too?" Pulickel braced himself as the skimmer slowed, approaching the shoreline.

"I don't think so." She eased the craft up on a narrow beach shaded by tall thin trees clad in striated blue bark and huge oval leaves that grew directly upon the trunk. Their coloring blended perfectly into the sky, an adaptive quality whose purpose he would have to discover at a later date. Near the crown of one bole small chittering things with eight legs hung upside down and gawked at him out of eyes like Persian turquoise. Each eye appeared to have three pupils.

"We have to stop here and walk." She climbed out of the open cab. "It's not far, but there's a bit of a climb."

He followed her over the side and studied the sloping terrain inland. "The skimmer should be able to negotiate this hill."

"Probably, but some of the older Parramati don't like to be around it when it's running." She smiled knowingly. "Because it sucks in air and kicks it back out they're afraid it might steal their breath."

"And besides," he grumbled as he studied the narrow trail that wound like a corkscrew through the dense vegetation, "no doubt it's against kusum."

"You got it. So I park it here." Reaching into the stern of the skimmer, she removed a couple of small backpacks and handed one to him. Slipping the other over her shoulders, she started up the trail. "As you've probably figured by now, the Parramati consider everything in the light of kusum."

"Who makes the interpretations? The local chief?"

"I told you," she reminded him, looking back over her shoulder, "the Parramati have no chiefs."

"Somebody has to make decisions."

"They all do. It's something like an Athenian-style democracy, only with internal gradations I'm still trying to sort out. There are big persons, and middle persons, and small persons, and the big persons have a greater say than the small persons, but if enough small persons get together they can override the opinion of the big persons."

"So the voting is weighted?" He'd always had plenty of stamina and the climb wasn't tiring him.

"It's not that straightforward. You'll see."

The trail was well maintained. He glanced back the way they'd come. "They won't bother the skimmer?"

"They'll look at it and peek inside, but they won't touch anything. They've seen what it can do, and no one wants to take the risk of it running off with them. I set the alarm anyway, just in case somebody's curiosity overcomes their adherence to kusum." She held up her right arm, showing him the communicator band encircling her wrist. "I can control basic functions from here. If some native were to start monkeying around with it, I'd just send it scooting out into the lagoon. Believe me, any intruder would abandon it in a hurry. The Parramati are brave enough, but they have a healthy respect for our technology, even if they don't want any of it for themselves." She grinned and pushed aside the branch of a succulent that had grown across the trail.

"Also, they have a healthy respect for ghosts and spirits, and I've told them that one sleeps in the skimmer at all times." She eyed him appraisingly. "You managing okay?"

"I'm fine," he replied irritably. "Just lead on and I'll be right behind you." Which, he decided, even though he did his best to focus his attention on the surrounding alien jungle, was not a bad place to be—provided he could get her to stop patronizing him. He might not be able to match her stride for stride, but he'd run marathons and could hike all day without stopping.

The jungle was an extraordinary place, frantic with motion and sound, brilliant with exotic colors and shapes. Surrounded by dwarf trees and gigantic flowers, it was often hard to tell which was which. In contrast to the great Terran rain forests, which boasted a thousand different shades of green, the jungle on Torrelau was painted with all the colors of the rainbow. Alongside blue-black branches and silver stems, red roots and yellow bark, some of the flowers looked positively intimidated. He mentioned his observations to his companion.

"Many of the plants here have the ability to concentrate specific minerals in their phylose." She indicated a brace of brilliant red-and-yellow bushes. "Colekoli. Sucks up cinnabar like a sponge. I hear that in the Puralyra Archipelago north of Ophhlia there's scrub that concentrates platinum." She grinned. "Makes me wish I had time to do a little gardening."

He stepped over a protruding root. "What about the rare earths here that have the commercial interests so excited?"

"Nice thought, but so far I haven't been able to find a flower with a passion for niobium. Too bad. Wouldn't stop the mining interests, though. They'd still want to dig the place up. Picking flowers would be too slow. Insufficiencies of scale." He reached for a loop of vine to help pull himself over a steep spot. "Don't touch that."

He withdrew his fingers. "Why not?" He studied the ropy liana. It looked innocent enough.

After she'd given him a hand up, she found a dead stick and carefully gave the section of vine he'd been about to grab a sharp whack. Instantly hundreds of small, hooked thorns that had lain flush with the smooth bark of the vine snapped erect, exactly as if she'd pulled a trigger. Which, effectively, she had.

She tossed the stick aside. "Not deadly, but extremely painful and difficult to shake off. Each thorn is lined with backward-curving barbs. If you're not careful or you don't know what you're doing, the harder you struggle to free yourself the more seriously entangled you become. The plant itself isn't carnivorous—the thorns' design is entirely defensive—but there are plenty of scavengers in the forest ready to take advantage of any critter that gets hung up in them and exhausts itself trying to fight its way free."

Pulickel leaned over to examine the vine, careful not to touch it. "I can see that you haven't been devoting *all* your time to studying the Parramati."

"They've taught me the characteristics of many plants. The teri-asti vine is just one of them. Others I've learned about on my own." Grabbing the hem of her shorts on her left leg, she pulled the fabric up almost to her waistline, adding to the enormous length of thigh that was already visible. Each roughly eight centimeters long, two parallel stars were etched into her flesh, pale white against her deeply tanned skin. She let the hem fall back.

"Those haven't healed completely yet. I'm not sure they ever will heal completely. I've tried half a dozen different reseptics."

"Another vine?" he asked as they resumed climbing.

"No. A tree-dwelling arthropod about a hundred centimeters long. It's got a dozen legs and a real interesting bite. I was picking jeru fruit and didn't see it until it was right on my leg. I must've disturbed its lair, or nest, or maybe I just caught it in a bad mood. The pain was so severe I thought I was going to fall out of the tree."

"Trouble in paradise." After first checking them for occupants, he pushed leaves out of the way.

"Senisran isn't paradise and neither is Torrelau. Since it was on me I couldn't get a safe angle with my gun. Had to cut its head off with my knife. Then I had to dig the head out of my leg. Strong fangs." She held up one little finger. "About half this long.

"Fortunately, the toxin works slowly. I'm sure that if I didn't have access to modern adaptive antivenins I would've died, or at least lost the leg."

"Sounds to me like you handled it admirably."

"The hell I did. I was screaming and flopping around like a burned baby. I'm surprised they didn't hear me all the way back in Ophhlia. I cried all the way back to the station and most of the rest of the day, until the analgesics started to bite. It felt like somebody was using my quadriceps for kindling. So watch where you put your hands and feet. This environment may look beautiful, but it isn't entirely benign."

"So even though indigenous dangers are abundant and modern weapons would help them cope, the Parramati won't accept them?"

"That's right." She ducked beneath an overhanging cluster of vines. "The big persons say it would violate kusum. This isn't a culture that allows for a lot of flexibility. Either you adhere to kusum or you abandon it. There doesn't seem to be much middle ground."

"Every primitive society hews to an inviolate set of moral imperatives. Flexibility comes in the interpretation. If we persist I bet that sooner or later we'll run into a big person or two who'll find a way to bend the absolutes to their advantage—and to ours."

She shrugged. "I hope you have better luck than I have. I understand that alien semantics is a specialty of yours."

He nodded. "There are times when I think that I get along better with aliens than with other humans."

"Due, no doubt, to your carefully moderated sense of humor."

He glanced up sharply, but she was turned away from him, her attention fixed on the trail, and he couldn't gauge the amount of sarcasm just from her tone.

"If it's any consolation," she went on, "the AAnn are even more frustrated than I am. I don't know that they've ever encountered aboriginals before who wouldn't accept free weapons. They're also frustrated because the Parramati don't do things quickly. Everything takes time since all the big persons have to be consulted on any major decision." She halted, took a deep breath, and gestured through the trees.

"We're almost there. No more climbing."

"It doesn't matter," he replied a little too quickly. "I'm not tired."

The ground leveled off and the forest began to thin. Raising her voice, Fawn called out in the singsong Parramati dialect. Stepping up alongside her, Pulickel was rewarded with his first glimpse of a live seni.

It looked exactly like the recorded images he'd been studying for the past several months. Smaller than expected, it exhibited all the specified characteristics of a juvenile of the species.

"This is Kirtra'a." Fawn made an elaborate rolling gesture of greeting with her forearms. "He's a young male on the cusp of sexual maturity."

"I can see that." While Pulickel studied the young seni, it gazed back at him out of narrow, solemn eyes.

Not yet fully grown, Kirtra'a's head barely reached Pulickel's chest. To the young native, Fawn Seaforth must have seemed like a true giant. The average mature seni would just be able to look the newly arrived male xenologist in the eye.

Leaping into the air on its powerful hind legs, the native did a complete backflip, landing exactly where it had been standing. Taking into account regional variations, this was a fairly universal form of greeting on Senisran. It was the gesture Fawn had attempted to simulate by rotating her forearms.

So both she and the seni were more than a little surprised when Pulickel promptly duplicated the native's athletic move. He staggered slightly when he landed back on his feet and attributed his unsteadiness to the presence of the small backpack. Without it he was certain he could have performed the flip perfectly. While Fawn could only gape, the young Parramati experienced a paroxysm of delight, barking and tootling excitedly.

"I couldn't do that if I practiced for a year. I'd break my neck." Fawn eyed him admiringly.

"You don't have a gymnast's body," he explained modestly. "Poor size-to-strength ratio." Kirtra'a continued to squeal and jabber in wide-eyed wonder. "Don't feel diminished because of it."

"I don't—but I really wish I could do that."

When the juvenile finally calmed down, Pulickel found he could understand it clearly. All the long hours spent listening to and mimicking language recordings paid instant dividends.

"My name is Pulickel Tomochelor."

"Pu'il To'chor." The youngster did his best to duplicate the sounds, many of which were more guttural than a seni could manage. "I am Kirtra'a. Welcomings to Torrelauapa, Pu'il. You do the Greeting!"

"A poor effort." His back had begun to throb but he was damned if he was going to wince. "Not as good as I could do when I was younger, I'm afraid."

The seni had long, narrow, blue, catlike eyes with slitted pupils. The meter-long tail that protruded from the back of the elegant woven skirt was naked as a rat's. Exotic, intricate patterns decorated the skirt, which was worn by both males and females, the individual designs telling another Parramati all there was to know about the wearer, from age to family lineage to status within the wearer's village.

Bipedal and completely hairless, the seni's smooth, featureless skin was the color of finely milled raw cocoa. Each of the two short arms ended in delicate hands that terminated in the three fingers, the central one being considerably longer than the other two. In contrast, the three toes on each foot were thick, strong, and of equal length. There were no nails or claws, fingers and toes alike ending in blunt fleshy pads. Crouching on powerful legs, the seni rested with elbows bent and both hands held close to the chest in an attitude resembling that of a hunting praying mantis.

The seni were the first intelligent species encountered by either humanx or AAnn explorers whose principal mode of individual locomotion was hopping. They were perfectly capable of taking one step at a time, but for anything faster than a crawl, they preferred to hop. They kept their hops short, though according to the literature they could, when startled, leap extraordinary distances.

The seni face was reflective of the species' gentleness and intelligence. Beneath the slitted eyes a long, narrow snout held a mixture of cutting and grinding teeth, terminating in a constantly active black nose. Snout and head were boldly striped, but the high, blade-like, independently rotating ears were not.

The seni were omnivores, taking fruits from the forest, edible invertebrates and coelenterates from the sea, and vegetables and tubers from their elaborate gardens. It was a robust mix, and by and large they were a healthy species. Epidemics were unknown. Clever and adaptable, it was no wonder they had populated nearly all of the larger island groupings and many of the smaller ones on the planet.

His ability to execute the traditional seni greeting had certainly started him off on the right foot with the youngster. Approaching fearlessly, Kirtra'a put both hands on Pulickel's waist and squeezed gently with all six fingers. The xenologist didn't flinch as the young native gazed into his eyes, the toothy snout not far from his face. What was it going to do next? he wondered. Kiss him, bite him, or lick him with the long, flexible seni tongue? That was one gesture he had no intention of returning.

It simply squeezed once and then retreated by means of a second backflip. With a contented squeal, it whirled and bounded off in the direction of the village, doing multiple front flips along the way, apparently for the sheer pleasure of it.

"Well, it looks like you've endeared yourself to one Parramati, anyway." Fawn started down the path. "It'll be interesting to see if you make the same impression on any of the big persons."

He trailed close behind, grateful they were no longer climbing. "Why? What do they do? Backward two-and-a-half gainers?"

"No, just the same single backflip. They're just a lot harder to impress. Harder than me, anyway."

"As an adolescent I was number two on my local gymnastics team. One doesn't have to be large to do well at athletics."

"Hey, am I arguing?"

By way of general conversation he inquired politely, "I suppose you also participated in physical culture?"

"Starting center for four years in my social matriculation group. All-regional. I got banged around a lot."

"Doesn't look like you suffered from it."

She smiled thinly. "I banged back. Hard." She lengthened her stride as they approached the village.

CHAPTER

5

As was so often the case with primitive species, he heard the village before he saw it, and smelled it before he heard it. The pungent odor was not unpleasant, however, and a few deep breaths sufficed to familiarize him with it. Between the cultivated gardens and the surrounding rain forest there were so many flowering plants in the immediate vicinity that the thick musk of the community was somewhat masked by a rush of natural perfume.

Fawn made a sweeping gesture. "This is Torrelauapa. Largest village on the island, though by no means the only one."

"How many are there?" he asked.

"Not sure. You have to delineate the number of houses and their proximity to one another that you want to use to define a 'village.' I'm still working on a definitive census."

It was hard to get a feel for the size of the community because the various structures were scattered among numerous tall shade trees. These were very different from the blue-barked growths he'd first encountered at the touchdown site and the beach. They had thick trunks of brown or yellow and dense overarching clusters of spatulate leaves. Clumps of maroon flowers burst like frozen fireworks from among the leaves. Obviously well tended, the trees served to shield the buildings and their occupants from sun and rain.

A narrow but fast-flowing stream wound its way through the village, drawing volume and energy from the high mountains in the distance. Upon leaving the last of the houses it tumbled, not into a freshwater pool, but over a fifteen-meter-high cliff directly into the ocean below. The watery finger of the steep-sided cove now visible off to the visitors' right was much narrower than the bay Fawn had used to access the station. Thousands of green, blue, and red growths clung to the sheer rock walls, overhanging the water.

The shallow cove was alive with a circus of sea-creatures, clearly visible as they swam back and forth in the transparent water. As well as being safe from large oceangoing predators, they could enjoy the mix of fresh and salt water in the aerated environment at the waterfall's base.

On the far side of the cove, he could see where narrow switchbacks had been cut into the side of the cliff. At the water's edge, where several large rocks protruded from the shallow inlet, a simple floating dock had been constructed of stripped small trees and reeds. Secured to this were several of the sturdy outriggers common to all of Senisran.

Each boasted double masts inclined forty-five degrees from the water and from one another. Not one or two outriggers, but a whole sequence splayed from the sides of each craft. The largest was attached to the side of the boat, the smallest the farthest distance away. The larger the craft, the greater the number of outriggers it deployed. When taken together, winglike sails and outriggers gave the boats the appearance of water birds at rest.

The village was comprised of elongated huts fashioned from local materials. All had thatched roofs while several could boast of raised stone foundations. None was more than ten meters in length, and each was a riot of color thanks to the brilliantly hued materials of which they were composed. The Parramati fondness for weaving was evident in the intricate patterns that decorated every wall and roof. It looked more like a circus encampment than a native community. The naked, bare, beige-colored flesh of the Parramati themselves was plain and dull beside their dwellings.

But the sight that literally took Pulickel's breath away, more than the magnificent little waterfall or the explosively tinted longhouses, were the wonderfully intricate gardens that climbed the terraced mountain slopes on the far side of the village. Now he understood what Fawn had been talking about when she had referred to them as an art form. The growing of food seemed incidental to the elaborate aesthetics that had been employed.

The few images that had been included in the research recordings came nowhere near doing the Parramatis' agricultural accomplishments justice. The actual terracing was comparatively unspectacular and, as expected, followed the natural contours of the mountainside. What distinguished them were the exquisitely carved and entwined trellises and arbors that protected them from damage by direct sun and wind. It looked as if the entire mountainside had been clad in a single gigantic, interlinked wooden sculpture. In intricacy and purity of design, it reminded him of the skeletons of microscopic foraminifera. In addition to the wondrous carving, every centimeter of the huge, rambling construction had been painted in delicate hues and designs.

Not merely decorative, the trellises provided protection for new, young plants and support for those maturing. Water lines handfashioned from hollow stems and branches irrigated the ascending gardens. Each as deeply carved as the trellises and arbors, they were perfectly integrated into the overall design.

From a distance Pulickel could make out large figures woven into the upper reaches of the vast, rambling structure. In all his years of study, he'd never seen anything quite like it.

"It's something, isn't it?" Fawn shouldered her pack higher on her shoulders. "Every pattern has traditional meaning, every outlined figure its own story. Once you know the Parramati, you can identify any family or clan by its piece of the communal garden. Kusum is right there, for anyone who knows how to read it. So are the roads."

"Roads?" He squinted. "I don't see any paths wider than the trail we're on now."

She looked back at him and smiled. "When the Parramati speak of roads, they're not talking about cleared strips of land. You'll find out. What do you think of Torrelauapa?"

"Very impressive. You were right. The few official recordings don't come close to doing it justice. These gardens must represent hundreds of years of work."

"And they keep adding to the artistic quotient every day. A section of carving here, a little paint there." She stepped over a dislodged rock. "The Parramati are quite a people."

As they entered the village outskirts, she began searching individual Parramati faces. "We're looking for a male named Jorana."

"Is he the chief? No," he hastened to correct himself, "you said there were no chiefs."

"That's right. He's just one of many Torrelauapa big persons. Someone who's respected by his fellows for any number of possible achievements. A big person isn't necessarily smarter than anyone else, or stronger, or a better fisherman. They just have respect.

Remember, no big person ranks another. Technically, they don't even rank the lowliest citizen. This isn't Ophhlia or Nalauevu.

"That's one reason why we're having so much trouble forging any kind of formal alliance with these people. Jorana could agree to put his name to a treaty, but Osiwivi or Massapapu might not. Since no one can compel anyone else, you practically have to sign a separate treaty with each adult Parramati."

Pulickel was nodding to himself. "I begin to see the scope of your problem here. Securing a treaty isn't impossible; it's just going to take time. Time and patience."

"That's right. And meanwhile, the AAnn are working just as hard to convince individual Parramati to bond with *them*."

"Controlled anarchy," he murmured.

"Isn't that a good definition of Athenian democracy?" She pointed. "There he is. Jorana's a famous carver."

The Parramati big person was seated at a simple bench whose upper surface consisted of the flat side of a split log. Shade was provided by an open-sided thatched roof, a shed without walls. Limber three-fingered hands worked with tools of bone, shell, beak, and stone. At the moment the native was working on one of three table legs. Each was roughly a meter in length and magnificently incised. One had already been inlaid with carved shell and bone and rubbed to a high polish.

Technology the Parramati might not have, but their culture was clearly of a high order. Pulickel knew the table legs alone would fetch a good price in Ophhlia. He couldn't imagine what the intact, completed table might bring from a collector on Earth or New Riviera. Aboriginal alien artifacts were one product modern technology couldn't synthesize, hence their continuing value to the cognoscenti.

And the art of each island group, each archipelago, was unique and different. Based on what he'd seen so far, that of Parramati could stand with the best of it.

Noticing their approach, the elderly big person put down his tools and rose from his working crouch. Placing his head upon the ground and flattening his ears, he executed a simple backward roll.

"Jorana can't do the flip anymore," Fawn informed her companion.

"What do I do? If I do the somersault will he be insulted?"

"You don't have to do anything," she assured him. "Jorana's used to my lack of acrobatics. It's not expected of humans." Raising her voice, she switched to the lilting singsong dialect of Parramat.

"Hello, Jorana! May your road be straight and clear."

"As may yours, F'an." Despite the slight quaver in his speech, Pulickel had no trouble understanding him.

"This is the coming of the other human I told you about." She indicated her attentive companion. "He is called Pulickel."

The old one's jaws ground slowly from side to side as if he was grinding bone. "Pu'il. A difficult name."

"I am sorry," Pulickel replied fluently. "Pu'il will be perfectly satisfactory."

"But your real name is longer. Will it satisfy you to be so identified?" Long cat-eyes gazed speculatively at the xenologist.

"So long as you don't confuse it with one belonging to one of your wives." Pulickel knew alien humor was always a difficult proposition, but he'd never been cautious where language was concerned.

A gargling sound came from the Parramati's throat, signifying not only acceptance and understanding but appreciation. Fawn looked on admiringly.

Jorana turned to her. "Is Pu'il a big person among your kind?"

"Bigger than I. Big enough to talk about things I cannot talk about."

The alien turned back to his work. "Well, it is always good to talk," he commented noncommittally. "Come and sit. I am working on a Pr'ithma ceremonial table."

The two xenologists accepted the invitation, settling themselves crosslegged close to the Parramati and beneath the shade of the thatched shelter. This left the alien squatting on its haunches, looking down at them. The seni used tables and beds, but not chairs. With their powerful hind legs, they could remain in a squatting/sitting position for hours at a time.

They watched quietly while their host used a wooden block lined with tiny sharp-edged shells to sand a rough section of tabletop. "One cannot reduce the beauty of the wood," he murmured. "But one can transform it." A slitted eye glanced at Fawn. "Ascela was asking for you."

"Who's Ascela?" Pulickel inquired.

His companion reverted to terranglo for the explanation. "Another Torrelauapa big person. Much younger than Jorana, not as big or as strong, but maybe smarter."

"But that doesn't mean he ranks Jorana."

She smiled approvingly. "Now you're getting the hang of it. And Ascela is female." Turning back to the woodworker, she swung her pack off her back and resumed speaking in the local tongue. "I have something for you, Jorana." Reaching into the carryall, she brought out a glassine envelope containing a dozen colorful titanium fishhooks. Pulickel was quick to note that the smallest was the size of his little finger. Apparently the Parramati diet included some fairly sizable denizens of the deep.

Taking the bag, Jorana made a show of inspecting the contents. Then, with a regretful yip, he handed it back. "I am sorry, Fawn, but I cannot accept these."

Her expression fell. "Why not?"

"Because we hunt the waters with straight points, not curved ones."

"I know, but what you do with these is put a little bait on them and tie them to a line. The coliat or metikim smell the bait and try to eat it. They catch themselves on the hook."

"But why wait?" Jorana was genuinely curious, his long, pointed ears arched sharply forward. "Any decent fisherman can go out on a boat, look into the water, and spear his quarry."

"But you don't always come back with something that way," Fawn argued. "Sometimes the spears miss and the boats come back empty."

"That is true." The carver scrutinized the package and its gleaming, high-tech contents. "And this works every time?"

"Well, no. The quarry has to take the bait and the fisherman has to make sure the hook is set before he tries to pull it in."

"I see." As Pulickel winced, the native emptied the bag's sharp contents into his open palm. Apparently that smooth, beige-hued skin was tougher than it looked. Jorana returned them to the gift-giver by placing the hooks on the ground in front of her. Then he held up the empty bag.

"This, however, is another of your wonderful carrying containers, and for this gift I thank you."

"See?" Fawn spoke again to her companion in their own language. "Any other seni society would have been glad to have the hooks, if only to trade with another island group. Not the Parramati. Here, a gift must be deemed immediately useful or it's refused."

"You should have this." Digging through a pile of wooden

shapes, Jorana extracted an exquisite carving a little larger than Pulickel's palm. Finely polished, the wood was jet black streaked with red. The carver had fashioned it into the likeness of a local animal with four legs, a stubby body, and two eyes protruding on stalks. The eyes had been carved so that they contained only the red grain, and a double set of external gills appeared made of lace, though they were also part of the single piece of hardwood.

Fawn was taken aback. "I can't accept that," she protested. "Not in exchange for a lousy plastic bag."

"Please." The native pushed the sculpture at her. "It is a fair exchange. I have many, many carvings and they are easy for me to make."

Professional considerations aside, Pulickel could see that Fawn wanted the delicate carving. Hell, he wanted it himself.

"Very well," she agreed reluctantly, "but to make it fair I must bring you more bags."

"Done." Pleased, the native handed her the little sculpture. Pulickel found himself wishing he'd brought along a few spare bags himself.

According to the information in the slim manual that had been prepared for him, now that official greetings, introductions, and gift-giving had been concluded, the conversation was open to any topic any of the participants might choose to introduce. Edging a little closer to the big person and avoiding something that scuttled along the ground on far too many legs, he watched appreciatively as the Parramati used a sharpened palm-size shell to etch traditional spirals and whorls into one table leg.

"I have come from my home, from my island in the sky, to . . ."

The native interrupted him with an expression that at the very least was suggestive of a smile. "It is not necessary, Pu'il, to explain. F'an has told us many things. Besides, the Parramati have always thought of the lights in the night sky as other islands, whose people set torches at night to show travelers the way through the ocean of darkness."

"Then I won't go into a lot of background. I know that my friend Fawn has already spoken to you about signing a treaty of friendship and commerce with our people. One that would allow us to move and trade freely among the islands of the Parramat and to search for and remove certain rocks from the ground. Such a treaty would greatly benefit the Parramati. You would be given access to many wondrous tools and learning devices.

"For example, you could learn how to better farm your gardens, how to produce more with less work. You would acquire weapons that would let you fight not only the forest animals that menace you but even the dangerous creatures of the sea. We can give you boats that would not sink in a storm and that could tell you always where you were, even in thick fog."

Jorana did not look up from his work, though both ears stayed turned in his guests' direction. His long snout twitched. "Why would one want to know where he is at all times?"

Pulickel smiled patiently. "If one knows where one is at all times, it is impossible to become lost."

"No Parramati is ever 'lost.' " Jorana knocked a shaving off the top of the table leg.

The xenologist frowned. "I don't understand. If a fisherman sails far, far out to sea, farther than he or any other Parramati has ever traveled before, could he not become lost among unfamiliar islands and places?"

"He would not be lost," the carver explained, "because he would know exactly where he was. Wherever he happened to be, he would be there. 'There' is always a place, and as long as one is in a place, one cannot be lost."

Pulickel fought down his impatience. He hadn't expected quite so sophisticated a rejoinder to what seemed the blatantly obvious. "But he would be lost in relation to his home, and might not know how to return."

"Nonsense. He would simply return the way he had traveled."

The xenologist decided to try another approach. "You've seen some of our kind's tools." He patted the sidearm snugged at his hip. "Our weapons, the boat that flies in air, our clothes. You've seen how they last. Wouldn't you like to have these things for yourself and for your people?"

"Not so very much." Wood chips spiraled lazily to the ground. "They are your weapons, your boat, your clothing. If we were to make use of so many of your things, it would mean that ours would be neglected. That would mean neglecting tradition, which is the same as neglecting kusum."

"Not in the least," Pulickel argued. "You could still use your traditional things. You would just have more choices."

The shell planer paused in mid-scrape. Bright, intelligent eyes peered directly into Pulickel's own. "Sometimes it is not a good thing for a people to have too many choices." Double eyelids blinked slowly. "People with too many choices might forget their kusum. We know that this has happened on other islands. The people there have changed and cannot go back. From what we hear, I do not know that they are any happier for this." He raised a three-fingered hand.

"We cannot talk through the air as F'an does, but neither are we ignorant of what happens elsewhere. Talk travels quickly enough, Pu'il. We have heard of what has happened to some who have accepted the big gifts from your people and from the shiny-skinned ones. We have heard what has happened to the Jimeri, the Corchosi, and the Trefaria. They have traded away their kusum, which is a bigger thing than trading bags and carvings."

Pulickel searched his memory. "There was an epidemic of food poisoning on Corchos. Commonwealth medicine saved many lives there."

Ears flicked, indicating that Jorana was not impressed. "There were too many Corchosi. Some must die so that others may live. The Corchosi who survive do so without their kusum. They are alive, but they are no longer Corchosi. Now they must rely on their trade to feed and support them. They have become wards of your kusum. This is bad for the spirit."

"I don't know that that's the case," Pulickel responded doubtfully.

"We do. Understand," the native continued gently, "I do not mean to criticize the decisions of the Jimeri, the Trefaria, or the Corchosi. They have done willingly what they have done. They have made their choices. But the Parramati choose the same road we have always chosen. Our kusum will stay pure. You may keep your boats that fly in air and bows that kill without arrows."

"I'm sorry you feel that way." Pulickel was not discouraged. After all, this was his first attempt. "Perhaps other big persons will feel differently." At this, Seaforth shot him a warning look, but he ignored her. It had been his experience that alien aboriginals of whatever intelligence favored directness.

Jorana was not offended. "You may talk to any of the Parramati that you wish." His left arm came up and three fingers spread wide in an eloquent gesture. "Some will not listen to you, but all will be polite. It may be that you will find one who can be swayed by what you have to offer. But it will be only one. Even if it is another big person, it will be only one."

"I understand. I, too, can be patient." To Fawn he added in ter-ranglo, "How the hell are we supposed to achieve a viable consensus here? Are they all going to be this stubborn?" As he spoke he continued to smile at the alien, who had returned to his carving.

"I hope not. I've had luck with some of the younger Parramati," she told him. "Maybe with your skills we'll be able to secure some firm commitments. I'm hoping for a snowball effect, especially among the younger and middle-level big persons, but I've had to learn patience."

He nodded. "That's the ticket. Get a fair number to come around to our way of thinking and let them do the convincing of the others. I can see why you wanted me to meet this Jorana: he's clearly an exceptional individual among his kind. But I agree that we might do better to concentrate the majority of our efforts on the younger, more flexible members of the tribe."

She nodded. "We can still try to convince Jorana and Ascela and the other elders. I have to confess that part of the reason I've spent so much time working with them is that I enjoy listening to them."

"That's okay," he replied. "We need to learn all we can about their society and culture, and for that you have to speak with the local elders. But I can see already that a political solution to our problem will have to be found in working with the more malleable islanders. We'll keep trying Jorana here and his counterparts; we just won't rely on them." He addressed himself anew to the alien.

"I am curious, Jorana. Do you think we offer you these things because it is our intention to harm you, or because we *want* to make you forget your kusum?"

The elder paused in his carving. "No, Pu'il. I am sure your people wish to do us good. That is part of *your* kusum. It means that you believe your kusum to be stronger than ours."

"Not stronger," the xenologist objected. "I choose to see them as different but compatible."

"You imply otherwise when you suggest that your weapons, your tools, and your learning should replace ours."

"Not replace. Supplement."

Jorana's ears twitched and his upper lip rippled like a wavelet on a shallow beach. "Listen well to me, Pu'il. The Parramati have their own weapons, their own tools, their own boats, and their own ways. Each has its own power, its own magic. The trees behind you, the bench you sit upon, the ground beneath your feet. It takes time to learn to know these powers and magics, to see the best way of using them. We have ours, you have yours. Ours does not need to be supplemented, not even by those good of heart and intention."

"Hierophanes," Fawn murmured.

Pulickel frowned at her. "What did you say?"

"Parramati society is based on hierophanes. Everything in the world is seen as a manifestation of the sacred. Each is a hierophane and each has power. With access to so much power, they see no need to invite in outside influences."

He nodded disappointedly. "It makes it difficult to convince a people to give something up if everything controls something else. But I still think that when some of the younger villagers accept access to advanced technology, Jorana and the others will come around." He switched back to the local dialect.

"I agree with you, Jorana. Everything in the world has a certain amount of power. Some have more, some less. Certain minerals that lie beneath the Parramat have very much power. My people have spent a lot of time learning how to make use of these, while the Parramati have not. So you see, our kusums are not so very far apart."

The old carver considered. "F'an has spoken of such. As you say, I would not know of such powers. I am a wood person, not an earth person. My road leads through the forest. To learn the value of certain rocks you would have to talk to someone whose road is of the earth."

"But if no one is using these minerals, why would the Parramati object to my people doing so?"

Jorana blinked double lids. "If the earth is turned up too much, it is bad for growing things."

The xenologist had had enough. "I think that's plenty for one day. We don't want to tire the old fellow, or irritate him. I'm happy with the progress we've made. Let's leave him to consider what has been said." He brushed wood dust from his shorts as he rose.

Fawn straightened. "You don't want to talk to anyone else in the village?"

"Not today. I don't want to get a reputation for being insistent or demanding. Nothing puts primitive peoples off more quickly. Better they should grow curious about me. That way, hopefully the next time they'll be anxious to see me, instead of simply polite."

Stretching, he bid the elder big person a polite farewell. "It has been good to talk with you, Jorana."

"And with you, Pu'il. F'an, I am always warmed by your presence." He bent low until his nostrils skimmed the ground. It was as close as he could come to performing the traditional flip.

"I am pleased by your happiness." She duplicated the elder's motion, bending double at the waist.

"Then I will see you both again?" Vibrantly colored alien eyes regarded them both.

"Very soon, I hope." With a hand gesture, Fawn turned to leave.

They headed out of the village and back toward the forest. A clutch of boisterous, barking juveniles escorted them. With powerful legs and feet too big for their still immature bodies, they tumbled and fell over one another in their eagerness to accompany the strange visitors. Only when dense vegetation closed in around the humans did the pack fall back, in twos and threes, toward their home. Their playful, high-pitched singing followed Pulickel and Fawn for long moments thereafter.

"You did pretty good for a first encounter." She stepped over a hollow that had filled with rainwater. "Just the right mix of conviction and understanding. I was afraid the stiffness and formality of your character would carry over into your fieldwork."

"But it didn't," he responded, "which means I'm just stiff and formal the rest of the time, right?"

"Not exactly," she demurred, trying to backtrack.

"It's all right. I know that I'm something of a cold fish. Like I said before, I relate much better to aliens. There are no preconceptions on either side."

She changed the subject. "I know it's premature, but do you have an opinion of the situation so far?"

He shrugged. "If this Jorana is a typical big person, then I don't foresee any further extensive delays. They're stubborn, but they seem to enjoy debate. Any creature that will talk with me is one I can eventually persuade to see reason. I sense exploitable openings already. Conclusion? It will take more time than I'd hoped but less than I'd feared."

She shoved a branch out of her way. It promptly exuded a cloud of perfumed dust. Since she walked right through it, Pulickel saw no harm in doing likewise. For a delightful moment, the world smelled of sandalwood and myrrh.

"Jorana's right, of course. If the Parramati give their consent to a full treaty, much of their traditional kusum will eventually be overwhelmed."

"I know that." He stumbled awkwardly down a slight slope.

"But the alternative is for them to fall under the influence of the AAnn. Better the Commonwealth than the Empire."

"Certainly. Unless they choose the third option and elect to remain unallied with either side."

He moved up alongside her and gazed flatly into her face. "There is no third option, Fawn. Not for primitive aliens. I'm not sure there ever was."

CHAPTER

6

"Why do I have the feeling?" he asked as they prepared to reboard the skimmer, "that there's a lot more to the Parramati and their kusum than you're telling me? You keep insisting that they're different. Of course they're different; they're aboriginal aliens."

Both hands on the ladder built into the vehicle's flank, she paused. "I've told you, Pulickel. I can't quite put my finger on it. Sure their society is unique among organized seni groups, but it's more than that. There's an assurance, a contentment that you can't find among the Eoluro or the Semisant, or even the Ophhlians. It's easy to see but hard to quantify." Effortlessly, she boarded the skimmer.

He followed and settled himself into the passenger seat. "I think you may be making too much of them, Fawn. The Parramati may be different from other social groupings on Senisran, but they don't strike me as particularly unique. Reactionary, yes, but not unique."

"I expect you're right." She powered up the skimmer's engine.

In response to the rising whine, something with a tail three times the length of its body went screeching off through the trees. With wings that were feathered in front and membranous in the rear, it had the appearance of a marvelous kite whose string was being given random jerks and pulls by a mischievous child.

The skimmer rose and pivoted to face the water. Fawn spoke without looking up from the console. "One thing I am sure of: we're never going to convince the Parramati to sign a treaty with us as opposed to the AAnn unless we can find a way to convince them that our road is the better one."

He blinked at her. "Our 'road'?"

The skimmer slid out over the calm water of the inlet. Small silver-sided cephalopods leaped into the air ahead of them, strips of mirror flashing in the sun.

"According to the Parramati belief system, everything in the universe—every person, every place, every dust mote—is connected by roads. These roads are fixed and immutable. Many are irrelevant to the scheme of things, but many others link places of importance and power. The location of these important roads are marked by special stones."

He turned thoughtful. "And each stone possesses certain qualities, powers, or mystic ascriptions?" She nodded. "A fairly basic and straightforward mythology, not especially remarkable. I could list a dozen analogies off the top of my head, others after doing a little research. Cultural specifics of primitive sentients often overlap, regardless of species."

They were out over the main lagoon now, accelerating as Fawn turned southward. "From my conversations with the Parramati, I've been able to make a short list of these stones. There are stones for healing, stones for fertility, for warding off disease or confounding enemies, and for forecasting the weather. There are stones that help in the steering of outriggers and stones for communicating with the spirits of dead ancestors.

"Control of the stones is strictly hierarchical. The patriarch of a family charged with the keeping of a planting stone wouldn't try to swap rocks with the matriarch of a clan holding a fishing stone. Stone magic is handed down through family lines and helps to keep the peace among the Parramati. You can't fight with your neighbors because you might want the assistance of their stones some day."

"Very convenient and ingenious, but I still see nothing that could be considered remarkable." Pulickel shifted in his seat, watching the clear water race past several meters below them.

As always, they found the station undisturbed. At their approach a gaggle of polutans—short, two-legged creatures with mournful dark eyes and incredibly ornate feathery crowns—went loping away from the trash pile like a flurry of midget extras from the last act of a Puccini opera.

"Cute little suckers, aren't they?"

Pulickel eyed the dark patch of vegetation where the creatures had vanished. "Very pretty. What are they, some kind of flightless bird?" Tired, he forbore from pointing out that she had once again neglected to activate the station's defensive perimeter prior to their departure.

"I'm not sure. I let the computer handle most of the taxonomic classifying, but it can't do anything unless I feed it information, and I've been pretty much preoccupied with the Parramati."

"I thought it was with improving your tan."

She gave him a sour look. "No, that's only my third priority. So you do have a sense of humor."

"I'm told that it's buried pretty deep, but occasionally it surfaces in spite of myself."

"Frankly, I'm surprised you'd noticed my tan. What's your opinion?" Seated, she still managed to strike a pose.

Thus invited, he allowed himself a long lingering look. "That you've been more successful with it than with the Parramati."

She snorted softly. "You're telling me." Using her feet, she drove the skimmer farther south.

Later that night, long after the evening meal had been concluded, he noticed her outside, walking the station perimeter. At his touch of a switch, one of the wide window panels slid aside. Warm, humid air meshed confusingly with that of the air-conditioned station as the night sounds of Parramat entertained his hearing.

"Lose something?" he called out and down to her.

She looked back and up. "Just checking the alarm stanchions. I didn't mean to distract you."

"You never distract me," he lied. Staring down at her, he was rewarded with a sardonic pout. From the night-shrouded forest, something declared its alienness with a hair-raising howl. "I thought you didn't worry about the local life-forms, even the dangerous ones."

"I don't. It's the AAnn who concern me. Them, and your desire to always have this damn thing turned on." She knelt to run a hand-held analyzer down the length of an activated stanchion.

He leaned out the open window. "I suppose I can imagine them trying to engineer an 'accident' in the field, but surely they wouldn't approach the station itself."

"Why not? Since neither side has any kind of formal agreement with the Parramati, they're as free to move around Torrelau as we are. By the same token, I could go clomping around Mallatyah—if I didn't mind being shot at." Rising, she moved to another stanchion and began repeating the inspection procedure. "But we can legally keep them away from the station itself and from cutting our throats while we sleep."

He shifted his arms against the sill. "That wouldn't look very good in light of the agreement on mutual cooperation for extraseni affairs that both the Commonwealth and Empire governments have signed."

"No, it wouldn't, but we wouldn't be around to chortle over the final resolution. I have no interest in becoming one of the triumphant deceased." She touched the analyzer to the top of the stanchion. Both devices promptly responded with a satisfying green flash. "On the other hand, if we were to be massacred in our beds, dragged out of the station, hauled onto a skimmer, and dumped into the ocean, seagoing scavengers would quickly eliminate the evidence. That's a chance I'd rather not take. In spite of what you think, I do occasionally leave the system running, especially at night."

Noting that she was more than half finished, he let his gaze roam skyward. Alien constellations teased his contemplation with suggestions of fantastical shapes that would have delighted the ancient Greeks.

"Beautiful night. Too pretty for homicidal speculations."

"Not where the AAnn are concerned. Forgive me if I seem a little paranoid on the subject, Pulickel, but you have to remember that I've been here alone for quite a while. Is the defensive screen on, is the defensive screen off—you can go crazy trying to keep up with your fears. Of course, now that you're here to protect me, I guess I don't have to worry about it anymore."

"Mock if you will. But I'm actually reasonably handy with a gun. It's a necessary component of the job." He smiled down at her. "But I don't shoot very well when I'm asleep."

"Precisely my point. We wouldn't be the first fieldworkers to vanish with the AAnn offering protestations of innocence in response to follow-up inquiries. I'm not saying they're responsible for what happened to the Murchinsons on Bandameva last year, but no one can prove that they weren't, either. Me, I have no intention of disappearing without explanation, or even with one.

"As for the station and you, they're both technically my responsibility."

Something fist-size and bright orange came whizzing out of the darkness to circle him twice before darting back into the night. Instinctively he swatted at it, but his slow-motion flailings didn't come close to hitting the creature, whatever it was.

"Why am I your responsibility?"

"Because even though you rank me within the Department, I'm the one in charge of Parramat station." Her tone was firm. "I'm the one who helped set it up, I'm the one who's been here for months, and I'm the one charged with the care of all local Commonwealth facilities."

"Dear me," he responded with mock uncertainty. "I don't think I've ever been referred to as a facility before."

"Go ahead and laugh. The AAnn have made several visits to Torrelau. They're concentrating on Mallatyah, of course, but they're not neglecting the other inhabited islands. Have I mentioned that their base commander is a slimy sort? Essasu RRGVB. An irritable character, as if the average AAnn wasn't testy enough."

"The AAnn aren't slimy," he reminded her.

"I was referring to his personality, not his epidermis."

Pulickel pondered. "How are they doing lately?"

"As near as I've been able to tell from talking with Jorana, Ascela, and other Torrelauans, no better than me. On the days and weeks when I feel that I haven't made any progress, I comfort myself with that thought. They have a full contact unit on Mallatyah, whereas until now there's just been me here on Torrelau."

"Well, now that there's two of us," he responded, "maybe we can double your progress."

"Sounds good to me." She was nearly finished with her inspection. "You know, I don't give a shit about the ytrrium, and niobium, and all the other 'iums' that the Commonwealth wants to dig out of Parramat. It's the Parramati themselves who fascinate me. That's why I've stayed on here for so long instead of putting in for a transfer. These people are hinting around at something of major importance, and I'm not leaving here until I figure out what it is.

"As for the AAnn and the danger they present, that's something I've learned to live with. One day I was out doing some collecting on the far side of the lagoon when the remote alarm I had connected to the skimmer went off. Let's just say that if I hadn't been alert and prepared, the skimmer might have 'drifted' off, leaving me stranded out too far to swim back against the prevailing currents. There have been other potential accidents that I've managed to avoid. Doesn't do any good to yell or complain or say anything about it, of course. The AAnn are consummate deniers."

"Alternatively, if they succeeded in doing away with us, they might choose to dispose of the evidence by consuming it."

He started. "I've never heard of the AAnn eating a human, or a thranx."

She grinned up at him, her face illuminated by the monitor lights that were an integral part of the armed stanchions. "They wouldn't rush to publicize a taste like that, now would they? Personally, I don't understand your reaction. Meat is meat. If I was hungry enough I certainly wouldn't hesitate to eat an AAnn, provided it had been properly cooked."

She might look like a goddess, he mused, but there were aspects to her that were decidedly un-Olympian. For these he was grateful. They helped to keep his thoughts focused where they belonged.

The inspection concluded, she started back toward the lift shaft. "The AAnn may not be having any better luck at persuading the Parramati to see things their way, but they're certainly more active in their attempts to eliminate the competition."

He had to lean out and look down to follow her progress. "Surely they know there'd be an investigation."

She paused to look up at him. "Uh-huh. Which means they wouldn't follow through on anything unless they were pretty confident of getting away with it. Which is why I check the equipment alarms and my weapons regularly." She vanished beneath the building's overhanging edge. A moment later he heard the muted whine of the lift as she started up.

Raising his gaze, he stared out into the squeaking, squalling, chittering rain forest, with its multihued trees and tremulous undergrowth. Were there night-camouflaged AAnn slinking about out there even now, watching him as he relaxed there at the open window, training night sights on his forehead preparatory to blowing his brains out?

He stepped back and closed the window. Not for the first time, Fawn Seaforth had given him something else to think about before retiring besides herself.

As warm, languid days came and went, progress in persuading the Torrelauans to formalize relations with the Commonwealth advanced at the philosopher Russell's two classic speeds: dead slow and slower than dead. Jorana, the other big persons Pulickel talked to, even those with the least status among the villagers: all were unvaryingly polite, cordial, and obstinate. They expressed respectful interest in all the benefits Pulickel and Fawn claimed a formal treaty would bring to the people of Parramat. They were willing to listen to comparisons of what both the Commonwealth and the Empire had to offer. And they absolutely, uncategorically, refused to agree to anything.

It wasn't long before Pulickel came to the conclusion that many, if not all, of the natives he had established a personal relationship with listened to him purely out of courtesy, and that they had no intention of giving serious consideration to the proposals he so carefully presented. Just as Fawn had warned him, they wanted nothing to do with the benefits being proffered either by the Commonwealth or the Empire.

One morning he confessed as much as they walked the mountain-side southwest of the village, continuing their study of the extraordinary gardens of Torrelauapa. Middle and small persons worked the terraces while youngsters, their antics patiently tolerated by the busy adults, bounded and chased one another through the lush growth and elaborate arbors. Damp earth squished beneath the xenologists' field sandals and they had to duck repeatedly to avoid bumping into the intricate, decorative trelliswork.

"Now you know," Fawn was telling him, "why from time to time I've been less than fanatical about my work here. If the Parramati ever agree to a formal treaty with the Commonwealth, it's not going to happen in a sudden burst of enthusiasm. It's going to be the result of a long, tedious grind."

Pulickel stepped carefully over something that looked like a meter-long yellow squash. "I'm sorry, Fawn, but I can't accept that. I'm not the long, tedious grind kind of person."

"You don't say." She started up a line of stone steps. "I never would've guessed. Listen to me: like it or not, you'd better resign yourself to the idea. Impatience here will only result in greater and greater frustration. No matter how clever or persistent you are, you can't rush the Parramati."

He followed her with his eyes. "The longest it's ever taken me to resolve a xenological impasse was three months. It's a record I'm quite proud of, and I do not intend on losing it here."

Idly waving at something small and fast that persisted in hovering in front of her face, she looked back over a shoulder at him. "I'd like to think you're right. Unfortunately, experience tells me otherwise. And, there's the big person I wanted you to meet."

Their climb had taken them to the topmost terraces and both of them were breathing a little harder in the thick, humid air. "What is she," he asked as he caught sight of the alien in question and was able to sex it, "a hermit?"

"No. Ascela and her relations just prefer to live up here. Think of it as a one-family suburb."

Approaching, Fawn lowered her head toward the earth. Several of the younger seni in the vicinity responded with neatly tucked forward flips. When Pulickel duplicated their efforts, as he was now known to do, their delight was joyous to behold. The senior Parramati the xenologists had come to meet yipped appreciatively.

"I had heard that you could do the greeting, friend Pu'il." Lips rippled eloquently.

He studied the mature female. She appeared to be approaching late middle age, though it was hard to be sure. The species did not manifest many outward indications of advancing years until they were quite elderly, but he was gradually learning to recognize the subtle indicators. She was a little less erect, a shade less bouncy on her hind legs than most of her brethren.

"It is pleasing to meet you." He extended both hands palm upward. Three long, smooth fingers did their best to cover four of his own, ignoring the thumb. The seni found that extra afterthought of a digit quite amusing. Finger-out-of-place, they called it in their own language.

Fawn was speaking. "I have brought my friend Pulickel to talk with you because he wishes to learn about roads and about stones."

"I am not surprised." The senior Parramati withdrew her hands. "It is said that you have no stones of your own and must use other things instead."

"This is true." In terranglo she told Pulickel, "I've tried to explain to these people what a computer is and what it does. It's not a concept that translates well to a culture with low-end technology."

"How did you finally do it?"

"Told them they were like flat stones that were connected by roads through the air. That's pretty simplistic, but it's a concept they can handle."

Ascela was picking some kind of oval-shaped blue berries with pink spots, her long middle finger snapping them off the vine and placing them in a basket she carried beneath one arm. "Did you come to me now because there is going to be a mastorm tonight?"

Pulickel's expression twisted slightly. "A mastorm? How does that differ from any other storm?"

"In the same way," Fawn explained, "that a big person differs from a small person, or a stone master from one who can only sift gravel."

"Then it's just a bigger storm."

"Not hardly." She walked alongside the busy elder, towering over her and the other Parramati. "It's a unique local meteorological phenomenon, sort of a pocket hurricane. Too compact to be a typhoon, too extended to be tornado. They form in the southwest at regular intervals and sweep over the archipelago. Riding one out is quite an experience. They're intense, and dangerous, but they're over fairly quickly. I haven't had time to analyze the mechanics very closely. When one sweeps in, I'm usually too busy seeing to the integrity of the station to spend time making observations."

He brooded on the consequences of this possible new disruption of his work. "But it's just a storm."

She nodded. "Insofar as I've been able to determine. If you want a local take, ask Ascela." He proceeded to do exactly that.

"The mastorm is a break in the roads." Three-fingered hands continued to pluck berries with the delicacy of a surgeon. "During such times, certain stones do not work properly and people must be careful."

"I can imagine," he murmured. "There's nothing worse than a defective stone." Fawn frowned in his direction but, as usual, he ignored her.

Ascela took him literally. "That is very true." She raised her penetrating gaze to the southwest. "This one will be difficult."

He eyed her tolerantly. "Are you the local weather forecaster?"

She turned bright seni eyes on him. "There has been a weather stone in my family for a hundred generations."

"There are two others on the island," Fawn told him. "Each island has its own complement of weather stones, fishing stones, growing stones, and so on."

"I remember." To the female big person he said, "I wouldn't mind seeing your weather stone."

Fawn missed a step, but Ascela didn't hesitate, gesturing elaborately with one delicate hand. "I would be pleased to show it to you, friend Pu'il. You must not touch it, of course, since you are not a stone master."

"I quite understand." Bending, he removed a glittering piece of quartz from the narrow paved path along which they were walking. "I have my own stones."

"Come with me, then."

Her simple home commanded a panoramic view of the terraced hillside, the surrounding green-clad mountains, and the village below. From such heights, the magnificent waterfall that tumbled into the narrow inlet beneath the village was a mere distant trickle.

There was nothing different or striking about the sparse, clean, artfully decorated structure. It sat on short stone legs and looked out on several smaller outlying buildings that were used variously for storage and hygiene.

The sacred stone was kept in a small rear room of its own, atop a wonderfully carved and fluted pedestal of richly polished, dark purple metaria wood that spiraled up from the floor like an amethyst whirlpool. As near as Pulickel could tell, the stone was not guarded, alarmed, rigged, fastened, or otherwise protected from intruders.

Ascela confirmed this by simply reaching out and picking it up. Any youngster could have done it.

It wasn't quite what Pulickel had expected. Uncarved and apparently unworked, the head-size, irregularly shaped lump of dark greenish glass hinted at a volcanic origin. Flung out by some ancient eruption, the stone might have come from any of a number of highly visible peaks that poked their dead or dormant crowns above the islands of the archipelago.

Ascela held it out for his inspection. One end was slightly flattened while the other exhibited several sharp edges where the material had been cut or fractured. There were hints of multiple inclusions within the material, no doubt other minerals that had formed in the course of the eruption. As a specimen it was interesting but hardly revelatory.

He watched as she turned it slowly in her hands. "This helps you to predict the weather?"

Ascela's long fingers twisted. "When it becomes necessary."

"That's nice." Having been invited in, the disappointed xenologist struggled to show interest. Now that he was actually seeing one of the fabulous sacred stones of Parramati mythology, he was distinctly underwhelmed. "The other stones all look pretty much like this one?"

"All the ones I've seen." Fawn was watching him closely. "Shapes and sizes differ, but I think they're all fashioned from the same favored material."

"That figures." He turned back to the big person who was their hostess. "Thank you for showing me the stone. We have to go now."

"You see how they avoid fighting among themselves." Fawn was explaining as they exited the simple but sturdy structure and started back down the mountainside. "Since different families 'control' different stones, it forces cooperation on them. The masters of the fishing stones need the help of the masters of the growing stones, who need the help of the masters of the weather stones, who often consult the masters of the healing stones, and so on. You can steal a stone, but not the generationally accumulated knowledge of how to use it. So you cooperate. That's the beauty of the setup. The Parramati aren't so much pacific as they are sensible."

"It's a good system that obviously contributes to a more stable culture than is to be found on many of the island groups." He was staring southward, where billowing cloud masses were gathering. Several were starting to show dark undersides.

"Of course, if you're going to lay claim to the position of tribal meteorologist, it doesn't hurt to live near the highest point on the island so that you can see approaching weather before anyone else." He smiled knowingly. "It's my guess that the Parramati are more than just secure in their kusum; I suspect they can number some intuitively clever individuals among their tribe, as well. I wonder if old Ascela would be quite so good a weather predictor, stone notwithstanding, if she lived at the base of the village waterfall instead of up on the ridge."

A trio of Parramati youngsters came hopping past them, clearing several of the broad stone steps with each bound. "Do you know if the stones were found locally, or have the Parramati acquired them through trade?"

"I don't know." They were almost at the bottom of the slope now, nearing the village, and she gestured. "I see Jorana chatting with Khoseavu and Uremila, two other big persons. Why don't we ask them?"

He considered. "Then they're not reticent on the subject?"

"Not if you're polite and respectful."

"I'm always polite and respectful."

"I'll bet," he observed cryptically as they descended the last of the stone steps and headed for the trio of big persons.

CHAPTER

7

Pulickel wasn't quite sure what to expect from the line of dark clouds: sheeting rain, driving wind, perhaps some isolated bursts of hail. At the very least, a vigorous downpour. In addition, he allowed as how his normal expectations might also be unexpectedly modified by unfamiliar local geologic and oceanographic conditions.

Yet despite Fawn's best efforts at describing a mastorm, the sheer suddenness and fury of it still took him aback. He'd weathered violent thunderstorms before. Even bucolic Denpasar, back on Earth, lay within the equatorial cyclone belt and was subject to annual extremes of weather.

It was the speed rather than the violence that dazed him. The sky darkened from clear blue to coal black in less than a minute, as if he were watching a many-times speeded-up vit. Gentle breezes metamorphosed into roaring winds capable of snapping sizable trees off at their roots. Rain fell not in sheets but in torrents, so heavy it completely obscured the view out the station's ports. Frequent lightning silhouetted the forest in tones of damp, diffuse gray. So thunderous was the downpour on the station's roof that he feared for its structural integrity.

"How do you prepare for these?"

Fawn was kneeling on a couch, resting her forearms on its padded back while staring out at the deluge. "You don't. Whenever they catch you, you just try to get under cover and stay there till it stops." She looked back at him and grinned. "That is, unless you have the chance to ask Ascela or another weather person what they think the day is going to be like."

Even inside the heavily insulated installation he had to raise his voice to make himself heard above the roar of the wind and the heavy drumming of the rain. "And these blow in how often?"

She considered. "They're fairly regular but unfortunately fall short of being predictable. What you've got is a miniature supercell. The clouds coil themselves into a frenzy, go crazy for a little while, and then the whole meteorological business just unwinds and the sun comes back out." She gave a little shrug. "Meteorology is another of my nonspecialties. If the mechanism responsible is half as impressive as the consequences, there's a dissertation in it for someone. But not me." She glanced down at her chronometer.

"Their saving grace is that they never last long. I give this one another fifteen minutes, max."

He turned away from the arc of windows and blinked. Lightning was now flashing frequently enough to have a strobing effect. In response to his query Fawn assured him that everything was properly grounded and shielded, both inside and out.

"Besides," she added with a grin, "Ascela has told me that my house is under the protection of her weather stone and immune from serious damage."

A wind-tunnel strength gust of wind rattled the triple-paned windows and he flinched involuntarily. "Some protection!"

"Consider what it might be like without it," she argued. "Consider, also, that the houses of Torrelauapa, though they're constructed wholly of woven matting over vine-bound frames, never seem to suffer any serious damage from these storms."

He looked at her sharply. "I've seen analogous primitive structures survive worse weather than this. It's a matter of simple but sound engineering, not magic." The windows shook again.

"I don't doubt that for a moment." She looked away, back out at the storm. "Still, it's amazing when you consider that all their intricate garden trellis- and latticework manages to survive intact, as well. So do those of the other villages."

He strove to make himself sound stern. "I saw the sacred, magic 'weather stone.' It's a rock, plain and simple."

She replied without looking at him. "Didn't the Curies say something similar?"

Together they watched the mastorm rage. After a while he commented, "You said that Ascela is willing to talk about the history and use of the weather stone."

She nodded. "Frequently. The problem lies in acquiring sufficient cultural referents to understand her. Most of what she says has to do with kusum, not meteorology."

"I think it would be useful to know more about the life and work of a stone master."

She eyed him speculatively. "With an eye toward persuading her to accept Commonwealth teachings on the subject of weather, and thereby endorsing a formal alliance with same?"

He pursed his lips. "The possibility has suggested itself."

"Pulickel, right from the start I suspected you might be guilty of intelligence. But I never imagined you being devious."

"It's nothing of the sort," he protested indignantly. "I merely seek opportunity wherever it presents itself." A slight smile parsed his fine, delicate features. "See, it's part of my kusum."

For fully five minutes the wind held at one hundred and twenty kph, with gusts topping out at over one-sixty. From the first blast of the brief, wild, mad storm to the last, twelve centimeters of rain fell at the station gauge.

Throughout it all a small part of him, usually shunted aside, was screaming, shouting, declaiming at him that while an intense, even romantic tempest was raging outside, he was restricting his conversation with the most beautiful woman he had ever seen to matters of meteorology and native culture. This overlooked and largely ignored portion of himself grumbled insistently about why, instead of wondering at the way the storm was rattling the station, he did not put his arm around her shoulders and put aside the matter of local weather conditions entirely. The notion, as thoroughly as the reality, stayed buried deep inside him.

They remained apart, separately contemplating the mastorm, which by now had begun to dissipate as rapidly as it had first burst upon the island.

Unlike the humanx station on Torrelau, the more extensive AAnn complex on Mallatyah consisted of half a dozen interconnected buildings. Prefabricated and ferried in by hevilift skimmers, they had been buried in sandy soil facing a small, curving beach. Only the upper third of each structure showed above the gently undulating loam, while the passageways and subsidiary modules that connected them lay completely beneath the surface.

The complex faced a sheltered lagoon that lay on the northeast side of the island, protected from the main thrust of prevailing mastorms. Higher ground would have been safer still, but contrary to AAnn preferences and architectural aesthetics. No AAnn would choose to live in jungle when an expanse of clean, open sand was available. Indeed, following the installation of critical structures, the first secondary project had been the construction of recreational facilities in and about the traditional sloping pit.

Proximity to the sea did not bother the servants of the Emperor. While no match for humans in the water, they were infinitely better swimmers than the thranx, and particularly enjoyed wading in the sandy, tepid shallows. Aside from the isolation, the atmosphere at Mallatyah base was nearly homelike.

At any given time the installation might be occupied by a dozen or more specialists and technicians, whose combined efforts were directed toward inveigling the resident Parramati into signing a formal treaty of alliance with the Empire. Their natural impatience demanded even more restraint in negotiations with the locals than that required by Fawn Seaforth and Pulickel Tomochelor. The uniquely diffuse nature of the Parramati hierarchy had driven more than one AAnn contact specialist to distraction.

Only the comparatively pleasant ambiance of the site made assignment to Mallatyah station tolerable for any length of time, provided one ignored the uncomfortably high humidity. As for the resident jungle, it had been razed to a respectable distance around the complex.

Presently, a disgruntled group of techs were cleaning up from the previous night's mastorm, gathering debris and dumping it in tagalong carryalls for later disposal. Two of the partially buried buildings had suffered minor damage, which another crew was engaged in actively repairing.

It wasn't the mess that discouraged them so much as the depressing regularity of the brief, intense weather disturbances.

They occurred year-round, regardless of whether it was the dry or wet season, and the danger they presented prevented anyone from ever relaxing fully. This was more emotionally than physically taxing. Besides, the need to continuously do repair and clean-up work cut into time better spent on research and social diplomacy.

Essasu RRGVB was as frustrated as any of those under his command. While no anticipator of miracles and fully cognizant of the special problems establishing formal alliance with the locals entailed, he still felt that the pace of progress was too slow. It was further frustrating to know that according to the reports he had received, the single human female the Commonwealth had assigned to Torrelau was doing no worse than his entire staff.

And now it appeared that the human delegation to the Parramat archipelago had just been doubled.

He couldn't understand it. Aside from having a smooth, bare epidermis instead of shiny scales, the seni looked far more like the AAnn than they did humans. Both species possessed long snouts, vertical instead of round pupils, large feet, and tails. A seni would fit into an AAnn spacesuit far more readily than a human, provided the gear was proportionately downsized to fit their much smaller stature. Compared to the average human, the AAnn looked positively senilike.

Yet so far, physical similarities had not proved an advantage in negotiations. A few contact specialists were crediting the locals with unexpected sophistication in their dealings with both sets of offworlders, but Essasu refused to countenance it. As far as he was concerned, the Parramati were simply showing the stubbornness of the true primitive.

And as if the recalcitrance of the natives wasn't frustrating enough, there were these damnable, damaging recurrent storms to deal with. He'd found himself wondering on more than one occasion how the single human female managed to keep her far more exposed installation operating efficiently in the face of the periodic tempests. It couldn't be the basic design. Other, unknown factors had to be at work.

Not that discovering them was a priority. It was merely a cause for puzzlement. A sibilant hiss emerged from between his teeth, his kinds' analog of a chuckle. Perhaps she has mastered a weather stone, he thought amusedly. The hiss faded. Offered the opportunity, it would give him great pleasure to gift the human with a different sort of stone—preferably one dropped from a great height.

None of which he betrayed during their occasional exchanges of communications, which were invariably conducted in an air of stiff politeness if not outright courtesy. From the first contact she'd shown herself to be indifferent to subtle sarcasm and insult. This suggested a lack of sophistication that immediately placed her beneath his serious notice. Her presence was an irritation to be tolerated—until it could be properly cleansed.

About the new human he knew little save that he was a highly regarded specialist come all the way from Earth itself. That suggested a more worthy opponent. Like all his kind, Essasu liked nothing more than a good fight, be it physical or verbal. As soon as time permitted he would have to call this new human and test him. It would be intolerable to have to kill him before learning what sort of person he was.

The humans couldn't be allowed to succeed, of course. If they somehow managed to secure a formal treaty of alliance before his people did, it would mean an end to any hope of personal advancement or promotion. His family name would be extended, a form of syllabic mortification. And that would be the least of his abasement.

He wasn't worried. His team would succeed long before the humans. The AAnn had superiority in numbers, resources, everything. It was only a matter of time. Patience was one of the hardest things for an AAnn to master, but to his credit, Essasu was trying.

He imagined the human female's soft, scaleless neck beneath his fingers, the sharpened points of his claws digging into the flesh, the thick red blood spurting. It helped him to relax.

Turning, he peered out through the long, narrow window set just above ground level. Beyond the down-sloping sand he could see the pale blue of the lagoon, backed by azure sky and a few isolated clouds. Within the office it was pleasantly hot and dry. Buried in the ceiling, dehumidifiers hummed efficiently, working around the clock to give the station's living quarters the desiccated feel of the deserts of home.

The door rustled insistently. With a rueful hiss, he turned from the window to face the portal as it parted to admit Piarai, his first assistant.

"The damage is not too bad. The nye grumble, but we have suffered far worse storms."

"Bad enough." Essasu curled up in the bowl-shape lounge that fronted his work pillars. "They should have placed the installation entirely under ground."

Piarai responded with a gesture indicative of third-degree commiseration accompanied by overtones of second-degree understanding.

"There was no precedent for it." The second-in-command did not add an honorific. The difference in rank was not enough to require it, and Essasu was not yet of the nobility—though everyone who worked under him knew of his aspirations. Truly, these differed little from their own.

Anyway, at a posting as obscure and isolated as Mallatyah, protocol tended to suffer.

"That is so," Essasu agreed. "Unless we suffer more severe

damage, we cannot properly request reconstruction. So we are forced to chew constant irritation." He squirmed in the lounge, enjoying the feel of the gritty surface against his back.

Loungeless, the first assistant squatted. "What do you think of the new human?"

"I prefer not to think of him. What I do think is that it is time we did something about the humanx presence here. If we can do nothing about the weather, perhaps we can remove a more tractable irritation." His eyes glittered, the slitted pupils narrowing.

Piarai's enthusiasm was muted. "Is that wise?"

"Not only do I think it wise, I deem it imperative. Now that a second human has come, others may be soon to follow. Best to halt this inclination to enhancement before it spawns a greater infestation still harder to excise."

Tilting back his head, he gazed at the ceiling, which had been designed to resemble the early morning sky of his home world. Carefully placed points of light duplicated familiar constellations while a single rust-hued moon gleamed not far to the right of his visitor's head. The pleasant vista never failed to soothe his liver.

"What do you have in mind?" Piarai waited expectantly.

Essasu lowered his gaze. "The humanx station has survived many mastorms, but it is not invulnerable. Surely successive blows have weakened it."

The first assistant made a perfunctory fourth-degree gesture of comprehension. "I see your thinking. You wish to eliminate not only the personnel but the installation itself. Is it truly necessary?"

The movement of Essasu's lips conveyed second-degree insistence. "Their presence here is a burr, their progress an embarrassment. Our contact specialists have enough to do without the added burden of competition weighing constantly upon them. I am convinced the time has come to remove that." He gestured importance.

"Something must happen first to the inhabitants of the humanx station and then to the structure itself. This something must occur discreetly and unnoticed by talkative locals." He picked at his teeth. "During severe weather would be the best time. It would provide impenetrable cover."

Piarai was visibly alarmed. "Surely you cannot be thinking of putting a readjustment party on Torrelau in the midst of a mastorm? Even the best stabilized floater would be hard-pressed to make the journey."

"I know that." Essasu shifted again in his lounge. "The readjustment party will stand ready to depart at a moment's notice. At the first sign of an approaching mastorm, they will move at maximum speed to Torrelau. It is a high, rugged place and offers ample room for concealment. According to the reports there are areas where even the locals choose not to go.

"I am thinking particularly of certain high sea cliffs on the east shore that the natives find negotiable but unattractive. A cut in the enclosing reef there allows large swells to break against the rocks, making fishing or any other gainful activity difficult. An expertly piloted float craft could make the approach and land atop the cliffs. From there a landing party could make its way unseen and on foot to the site of the humanx station." Teeth flashed. "Cleansing should not take long."

Piarai indicated assent. "The humans will not venture out during a storm."

"Just as we would not—normally. I myself will lead the team." He reeled off a handful of names. "Chosatuu should certainly participate. I believe she is adept with explosives."

The first assistant emphasized his words with a gesture of third-degree concern. "When the station goes silent, investigators will be sent from Ophhlia. If they find any evidence of explosives, blame will not fall on the Parramati."

"Appropriate care will be taken." Now that he had made the decision, Essasu was not to be denied. The AAnn commander clicked the claws of one hand against those on the other. "Signs of severe storm damage will be present in abundance. Have confidence in our technicians."

Piarai remained uncertain but did not show it.

"For example," Essasu went on, trying to reassure his visitor, "the humanx station includes the usual equipment for monitoring and recording the weather. We will adjust these on site to reflect a mastorm of exceptional intensity. Appropriate explanations in abundance will be provided for any who arrive seeking enlightenment. The destruction will be seen as a consequence of a freak storm among freak storms."

In light of the base commander's unshakable confidence, the first assistant's enthusiasm rose. "And the bodies?" One sandaled foot shuffled against the floor.

Essasu's gesture was imperceptible. "Seeking shelter from the storm elsewhere on the island, their skimmer will have an accident. It may be found. Their physical remains will be offered to the voracious ocean scavengers of this world. I am confident they will *not* be found."

Piarai began to pace. "A tricky undertaking, this."

"Anything to alleviate the boredom and frustration of this assignment. Kill plans stimulate the mind. It will be beneficial to those fortunate enough to be taken along."

The first assistant glanced meaningfully at his superior. "The Parramati of Torrelau may want to know what happened to their humans."

Essasu let out a derisive hiss. "Why should they care? They are interested only in their 'roads.' None bind them to the humans. What happens between us and them lies outside the boundaries of Parramati kusum. They will be less concerned than you think."

A tapping on the narrow triple-paned window caused both AAnn to turn. A gaily colored hopiak was pecking at the transparency with its short, sharp beak, wings half feathered and half membranous flapping awkwardly against the sand. Beneath the beak a bright pink eye regarded them curiously, while atop the smooth oval skull a second eye kept independent watch on the sky above.

Like so many of Senisran's native life-forms, the creature was engaging to look upon. It could not break the window, of course. Such colorful intrusions were welcome diversions from the monotony of daily routine.

Turning back to his first assistant, Essasu gestured in such a way as to express self-satisfaction in the second degree. "When questioned by visiting investigators, the Torrelauans will undoubtedly insist that the regrettable loss of property and life was a direct consequence of the deceased humans not mastering the appropriate road, or failing to consult with the relevant stone masters. While expressing our own regrets we can, as interpreters of local kusum, do no less than concur with this somber assessment. It may even serve to strengthen our ties with the locals."

"The humanx will send others. They will reestablish the station."

"Of course they will." Essasu slid out of the lounge and dug his bare feet into the heated sand heaped at its base. "But by that time, in the absence of any competing voices, we should be able to achieve our objective here. If not, we deserve to wear the stigmata of failure."

Piarai stiffened, his teeth clenching. "Truly."

The base commander came out from behind the work pillars. "The human female is the only one with a working knowledge of Parramati kusum. With her eliminated, the humans will have to start over again. As they do so, we here on Mallatyah will patiently emphasize their clumsiness and mistakes. We will have our treaty and the humanx will be forced to concede this important corner of Senisran to the Empire."

He moved to the window. As he did so, the startled hopiak pumped hybrid wings and flapped out of sight, precipitously abandoning its attempt to burrow into the room. It left Essasu with an unobstructed view across the beach to the pale blue water.

"For once I look forward to the next of these interminable little mastorms. Calm weather only means delay, and now that I have determined upon this course I wish to pursue it with utmost vigor to a satisfying conclusion."

"Have confidence, Commander. It will turn nasty soon enough." Piarai, too, peered through the window. "It invariably does." The first assistant gestured second-degree jocularity. "If you wish, I can find a local to consult a weather stone."

Essasu was not submerged so deeply in his killing vision that he missed the jest, and he was quick to respond with his own hiss of amusement.

CHAPTER

8

The longer he had contact with them and more comfortable he grew working in the village, the more Pulickel came to admire the Parramati. From his preparatory research he'd known in advance that their culture was special: different not only from the other aboriginal alien societies he had previously encountered, but from that of their fellow seni, as well. How different, the reports could not accurately convey. As always, there was no substitute for being in the field.

It was captivating to observe them at work and at play, to see how content they were in their nontechnological lifestyle and how secure in their zealously maintained kusum. The serenity of Parramati village life stood in sharp contrast to the sometimes wrenching cultural changes being undergone by the seni who had opened themselves to humanx and AAnn influence. He found himself reflecting on more than one occasion that, unlike so many other tribes, the Parramati knew themselves.

He and Fawn were making recordings of youngsters at play near the base of the waterfall that tumbled over the steep cliff into the shallow lagoon below the village. With their oversize hind feet, powerful legs, and short muscular tails to aid in steering, the seni were quite comfortable in the water. Their swimming strokes were more akin to those of frogs than humans. They hardly used their three-fingered hands at all.

The volume of water cascading over the cliff was sufficient to keep the youngsters away from the base of the sheer rock walls. Pulickel could hear them playfully taunting one another. The game consisted of seeing who could swim farthest under the falls without being shoved to the bottom of the lagoon by the force of the falling water.

This natural aeration attracted a phantasmagoria of sea creatures, most of whom scooted about the lagoon by pumping water through an astonishing assortment of valves and chambers. Considering their numbers and relative velocities, it was something of a minor miracle that they managed to avoid running into the silicate pseudocorals or one another. The swimming youngsters tried to catch the more brightly colored visitors, rarely with any success. Quick as the natives were, the jet-propelled denizens of the sea were far faster.

The small inflatable the two scientists were using allowed them to move in for closer shots. Behind them, the skimmer sat motionless on the transparent water, secured to the same floating pontoon dock the Torrelauapans used for berthing their wonderful outriggers. Swimming young villagers frequently moved to touch and inspect the alien craft, but they were forbidden by the local big persons to board it.

Pulickel knew the temptation must be great. The seni were a naturally curious species. He could see them examining every centimeter of the vehicle, their vertical pupils fully open, high pointed ears flicked sharply forward, fingers eager to probe. But not one of them was bold enough to violate the prohibitions laid on the craft by their elders.

"I believe that a lot of the Parramati's success is bound up with the way they order their existence," Fawn was telling him. "The Herimalu and the Poravvi who live on the islands to the west have a genealogically stratified society. Everything is determined by who your relatives are, and were. The Soroaa elect chiefs and clan leaders. The Parramati organize their existence spatially."

He watched her as she aimed her recorder at a pair of adolescents frolicking in the water. She was wearing only the skimpy bathing costume she'd had on when they'd first met. Comparative nudity was funny that way. The more of it there was, the less attention it drew after a while. He found that familiarity now allowed him to almost ignore his colleague's physical attributes. Almost.

She turned to look back where he was seated at the rear of the inflatable and he reflexively shifted his gaze. "It's all bound up with their mythology of roads, of everything being connected to everything else. It's just not a concept you find in the Narielle Islands, or the Suruapas, or even in the outer reaches of the Helemachus shoals. Like so much else, it's unique to Parramat."

He found himself nodding. "You might be able to steal someone else's stone, but you can't steal another person's space. What about forcing someone off their land?"

She grinned down at him. "Doesn't work that way. A person's space moves with them. Roads aren't fixed; they move with individuals, as well. By the same token, no one owns their individual space. The Parramati don't believe you can possess space. You can only make use of it."

He checked the charge on his recorder. "No wonder you've had so much trouble here."

She nodded. "That's why they're having such a hard time agreeing to what we want. A mine would make use of space, but the wording of the proposed treaty talks about owning it. That's the concept they have trouble with."

"The Commonwealth doesn't want to own the space. Just the minerals that occupy it. But I follow your reasoning."

He let his legs dangle over the side of the inflatable. The water in the lagoon was too shallow to admit large predators like the apapanu, and he could cool his feet in safety while electrically hued cephalopods and mollusks darted back and forth beneath them. A nearby bommie consisting largely of blue pseudocorals attracted schools of swimmers. The upthrust tower seemed fashioned of azurite crystals: dark blue spears thrusting up through the crystalline water.

He felt himself becoming altogether too relaxed. The temperature of the lagoon water flirted with thirty degrees. Easy to lie back in the inflatable, forget about work, and go to sleep in the warm sun. No wonder Fawn Seaforth had lost her inquisitive edge. A few months here could turn the most compulsive researcher into a beachcomber.

Resolutely but not without reluctance, he swung his feet back into the little boat. He had a job to do here. It was up to him to resist the exotic blandishments of the local atmosphere, however seductive.

The tropical sun soothed and warmed him. He felt as if he were trying to run through gelatin. At the same time, he couldn't escape the feeling that there was one key, one discovery, one cultural Rosetta stone that would allow him to deal successfully with Parramati society. When he discovered it, Fawn Seaforth would be impressed, he would be commended and transferred, and the AAnn would again be confounded.

All he had to do was find it.

"This is the most difficult culture to get a handle on I've ever dealt with," he told her. "Everywhere else, irrespective of species, there's always been a chief, a leader, a senior teacher, an elected representative, a head priest, a respected philosopher, a senior matriarch, even a local mob boss. *Someone* charged with making decisions. You work up to them and they speak on behalf of those below. This polite semianarchy is frustrating as hell." He watched something like a rocket-propelled banana with eyes go flashing past beneath the boat.

"Sometimes I wonder if either we or the AAnn will ever persuade these people to agree to anything."

She turned off her recorder and sat down opposite him, on the curving flank of the inflatable. "And it's not just individuals you have to convince. You might get a majority to agree to a treaty, but then the clans have to debate it. If the clans agree, then the population of each island in the archipelago has to vote. The power to decide is dispersed through multiple layers."

"It's not necessary to remind me," he complained. "Talk about your fragmentary processes . . ."

"Roads." She tried to sound encouraging. "All we have to do is find the right road. The road that leads to general agreement."

He looked up. "You really think such a 'road' might exist?"

"Why not?" she replied cheerfully. "There seems to be one for everything else." She lay down on the side of the inflatable, a strip of dark photosensitive plastic protecting her eyes.

He looked away from her, to where Parramati youngsters were doing acrobatic flips off a small ledge that projected out over the lagoon. Behind the inflatable, one of the large outriggers was just returning from an extended fishing trip. Its crew rushed to reef the double sails. It was always interesting to view the daily catch. Much of what the Parramati caught resembled outtakes from a fever dream. They were invariably tasty dreams, though, with rarely any bones to deal with.

Something green and yellow and blue-spotted tried to climb into the boat, its four small tentacles groping. Gently, Pulickel nudged it back into the water, discouraging the intrusion. Sometimes the sea life was as curious as the natives.

Parramati wasn't paradise. Roads notwithstanding, ordinary everyday arguments were common enough among its inhabitants. Sometimes disputes were settled violently. But when it came to dealing with outsiders, be they human, AAnn, or other seni, the locals presented a united front. That was the strength of their kusum. They were aggressive only among themselves. What was the point, anyway, of trying to conquer an outlying island when you could not possess its space?

The Parramati had their stones and their roads. Use the stones, follow the roads, and life would be good. Watching them at their everyday tasks, seeing the joy they took in life, who could argue with them?

The sacred stones were the key, he suspected. Understand the stones and you would understand the roads. Understand the roads and you would know what bound the Parramati together. Learn that and you might get them all to agree on something. Perhaps even a formal treaty.

Medicine stones, love stones, fishing stones, planting stones. Weather stones and birthing stones, blessing stones and building stones. Stones of war and stones of sleeping. Tired, he shook his head. Maybe what was needed here was not a xenologist but a mason.

Stones and the roads that connected them. Imaginary lines of power linking all of Parramat and Parramati society. What was his stone, what was his road? The Parramati couldn't tell him and he couldn't tell himself.

Whichever road leads to a treaty, he thought. That's the one I want to find. He smiled to himself. It was there: of that he was certain. It was just in poor condition, full of ruts and potholes, forcing him to go slowly and carefully instead of speed along.

If only he could be as facile with solutions as with metaphors, he mused.

The hell with it. Slipping on mask, rebreather, and fins, he flopped over the side. Fawn ignored him, intent on her work. As he slipped blissfully beneath the surface he felt the warm water envelop and refresh him.

Curious creatures surrounded him, staring and touching. His mask dimmed the glare from the glistening pseudocorals. Reaching the sandy bottom, he sat down and contemplated his utterly alien surroundings, hoping to find inspiration somewhere among the sea-dwellers.

Not long thereafter, a long, lithe shape shot past him, trailing blond tresses. The hydrojet attached to Fawn's rebreather pak allowed her to keep pace with many of the lagoon's denizens. Rolling over like a porpoise, smiling beneath her mask, she beckoned to him.

All thoughts of treaties, cultures, and serious contemplation fled, as he activated his own unit and pushed off the bottom to join her.

The business had been carefully organized and rehearsed, so that when the first signs of an approaching mastorm manifested themselves, each AAnn who had been chosen for the expedition knew just where to go and what to do.

A single floater was all that was necessary. With three to choose from and stability more critical than speed, Essasu had settled upon the largest. Designed for ferrying bulk cargo, it was capable of transporting far more than the small group of fully equipped technicians Piarai had assembled from the pool of willing volunteers. It would make the run from Mallatyah to Torrelau with ease while remaining stable even in the heaviest weather.

The plan was to finish the work on Torrelau as quickly as possible and then retreat to the shelter of Iliumafan, a small high island located not far offshore. There the cleansing expedition would wait out the worst of the mastorm hidden from view of any possible Parramati witnesses. When the unpredictably violent weather began to settle down, the AAnn would retrace the rest of their steps back to base.

It would be a quick, invigorating, surgical strike, carefully designed to leave no evidence and no witnesses. They would go in under cover of the mastorm and be out before it abated. Just rerunning the details over and over in his mind left Essasu feeling better than he had in months.

He found himself paying more and more attention to the weather reports, anticipating the abrupt drop in pressure and increase in wind speed that traditionally portended the buildup of the next mastorm.

Everything was in readiness when the first towering thunderheads appeared on the southwestern horizon. Meteorology confirmed what everyone suspected: the weather was about to turn seriously bad, which for Essasu was all to the good.

He personally supervised the loading of the floater, checking each tech and all the gear himself. The latter was important, since they didn't want to take the chance of alerting the natives to their activities. Manual tear-down of the humanx installation would be harder and take more time than simply blowing the whole thing up, but the results would more closely approximate the kind of severe storm damage Essasu intended to simulate. Relying on surprise and expecting no resistance, the techs brought only sidearms and a couple of rifles. Essasu was thorough, and a firm believer in insurance. While not anticipating any trouble, he prepared for it anyway.

Bound, drowned, released, and not found was what he had in mind for the station's inhabitants, but gunshot wounds of any kind were to be avoided, just in case. Recriminations might fly between diplomats, but he had no doubt that he and his staff would secure absolution early on in the inevitable follow-up investigation.

There was only one possible complication: what if when the team arrived, the humans were nowhere to be found? Hard to imagine them not preparing for and taking refuge in their station during a mastorm, but humans were nothing if not unpredictable. In that unlikely event, he would have no option but to abort the mission. He didn't expect that to happen. Humans had no more love for mastorm weather than did the AAnn.

By this time tomorrow he would be free of competition for the hearts and minds of the Parramati. Turning his gaze to the southwest while the technicians settled themselves in the floater's enclosed cabin, he studied the rapidly building storm. The crossing promised to be uncomfortable but not life-threatening. They would hold to the lee of as many intervening islands and reefs as possible.

Like any mature AAnn, each of the technicians chosen for the mission were fully conversant with military procedures and equipment. All knew how to handle the weapons they had been assigned. Even if a worst-case scenario materialized and they forfeited the element of surprise, the humans would still have no chance against his experienced and determined team. As near as he'd been able to discover, neither the female nor the male had received any military training whatsoever. In any event, they would find themselves overwhelmed before they had a chance to react. Eager to begin, Essasu signed himself several gestures of pleasure and satisfaction.

They were almost ready. Seated in the pilot's lounge, Technician Turikk had activated the engine and was methodically checking readouts. Final supplies were put aboard.

Already the floater was vibrating slightly in the rising wind. By sunset they would be standing off Torrelau, the floater's stabilizers holding it steady in the midst of the storm as her passengers disembarked. The unsuspecting humans would be ensconced in their station, snug in their misplaced security, perhaps even asleep. If all went as planned, they would never even have the chance to wake up.

He threw Piarai, who had been left in charge of the base, a farewell salute. For an AAnn, this involved half a sweeping, intricate pantomime that more closely resembled a dance than a salute. It was returned with reptilian panache.

The entryway sealed behind him and the transparent shell of the floater misted temporarily as the onboard dehumidifiers sprang to life. At his sign of assent, the pilot fed energy to the engines. The big lifter rose a body-length off the sand, pivoted, and moved out over the still-calm shallows of the lagoon.

The surreptitious journey to Torrelau could not have been smoother had it been simulated by computer. While continuing to build massively until it obscured the entire southwestern horizon, the fury of the storm remained held in check until the lifter reached Iliumafan. There they waited, running last-minute equipment checks and enacting procedure, until cloaked in deep night.

By the time they were ready to move, the mastorm had broken over the archipelago. Despite the pilot's skill and care, it made the crossing to Torrelau, which under normal conditions would have taken five minutes, require twenty. With the floater rocked and bucked by the roaring winds, several of the stolid soldier/technicians were unable to maintain their internal equilibrium. Wordlessly the others shunned their sick companions. There was nothing they could do for them in any case.

It was no less than Essasu had expected. Finally shielded by Torrelau's bulk, the transport steadied. Medication settled unsteady innards as the invaders disembarked, their features obscured by protective raingear. Internal suit dehumidifiers struggled to keep them comfortable as they leaped from the ramp to the sodden ground atop the sea cliff. Night-vision lenses revealed trees and bushes bending and rustling in the wind, colorful blossoms beaten down by the driving rain. Of humans or natives there was no sign.

Detailed maps revealed every rill and depression on the island, overlaid with vegetation and moving streams. Preprogrammed markers placed every member of the expedition on the same map. These markers shifted as individuals advanced, enabling every technician to locate their companions' positions instantly.

A brief, slippery ascent took them over a high ridge, then down the far side to a heavily vegetated plateau. Crossing a less difficult rise found them descending a moderate slope that eventually led to a wide ledge that overlooked the humanx station. As rain drummed on his drysuit, Essasu increased the magnification factor on his night lenses.

There being no need for privacy shades on an island inhabited solely by locals, he was able to see the interior of the station quite clearly. It was well lit from within and the curving windows that marked its circumference were mostly unobstructed, except for a few places blocked by botanical specimens that seemed to be growing wild.

Shifting his line of sight to his right, he noted that the humans' skimmer was parked in its shed, inert and powered down. He could find no reason to hesitate.

"Should we move in now, Commander?"

He glanced back at the tech who had spoken. "We will wait awhile longer. There are many lights on within the station. Their illumination may be an afterthought, or it may signify that the humans are still awake and active. Let us give them a chance to retire." He checked the weather station on his wrist. Pressure was still phenomenally low, indicating that the mastorm wasn't about to abate any time soon.

"Humans tend to stay awake longer than we do and rise later, though they hew to no hard and fast biological schedule. I do not expect much trouble, but whenever possible I prefer to minimize it. We will wait."

The technicians huddled together, dry and reasonably comfortable in their field suits but impatient, waiting for the lights within the station to go out. Ten minutes later, just as Essasu was about to order the advance, the structure darkened. This occurred in stages, a good indication that the occupants were retiring for the night. He was much pleased.

Voicing the command softly, but with overtones of second-degree anticipation, the AAnn commander led his group down the slope toward the clearing. No one remarked on their approach, no one overheard the muttered curses and sibilant hisses of tense techs as they slid and scrambled down the soggy ground. Wind wailed around them and hurled rain sideways with impressive force. Neither slowed their progress. Each member of the group was eager to conclude the matter and return to the floater. More than bloodlust or tradition, thoughts of the soothing, dry heat of their respective sleeping lounges spurred them on.

While the rest tensely kept watch, a pair of specialists deactivated the station's defensive perimeter without setting off any alarms. Designed primarily to prevent the intrusion of primitive but potentially dangerous endemic life-forms, the system was efficient but not especially sophisticated.

In-suit communicators allowed the invaders to talk despite the storm's unceasing bellow. Thunder rolled through the forest while the almost constant lightning rendered the need for artificial illumination superfluous.

Responding to a prearranged gesture from Essasu, team members poured through the breach in the defensive perimeter and proceeded to prearranged positions. Spreading out, they readied themselves to intradict any desperate flight from the installation. Ever thorough, Essasu had prepared in advance for the unexpected.

Taking three techs with him, he advanced on the single entrance at the base of the station. No AAnn would have been comfortable in a structure with only one way in and out, but humans had evolved from tree-dwellers while the ancestors of the AAnn had come up from interlocked burrows. No matter how advanced the species, certain evolutionary idiosyncrasies were hard to shake.

Know one's enemy, he told himself.

Despite their ancient arboreal origins, he didn't expect fleeing humans to come leaping out of any open windows. They could climb far better than any AAnn, but they couldn't fly. By now they should be falling asleep. Surprised in their sleeping quarters, paralyzed by a couple of short bursts from neuronic pistols, they could be carried out conscious and aware but unable to resist.

A short if bumpy floater ride would take them out beyond Torrelau's fringing reef. Dumped overboard, unable to swim, they would immediately attract the attention of eager pelagic predators, who would dispose of his persistent headache once and for all. Torrelauan scavengers were efficient. Not even the bones would be overlooked.

It would take time for them to be missed, even longer for a reconnaissance team to be sent out from Ophhlia. By then less than nothing would remain of the fading drama in the Torrelauan jungle.

The secondary security system that sealed the doorway proved even easier to bypass than the perimeter fence. The techs stepped aside as the door slid clear, making way for Essasu to enter first.

As he was preparing to do so, a shape appeared on the edge of his vision. Turning sharply, he saw that it was not alone. There were three of them altogether, exposed to the fury of the mastorm, standing there watching. One took a couple of steps toward him. It hopped rather than walked.

Parramati.

The voice of the tech on his immediate right hissed over the communicator. "Commander, what should we do?"

Startled by the unanticipated confrontation, he snapped an order. "Ignore them. Keep arms at the ready but do not fire unless I so order it." His thoughts were churning.

Disposing of three natives would be time-consuming and tiring but hardly calamitous. They certainly couldn't be allowed to observe the nocturnal goings-on and leave. A few local scavengers were going to feed especially well tonight, he mused.

The one who had stepped forward raised a three-fingered hand in greeting. Narrow, slitted eyes stared unblinkingly. The native ignored the rain that coursed in gleaming rivulets down his bare skin.

"What is it you wish here?"

Though it was hardly the most propitious time for exchanging pleasant inanities, Essasu felt obligated to at least try to talk the natives away, as opposed to shooting them outright. Wind whipped their sharply pointed ears sideways as they awaited his reply.

"Why, to check on our human friends and make certain they are all right. It is a bad storm and we feared for their safety." He was pleased with his practiced fluency in the native tongue.

The seni exchanged a look. "They have never had trouble during any other storms," remarked the female member of the trio. "Why would they need your help now?"

Essasu restrained his impatience, not to mention his anger at being spoken to in such a fashion by a member of a lesser species.

"We are simply paying a courtesy. You wouldn't understand. It is—*sssish*—part of our mutual kusum."

The younger male spoke up. "We have listened often to the humans speak of their relationship with your kind. The road between you is difficult, and broken in many places." Eyes double-blinked. "You come with many weapons."

Essasu hissed under his breath but remained polite. Above him, the station's inhabitants continued to evince no knowledge of the AAnn presence. "We must protect ourselves against the creatures of the night. Surely you can understand that."

The leader of the trio replied. "The creatures of the night are denned up out of the mastorm." His eyes were fixed on the AAnn's.

Essasu glanced at his wrist. Barometric pressure was starting to rise. The fury of the mastorm was always brief. Lose the storm and they would lose their anonymity.

The native was right, of course. All sensible creatures took cover at the first sign of an incoming mastorm. So—what were he and his three companions doing out here, exposed and unprotected? He posed the question.

"You were seen coming from Iliumafan and it was decided to

find out what you wanted. The humans did not warn us of your intended arrival."

"It is only a courtesy call. There is no need to announce such things." Essasu's exasperation was starting to boil over. His finger twitched on the trigger of his pistol. "We apologize if we have violated any protocol."

"Not ours." The female glanced upward, her long snout pointed toward the underside of the station. "You come at night, at the height of a mastorm, with weapons showing. That is not the manner of visitors intent on help."

He'd had about enough of this aboriginal interrogation. "It is really none of your business. You would not understand such things."

"But we do understand such things," the younger male declared. "Anyone who appears uninvited outside the hut of another in the middle of the night with weapons drawn can only mean mischief."

"Why are you interested? The motivations of our visit remain a matter between us and the humans. It does not concern the Parramati."

"But it does." The senior male was insistent. "You have come into our space."

Essasu indicated the station. "The humans live in it."

"By our leave. You do not have permission to enter. You must apply through the appropriate village. Your people have followed the appropriate procedures before and know them well."

Barometric pressure continued to rise while Essasu's anger began to soar. For a moment he considered composing a formal apology and calling the whole business off. But sooner or later these three were bound to inform the two humans of the nocturnal intrusion. However much Essasu might deny it, upon receiving the information the pair of softskins would surely intensify their guard. And there was the little matter of the breach his techs had made in the station's security perimeter.

He took a step forward, gesturing with the pistol. "Let us alone. We have business here that does not concern you." Unlike the neuronic pistols carried by two of his companions, the explosive projectile weapon in his hand would make no fine distinction between human or seni. He didn't want to kill these natives, but he was tired and running out of time.

The three Parramati took an impressive hop backward and immediately raised objects in front of them. Expecting spears or knives, Essasu flinched, then relaxed. The natives held only samples of the familiar, etched glassy stones that formed such an important part of their kusum mythology. If thrown, they wouldn't make much of an impact.

His voice gentle and reassuring, he addressed the trio's wary leader. "You are not really going to throw those at us, are you?"

"The sacred stones are not for throwing," the senior native declared with dignity. He held out his own. "This is a road stone, and that—" He indicated the irregular mass reverently cradled by the other male. "—a stone of the earth."

"A seeing stone." The female displayed her own modest burden.

"Very interesting." Undertones of third-degree humor crept into the commander's voice. The subtleties were lost on his audience, of course. "Then you should be able to see the path we intend to take."

The native leader's lips rippled. "You must find another road. Yours does not come through this place."

"Why do you care? Ah, yes. This business of your space."

One of the techs impatiently shook water from her headgear. "Enough, Commander. Let us be done with this."

"I agree." Essasu raised his pistol. "We must finish what we came for, and I regret that your interference requires a response. All space is our space, and within it the AAnn go where they please."

"This is not your road." So saying, the senior male turned his back on the commander. As a threatening gesture, it didn't carry much weight. Essasu aimed carefully and assumed that his companions were doing likewise. A single silent shot to the back of the head would end this unfortunate dialogue cleanly.

All three Parramati tossed their stones into the air. They aimed them not at the scaly intruders but at one another. There were many times thereafter when Essasu carefully reviewed what had happened. It was very clear. It just wasn't very believable.

Spinning through the night toward one another, the three stones appeared to slow. Silently they struck. Instead of tumbling to the ground, they stuck and hovered, the resultant unified mass visibly altering its shape like the parts of a completed puzzle. A pale yellow-green efflorescence emanated from the amorphous lump, intensely bright in the darkness of the storm-swept night.

A disk appeared beneath the suspended mass. Several body-lengths in diameter, it formed a translucent barrier between AAnn and Parramati. The reflective surface was bright with stars. Beyond, the natives could be seen huddled together and chanting softly.

A projector of some kind, Essasu thought in disbelief. How had these primitives come by such a device? One of the techs was jogging his shoulder.

"Commander? The storm is ending."

"I know." He gestured. "Step through this. Shoot all three natives but do not damage their interesting device. We will take it back with us and let the appropriate specialists examine it."

Did the humans know anything about this? he found himself

wondering. If so, all the more reason to eliminate them. An upward glance showed the station still quiescent, its inhabitants still oblivious to the little drama being played out below them. It wasn't surprising. The violence of the storm would have smothered the sounds of a small war.

"Choose!" The senior male was speaking again, from behind the disk. "The road that leads back to Mallatyah—or this one."

"Some kind of mirror device," Essasu murmured aloud. "I wonder how they came into possession of it? Well, we will find out later." He gestured sharply.

Two of the tech-soldiers stepped forward, simultaneously crossing the lip of the disk. A couple of brief, startled screams resounded over the communicators just before they fell out of sight. It was exactly as if they had stepped into a hole. The disk swallowed them as neatly as if they'd gone over a cliff.

Darting forward, Essasu and his remaining companion peered cautiously into the swirling translucency. They could see the pair who had gone in and over, flailing and kicking madly as they tumbled out of sight. Not down, he thought. They weren't falling down so much as up. He started to put out a hand.

The remaining tech restrained him. "Commander, don't." She struggled to pull Essasu back from the brink.

Shaking her off, he reached out. His hand and forearm entered the translucency. His suit sensed nothing unusual, but something pulled forcefully on his arm. With an effort, he drew it back. At the same time he recognized the pattern of stars revealed by the disk, remembering it clearly now from the standard manual on Senisran. The faint memory had been nagging at him ever since the disk had first materialized.

The constellations depicted in the disk were exactly what would be seen if one were standing somewhere in the planet's southern hemisphere and looking up at the night sky. He could not pinpoint the exact location. The Seurapan Reef system, perhaps, or the Challooriat Atolls. Those locales and others were known to him from official familiarization scrolls that suddenly seemed no longer immaterial. Both island groupings were situated almost exactly as far below Senisran's equator as Parramat was above it.

The disk *was* a hole, or if one chose to use the Parramati definition, a road. Right through this side of the planet.

CHAPTER

9

The two unfortunate tech-soldiers? They had fallen, all right. Right through Senisran into the night sky in the southern hemisphere. Shaken, Essasu lifted his gaze to the three Parramati. They were watching him silently.

The storm in his mind mirrored the greater, darker one raging about him. Three stones come together: earth, road, seeing. A way of seeing a road through the earth to the sky?

But how? Though more administrator than scientist, Essasu still was aware that several important laws of physics had just been violated directly in front of him. Not magic. He was no believer in superstition. It was technology, but of another order. Three stones. Surely the Parramati weren't responsible for them.

Then who were? How had they come to be here, on this backward watery world? Clearly the locals had learned how to make use of them. Had they been instructed, or was learning the properties of each individual stone a matter of trial and error? He'd seen no switches thrown, no surreptitious controls nudged. The Parramati had simply thrown the three objects together.

To become useful they had to be combined. A single stone was nothing more than a lump of inscribed slag. But when pushed against another, or several others, it helped to open a gate. In this case, a gate to another part of Senisran.

His thoughts reeled. Mallatyah and Torrelau were each home to dozens of the sacred stones. Many more were held and cared for on the other islands of the archipelago. Were some inert, no more than what they appeared to be, or were all potentially capable of equally inexplicable higher functions?

What else could the sacred stones do? What would happen if a sea stone was combined with a pair of road stones, or growing stones with sky stones? Did only certain specific combinations have a higher function, or would any work?

Puzzle pieces, he told himself. Hundreds of them, scattered the length and breadth of the Parramati archipelago. Each one looked after by a designated individual, or family, or clan. What else, if anything, besides the sky disk transporter could the stones become?

He had a thousand questions, the answer to any one of which was more important than the elimination of a couple of bothersome humans.

The female was speaking. "We are sorry for your friends, but they chose their road."

"Yes. Yes, they did." Mumbling, Essasu and his remaining companion backed away from the glistening sky disk. Rain was sucked into it as readily as bodies, he noticed. How much control did these primitives have over a device clearly not of their own making? Could its locus be shifted? Toward him, for example? What if they pushed it forward and it slid under his feet? Would he, too, fall through to the sky in the southern hemisphere?

Madness it was, utter and complete. Except that he'd seen it happen. As she retreated, the surviving tech stumbled slightly, reminding him that he was not alone, that another had witnessed the impossibility.

Tilting his head slightly within the protective hood, he tried to raise the pair who had vanished into the disk on their communicators. When there was no response, he addressed the other members of the expedition who had taken up positions just inside the station's breached defensive perimeter.

"Interdiction is aborted. Return to the floater. Any who delay will be left behind. I repeat, return to the floater."

The tech glanced at him. "Commander, the mastorm . . . should we not wait awhile?"

Essasu continued to back away from the three Parramati. "We are leaving *now*." Suddenly nothing, not even the roaring storm, posed nearly the threat implied by the inexplicable translucent disk.

"Did you see it? Did you see what happened?"

The tech responded with a gesture of first-degree concurrence, massively emphasized. "I saw, Commander, but I do not understand. What happened to Suugil and Rieibaa? Where did they go?"

"On a journey from which I fear they will not be returning." Again he addressed himself to his suit pickup. "Assemble at the prearranged point. Do not, I repeat, do not attempt to question or interfere in any way with any natives you may encounter."

Moments later the remainder of the assault team had reunited outside the station's defensive perimeter. The senior among them eyed the commander searchingly.

"What happened? Why have we aborted?"

Essasu stared back evenly. "It seems we have chosen a wrong road." At this, the other members of the group looked uncertainly at one another. Essasu did not elaborate. Let them query their surviving companion. Other thoughts occupied his thinking.

The first thing he intended to do upon returning to Mallatyah was institute a thorough survey of all the sacred stones on the island. Then he would initiate careful, nonthreatening discussions with their caretakers. It should be possible to secure additional, nonhostile demonstrations of the stones' abilities, under conditions that would permit proper scientific study and analysis.

This was big, he knew. Major. *Ra'selah miscaf nye.* Much more important than some trifle of a treaty. And he, Essasu, would be responsible for its discovery and subsequent exploitation. The noble title to which he aspired was no longer a distant dream but an imminent reality. Such a destiny was worth the sacrifice of a couple of technicians. In gratitude, he would incorporate their names into his title.

Their number reduced by two, the group pushed their way back through the storm, up over the ridges, doggedly retracing their path. Essasu found himself glancing back over his shoulder on more occasions than he cared to admit. He suffered from a quiet horror of looking around only to see a glistening disk full of stars bearing down on him, swallowing rocks, trees, and everything else in its circular path as it sustained a remorseless pursuit.

Some kind of transport mechanism, he knew. One that the Parramati could call into existence but not manipulate. That would be for imperial scientists to master. Surely the system was designed to allow travel from one part of the planet to another and not to dump would-be travelers into an empty slice of sky! No doubt it was all a matter of proper alignment, the details of which time and study would resolve.

He wondered if the two unfortunate technicians who had been swallowed up by the disk were still falling, and he shuddered.

The origin of the disk-generating stones intrigued him almost as much as their operation. Who had manufactured them, and when? Those parts of Senisran that had been explored had revealed nothing in the way of a civilization predating that of the primitive natives. There was nothing; not a wall, not a statue, not a crumbling ziggurat. Nothing to indicate the earlier presence of a technologically advanced society.

That the stones were not recent arrivals but had been on Senisran for some time was clear from the extensive mythology that had been developed around them by the Parramati. The fact that the devices were still functional was yet another testament to the achievements of their designers. Galactic archeology was not a subject that had much interested him, and he knew next to nothing about it, but there was clearly work here for specialists in many disciplines. He had to move with care and caution lest he overload his brain.

Focus on the immediate, he decided. Concentrate on surmounting this wet, slippery slope without breaking a leg. Understanding, great acclaim, and noble titles could come later.

One of the first steps must be to get hold of a stone and subject it to rigorous examination and analysis in the lab. Facilities denied to the station were available at Chraara. Other stones could be sent offworld for study, preferably accompanied by their respective stone masters. It would not matter if their relations with the Parramati suffered. From now on, it was the stones that mattered.

Would he be believed, even with a witness to corroborate his statements? If only they'd had recorders going! It being, of course, inappropriate to make a record of a double assassination, there were only his personal observations and those of the surviving technician to attest to what had happened. It would have to suffice.

Did the Parramati know more about the stones than they were

saying, or were they akin to children who knew how to operate a complex machine but could not have begun to explain how it actually worked? Those questions too would yield to future scrutiny.

"Be careful there!" he warned those ahead of him. "Watch your step." Irony would not be a strong enough concept to describe their situation if, having just made the discovery of the age, they succumbed to the vicissitudes of bad weather.

Whirling abruptly, he saw only wind-whipped trees and sodden ground. The image of the disk swallowing his two technicians was one that was going to be difficult to dislodge from memory. The sight of them stumbling, falling, screaming as they shrank into the starfield . . .

Angrily, he returned his attention to the trail ahead.

The four big persons squatted comfortably on their haunches. Torrelauapa lay below the slope on which they sat and off to their right, the waterfall and its narrow lagoon to their left. Three outriggers were heading out to sea, their nets draped neatly over their sides, while females came and went from the intricate mountainside gardens.

Ascela, Jorana, Osiwivi, and Massapapu had gathered to discuss the incident of the previous night. Overhead, the tropical sun shone down through a perfectly blue sky storm-swept clean of particulates.

"Are the stones safe?" Jorana inquired of Osiwivi.

"All have been returned to their keeping places," his friend replied. "To use them together was a difficult decision."

"But one that had to be made." Massapapu was employing a middle finger to clean one ear. "We could not let the two humans be killed. Not while they were living in our space."

"Bad kusum." When Ascela grunted, her whole body lifted slightly on powerful hind legs.

"A violation of hospitality," added Osiwivi.

"But now the shiny-skinned ones, these AAnn, know the power of stones." As was each of them, Jorana was openly concerned. "They will trouble our Mallatyahan relations and return to harass us as well."

"Perhaps not." The others looked to Ascela, who while carrying no more weight in discussion than anyone else, was senior in years among them. "It may be that none of their big persons will grasp the true meaning of what was seen." She barked gentle amusement. "After all, unless one knows the ways of using, the stones are only stones. Except for what the Mallatyahans choose to tell them, the shiny-skinned AAnn are ignorant of kusum."

"That is so," Osiwivi agreed, "but I still think as does Jorana. They will trouble us unless we make them all go away."

Massapapu considered the problem. "We could send them all down a road from which they would not return."

Ascela gestured agreement. "That is easily enough done. But from talking with the humans, I believe that others would come to take their place. These who would come after would be more cautious as well as more ready to use weapons."

"Just as a human male has come to join the female." Jorana's nostrils flared slightly. "Do you think they will mate?"

"I do not know. They don't speak of such things to me. If I think of it, I will ask them sometime. They seem mismatched as to size."

Massapapu considered. "Maybe among their kind the female is always larger than the male."

Jorana made a low chittering sound deep in his throat. "It seems that we are going to have to learn how to live with these visitors among us, humans and AAnn alike. But that does not mean we must agree to let them come and dig out what they want from the land." Double eyelids blinked. "Better for kusum to keep playing them off one against the other."

"Yes," agreed Osiwivi. "Contact and trade is supportable—so long as *we* control it."

"But they will want to manage things." Ascela shifted on her haunches. "Both believe that they speak from a position of strength, but neither has any stones." She snorted derisively. "They are not stronger than us, but it is better to let them think that they are."

"They will continue to harangue us to choose between them," Massapapu argued.

"Let them." Ascela let her gaze wander to the relaxing symmetry of the terraced gardens. "We will continue to play no favorites. Access to all islands of the Parramati will be controlled, and we will not allow them to dig on our lands. We will pass judgment on every soft- or shiny-skin who wishes to reside among us."

"For how long?" Osiwivi was not afraid to let uncertainty show. "They have powerful weapons and machines."

"But they do not know the right roads." Jorana half closed his eyes, squinting into the sun as he watched the last of the fishing outriggers vanish around the northern point. "Perhaps if we were to show some of them a true road, they would come to understand what preserving our kusum means to us."

"Yes!" Massapapu was immediately enthusiastic. "Show the two humans the great road. See then if they do not become more like us, more attuned to true kusum. Show them the great road and they will understand why we do not need their treaty and their trade goods."

As Ascela mulled over this proposal, she sifted soil through her fingers, studying the small lives it had to offer. Occasionally she nibbled.

"An idea worthy of further consideration, but are these two humans the proper candidates? They do not strike me as big persons among their own kind. Wise, yes. Understanding and sometimes even sympathetic. Intelligent and knowledgeable, or they would not have been sent among us. But after much talking with them, I do not believe that they are persons of influence or power."

"We can add to their power as well as to their knowledge by showing them the road," Jorana pointed out. "Once they have seen, then big persons of their own kind will have to listen to them."

Ascela rocked backward, using her short tail to form the third leg of a tripod on which she could balance. "Well, on one thing we are all agreed: something must be done about these persistent soft- and shiny-skinned visitors. If we cannot drive them away or kill them all, we must make them understand what it is to be Parramati. If that means they must be shown the great road, then so be it."

Bathed in warm sunlight, their naked skin caressed by the occasional warm breeze off the lagoon, they fell to discussing the details.

Fawn frowned at Naharira, a Torrelauapan big person she knew only by name. Repairs to that part of the station defensive perimeter that had been damaged during the last mastorm were taking longer than she'd calculated. Straightening and wiping sweat from her forehead, she peered across the cleared area to the far side of the defensive fence where Pulickel was methodically checking each newly refurbished stanchion with a hand-held monitor.

So far, only the one she was working on seemed to have suffered any serious damage. It was the first time any part of the defensive fence had failed. Given the fury of the periodic mastorms and the debilitating nature of the climate, it was surprising it hadn't happened before.

Personally, she thought the energized perimeter excessive. No local predator could force an entry into the station. But it was SOP, and she'd had no say in the station's construction. Even so, she was making immediate repairs only at Pulickel's insistence.

Of more interest was the bare piece of land near the main entrance to the elevator shaft. A circular patch of ground had been wiped clean of soil and all plant matter to a depth of several centimeters, right down to exposed rock. She and Pulickel had discussed possible explanations ranging from a miniature tornadic touchdown to a freak bolt of lightning. Most puzzling was the near perfection of the circle.

Save for the single perimeter post, the station itself had come through the mastorm undamaged as always, a tribute to its designers and builders. Despite delays, she expected to have the fence up and running within the hour.

It was while they were out sweating and straining in the heat of late morning that Naharira had come to stand and stare. And to make conversation.

"I'm afraid I don't understand," she told the attentive villager. "What are you trying to tell me?"

The big person leaned on his simple hoe, rocking slightly on his huge feet. "We want you and Pu'il to understand what it means to be Parramati. We want you to understand why we don't want a treaty that will bring others of your kind, or of the shiny-skinned ones, here to dig up our land."

Fawn was on her knees, peering into the eviscerated interior of the damaged stanchion. As she listened, she removed a replacement module from its clear plastic casing and carefully snapped it in place. Within the stanchion, a pair of tiny green lights winked to life.

"There will be a treaty." She snapped connectors back into place. "Either with us or with the AAnn. It's going to happen, so the big persons in Torrelauapa and the other villages might as well get used to the idea." She made a face. "It's called progress."

Naharira scuffed the ground with his hoe. "Let me put it another way. The Parramati feel that any such treaty would constitute a defacement of kusum."

Blinking away sweat, she looked up at the native. "I don't see that it damages kusum at all. The proposals don't ask the Parramati to change their way of life in any fashion. They simply enshrine an already existing friendship."

"It would lead to the opening of other roads and other ways. Roads that lead to attractive options and new things that are appealing to youth who have not yet been instructed in the fullness of kusum. Tradition would be eroded. We have heard how this has happened elsewhere. Heritage has been sacrificed for shiny toys that honor no kusum." He shifted on his hoe.

"You and the shiny-skinned AAnn have knowledge, but the Parramati have life. Knowledge without life is nothing. Everything we have, everything we are, arises from our kusum. Change that, substitute for it, and we will lose that which makes us what we are. Our kusum has kept us safe in war and drought and bad times while many around us were suffering. That is because other seni have forgotten or put aside their kusum in favor of new fads and tempting ideas. Only the Parramati still hew to an unchanged kusum. We have done so for as long as memory serves. We must continue to do so."

"You don't need to tell me. I've heard the same liturgy from Ascela and other big persons." She was trying to be polite to the native while concentrating on the repair job. "I see your point."

"I'm not sure that you do." Naharira was being very direct this morning. "But we would like you to. We are not like the Eolurro or the Simisant. Only the Parramati know well the roads. It is because of this, because of our kusum, that we see the world as it truly is."

Fawn carefully closed a connection, smiled to herself as a last green light came to life. "And how *is* the world, according to the Parramati?" High up a flaring ulawari tree, a chiji squealed like a bagpipe badly in need of tuning.

"The Parramati see everything in terms of space." The big person gestured broadly to encompass the surrounding forest. "Each location in space has its own access point, and each point has power. The big people among the Parramati can recognize these points of power. Most of them are concentrated in the stones. Those who know the ways can use the stones to open the roads to these other spaces. We do not always use them, but we know they are there. Our kusum has always allowed us to do this. Others do not know the ways, or do not possess the right stones."

"That's all very interesting." She leaned back and began buttoning up the refurbished stanchion. "But what does it have to do with the proposed treaty?"

Naharira sighed. "We are hoping that if you come to see space as the Parramati do, you will better understand why we do not want, do not need, and cannot afford to have closer ties with your civilization. We would like for you to agree to become more Parramati."

Its integrity restored, the perimeter fence could be switched back on at any time. Satisfied, she rose, towering over the attentive big person. "I'm still not sure that I follow you. Are you proposing that Pulickel and I undergo some sort of initiation ceremony?" It took a moment to find the right words.

Naharira showed the many teeth in his long, narrow snout. "It is more of a demonstration, so that you may better comprehend certain things that are difficult to convey only with words. It was not a decision easily arrived at, but it is felt that something needs to be done so that you may understand. Your ignorance is not your fault."

The sardonic tone of her reply was lost on the native. "Gee, thanks."

"You are welcome. It is felt that when you see that our ways are stronger, you and your people will understand our desire to be left alone and our wish to forgo the benefits of your society."

"If it's that important to you, then of course we will participate in your show, or demonstration, or whatever it is." She yelled and gesticulated in Pulickel's direction. Almost finished with his inspection, he turned and waved casually back.

Naharira continued. "Tomorrow there will be a ceremony marking the planting of the pohoroh root. A growing stone will be used to ensure a bountiful crop. At that time you will be shown the relevant road. When you see it open, perhaps then you will understand why we do not need your ways, your machines, or your treaty." He straightened proudly.

"It is a great honor. Only big persons may use the stones to open the roads. Only they know the ways of power that are handed down from generation to generation."

"We're flattered to be included," Fawn replied, not knowing what else to say. "I'm sure Pulickel will feel the same way." The crop-blessing ceremony, or whatever it was, sounded interesting. Anything that expanded their insight into Parramati sociology was worth recording, just as anything that solidified the developing relationship was to be encouraged.

Hefting his hoe as he turned to go, Naharira eyed the much taller human curiously. "Tell me one thing, F'an. You and the male human live together but are not mated. You have no cubs. This is a thing much speculated upon in the village. Do you plan to mate?"

The abrupt change of subject caught her off guard. "Noooo, I don't think so."

"If you do, Ascela said to tell you that she would be honored to perform the ceremony."

She smiled. "Tell her thank you, but we have no plans to, um, mate. Our relationship is strictly professional. Different families can till the same hapirri patch."

"Yes, that is so," the big person agreed.

"Pulickel," she added, gesturing in her associate's direction, "is not what, among my people, would be called my type."

" 'Type.' " The native looked thoughtful. "We have much still to learn about the meanings of words."

She strove to return the discussion to more significant and less personal matters. "We'll be happy to be initiated as stone people, or whatever, and to learn more about the ways of the Parramati and your roads."

"Then it is settled. Tomorrow at first sun."

Not being much of a morning person, she winced internally. "First sun?"

"It is the proper time, when the flowers of the pohoroh first open to the light."

"Of course. That makes sense. You must excuse my ignorance." Bending, she picked up her repair kit. "Tomorrow at first sun then, in the village."

"You must be at the base of the gardens before first light so you can be on the mountain when the sun shows itself." Naharira was insistent.

She winced again. "We'll be there."

Exhibiting wonderful flexibility, the long snout twisted sideways. "I will come and guide you. It will not be hard for you to find your way. You have lights that let you see in the dark."

"That's right." Unable to resist, she added, "If you agreed to the treaty, you could have such lights for yourself. You could turn night into day for every village in the archipelago."

"Why would we want to do that?" With a vertical hop and midair pivot, the native turned away from her. "If the night was made into day, how would a person sleep?"

With that the visiting big person headed off toward the trail that led through the forest and back to the village, covering the open sections of ground in long, graceful bounds. Fawn watched him go.

A simple folk, the Parramati. Straightforward and stubborn, but they'd come around sooner or later. Meanwhile, attending this planting ceremony or whatever it was would establish one more bond between them. It was important, she knew. Anything involving the sacred stones was important. It would probably prove interesting, as well, except for the part that involved rising before sunup.

She called across the clearing beneath the station. "Better turn in early tonight, Pulickel! We have an early-morning appointment."

His querulous reply rose above the background mutter of the jungle. "What for?"

"To look at roots, and rocks. Would you rather be a root person or a rock person?"

"What's that?" He put a hand to one ear, but she only grinned at him. She could give him the details later. There was no urgency.

After all, nothing exceptional was going to happen.

CHAPTER

10

It was very early indeed the following morning when Fawn learned that she had misconstrued Naharira's invitation.

"Only females," the big person explained apologetically, "are permitted to participate in the pohoroh ceremony. It is they who master the growing stones. Only they may attend."

"Not a problem." It was still night-black outside the station, and Pulickel smiled jovially at his associate. "I can live without watching the locals stick a bunch of seeds in the ground and pound them with a sacred stone. You do the recording, Fawn. Me, I'll just have to go back to bed."

"Get some sleep for the both of us." Her tone belied her expression. Given the choice, she would gladly have swapped places with her companion. That was not possible. Naharira was insistent as ever.

The sky was only beginning to show signs of lightening when she finally halted just beyond the village, at the foot of the magnificently terraced mountainside that the Torrelauapans had transformed into one vast, intricate garden. There Naharira turned her over to Jariill, the female big person who had care of the growing stone. Together they started up the laboriously worked slope.

Three-quarters of the way along, they halted on a small plateau. A large section of terrace had been cleared for planting. Reeds, vines, fronds, flowers, and stripped bark lay in neat piles nearby, ready to be woven and sculpted into protective, decorative trellises and arbors as soon as the planting was concluded.

Among the assembled Parramati females, Fawn stood out like a construction crane surrounded by busy earthmovers. Switching on her recorder, she followed the beckoning Jariill to the middle of the clearing. Exotic native fruits and vegetables grew in profusion on the terraces below while immature growths greened the remaining levels at higher altitudes.

From the vantage point provided by the plateau, she could see much of the western half of Torrelau. Swathed in shades of emerald and vermilion, carmine and yellow, it lay like a blaze of energy against the framing azure blue sea. The village lay below, peppered with the small moving shapes of other Parramati beginning the day's work. Off to the left, the clear, cool course of the river cast its singular torrent into the svelte inlet of the lagoon. All in all, it was a grand vista.

"Stand here, F'an."

Turning, she nodded understandingly at Jeriill and walked to the indicated location. She wondered if she would be allowed simply to watch or if she was expected to participate in the ceremony. Other females crowded close around her, forming the balance of a semicircle that faced the center of the plateau.

Holding the growing stone out before her, Jeriill advanced from one end of the crescent. Carrying an earth stone, the big person known as Ululiapa approached from the opposite direction. Fawn strove in vain for sight of any seeds or cuttings.

Meeting in the center of the plateau, the two females squatted low. Setting the stones aside, they began to dig a small hole.

Fawn leaned over to whisper at the middle person standing on her right. "I don't understand. Where are the seeds or seedlings?"

The younger Parramati looked up out of bright blue eyes. "Why, the pohoroh cuttings are already in the ground, of course. They were planted all last ten-day."

Fawn switched off her recorder. "If the planting is already finished, then what's the purpose of this ceremony?"

"Why, to bless the health of the crop and ensure that it is fruitful."

"I see." Fawn was still disappointed that she'd missed the actual planting. Apparently she'd been brought here simply to witness some chanting and speech-making. At least it shouldn't last too long, she rationalized.

Near the far end of the female crescent, several of the villagers were removing musical instruments from their carry bags. She recognized the important kes flute, a set of small, vibrantly carved goralau drums, and a pair of balatingting harps. Even though the sun had not yet peered over the horizon, she was sweating. Torrelau's humidity did not vanish with the daylight but persisted around the clock.

Running a hand around the inside hem of her halter top, she made the decision to switch the recorder back on. If nothing else, the music would provide an enjoyable subject for study. Too bad the ceremony had to take place out in the open instead of beneath some shady, finished pergola. She gazed longingly at the wisps of twisted and shaped reed that darkened a row of simwhila snaps only meters distant.

Pulickel didn't know what he was missing, she groused silently.

At a signal from Ululiapa the female crescent began to snake and wend its way back toward the edge of the clearing, accompanied by an unmelodic but rhythmic drone from the musicians. Caught up in the Senisrani chorus line, Fawn raised her arm so the recorder could shoot over the heads of the gyrating natives. She was hard put to avoid their enormous feet, which stamped in unison first to the left, then to the right. This uniform pounding made a drumming upon the earth that bordered on the dynamic. For the first time all morning she was glad that she'd allowed Nahariri to talk her into coming.

Having finished their excavation, Jeriill and Ululiapa straightened. Sweat streaming off her face, Fawn struggled to aim the wristmounted recorder in their direction. As soon as the ceremony ended, she promised herself, she would sit down in the shade and take a nice, long drink from the condenser in her backpack.

The female dancers had begun jumping up and down, matching their prodigious leaping ability to the beat of the goralau drums. In their enthusiasm several sailed cleanly over Fawn, clearing the top of her head by no less than half a meter on each occasion. It was a supremely athletic demonstration. The loud *whump*s the natives made when they landed complemented the percussive quality of their chanting. It was one of the more impressive demonstrations of traditional kusum Fawn had yet witnessed.

As she absently let the recorder run, she found herself wondering how much real work she could still accomplish before nightfall. There was so much that needed filing and organizing—but at least Pulickel had stopped nagging her about it. Most of the time, anyway.

A glance skyward showed that the sun was peering over the western ridges. A few isolated cumulus clouds hovered overhead, blotting up excess blueness. By late afternoon they would have solidified their hold on the firmament and it would rain for an hour or so. Now if one of the early arrivals would only interpose itself between her and the sun . . .

The ceremony seemed to be winding down, the music growing less intense. Good, she thought. Jeriill and Ululiapa bent to pick up their respective stones. Switching to a slower, more sedate chant, the Parramati females gathered behind the musicians.

The two big persons solemnly bent to place their respective stones in the hole they had dug. What followed happened so quickly Fawn wasn't sure she'd actually seen it, and could only hope that the recorder had done its job.

The two stones appeared to jump toward one another. Fawn was positive the females hadn't thrown them. It was as if the glassy lumps had become suddenly and powerfully magnetized. What happened next was more astonishing still.

Emitting a sea-green glow, the stones fused together. For a mad moment she thought they were going to pass through each other. What resulted was a single stone that looked larger than the two separate stones combined. That was impossible, of course, but then so were rocks that exhibited green efflorescence and independent motion.

She considered the possibility that she might be the victim of some primitive tribal sleight-of-hand, but that wouldn't explain the light that continued to emanate from the glassy mass. As she stared, the two female big persons squatted and began to throw dirt onto the lump, covering it up and filling in the hole they had dug.

Behind her, the chants of the singers and the steady rhythm of the musicians was an unvarying drone in her ears. Her head was pounding. Heat and perspiration were no longer uppermost in her thoughts.

Dropping to their knees, the two stone masters placed both open hands on the ground, above the buried stones. They seemed as oblivious to her presence as to the singing and the music. The recorder caught it all.

Faintest of the faint, a pale green light emerged from the earth beneath Jariill and Ululiapa's hands. Like ink in water, it spread out across the carefully prepared field, seeping beneath walking paths and retaining walls until it covered the entire planting.

Fawn barely had presence of mind enough to check on the recorder. It continued to function efficiently and independent of her attention. By now the entire upper third of the mountainside was lit from within by the dissipating lime-green glow. Looking down, she could see it trace an olivine arabesque of mysterious beauty beneath her sandals.

That's when she recognized the pattern in the earth. It was a restatement of the intricate scrollwork that dominated the overall design of the Parramati arbors and trellises.

Her feet had begun to tingle through the soles of her sandals. It felt as if she were standing in a shallow, carbonated bath. A glance down revealed that her toes were not glowing green. At that point, it would not have surprised her.

Jariill and Ululiapa continued to kneel, their hands pressed to the earth, their heels high in the air. They must be feeling the tingling much more strongly than she, Fawn knew.

The efflorescence persisted for another five minutes before it finally began to fade. As it vanished, soaked up by the intensifying sunshine, the chanting slowed and finally ceased altogether. The musicians put up their instruments. The two female big persons rose solemnly from their kneeling positions, wiping dirt from their three-fingered hands. Fawn reached for the controls on her wrist recorder, then hesitated.

Let it run, she decided. Despite the look of things, she might miss something.

Jariill was beckoning to her. Uncertainly Fawn moved forward, treading lightly on the soil as if it might without warning turn amorphous beneath her feet. She felt as if she were in a trance. Long lips rippling, the two big persons indicated that the tall human could join them if she wished. The invitation concluded, both bent and began to dig at the spot where they had buried the two stones become one. Restraining the hundred questions she had already formulated, Fawn joined them.

Soundlessly they dug. No music accompanied them now, no enthusiastic dirge. Not far below the surface they uncovered the stone. The glow had nearly vanished, as if its brief sojourn in the earth had drained it of some inherent inner vitality. In the vicinity of the misshapen mass the soil was dark and moist.

"Pick it up, F'an." Ululiapa gestured encouragingly. "You are female. You should be comfortable with all things that are of the earth and of growing."

Taking a deep breath, she reached down and picked up the stone. A surge of warmth promptly coursed through her whole being, from her fingers down to her toes. Startled, she dropped the mass. Jariill caught it in one smooth gesture before it could hit the ground.

The xenologist felt foolish. What harm could it do to hold the object? It was just a rock—wasn't it? Sure it was. A rock that changed shape and tingled to the touch and infused an entire hillside with energetic green light.

Okay, so it was more than just-a-rock. What the hell *was* it?

When she reached out, smiled, and made the proper gesture, Jariill freely handed the stone back. Holding it up for a closer look, Fawn found she could see partway into the vitreous mass. The interior was highly stratified, suggesting organization of a type only nature was capable of imparting to the interior of an ordinary rock. If, she found herself thinking, it was an "ordinary rock." But what else could it be?

Her eyes widened and she brought the mass closer to her face. Was that something moving, deep within the stone? Coils and flashes of energy, fluctuating lines of force? Were they lingering echoes of the green radiance that had suffused the field, or the cause?

The big persons, the wondrous isle of Torrelau, the cradling sea, Senisran itself: she held all of it in her cupped palms. The sensation of life force, of prodigious fecundity, was overpowering. It enveloped her whole being. While her mind reeled, her body felt more alive than when she was making love. That was exactly what it was like, she thought dazedly. She was making love to the earth, and the earth was responding. Nurturing, giving back, through the power of the stones.

She stumbled slightly and blinked, the delicious fog that had blanketed her thoughts vanishing. Looking down, she saw that she now held two stones, one in each hand. They were the original stones, inert and immutable. No light, green or otherwise, emanated from their irregular, glassy surfaces.

Gently the two female big persons retrieved their stones. Wiping at her eyes, Fawn turned to examine her surroundings. No remnant of the radiance remained. Bathed in early-morning sunshine, the cleared field and surrounding gardens shone only with natural color. No supernal hues attached themselves to growth or soil. The world was as it had been before.

Looking down, she found that she was unable to see into the interior of either stone. When separated, their surfaces were opaque and impenetrable.

"What—what was that all about?" she heard herself inquiring of Jariill.

The smaller female gazed unblinkingly up at her, both eyelids fully retracted. "When a growing stone and an earth stone are put together, it ensures a good crop. The continuity of life is preserved."

Continuity. That seemed inadequate to describe the sensations that had raced through her when she'd held the commingled stones. She felt a touch, looked down to see Ululiapa resting a three-fingered hand on her wrist. Slitted alien eyes peered up into her own.

"Are you all right, F'an?"

The xenologist put a hand to her forehead. "I think so. I—I saw some things. I feel fine. I'm just a little confused about what I saw. Or what I think I saw."

"You saw life." Reassured, Ululiapa stepped back. "The life the stones give." She gestured downward. "Look at the earth. Look at the ground beneath your feet."

Fawn complied—and her jaw dropped.

Where moments ago there had been only bare, freshly turned soil, green shoots were now poking their heads through the surface. As she gaped, they coiled upward, seeking the sun. Uniform neither in size, shape, color, nor speed of growth, they represented more than two dozen cultivated varieties of fruits, vegetables, and tubers. Lifting her gaze, she saw that the entire field was involved, alive with new growth that was maturing at astounding speed.

Within minutes, the first burst of new life had manifested itself and slowed. The frenzy of growth moderated. But the stones had done their work. The formerly bare field was now covered in healthy green, yellow, carmine, and brown shoots and stalks.

It was insane, she knew. There wasn't a fertilizer or growth-stimulant known that could turn a naked hillside this fertile in mere minutes. Yet it had happened, and with her standing smack in the middle of it. There was chemistry at work here beyond the comprehension of Commonwealth agronomists.

"We are done." Ululiapa put an arm around Fawn's waist, having to reach up to do so. "Now you are one of us."

"One of what?" Allowing herself to be guided, she gazed down at the kindly seni. "A stone master?"

"No." The female big person barked gentle laughter. "A human person could never be a stone master, could never understand or channel the energy of a stone. What you are become now is a Torrelauapan female person."

"I'm honored, but you say I could never learn how to channel a stone's energy. How do you do it?" Nearby, the musicians were packing up their instruments.

"The knowledge is passed down through the generations, from mother to daughter." Ululiapa gestured eloquently as she spoke. "It is a way of handling and of touching. A way of believing and of seeing. Every stone master learns these things at the feet of those who have gone before. How a stone is to be manipulated, how it is to be cared for, what are its limits."

She didn't press the issue. Unless something unforeseen went terribly wrong, it was all there on the recorder, available for study at leisure.

Of one thing she was already certain. The stones of the Parramati weren't "stones." They were something more, much more, and it had nothing to do with autochthonous magic. Physics and chemistry of an unknown order, yes, but not alchemy. During her stay on Torrelau, Senisran had revealed many of its secrets. Now it was clear that the stones of the Parramati contained the deepest secrets of all.

Not all indicators of technologically advanced species took the form of towering obelisks and extensive tunnels. Important artifacts could be small, even tiny. Who had been on Senisran before the seni? Before humanx and AAnn?

No, not magic. There was science in the stones. She needed to get one or two into the lab and under instruments capable of providing answers.

The Parramati could help—if they were so inclined. How many effective stone combinations were there? Did other amalgamations produce different results, or were stones useful only for stimulating new crops? What revelations did the stones contain that she couldn't even imagine?

What of all the other stones? How did, for example, a fishing stone work? Or the love stones, or the weather stones, or the stone that supposedly helped its master to think more clearly? From her time spent among the Parramati, she knew of sacred stones with at least a hundred different, specialized designations. What multiplicity of combinations were possible? Could a thinking stone be put together with an earth stone, and if so, what would be the consequences? Or a fishing stone with a weather stone?

Treaties no longer seemed important. Neither did geology, or a host of other disciplines she was supposed to be practicing. The demonstration in the field had opened up an entirely new avenue of research for her and Pulickel.

Pulickel. He was ignorant of what she'd just experienced, knew nothing of the revealed wonder of the stones. She had to tell him. He wouldn't believe a word of it, of course. She'd be disappointed in him if he did. But she had the recording.

Anxiously she checked the compact instrument. It appeared to have worked perfectly, but she knew she wouldn't be able to relax until she had played back and checked every centimeter of the visuals. Despite her concern, she deferred the replay out of fear of offending or upsetting her escorts. It might be considered improper, or disrespectful. She would hold off until she got back to the station.

Even if the images were insufficient to convey the wonder of what she had seen and experienced, she knew she would convince Pulickel somehow. She had to. After the truth of the stones, everything of consequence that had been learned about Senisran paled to insignificance. Understanding the stones was vital not only because of what she had seen but because of what it implied.

Did the AAnn have an inkling? Did they know anything of the real nature of the stones, or did they continue to believe, as she had until the episode in the field, that they were no more than inert ingredients for primitive aboriginal ceremonies? The latter seemed more likely, or she and Pulickel probably would have heard otherwise by now. Commonwealth intelligence was very efficient.

No, this was something new, a discovery unique to her and soon to be shared with her associate.

How could they obtain a sacred stone or two for lab work? No stone master would part with one, much less if they knew it was going to be subject to bombardment by strange radiation or immersion in alien liquids. The notion of breaking one open to examine its insides would fill the least pious Parramati with horror.

To surrender a stone for study, she knew, would be akin to giving up access to a road. It would leave the stone master thus deprived feeling blind and stranded in space. No gift, no revealed knowledge, would be sufficient to persuade a stone master to part with his or her legacy.

She lengthened her stride in order to keep pace with the long hops of the Parramati. Everything depended on acquiring at least one stone for detailed study. Perhaps Pulickel would have some suggestions. He always did.

CHAPTER

11

Back at the station, her colleague and companion listened patiently to her rushed, out-of-breath description of what had taken place on the flank of the mountain above the village. From time to time he had to remind her to pause and catch her breath; not only so that she wouldn't hyperventilate or fall over in a dead faint, but so that he could understand her.

"I don't know how it works or what kind of physics are involved. I only know what I saw, and what I saw is impossible." She leaned back against the couch and chugged half the mug of cold carbosugar drink he'd brought her. "It happened, Pulickel. I didn't imagine it."

"No one's saying that you did." He indicated the wrist recorder that was lying on the table between them. "I must say that I'll be more inclined to believe you after I've seen it for myself."

"Can't blame you. I'd feel the same." Finishing the last of her drink, she snatched up the recorder and led the way to the lab.

Removing the recording sphere, she popped it in the playback unit. It turned on automatically, filling a corner of the room with light. Reduced in size but fully three-dimensional, the field blessing ceremony played itself back for an audience of two.

The recorder had worked perfectly. It was all there: the snake dancing, the chanting, the music, and, climactically, the melding of the two sacred stones and their consequent astounding effect on the newly planted earth. Pulickel sat up very straight when the green glow suffused the ground, then muttered something under his breath when plant shoots began to erupt from the soil with preternatural celerity. At the conclusion of the recording, he turned unhesitatingly to Seaforth.

"One thing is immediately obvious. The sacred stones are not stones at all. They may look like stones and feel like stones and behave like stones ninety-nine percent of the time, but they are not rock. They are devices, individual components that when joined in specific combinations have remarkable consequences. What is your take on this?"

"I haven't thought about it much. The whole business is so unbelievable that I've spent most of my time working to convince myself that it actually happened. Up to now my main concern has been convincing you."

"You don't have to worry about that anymore. I'm convinced." He indicated the now-empty corner of the room where the recording had played itself out. "Whatever you saw, it wasn't the result of some clever Parramati sleight-of-hand. It was real. The stones contain some kind of stored energy, or . . ." His voice trailed away.

"Or what?" she prompted him.

"Or I don't know." He spoke to what he did know, or what he thought he knew based on what he'd seen. "It's clear that single stones have no power to affect their surroundings. They only function in combination. You saw them change shape. The natives don't even need to know how to fit the stones together. The appropriate adaptive mechanism is inherent in the devices themselves."

"How do you program a rock?"

"I told you; I don't think they're rocks. For all we know, their internal composition may be as malleable as their shape."

She found herself nodding agreement. "I tried to take a closer look at these. Their internal structure is complex. My first thought was of fracture lines, cleavage planes, and weathered striations . . . ."

"Naturally," he commented approvingly.

"But obviously there's more to it than that."

"What about their composition?"

She pondered. "You saw the recording. These two look just like all the other sacred stones. It's that same volcanic-glassy material we've seen before. For what it's worth, they didn't feel any more ductile than they look. Smooth and hard, both of them."

"We can freeze and enlarge individual segments of the recording."

Her energy restored, she rose and began pacing the room. "I know, but they were throwing off so much light it's going to be damn hard to manage a good look inside. I don't know how much structure we'll be able to see."

He smiled encouragingly. "I'm pretty good at manual enhancement procedures. We'll give it a try, anyway." He hesitated a moment before continuing. "It could be an entirely natural phenomenon, but the more I see of it and the more you tell me, the more inclined I am to think of these stones as machines. As things that were made, not formed."

"But who? What species?"

"What species indeed?" he murmured. "Either the Parramati

have fallen to their present circumstances from a great height, or else—" He stared evenly at her. "—some other race has called this world home at some unguessable time in the unimaginable past."

"In the absence of any large-scale ruins, I think we have to incline to the latter."

"*Will* you be still?" Her endless pacing was making him nervous.

She plopped herself into a lab chair and threw her long legs over one plastic arm. This did not make him less nervous so much as it changed the nature of his unease.

"What kind of civilization manufactures devices like the stones but leaves no other sign of its presence, much less its passing? No buildings, no tools, no mines or other marks on the earth."

"There's a lot of erosion here," he pointed out. "Wind, rain, the sea."

She was less than convinced. "You're reaching, Pulickel."

"Don't you think I know that?"

"No crumbling towers, no ruins, no corroding subaqueous constructions: nothing but the stones." She made a face. The woman was a ferocious attacker of puzzles, Pulickel knew.

"The stone, the whole stone, and nothing but the stone. I wonder if weather stones let you manipulate storms." He half grinned, because he was only half joking.

Based on what she'd seen on the mountainside, Fawn was ready to entertain the most outrageous speculation. "Hell, how do we know? Maybe the weather stones are responsible for the mastorms."

He frowned. "I don't think so. The mastorms cause too much damage. I admit that in light of such a discovery it isn't easy to be restrained, but let's not get carried away here."

"Get carried away?" She threw him a don't-make-me-laugh look. "We have found what may be the final relics of an unknown, technologically advanced civilization, of unknown potential, and you tell me not to get carried away?"

Under her enthusiastic assault he backtracked slightly. "All right. You can get carried away a *little*."

She snorted. "That's better. But you're right. If the weather stones were capable of anything like that the Parramati would surely use them to prevent storm damage to their villages. Although—" She turned suddenly thoughtful. "—if you think about it, considering the ferocity of your average mastorm, the Parramati communities really *don't* incur that much damage."

Placing both clenched hands together, he leaned his chin against them. "One's imagination reels. I wonder, for example, what a health stone does in proper combination with another? Can it cure a revavuaa bite? Heal necrotic tissue?"

She laughed; a little unsteadily, he thought. "Why think small? Maybe it can resurrect the dead." Her expression turned sober. "You're right; I'm getting carried away. Plenty of Parramati die, of everything from drowning to old age. Whatever the health stones do, they don't convey any special protection against natural demise."

"They appear to utilize the stones only on special occasions. It seems reasonable to assume that whatever energy powers them is finite. If as we suspect they are ancient, then restricting their use may be a way of preserving their useful life. Perhaps letting them lie fallow, as it were, allows the devices to recharge somehow." He eyed her hard. "You realize that we must now redirect our efforts here."

She nodded vigorously. "Absolutely. This alters all priorities. We can still work on the treaty, but only in the context of researching this much more important discovery." As she speculated, she thrust both long legs straight toward the ceiling and commenced a sequence of exercises in place. He found himself speculating, as well.

"Obviously, the first thing we need to do is try to get hold of a stone for detailed study. That's not going to be easy. No stone master will consent to it. Too much kusum at risk."

"We have to be careful," he declared. "We don't know what we're dealing with here. Putting the wrong stones together might have unpleasant consequences. Or no consequences at all. Native traditional knowledge would be a great help in our studies."

Legs up, legs down. Legs up, legs down. She spoke as she exercised. "We already know that the Parramati will do nothing that they feel compromises kusum. Letting me witness the ceremony in the field shows how far we've come in gaining their trust, but we've still a long ways to go before anyone offers to tutor you or me in the ways of stone mastering. Nor do I see anyone letting us stick a stone in a spectroscope or a matrix disseminator."

Rising, Pulickel walked to the nearest window and stared out at the surrounding riot of color that was the tropical Torrelauan forest. Thousands of new specimens lay there, just out of reach, waiting only to be collected and classified. But the only type that interested him now was one to which they would be denied access. He turned abruptly.

"If the Parramati won't lend us a stone or two, then we'll just have to borrow them."

That brought Seaforth's legs down. She gawked at him. "Pulickel, are you talking about stealing a stone? First of all, if the Parramati find out, that'll be the end of our work here. Work, hell; it'll mean the end of the station. The AAnn will have a clear field. As far as any kind of treaty goes, the Commonwealth will have to forget about it. You know the Parramati. They'll never trust us again."

"Not if they don't find out," he snapped. "I'll handle this myself. If something does go wrong, you can tell them that you had nothing to do with it, that you were against it from the inception, that it was all my idea, and that I did it on my own. Which happens to be the truth."

"Damn right it is," she complained.

"If this fails, you can have me replaced. That ought to mollify any outraged Parramati."

"They may not accept that explanation. Yours *or* mine."

"We'll make sure that when I'm carrying out this little bit of fieldwork the Parramati know your whereabouts. They'll see that you're not helping me, that you're not involved in my efforts. They may be suspicious, but I think they'll accept your protestations of innocence." He straightened. "It doesn't matter anyway, because this is going to come off. Unless you've got a better idea."

Seaforth was chewing on her lower lip. "I don't, but I don't much like your idea, either. I wonder if we shouldn't clear it with Ophhlia first."

"Sure. Send them the recording. You think that after reviewing that they'll let us proceed in a quiet, studious manner? As soon as that recording's integrity has been verified, a hundred researchers will descend on Torrelau and the other islands of the archipelago. They'll be accompanied by armed peaceforcers. Lest the AAnn get wind of what's happened and try to muscle in, heavy weapons will accompany the research teams. So much for the easygoing, pastoral Parramati lifestyle. You want to see that happen?"

She was still reluctant. "You argue persuasively, Pulickel. You always do. But I still don't like it."

He turned slightly from her. "You think I do? I'm a xenologist, not a sneak thief. But viable alternatives elude me. We can't do a proper study of the stones without a specimen or two. What do you think a team from Ophhlia will do? They'll acquire the necessary research material by whatever means necessary. Maybe it's a Hobson's choice, but I prefer thievery to coercion." He did his best to cast the proposal in a benevolent light.

"When we've completed our studies, or at least acquired enough material to work with, I'll return the stones. The Parramati will be none the wiser and their way of life, their kusum, will be minimally impacted, if at all. Isn't that better than subjecting them to an armed scientific invasion? Subjected to that kind of pressure, I wouldn't be surprised to see them throw every one of the sacred stones into the deep ocean. That sort of thing has happened before. Many primitives will destroy their culture before they surrender it to force."

Fawn thought of Jariill and Ululiapa and the reverence with which they had handled their stones. "It would be terrible," she agreed tentatively, "if the stones and the knowledge they represent were to be lost."

"Exactly."

"So by stealing a couple of stones you're actually doing the Parramati a service."

He beamed at her, his teeth white against his dark-olive complexion. "That's right."

She shook her head, her tone sardonic. "I'm not sure that you chose the right profession, Pulickel. Okay, I'll buy your reasoning, but I still don't want any part of this."

"Excellent. It's my intention that you do not. You'll stay well out of it. We'll retain the stones for the absolute minimal amount of time necessary to learn what we're dealing with and then I will return them."

"It better be minimal," she declared. "Sacred stones don't just go missing. Their absence will be noted immediately and the Parramati will start looking for them."

"I know. We should be able to acquire enough basic information in a couple of days to give us something to work with. Three days at most. After that we can process readings instead of the actual stones."

Looking resigned, she swung her feet back onto the floor and stared at him. "You've admitted that you're not trained as a thief. How are you going to steal a stone?"

"No Parramati would think of making off with one, would they?"

"Of course not. The penalty would be ostracism and exile. If the stone was important enough, maybe even death. No villager would think of touching a stone without permission from its master, much less the family or clan responsible for it. No stone master will even touch another master's stone. It would be an appalling violation of kusum and an invasion of personal space."

"So they're looked after and cared for but not really guarded."

She conceded the point reluctantly. "That's right."

He brightened. "Then all I have to do is wait until everyone in the vicinity is off working in the fields, or fishing, or visiting relatives; then walk into the appropriate longhouse, pick up the stone, stick it in my backpack, and leave. Without being seen, of course. There's no guard to battle, no traps to avoid. Kusum is protection enough."

"I suppose you're right. But how do you plan to carry this off without being seen?"

"By no means are all the stones kept in the larger villages. We know of many stone masters who live in family-size communities, or even isolated and alone. Those are the ones I will "borrow" from. Not only will it improve my chances, it will greatly reduce the likelihood of my being seen."

She rose and moved to the nearest table, began idly fingering the wrist recorder. "You probably won't be able to acquire the kind of stones we'd most like to study."

He shrugged. "It's the nature and operating methodology of the stones we need to learn, not the specific individual functions. The how more so than the what. I'll be perfectly happy with a couple of growing stones or water stones. As for trying them in combination, what's the worst that could happen?"

She turned to stare back at him. "I don't know, Pulickel. I suppose that depends on the type of stones you bring back."

"We must have at least two. Three or four would be better. That would allow us to experiment with a number of different combinations. After we have exhaustively analyzed their internal structure and composition, of course." He smiled expectantly. "Then we are agreed?"

She hesitated before letting out a long, heartfelt sigh. "In the absence of any viable alternatives, I suppose so."

He moved to a computer station. "Then the first thing we need is a list of all the known stone masters on the island. I could go elsewhere in the archipelago, but off Torrelau I'd stand out more. Being familiar with the local topography will also help." He spoke softly to the computer and the section of wall immediately above flared to life.

"There." He gestured at the readout. "The Vounea Peninsula is full of isolated farms and small villages."

"That's because it's one of the most rugged areas on the island," she reminded him. "You've only been there once."

"I don't mind a little hiking. Besides, the documentation is excellent. According to this, there are more than a dozen stone masters living in the area. They don't have as much contact with the larger towns like Torrelauapa. With traditional methods of communication, it will take at least a couple of days for word of the disappearances to travel across the island." He looked up at her.

"With luck we'll be able to return the stones we borrow before many Parramati are informed that any have gone astray."

"Which presents another problem," she observed. "Assuming you bring this off, you still have to return them without being seen."

He waved off her concern. "It's not as important. If I'm seen returning a stone I'll probably be hailed as a hero for making the recovery. This could even end up enhancing our standing among the locals. The Parramati will be so glad to have the missing sacred stones back they'll soon quit wondering about their mysterious and temporary disappearance. For all I care they can imagine the stones grew legs and went for a stroll."

He directed the computer to transfer the list on the wall to the portable unit in his locker, which he would carry with him. Appropriate map overlays were next on his research list.

"Twenty-four lab hours with a couple of stones: that's all I want. That should be enough time for us to get some idea of their composition and internal structure. From that we ought to be able to put together a presentation sufficient to interest Denpasar. If we can bypass the imported scientific bureaucracy in Ophhlia, we might be able to keep this to ourselves for a while and prevent Parramat from being overrun by the curious. Otherwise it will be impossible to do rational ethnography—or much of anything else."

"I agree with that much." Fawn poured herself a glass of fruit juice from a refrigerated pitcher. "What happens if you get caught in the act?"

"I'll say that I was just looking to satisfy my curiosity. Since no Parramati can conceive of stealing a stone, it's reasonable to assume they'd think likewise of us. I might have to sit through a lecture on proper stone-visiting procedure, but I think the locals will make allowance for my ignorance." He smiled blandly. "The natives can be very forgiving."

"They won't be," she warned him, "if they confront you on a trail and find a couple of missing stones in your backpack."

"You postulate a worst-case scenario. I'll cope with it if and when it happens." He rose. "You can drop me off somewhere along the Vounea, stand out to sea, and pick me up later that evening. If there's any problem I'll contact you and we'll make other arrangements."

She brooded over the proposal. "You make it all sound so plausible."

"We've already contemplated alternative approaches and come up with nothing." His tone sharpened. "We can't just leave this alone, Fawn. Not after what you saw."

"I know. I just wish there was some other way."

"So do I. Keep in mind that we're not taking the stones. We're not packaging them up and shipping them off to Hivehom or Earth. We're going to look at them for a couple of days, take a few measurements and readings, and then put them back where they belong. That's all. If based on our initial findings more advanced analysis is called for, then we'll formulate a fresh approach at that time. Meanwhile we'll do things a step at a time."

She nodded. "I wish I could be as sanguine as you. When do you want to do this?"

"What's wrong with tomorrow?"

She drained her glass. "I suppose you're right. The sooner the better."

He tried to reassure her. "Don't worry. I won't take any unnecessary chances. If one stone is too closely attended, I'll just move on to the next. I'm more concerned about curious cubs than I am watchful adults." Once more he considered the view of the surrounding alien forest.

"We'd do well to rest for the remainder of the afternoon. Tomorrow is going to be frenetic."

"I hope that's all it is." She put the glass aside. "Weapons here are primitive, Pulickel, but an arrow or an ax can kill you just as dead as a needler."

"The last thing I want is to precipitate any kind of violent confrontation. I don't want to get hurt and I don't want to hurt any of the natives. It's not going to happen. Will you stop worrying?" He walked over and put his arm around her, having to reach up slightly to do so. "Unless someone sees me actually taking a stone there's no chance of any trouble."

"I wish I had your confidence." Reaching down, she messed his thick black hair. He kept it combed straight back in a utilitarian but not especially flattering coif. When she was finished much of it stood straight up or out, in spikes. Patiently he smoothed it back down.

Wish I had you, he thought . . . but did not dare even whisper it aloud.

CHAPTER

12

Daybreak found them speeding along the outer edge of the fringing lagoon, Fawn guiding the skimmer just inside the line of marching breakers. It took awhile to half circumnavigate Torrelau, but within the hour they were approaching the Vounea Peninsula.

Moving inshore, she cruised back and forth while Pulickel studied the terrain in search of the ideal place to land. With the aid of survey maps they found it in a tiny, rock-walled cove too shallow for fishing and too strewn with silicate and stone rubble to serve as a play pool for Parramati young. The inlet's slick wave-worn walls offered little in the way of hand or foot grips, and the crumbling rim overhung the water.

Fawn held the skimmer level with the top of the nearest cliff while Pulickel tossed his pack into a clump of obliging bushes. In addition to map and locator gear, he carried three days' worth of concentrated rations, a backup communicator, first-aid pack, wet-weather attire, shoe and clothing repair kit, and several padded sacks for carrying—and concealing—stones.

"I expect I have everything." He put one foot on the edge of the skimmer and prepared to step over the slight gap between the craft's outer edge and the heavily vegetated stone parapet against which it floated.

"Just one more thing." Leaving the controls, Fawn walked back to him. Standing on the side of the skimmer put his face level with hers, so she didn't have to bend to kiss him. It was a straightforward and chaste peck on the lips, no more lubricious than a handshake held long, but his mouth burned as if he'd gargled with sambal sauce.

Before he could react or say anything, she'd pivoted and returned to the controls. "Watch your step. And by that I don't mean look at your feet all the time. I don't want to go back to running the station solo."

The fire on his mouth lingered, and he wanted to say a great many things. What he said instead was "I will endeavor to keep myself intact." Though he commanded a large army of words, in the presence of women the ones he wanted to use always seemed to be AWOL when he was most in need of them.

After backing the skimmer out of the inlet, she threw him a perfunctory wave as she headed for the distant reef line. She'd find a sandy islet with shade and make herself comfortable until it was time to return and pick him up. It was how he'd first encountered her; exposing her nakedness to Senisran's tropical sun, blissfully indifferent to potential onlookers. Combined with the lingering taste of her on his lips, it kept him from concentrating on the task at hand.

He allowed himself to remain distracted for approximately four minutes. Only then did he put the delightfully unsettling farewell out of his mind and get to work.

A quick check of his equipment revealed that all was as he'd stowed it. Activated, his handheld showed the skimmer moving steadily out to sea. Disabling the unit's integrated vorec, he used silent manual controls to call up a detailed map of his present position. It indicated that it was a short but rugged hike to the small village housing the nearest sacred stone.

He eyed the steep, thickly vegetated slope in front of him and sighed. Better get going, he told himself. The sooner he obtained a couple of good specimens and had Fawn pick him up, the sooner he would be able to relax. At his request the handheld mapped out the easiest route up the ridge. Among other functions, the compact device could pinpoint his position, Fawn's, and that of potential specimens; compose a respectable weather prediction on-site; translate all known Parramati terminology; let him communicate with his colleague, the base station, or Ophhlia; access the small but rapidly growing *Encyclopedia Senisran*; and run a fairly thorough health check on human, thranx, or native. But it could not walk for him.

Keeping an eye peeled for dangerous animals and toxic plants, he slipped the pack onto his back and started up. In hopes of avoiding unwanted attention, he had selected a route that would take him to the most isolated stone repositories first. Only if these attempts failed would he risk borrowing from the larger villages. With luck, his first couple of tries would be successful, and he and Fawn would be back at base in time for lunch.

He encountered no one in the jungle. The rocky, heavily eroded terrain where the skimmer had touched shore was not conducive to terrace farming, and the vegetation was too tangled for good hunting. He welcomed it as an ally since it would slow communications when astonished stone masters began to spread the news to the rest of the island of stones gone missing.

Some of the plants and forest dwellers he encountered in the course of his climb were familiar to him. Others, being endemic to the Vounea, were new. Ignorant of their properties and capabilities, he treated anything unfamiliar with the greatest respect.

One who assumes that *everything* bites or stings is less likely to get bitten or stung, he knew. It would be worse than ironic if he were to effortlessly make off with a couple of prime stones and not be seen at all, only to be laid low through careless confrontation with a ravavuaa or tesamau. Incapacitation from natural causes would do nothing to protect him from Parramati wrath if they found him with the missing stones in his possession.

So he checked every burrow, every overhanging branch, every coarse leaf and stem, while his sweatcap struggled silently to cool his head and the back of his neck. In the rugged terrain the humidity seemed magnified. Acclimated he might be, but his body was less persuaded than his mind.

He could have chosen an easier route to more accessible targets, but the same topography that was presently making him curse under his breath would help to conceal him when he fled. Occasionally he was forced to change direction when confronted by a grade too steep to ascend or ground too broken to cross, but the handheld always brought him back on line.

The first stone was kept in a well-built hut that was located slightly upslope and isolated from a community of less than a dozen buildings. As he crept toward the back of the structure, he could hear the villagers' gentle barking speech rising from below. From its tone he inferred the presence of only infirm elders and immature cubs.

Vegetation grew right up against the hut, ideal for his purposes. He searched for a tractable section of wall, careful to watch where he put his feet. Seeking shelter from sun and weather, aggressively large arthropods with disagreeable demeanors often made their homes beneath the shady undersides of raised native dwellings. Neither querulous native nor inimical fauna materialized to interdict his efforts, however.

The back wall being high and well made, and having heard not a sound from within, he decided to try around front. The typical traditional wooden porch was likewise deserted. Still, he advanced with caution. Might be someone sleeping late inside, he knew, or an enfeebled oldster, or a sickling at rest.

With a glance in the direction of the village, he whispered a generic Parramati greeting. No response was forthcoming. Stepping through the open portal, he took note of sleeping quarters off to the left, living space in the center, and storage to the right. Hygienic facilities would be located elsewhere, somewhere deeper in the forest. It was a standard floor plan, repeated with minimal variation throughout the archipelago.

Heading to his right, he found himself in the family storeroom. There was no food. Dried seafood, meat, flour, fruits, vegetables, and other comestibles were kept in special communal storage buildings. What he did find were personal effects, fancy attire and accouterments carefully hung or laid out for use on ceremonial occasions, fishing gear, eating utensils, and cooking ware. There were no cabinets or drawers, everything being neatly placed on intricately woven Parramati floor mats.

Only at the far end of the room near the back wall did the building differ from those he frequented in Torrelauapa.

In stunning contrast to its simple surroundings, a meter-high wooden pedestal shone with the skill and craftsmanship of which only the best Parramati carvers were capable. Light brown and black-banded, every centimeter of the solid piece of toka root had been carved in relief. Bending close, Pulickel saw representations of village life, ancient clan battles, landscapes, seascapes, and wonderfully detailed portraits of unknown but obviously revered individual Parramati. The pedestal was a testament not only to the proficiency of its carver but to the shining spirit of the Parramati themselves.

To their kusum, he thought.

Resting atop this rousing work, which would have commanded a fortune from any of the many crafts dealers in Ophhlia, was—a rock. A distinctly green-hued, irregularly shaped, singularly uninspiring lump of what appeared to be volcanic glass. It was not fastened, glued, or otherwise attached to the pedestal.

Nor was it especially heavy, he found when he plucked it from its stand and slipped it into one of the empty sacks in his backpack. As he did so he found himself wondering what kind of stone it was. Externally, except for shape there was nothing to distinguish one sacred stone from another. His prize might be a healing stone, a growing or drying stone, or even a stone called upon to aid in resolving domestic disputes.

He checked the porch and its immediate environs carefully before fleeing the hut. Hastily he dashed to his right, cleared the edge of the porch, and disappeared into the jungle behind the building. As far as he could tell, no one had seen him arrive or depart. He was much pleased with himself. Whatever it was that he'd just added to the weight of his pack, it wasn't a burglar-alarm stone.

One more, he decided firmly. One more and he'd be away. After only his first try he was already ahead of schedule.

He held the tracker out in front of him and checked it frequently. There was no sign of any pursuit or indeed that the theft had been discovered. With luck it might be evening before the stone was even missed.

A passing shower was welcomed. Rain could not increase the

humidity but did somewhat alleviate the oppressive heat. Of course, it was worse when the rain ceased and the sun came back out, but he enjoyed it while it lasted. Disdaining the best efforts of his tropical cap and clothes, perspiration poured off him in thin, salt-rich rivulets.

Despite his caution he did encounter a tesamau, hunting alone, and had to fire a couple of bursts from his pistol to discourage it. Later he thought he heard a party of female Parramati berry-picking close by but couldn't be certain of it. Nevertheless, he waited until the distant murmur had faded completely before resuming his march.

The second stone proved much more of a challenge. For a long moment he considered passing on it and continuing on to the third of the six locations he had preselected. But there was no guarantee the next locale would be any easier, nor the ones after that. If he waited until he was down to the last one, he'd find himself trying to snatch a stone from the middle of a good-size village.

At first glance it didn't appear that difficult. There was no formal community, only three huts. Two of them were situated some distance from the house of the stone master. This sat on a small plateau that overlooked the sea. Hard as he strained, he couldn't hear a soul: not elders, not cubs at play, not females attending to domestic tasks.

The problem was the lack of cover for his approach. Thinned by the wind, the forest in which the huts sat was full of gaps where a strolling human could easily be spotted. Furthermore, the stone master's residence could be reached only by a series of a dozen or so steps cut into a rocky slope. The steps were wide and easy to nego-tiate. They would have to be, to accommodate the long seni foot. But they were completely exposed. Anyone ascending would be visible over a broad area.

A comfortable place to live, Pulickel thought as he tried to sketch out an approach. The same wind that thinned the foliage would cool the houses. On Senisran, any breeze was a welcome one.

Clearly he couldn't use the front steps. Even though there was no one around at the moment, it would take only one returnee to spot him leaving the house to ruin everything. Sacrificing some skin, he forced his way up the steep back of the plateau. Half the time he was tree-climbing instead of hiking. Branches and thorns ripped at him.

It was with considerable relief that he arrived at the level rear of the building. Since it caught the ocean breeze from the front, it had not been raised very high on supporting posts. Almost immediately, he found a frayed section of back wall and set about enlarging it until it was big enough for his purpose. The weathered fibers came away easily in his hands.

Crawling through the opening he'd made, he found himself in the familiar central living quarters. These were more spacious than the one he had visited earlier, this hut having been built to a larger floor plan. But the layout and design were the same. A curving bench fronted the cooking area, and thick, intricately patterned sleeping mats were piled outside the entrance to the bedroom.

Rising and moving to his left, he found a storage room that, like the rest of the structure, was larger than the one he'd previously explored. The usual utensils, bowls, and hand-carved household goods lined the walls or were piled on the floor.

The stone pedestal at the rear of the room was short, almost stumpy. Instead of wood, it had been hewn from the bone of some unknown creature. From the size alone Pulickel knew it had belonged to some large ocean-dweller. From base to top it was inlaid with highly polished strips of wood and the Senisrani equivalent of mother-of-pearl. It was another remarkable piece of Parramati craftsmanship, completely different from the one he'd seen earlier but executed with equal skill and love.

He allowed himself a moment to admire it before reaching down to pluck the fist-size stone from its apex. Into an empty sack this went, carefully placed alongside the first stone in the top of his pack.

Finished, he thought with satisfaction, and well ahead of the schedule he'd set for himself. He turned to depart the way he'd come.

Perhaps he shouldn't have spent so much time admiring the inlaid pedestal. With his mission nearly accomplished it was possible that he let down his guard, or that after the difficult climb he was more tired than he realized and not as aware of his surroundings.

Whatever the reason, he nearly knocked down the young female Parramati who entered the storeroom just as he was leaving. The seni of the Vounea Peninsula might have encountered Fawn once or twice before, but this was their first exposure to another human.

"Hey!" he blurted in involuntary counterpoint to her startled *"Sarkk!"*

She started to twist forward; head bending, snout aiming for the floor, the powerful hind legs contracting preparatory to boosting her into the familiar forward flip that served as a formal greeting among her kind. Before she could follow through with the gesture it suddenly struck her who, or rather what, she was confronting.

"Pardon me." By this time his mastery of the local dialect was as complete as it was possible for any human to manage. "I did not mean to startle."

Not yet mature, unsure of herself, and fascinated by the bipedal apparition that she had encountered unexpectedly, she had yet to notice that the stone was missing from its place of honor atop the pedestal. Shifting his stance to block her view, he used an arm to gently ease her out of the room.

Realizing that any attempt to explain himself would only further incriminate his presence while consuming valuable time, he departed in haste. If he hadn't been so rattled by the collision/confrontation, it might have occurred to him that in leaving by the way he'd entered he damned himself more thoroughly than he could have with any number of words. Had he fled via the unbarred front portal, it was just possible that she might have considered him an invited guest, however unusual. That chance vanished when he took off through the hole he'd made in the rear wall.

He could hear her shrill, staccato yips of alarm as he plunged back the way he'd come, throwing himself heedlessly into the tangle of branches and bushes behind the house. Was she sounding the alert over the presence of an intruder, or had she discovered that the stone was missing? If he had shoved her bodily back into the living area, would it have gained him enough time to set the stone back on its pedestal?

None of that mattered now. He could hear the voices of other seni joining that of the young female. They were full of uncertainty, concern, and something else. Something new. Something that until now he hadn't heard in a Parramati voice. It took him a moment to identify it.

Anger.

He tried to put it out of his mind as he concentrated on the difficult descent. All he had to do was retrace his path back to the inlet. Shoving and striking at obstructing branches as he ran, he forced himself to ignore the rising chorus behind as he concentrated on following the route laid out by the tracker.

He'd make it easily, he told himself. By the time any kind of formal pursuit was organized he'd be halfway back to the inlet.

Brush crashed behind him but he heard no voices. Surely they wouldn't just connect the missing stone with his unannounced presence? It would be most un-Parramatilike to account a visitor a thief without some sort of proof.

It struck him that he'd left many voices in his wake. More than would normally be found inhabiting three isolated huts. A fishing or hunting party come to pay their respects, perhaps, or a clutch of visiting relatives. Bad luck for him. He tried to increase his pace, wishing he had Fawn's stride.

Better contact her while he still had enough breath to do so, he thought. The sensitive autocontext had her on line in less than a minute.

"Well, that was quick." Her tone confirmed that she was blissfully unaware of the sudden downturn in his present fortunes. "How did it go?"

Panting hard, he tried to maintain his pace while replying. It was a good thing he was in decent shape. He gave silent thanks for all the marathons he'd competed in.

"The first stone was no problem." He cleared a small creek in a single leap.

The handheld was of excellent thranx manufacture. It conveyed every nuance of his speech, including his labored respiration. "Pulickel, what's wrong with you? You sound like you're out of breath."

"Not yet, but I'm going to be. I need you to meet me at the pickup point. *Right now.*"

"What the hell's going on? What's wrong?"

He ducked an overhanging branch, pleased that he was able to do so without either slowing or decapitating himself. "What makes you think anything's wrong?"

"Oh, I don't know. Maybe the fact that you sound like a diver sucking his last lungfull of air. So you got the first stone okay. Then what?"

A protuberant buttressing root appeared and threatened to send him sprawling. He escaped it with only a minor bruise, one of many that had begun to festoon his lower legs.

"Nobody saw me get the first stone, nobody heard me, and I didn't see or hear anyone, either. Same thing on the second attempt—except that in leaving I all but ran over an adolescent female. She must have entered the building while I was concentrating on acquiring the stone. Without thinking, I left the same way I'd entered—through a hole I made in the back wall. Stupid. I should have simply walked out the front, hands tucked in my suspenders, looking like I belonged."

"You don't have any suspenders," she snapped.

"If you're not waiting for me at the rendezvous, I may not have any fingers to tug them with, either." He stole a quick glance back over his shoulder. Nothing untoward disturbed the forest behind him.

"I think they're after me, but I don't see anyone yet."

"Keep moving. You may be able to outdistance them. On a beach or other open flat you wouldn't have a chance. I've seen competing young adult males clear ten meters with every bound, but in dense jungle those big feet slow them up and it's harder for them to hop. They're not so good at dodging trees, either. Maybe you can shake them."

"I don't have to shake them. Just beat them to the inlet."

"So they saw you." Seaforth's voice was resigned.

"Only the one adolescent. Given time, maybe we can cast doubt on her story. Insist in the face of all accusation that both of us have been back at the station all the time. Try to convince the local big persons that what she saw was a spirit and not a visiting human."

"But the stone is missing."

"She didn't see me with it. Unless they catch and search me they can only suspect. They have no proof."

"Then you'd better not let them catch up with you."

"What do you think I'm trying to do here?"

Understandingly, she ignored his angry retort. "I'm on my way."

Severing the connection, he returned his attention to the handheld's readout and the forest ahead. He was making good time, his small stature allowing him to dart around and under obstacles that would have slowed a larger man. His body was insisting that he rest, but he continued to push himself. Just because he couldn't hear or see any pursuers didn't mean they weren't a literal hop, skip, and jump behind him. If so, they were certainly conserving their voices.

On the handheld, the location of the inlet was coming up fast. He allowed himself to feel a measure of confidence. They could make up some kind of story, express their outrage at being accused of the crime, call on the influence and friendship of the Torrelauapan big persons they knew well, and generally do everything possible to cast doubt on the aspersions of the adolescent female. It would be his word against hers.

And in a few days, when they'd completed the lab work on the stones and had built up sufficient computer models for further research, both missing stones would mysteriously reappear at the appropriate venues. With the stones returned, any rising anger among the Parramati in general would dissipate before it could reach dangerous proportions. Polite as they were, they would probably point the finger of blame at one another before formally accusing the visiting humans.

Such a theft would make even less sense to them than if the stones had been taken by one of their own kind, for what use had an alien for a sacred stone? For example, no human knew how to manipulate the stones to locate roads. The whole idea was absurd.

There was a flash of color and light behind him and he nearly stumbled, but it was only a pair of harmless oronai darting through the trees. Always curious, they remained by his side, pacing him as he ran. As long as they remained relatively silent and didn't cry out, he welcomed their company. They would alert him to the presence of any truly dangerous predators. One turned in midair and continued flying on its back, bringing a smile to his face despite his increasing exhaustion.

His attention on it, he overlooked the hole and went down hard, his left leg plunging into the opening, his head slamming sideways into the dirt. The impact jarred his teeth and shook colors loose behind his eyes.

Rolling over, he sat up and took stock of his stunned form. Nothing broken. His left foot throbbed a little and he tested it gingerly, putting more and more weight on it until he was standing without pain. He thought he might have pulled something, but the leg was just sore.

Something was warming his back. It didn't feel like liquid. Not blood, then. Looking over a shoulder, he saw the glow. Pale green tinged with blue, it was strong enough to penetrate the tough material of his backpack, emanating strongly from within.

The stones, he realized quickly. In falling he'd twisted, and in twisting he'd landed partly on his back. Both sacks must have snapped open, throwing their contents together. His backpack had become an unintended incubator for the offspring of stone fusion.

Hurriedly he slipped free of the shoulder straps. The heat from within now verged on the uncomfortable. His hands hovered over the top flap of the pack, hesitating. What could he do to terminate the reaction? What was the accepted procedure for dealing with stones that had been unintentionally melded? Could he pry them apart manually? He unfastened the flap.

So intense was the green-blue light that spilled from the interior that he could barely stand to look directly at it. He could just make out the source of the light and heat: a single uneven mass where earlier there had been two. The individual specimens had melted into one, duplicating the reaction Fawn had described previously.

To what end? Aside from the heat, which might be nothing more than a residual by-product of the commingling, he felt nothing. His health was unaffected, as was the color of the sky and the pungent odor of the rain forest. Nothing sprouted dramatically from beneath his feet—or died, either, he noted with some relief.

He had a flash of inspiration. Maybe the bright light itself was the intended end product of the accidental conjoining. Perhaps this combination of stones was designed to illuminate the interior of caves, or long night-time walks through heavy jungle, or to attract nocturnal sea creatures to a fisherman's net.

His fingers hovered over the lambent mass. The heat was substantial but not unbearable. How did one separate commingled stones? Squint as he might, he saw neither seam nor crevice nor cleavage plane. How did the stone masters do it? Or did they simply wait until the reaction exhausted itself, at which time the stones would separate of their own accord?

Exactly how much control did the stone masters have over these devices anyway?

He felt he had to at least try. Maybe a good, strong, old-fashioned tug on both ends simultaneously, he speculated. Grabbing one side of the composite mass in each hand, he tried pulling. No luck. Interestingly, the heat seemed to dissipate through his palms rather than burn him. A twist, then, in opposite directions. As he worked his hands and wrists he thought he felt something give within the mass.

The stone exploded.

No, he decided, aware that he had not lost consciousness. The glassy mass had not blown up. In fact, he and the conjoined stones were the only things that had *not* exploded. They remained intact and unaltered.

It was the universe that had detonated.

Well, come apart, anyway. Disintegrated, dissolved, shattered. When eventually it reconstituted itself, he was someplace else.

The only constant in this mental and physical transposition was the stone, which continued to pour forth its intense, unrelenting radiance. Deciding to chance the heat, he slipped the pack back over his shoulders.

Odd sort of explosion, he reflected, during which the cosmos had seemed to disintegrate and re-form around him. Only, the process had produced some changes. Significant changes.

For one thing, there was no sign of pursuing Parramati. There was nothing to even suggest the presence of Parramati. He was still standing on a moderate slope in the midst of dense forest, but the foliage was not of the kind he had come to associate with the Vounea Peninsula. In fact, it was not of a kind he recognized at all.

There wasn't a sane trunk in the lot. Trees took the form of sharp curves, right angles, berserk spirals: anything but straight. Instead of leaves, the majority sported tiny red pustules. Some were no larger than the tip of his little finger while others were a meter and more across. Nor were these singular growths stable. They twisted and writhed as if in pain beneath a pale red sky in which hung suspended an orb of deepest crimson, whether sun or moon Pulickel couldn't tell.

There were other lights in the sky, but he balked at calling them stars. For one thing, most were purple, except for those that blinked lavender. Within arm's length of his right hand a cluster of narrow, blue-striped shoots quivered in the still air. As they trembled, they hummed.

Their murmuring resonated in time to the humming that was intensifying inside his head. It felt and sounded as if he'd been locked inside a steel cylinder full of bees. Stumbling to his left, he saw something thick and ropy slither out of sight below the surface of a tangerine stream. Glistening wetly as it moved, it resembled animate yellow slime.

A flock of flying creatures appeared, keeping less than a meter off the ground. Showing no sign of changing direction or swerving, the V-shaped formation headed straight for him. At the last instant he threw up his arms to ward them off.

Most sailed past on either side. The several that did not, penetrated his skin and passed completely through his body. No ghosts they, he could feel every centimeter of their passage. Gasping at the sickening sweetness that filled his belly, he bent double and grabbed his midsection. Only after the sensation had passed was he able to straighten and look behind him. The flock continued on its way, oblivious to the ineffectual human blockade it had so effortlessly ignored, penetrating anything that stood in its path with lugubrious ease. Hasty inspection revealed that the incident had left not a mark on him. Not a hole, scratch, bruise, or puncture. Atomic structures had been momentarily rearranged. His, or theirs? he wondered.

The scarlet orb that dominated the heavens was sinking rapidly toward the distant horizon. Much too rapidly, he thought. The purple sky-points brightened. They were stars then, he decided, but arrayed against the red-tinged firmament in no pattern he recognized. Certainly these were not constellations discernible from anyplace on Senisran.

Several of the energetic stellar formations resembled nothing in the canon of known celestial features. Riding in the pack on his back, the luminescent stones continued to radiate steadily.

Taking a couple of hesitant steps in the direction of the peculiar stream, he saw that it ran not with water but a much more viscous liquid that had the consistency of orange syrup. With each step the surface underfoot let out a quavery moan, as if he were treading the spine of some enormous, somnolent being. Those tortuous, serpentine growths he'd assumed were forest: were they trees—or hair? Was his presence here disturbing enough to make the earth complain?

His throat dry from running, he dipped an uncertain hand toward the orange current. It twisted away from him, retreating like a live thing. Insistent, he shoved his fingers sharply downward. The fluid flowed over and around his hand and forearm, never touching the skin. Whatever it might be, it was repelled by his humanness.

Defeated, he straightened. There was nothing inherently inimical about the place he'd been dumped. It simply didn't like him. Where was he, and where was Fawn Seaforth? For that matter, where was Senisran? The questions led him to an answer. He knew now what kind of stones he'd stolen. Not growing stones, or healing stones. Not stones for filling nets or imparting wisdom.

They were transportation stones. But—transportation to where?

Roads. Stones and spaces and roads. That was the core of Parramati kusum, brought home to him now in a manner as overwhelming as it was unexpected. He'd accidentally opened a road, only to find himself catapulted down its length utterly ignorant of his destination. As a demonstration of unfamiliar alien science, it was several orders of magnitude greater than enhanced garden growth.

The world on which he found himself resembled nothing he'd

ever heard about, read about, or researched. Certainly it wasn't in the Commonwealth catalog of known systems.

His orgy of speculation was interrupted by the appearance of a puffy pink fuzzball laced with delicate blue veins that materialized among the growths just in front of him. It was roughly half his size. After a moment's hesitation, it began rolling toward him. Wary, he drew his pistol and held it ready.

As it neared, the creature slowed. Halting, it exuded a strong pseudopod that terminated in a pair of impressively thick yellow lips. Approaching to within a meter, this flexible organ proceeded to scrutinize him intently, the lips making soft sucking sounds every time they altered position. His feet, legs, torso, arms, and head were all carefully inspected.

When he took a sudden step forward, the limb retracted completely into the round body. Avoiding him, the fuzzball rolled into a clump of dancing spines and vanished.

One faint hope was dashed when his communicator responded to his terse entreaties with the expected silence. He would have been shocked if Fawn had replied. Clipping the unit back onto his belt, he tried to decide what to do next. What *could* he do? He had been transported to a very elegant nowhere. Everything was off, outlandish, and unnatural, from the stream to the stars to the sun that had abandoned the alien sky with deviant precipitousness.

At that point the orange liquid inhabiting the creekbed began to flow out of its banks and head toward him. As he backed away warily, the whole stream lifted itself up and started looping in his direction like some gigantic candy-flaked sidewinder.

Having no intention of being strangled by a stream, he turned and ran, hoping as he did so that he wouldn't run smack into something worse. Swinging the backpack around in front of him, he half closed his eyes as he searched the surface of the pulsating stone for a significant depression, a crack, anywhere it might make sense to place a manipulative organ. A glance back showed that the perambulating tributary was closing on him.

A couple of the larger growths twitched and leaned in his direction. If the stream didn't get him, it seemed increasingly likely that the forest would.

Twisting the stone had brought him here. There was nothing for it but to try again.

Reaching into the pack, he secured a firm grip and wrenched hard with both hands. His greatest fear was that the mass would separate back into its component halves, marooning him here for what promised to be a very brief if spectacularly educational future.

How far was he from Senisran? A light-year or half a galaxy away? Not that it mattered. When nothing happened, he twisted hard against the mass a second time. The ambulatory orange tide was quite close now. When it caught up, would it try to choke him, or drown him?

For a second time, the cosmos fragmented on the fringes of his consciousness. When he could again focus and cogitate, he found himself once more transported. There was just enough time for him to breathe the proverbial sigh of relief before realizing that, while liberated from hostile rivers and neurotic woods, neither was he back on Senisran.

CHAPTER

13

The distant mountains were limned in black. Closer at hand stood a cluster of stark, gnarled trunks, leafless and forlorn, that on a lusher world would not have passed for trees. Bare-stemmed and ghostly, they thrust naked limbs at the sinister sky as if struggling to hold a hostile universe at bay.

Gaunt, spectral flying creatures twitched uneven paths through the oppressive atmosphere, dipping and soaring as if avoiding unseen, unpleasant lumps in the air. Beneath his feet the ground was pale gray. Rocks were a darker gray or charcoal-hued. Atop one, something the size and color of old sewer pipe was quivering with horrid life. Smaller, dun-colored young huddled close to its protective bulk.

Holding up one hand, an unsettled Pulickel saw that it had acquired the same unhealthy ashen pallor that permeated this place. It was cold, and his jungle shorts and shirt provided inadequate protection. Only the warmth that continued to pour from the sacred stone kept him from shivering.

Though no sun appeared, the sky began to lighten. Instead of blue it was white. Not a revelatory, illuminating white, but a dull, listless shift from gray to something else farther up the spectrum. Stars revealed themselves in a night that was brighter than the day. They were black. Instead of blinking, they regarded the stark landscape with a steady, baleful glare.

Ahead, the sun began to emerge from hiding, and it was as caliginous as the misbegotten stars. A sickly gray effulgence ghosted the rim of the burning black orb.

Slowly Pulickel brought his hand toward his face and found that he could see *through* the pale, wan flesh. Black bones stood out as clearly as in an old-fashioned X ray. But the sky was worse— the ghastly white sky splotched with unhealthy constellations of black stars.

Color had been banned from this world and no suitable replacement found. Or was everything normal and only his vision damaged, or his mind? Had the universe gone mad, or only he?

Was this the view from the bottom of a black hole? he wondered. A place where color as well as matter was crushed out of existence? But if the latter, how could he still stand, still feel his body, his face?

Here I am dragging the bottom of a gravity well, he thought wildly, *and it's dry.*

The stone had cast him into the realm of unnatural law. Physics here were not merely different: they were *other*. But he could still see color. He knew that to be true because the radiance from his backpack remained that steady, unvarying green-blue. Whatever powered it was strong enough to resist even the morbidifying effects of this place.

His eyes hung gratefully on that green glow as he gripped the glowing mass for a third time and twisted, his effort this time driven more by desperation than hope. When nothing happened a deep shiver of sheer panic raced the length of his spine.

Shaking, he fought to keep from losing control completely. Remembering that his first effort immediately prior to this one had also failed, he steadied himself for another try. The stone *had* to work. Around him, the pallid gray emptiness shouted death. His fingers convulsed on the softly glowing mass.

The universe came apart in a shower of coal and snow, shimmering shards of white and blackness. They pierced like knives and he gasped in pain.

Only to find himself saturated with color, beneath a sunset sky, standing on grass.

Red grass.

The bushes were round and yellow, the herd of hexapods browsing them burnt umber with camouflaging canary stripes. Multiple mouths paused in mid-nip as bulging pink eyes swiveled sharply to regard him. Limpid stares reflecting sudden shock at his unannounced appearance, the entire herd promptly lumbered past the line of foliage and disappeared into the distance in a cloud of eyes, legs, cud-chewing mouths, and red dust.

He was alone again.

Except for the occasional patch of dense, fiercely colored vegetation, the land in which he found himself was perfectly flat. Not a ridge, not a mound, not even an anthill interrupted the horizon. It was as hot as the previous world had been cold, but devoid of humidity. The red grass formed a thick, lush carpet beneath his feet.

Blissfully blue, the sky was vacant of cloud. While not a comforting yellow, the single ripe red-orange star that dominated the firmament did not inspire dread, either. It wasn't Senisran—but it was better. He wasn't home, but it felt like he was back in the neighborhood.

Something irritated his throat and he suffered through a brief coughing jag. The red dust, down in his lungs, or some impurity in the atmosphere? Attractive as his new surroundings might be, he knew he couldn't stay long. With a sigh, he fondled the conjoined stones.

How extensive was the route it followed? How many worlds could it access? Undoubtedly it offered a means of selecting one's destination, but he didn't have a clue as to how that might work. He'd found the ignition, but steering remained a mystery to him.

He might die of hunger or thirst before he twisted his way back to Senisran. Or it might be the next stop on a preprogrammed, alien itinerary. Meanwhile, as the old saying went, he might as well try to enjoy the ride.

Was the green glow fading slightly? If whatever powered the system failed, he would be marooned forever. Marooned by the side of a Parramati road, he mused, with no one likely to come along and offer him a lift. The source of the stone's energy remained as much a mystery to him as its alien engineering.

Maybe the glow wasn't weakening. Maybe the color change was due to some quality of the local atmosphere. Forcing himself to accept that comforting hypothesis, he took a deep breath and twisted hard on the stone.

His hands came loose and went drifting slowly off over the grass. They were followed by his forearms, which broke free at the elbows and began to spin lazily end over end in the direction of his peramubulating hands.

There was no blood, no pain. Just an unmistakable physiological parting of the ways. As he lunged instinctively after his escaping body parts, his torso detached from his hips and his legs came apart in sections. Last of all, his head popped free of his neck.

Obeying some unknown, unimaginable herding instinct, his component bits and pieces remained in the same general vicinity. Too focused to scream, he strove to will his corpus whole again. Though fully functional, his disembodied head no longer exercised any control over the muscles in his limbs. His hands seemed to have the most mobility. Fingers fluttering like thick cilia, they darted in and around the rest of him, kicking backward through the air. One hand latched onto a forearm and rested there like a bird taking roost on a branch.

As he stared dazedly, the yellow bushes began to detach themselves from the ground and drift off into the sky. Pulling themselves free of the soil, roots separated from branches and drifted off on their own. Indeed, the soil was beginning to separate from the ground.

Caught by a rising breeze, clumps of grass were whisked toward the eastern horizon. Elevated from their subterranean homes, burrowing creatures twisted helplessly in the air, only to be preyed upon by flying teeth that seemed to have no trouble coping with the jabberwockean change in conditions.

Overhead, the orange-red sun was coming apart, fiery prominences dancing in all directions. In the distance he saw the handsome brown and yellow grazers coming apart, only to re-form as a spherical mass of floating eyes, legs, horns, and bodies.

This time only the absence of lungs prevented him from screaming.

In the center of rising chaos hovered his backpack, the stone pulsing peacefully within. It didn't matter, since he was no longer in control—or even possession—of his hands. He closed his eyes. That he could still do.

When he opened them again everything was coagulating. The spherical herd of grazers separated back out into its component parts, reformulating animals instead of insanity. Branches returned to bushes, bushes to roots, and roots to their place in the earth. Feeding time over, the flying teeth disappeared.

The surface resolidified beneath him. Up in the sky, the local star became once again a familiar rounded ball of burning hydrogen. As he stared mutely, the rambling bits of his body re-formed. Only his hands resisted, waiting until the last instant to reattach themselves to his wrists. He had a bad moment when he thought they were going to hook up with his ankles instead.

Slowly turning to left and then to right, he found his head once more firmly positioned on his neck. Arms and legs responded to mental command. He took incalculable pleasure in being able to execute a short hop.

Next time the effect might last longer, the consequences prove more severe, the distances between liberated limbs turn out to be dangerously greater. Given another taste of freedom and independence, his hands might not return. As if in confirmation, they seemed reluctant to grasp the stone and twist on its ends.

Finding himself arguing with his own body, he forced them to obey. Chaos might be a liberating place to visit, but he didn't want to live there.

Was he any nearer Senisran? Was he even in the same galaxy? The same universe? Already he'd visited corners of the cosmos that defied natural law as he knew it. He wanted *out*.

That's what he got.

As his fingers relaxed on the stone, he found himself in a place of utter blackness. No, he decided, it was blacker than black. It wasn't an absence of light so much as the fact that in this place it seemed never to have existed. It was an abstract concept, a fever dream, a product of delirium.

He could not see, could not perceive. Sensing that he was floating, he felt with his feet and hands for a solid surface and found none. There was nothing to orient himself against, no point of reference. He could not see but was not blind, could not hear but was not deaf. His nose wrinkled. That sense, too, was functional. He wished it wasn't.

His incomprehensible surroundings stank of the charnel house.

He could still feel. The backpack was heavy against him, but for the first time he could not see what had come to be the solacing glow of the stone. Groping within the pack, he felt of its outline, its weight, reassuring himself of its reality.

Enveloped in an all-consuming shroud of tangible corruption, he drifted helpless and alone. Or was that a Presence he now sensed? Deprived of the majority of means of exploring the space around him, he couldn't be sure.

It touched him.

Though he couldn't see It, his eyes tried to shrink back into his skull. Though he couldn't hear It, his mind was drowned in a chorus of horror. The suddenly overwhelming odor pierced the core of his being.

Disoriented and slightly deranged, he fumbled for the stone. Colossally indifferent, a minuscule portion of the Presence began to examine the insignificant splotch of protoplasm nearby.

This was not a place that was simply bad for him, where there was no water to drink or comforting sunshine to warm his bones. He had come to a blasted place in the cosmos, where any organic life-form, be it worm, human, or blade of grass, was not welcome, did not belong, and could not long survive. Could a blade of grass go insane? He knew that he could.

He Needed to Get Away.

As the infinitesimal extrusion of the Presence stepped between two dead stars to close in around him, his fingers twisted convulsively on the ends of the stone. A sickly clamminess enveloped him as he sensed something sandpapering his soul. It promised a primal and intimate experience worse than death. His self threatened to fly apart. In the Presence, even atoms could not long remain coherent.

It was evil incarnate, an evil that transcended theology, physics, and metaphysics. Possessed of a loathsome purity, it left no room in its Presence for anything that smacked of the natural universe. Only Pulickel's insignificance saved him. Of next to no consequence, he was overlooked.

But that was changing.

He couldn't run because he had no legs, couldn't flail because he had no arms. In the absence of lungs he couldn't scream, and in the absence of sanity he could not conceive. All he could do was react instinctively. More fortuitously than he could imagine, his reaction took the form of wrenching on the stone.

He knew a little about the subatomic forces that bind the cosmos together. There was taste, and there was flavor. There was up and there was down. Here was something else, something new. Something previously unquantified. A different state of not-matter, not-energy, not-plasma, not Einstein-Bose conjunction. He could not give a name to it because his mind was not working very well. He knew only that He Had to Get Away from It.

Insignificant speck that he was, it would annul him, reduce him to a single tiny scream that would float forever in this place. It wanted him nothing because it abhorred anything that was not itself. His fingers weakened in tandem with his resolve.

In the distance, impossibly far off and yet proximate, a subdued flash of green. Beyond sickliness now, he felt little. Exit left, shrieking. But the Presence went away. Or rather, he went away from It.

Fawn stared down at him. She was not alone. Parramati stood on either side of her. Several were inspecting the station's greeting lounge, examining the alien surroundings. Most, like Fawn, focused their attention on the figure that lay prone on the couch. Senisran's comforting sunlight filtered in through the bank of windows that lined the station's exterior.

"He looks better." At the tip of his long snout, Massapapu's black nose twitched as he inhaled of the reclining human. "His eyes are open."

"Yes, but he's still not reacting." The expression on Fawn Seaforth's face was one of grave concern. She waved a hand slowly back and forth over her comatose companion's eyes. He blinked but gave no sign that he actually saw her. His gaze was locked other-where. Sight of a sort had returned, but not perception. "There's eye movement, and he's breathing, but that's about it. I don't like his color. He's white as a sheet." She turned to the Parramati clustered closely behind her.

"Has he been like this ever since you found him?"

Massapapu signed his agreement. "You know, F'an, that he had taken two stones."

"Yes, you told me." Uncomfortable, she looked away. So far the Parramati hadn't implicated her in the thefts. Thus spared, she immediately denied any knowledge of them. If they accepted her protestations of innocence, then her work on Torrelau could continue unhindered. Despite his undeniable expertise and ability, Pulickel could be replaced.

What had happened to him? It was impossible to get a straight answer out of the Parramati who had brought him in. She thought she'd mastered the nuances of their language. Now she wasn't so sure.

They claimed to have brought him back not just from the Vounea Peninsula but from another place entirely. Upon learning that two stones had gone missing, the affected stone masters had contacted their brethren across the island. Working in concert, Ascela had explained, allowed them to conduct a proper search for the thief. Or overeager researcher, as Fawn had striven to characterize her comatose companion, doing her best to exonerate him even in unconsciousness. With the aid of other stones, they'd found him and brought him back.

Jorana's tone was admonishing. "We understand Pu'il's thirst for knowledge, but he should not have taken the stones. He most especially should not have tried to use the stones that he did take."

"That's obvious," Fawn conceded.

Ascela's wizened eyes shifted periodically between the prone figure and that of the tall woman standing next to her. Luminous vertical pupils flexed. "He is fortunate that we were able to bring him back. He is very lucky."

He didn't look lucky, Fawn thought as she studied her friend and associate. He looked terrible. What had happened out there? Where had they brought him back from? When they spoke of it, the big and middle persons who had brought him in used verbs inflected in a fashion previously not encountered. She *thought* she knew what they meant but wasn't entirely sure.

Standing out on the reef, studying its inhabitants while waiting for Pulickel to call in, she'd been alerted by a warning tone from the skimmer's instrumentation. A check revealed that Pulickel's transmitter had gone dead. She couldn't even raise a carrier wave. While it was possible for a field transmitter to fail completely, it was highly unlikely. For one thing, the locator unit carried its own emergency power source.

But it was possible. For example, he could have dropped the unit and accidentally rolled a boulder on it. It would have to have been a sizable boulder, she knew, but such things did happen. Exhausting all efforts to raise a signal, she took the dangerous step of returning to the inlet and leaving the skimmer parked on hover while she searched the immediate vicinity.

Fatigued and frantic, she had finally returned to the station, only to find Ascela, Jorana, and Massapapu waiting for her outside the activated defense perimeter. They were accompanied by half a dozen Parramati she did not know. On a woven stretcher in their midst lay Pulickel: eyes open, visibly intact, but utterly unresponsive. They had carried him all the way across the island from the Vounea. Or from wherever it was that they claimed to have found him, she reminded herself.

A check of his person revealed that the stones he had taken were missing. No surprise there, she knew. Doubtless they had been returned to their appropriate resting places. When she had protested her ignorance of Pulickel's intentions, several of the Vounea Parramati had eyed her suspiciously, but none challenged her openly. Ascela, Jorana, and the other Torrelauapans had vouched for her, bless them.

"It is not easy to find someone after they have used these stones," Ascela was saying. "Particularly someone who has not been instructed in their use. The roads they open are difficult to travel."

"It takes many, many generations to learn how to use the stones," added one of the visiting Vouneans.

She desperately wanted to hear Pulickel's side of the story, but he couldn't even look in her direction, didn't respond to her voice. He continued to breathe, slowly and evenly, his eyes staring off into the distance and blinking occasionally. He was present, and yet he was not. Something critical, something vital, was missing.

If he didn't respond soon, she was going to have to hook him up to an IV and request medevac. She didn't want to do that. For one thing, it would be an admission of failure. Nor did she want to deal with the questions that would inevitably accompany such a procedure. But if she was going to be able to avoid making the call, he had to react to her presence, had to show some progress. She couldn't let him lie there and starve to death. Dehydration would be the first problem, she knew.

She turned to Ascela. Of all the Torrelauapan big persons, she felt the strongest rapport with the senior female. "I still don't understand. The Vouneans claim they found him just lying in the jungle like this?"

"Not just like this." A Vounean big person of equal stature stepped forward. Ears thrust forward, he swapped a series of rapid finger movements with Ascela, too fast for Fawn to follow. "When the stone masters found him he was screaming and kicking. This was understandable, as he was in a bad place. A very bad place."

"What kind of bad place?" The xenologist tried to remember the proper gestures. "Did he fall and hit his head?" But that didn't make sense, she thought. If he'd tumbled into a ravine or something, they wouldn't have found him kicking and screaming. Besides, except for a few minor cuts and scrapes, he appeared unharmed. There was no blood showing, and the station's medical scanner had revealed no broken bones or torn ligaments. If he'd suffered some kind of concussion or contusion, it was too subtle for the scanner to detect.

"The worst place," the Vounean explained without explaining anything. "Our stone masters had to use other stones to bring him back. I am not a master so I did not participate, but those who did tell that it was a near thing."

"Well, there was certainly something bad about it." Whether through means chemical or otherwise, her companion's previously jet-black hair was now streaked with white. Nor was the change superficially cosmetic. Close inspection had revealed that the color change extended right down to the follicular roots. It didn't wash out when she was cleaning him up, either.

That had been her first priority, and it had been a job. The smells that clung to him didn't want to wash off. No doubt he'd picked up several exotic odors while stumbling through the jungle in his attempt to avoid the Vouneans. With the aid of the Parramati, she'd managed to wrestle him into some clean clothes, and that had helped. But a faintly disquieting odor still hung about him, a miasma that wouldn't go away. It seemed familiar but she couldn't quite identify it. It made her skin crawl, and she had to work hard at ignoring it.

"We did what we could for him," Jorana was saying.

"Don't get me wrong," Fawn responded. "I'm grateful for everything you've done, for bringing him back and doing your best to help him. I'm just trying to understand what happened and to figure out what's wrong with him." She studied the prone form. Perhaps he'd been bitten and paralyzed by some unknown denizen of the forest. But there were no bite marks that she'd been able to discover, no swelling or redness that would indicate the site of a sting. What was responsible for his present condition? Again she confessed her bafflement to the watching Parramati.

Jorana, too, was searching for an explanation. "Sometimes one who tries to use the stones cannot stay on the proper road. Then the stones may choose the road instead of the user. There are many roads and not all of them are benign."

"I could've guessed that much." Fawn spoke more harshly than she intended. "What am I going to do with him? What *can* I do?"

Her colleague lay as limp as one of the dozens of cephalopods the Parramati fished daily from the ocean. It was as if all the bones in his body had melted away.

Perversely, she envied him that part of his condition. At least he looked at ease. His vital signs remained strong. Nothing critical would relax, she hoped. Like his heart.

"There must be something we can do," she insisted.

"Perhaps a healing stone . . ." Massapapu began.

Fawn looked over sharply. "No! No stones. Not until I've exhausted the medical program's recommendations."

Unmoved by the sharpness of her reaction, the Torrelauapan big person indicated understanding. Turning away from her, he proceeded to discuss the matter with his companions and the Vouneans. Fawn strained to overhear, without much success.

She'd pumped an assortment of stimulants into Pulickel, but without knowing the cause of his condition, the station's pharmaceutical program could only prescribe the most general range of medication. She'd even chanced a dose of buffered adrenaline. It made him twitch briefly but did nothing to restore awareness. At least the occasional blink meant she didn't have to drop-treat his eyes to keep them moist.

In addition to taking no nourishment, his body generated no wastes. It was as if his entire system beyond that necessary for the maintenance of life was locked in a kind of physiological as well as mental stasis. Nothing she had done showed any signs of bringing him out of it.

She became aware that the Parramati had concluded their discussion. They stood by patiently, waiting for her.

"I can give you an idea of what happened, F'an." Jorana regarded her out of dark eyes. "Pu'il traveled down a road he shouldn't have, to a place that should not be visited."

"How did you—how did the stone masters find him if they didn't know what road he'd taken?"

This time it was Ascela who responded. "One stone knows another, even as the stone masters seek to know them. Stone follows upon stone."

"I see," she muttered, not seeing at all. "So some Vounean stone master used another stone to track Pulickel down, and then you brought him back?" Did certain stones give off a resonance only the seni could detect? The idea seemed farfetched. The glassy material looked utterly inert. Almost as inert as Pulickel, who at the moment wasn't resonating very much himself. Certainly the stones didn't smell. So how had one stone master tracked down another stone?

Light, she thought, and wondered why the answer hadn't occurred to her earlier. During the demonstration she'd been privy to, the growing stone and earth stone had conjoined to form a single mass that had given off an intense green luminescence that had spread throughout the newly planted field. Somehow, intentionally or otherwise, the pair of stones in Pulickel's possession must have come together. In addition to his present condition, one of the by-products of that mingling had probably been light similar to that which she had witnessed. If bright enough, it would have generated a beacon easily followed even at midday.

"Not all of him." Ascela nodded somberly at the motionless body on the couch. "A part of Pu'il has not yet returned. Now that we have most of him, the rest must be brought back."

"Yeah, I can see that. But I'm not ready to try a healing master. Not yet."

"Then we will leave you to your friend." Jorana gestured at the Vouneans, who were still fascinated by their alien surroundings. "Our friends from the peninsula will stay with us tonight. We will go back to Torrelauapa but return tomorrow with proper help. If you wish it then, we will try to heal Pu'il."

"If there's been no change by tomorrow," she replied listlessly, "I'll need your help."

She bade farewell to the concerned Parramati. Once they had departed and she had reestablished the defensive perimeter, she resumed her vigil over the diminutive xenologist.

As she watched and waited and hoped for the pharmaceuticals she'd pumped into him to take effect, she reviewed in her mind the confrontation and conversation with the Parramati. Though she felt sure that much that had been said bore importantly on Pulickel's recovery, she was unable to penetrate the natives' multiple layers of meaning.

Or else, she concluded tiredly, she simply did not possess the necessary cultural referents for understanding.

CHAPTER

14

She stayed awake until her body demanded sleep, and then she gave it little enough of that, rising immediately after the sun to check on her patient. Pulickel lay as she'd left him, prone and motionless on the couch, blinking at the ceiling. According to the scanner, his vital signs were unchanged. Small comfort, she mused.

At her invitation, the Parramati who had been waiting patiently just beyond the defense perimeter filed somberly back into the station. Ascela performed a respectful introduction, following which the oldest seni Fawn had ever seen stepped forward.

His name was Ijaju. His back was bent and sharply curved forward, his tail broken so many times it no longer was held out stiffly but hung down, limp and flexible, behind him. Incapable of hopping, he could advance only by shuffling, sliding forward one huge foot at a time. Instead of being held erect and alert, his ears lay flat on the top of his head. When he spoke, the double eyelids opened no more than a crack. It gave him the appearance of being perpetually asleep. The long snout was shrunken and wrinkled, the lips cracked and blackened, and most of his teeth were missing. Those that remained in the aged jaws looked none too healthy.

But the delicate three-fingered hands did not shake as they traced the length of Pulickel's comatose form. Fawn kept silent for as long as she could stand it before finally stammering, "Can you help him?"

Ancient eyes turned to meet her own. The healer's voice was a lacework of whispers, and she had to strain to make out the words. "I do not know. One who has taken to such roads in ignorance may be doomed to wander them forever."

"Wander—but he's *here*," she protested.

The elder didn't argue with her. "I will try. But not here. To heal, two stones are necessary. Two stones and two masters."

That much made sense. Based on what she now knew, no stone functioned on its own. At least two were required and for all she knew, sometimes more.

"Where, then?"

"Torrelauapa." As he said this, several of the assembled big persons indicated solemn assent, executing in unison the gestures she had come to recognize as the Parramati equivalent of a nod.

Insisting that the patient be stretchered so that Ijaju could watch over him, and leery as always of the skimmer, the Torrelauapans carried Pulickel over the mountain trail back to their village. Lesser males and females looked on in silence as the line of big persons conveyed the body to the longhouse of Solinna. Though subordinate in age and status to the visiting Ijaju, her healing skills were respected throughout the region.

No feasting, no celebration preceded the treatment. The villagers went about their daily tasks as if nothing out of the ordinary was going to take place. This was very different from the ceremony of the blessing of the planting that Fawn had witnessed. Those youngsters whose innate high spirits could not be restrained were gently guided away from the healer's longhouse. Several elders whom Fawn had come to know well came up to her to offer condolences. Their concern made her feel ashamed. None of this would have happened if they'd simply left the stones alone.

Which they couldn't do, she knew with equal certainty. Not after the planting ceremony, and especially not now. Pulickel would agree with her absolutely—once he was able to agree to anything again.

She refused to countenance the possibility of that never happening.

Pulickel was placed on one of the most finely woven Parramati mats Fawn had ever seen. Incense pots were placed at the four corners of the mat and lit. Aromatic smoke filled the room, drifting out through a hole in the sharply raked ceiling.

With two young villagers supporting him under either arm, Ijaju settled into a resting squat close by the motionless xenologist's head. Solinna assumed the lesser position, at the human's feet. Chanting and waving pucici fronds, they set their respective healing stones down in front of them. These were typically unimpressive lumps of the same glassy green material Fawn had seen before.

The chanting continued without a break, monotonous and uninspiring. Waving at the smoke, she frequently stepped outside for some fresh air and sunshine. No one could give her an idea of how long the ceremony might last. She knew that by nightfall her companion's body would be demanding fluids even if he couldn't come right out and ask for them. That would mean a return trip to the station for the necessary equipment. Whether it interfered with the healing ceremony or not, she had to at least get some sustaining glucose solution into him.

She intercepted Ascela as the big person was bounding past. "I can't see that anything is happening or that this is doing Pu'il any good. When does the healing start?"

The weather stone master eyed her sympathetically. At least, Fawn thought it was sympathetically. Her knowledge of Parramati expressions was less than perfect.

"The healing has already begun, F'an." She took one of Fawn's hands in hers, the long fingers wrapping completely around the smaller human hand, the middle one twice. That gesture, at least, needed no interpreting. "They are seeking the right road. Challenging or otherwise interrupting them may divert them from their course and make the healing more difficult."

Frustrated and less than reassured, Fawn debated whether to call a halt to the ceremony and have Pulickel returned to the station. Assuming he'd shown no improvement by then, she'd have no choice but to call for a medevac. Her options were limited by his condition.

She ducked back into the longhouse, waving at the pungent smoke. His color was unchanged, which meant that it was still not good, but otherwise he appeared physically healthy. While this could not be allowed to go on for days, recalling the effectiveness of the planting ceremony convinced her to give the Parramati healers until the following morning. At that time she would have no choice but to have Pulickel evacuated to Ophhlia.

Meanwhile she could only try to contain her frustration and nurture a hope that she didn't feel. With a start, she realized how much she missed Pulickel's quiet confidence, his assurance that any problem could be solved, any obstacle overcome. What she had initially perceived as blind stubbornness she now saw as conviction born of experience and knowledge.

Maybe he wasn't the liveliest or most entertaining of

companions—but he was human. Once more she had only aliens for company. She found that she'd grown used to conversing in terranglo again. She even missed his implied insults.

She doubted if analysis of the stones he'd taken would have provided any clues to his present condition. It did not matter in any event because they had been returned to their respective stone masters. By now she'd seen many of the sacred stones. Irrespective of function and while differing in size, all were similar in shape and composition. Even had they been available for analysis, she doubted they would have provided the necessary answers.

Night had crept in quietly and the Torrelauapans had prepared and consumed the evening meal. Too troubled to be interested in food, she had declined polite invitations to join them. Bathed in torchlight, she stood outside the longhouse listening to the chanting from within. It did not seem to have changed much, if at all. In her mind she had begun to compose the evacuation request that would have to be sent to Ophhlia in the morning.

She forced herself to chew a couple of concentrate bars and drink some supplement-enhanced juice. It wouldn't do Pulickel any good to let her own system run down. A glance at her chronometer suggested it was time to make yet another check on the xenologist's condition. Knowing in advance what it would be, she took a deep breath and bent low to reenter the longhouse.

She'd grown semiused to the smoke, and it no longer stung her lungs as badly as the first couple of times. What she saw through the lingering haze snapped her out of her lethargy faster than any energy bar.

Ijaju and Solinna had moved. Instead of squatting at Pulickel's head and feet, they now faced each other across his chest. Each held arms straight out toward one another, the fingers not quite touching. Ijaju's trembled slightly but did not falter.

Resting beneath their hovering hands on Pulickel's chest was a single vitreous mass: their respective healing stones fused to become one. From it emanated an intense halo of pinkish-green incandescence that had spread out to infuse the motionless xenologist's entire body. The light was brighter than that of the torches outside, brighter than that put out by the portable illuminator she carried in her backpack. So intense was it that his features were partly obscured, as if by a translucent pink-green wave. The concentrated effulgence cast strange shadows on the squatting bodies of the attendant stone masters.

Afraid of disturbing them, she tiptoed inside and edged slowly along the interior wall until she found a place where she could see everything clearly. As she stared, Pulickel's body twitched sharply. Not adrenaline shock, she decided, but something else, something much deeper. He began to moan then, and it was the most horrible sound she'd ever heard emerge from a human throat. A shiver ran like ice water down her spine, and it took a considerable effort of will for her to keep from rushing forward and terminating the ceremony. All that stopped her was the realization that the stone masters had managed to induce a reaction, albeit a terrible one.

The moan changed to a high keening, sharp and measured. It was repeated at unpredictable intervals as the chanting rose to fever pitch. She stood motionless, unable to decide whether to rush forward, reach for her medikit, or flee. Ascela's warning loomed at the forefront of her consciousness. If she interrupted, the stone masters might have to start all over again. She didn't know if Pulickel could take that. Hell, she thought, she didn't know if *she* could take it.

Several Parramati big persons pushed their way into the room with uncharacteristic abruptness. Usually they were unfailingly courteous, but this time they ignored her as if she weren't there. So intent were they on their purpose that she was convinced they would have shoved her aside had she been blocking the doorway.

While Solinna sustained the chant, Ijaju leaned forward and grasped the conjoined stones with both hands. As he did so he barked instructions to the new arrivals. At that moment he seemed not ancient, but young and vigorous.

The Parramati clutched Pulickel's flailing arms and legs and held him down. One did her best to keep his head from banging against the thick mat and the floor beneath. Meanwhile that hideous keening continued to issue from the xenologist's throat.

As Fawn stared wide-eyed, the wailing began to soften and fade, the violent thrusting and thrashing of limbs to lessen. Pulickel's movements grew less pronounced, the terror in his throat less compelling. Then, with a deep sigh, his entire being seemed to relax and slump back against the mat.

Solinna bent forward and put her six fingers on the stone. The radiance vanished and the mass came apart in her hands, separating once more into two dull green lumps. Taking hers, she rose and moved to the right side of the longhouse. Ascela and Massapapu helped Ijaju to his feet while Osiwivi reverently picked up the remaining stone.

Something wonderful had happened in the longhouse, Fawn knew. Something that had very little to do with burning herbs and traditional chants and a great deal to do with a couple of seemingly static bits of rock.

Approaching tentatively, she confronted the exhausted senior healer. Ijaju responded with the Parramati equivalent of a smile, more subtle than the analogous human expression but distinctive and recognizable nonetheless. He continued to lean on the two Torrelauapan big persons for support.

"Your friend will be alive now."

She blinked uncertainly. "I don't understand. He's been alive all along."

The venerable healer turned to look at the prone form of the xenologist, whose eyes were closed for the first time since the Vouneans had brought him back into the station.

"No. He was not alive. His form was here, but the part of him that constitutes life was elsewhere, lost between here and the bad place where he was." Wizened slitted eyes gazed up at her. "He had started back down the proper return road, but somewhere along the way that part of him slipped off and could not find its way back on. Solinna and I had to help him back onto the road."

It didn't make any sense, Fawn thought. But then, very little had since Pulickel's signal had vanished from the skimmer's pickup. Stepping past the healer, she knelt close to her companion and put a hand on his right shoulder.

"Pulickel? Pulickel Tomochelor, can you hear me?"

There was an extended moment of awful nothing. Then he blinked, opened his eyes, and turned his head toward her. For an instant, the briefest of instants, she felt that his gaze focused not on her but on something behind her. Behind his eyes there was a flash of panic the likes of which she'd never seen before. Then it was gone, replaced by fond recognition, and she knew he was looking only at her. He smiled weakly.

"Hello, Fawn Seaforth. It's good to see you again."

"Good to see you, too." She squeezed his shoulder. "What happened?"

"Where am I?" Pushing himself up on his elbows, he surveyed his surroundings.

"Torrelauapa. I had to bring you here to bring you back."

With her hand at his back he was able to sit up all the way. "Do they know about the stones I took?" he asked in terranglo.

She nodded. "They've taken them back. I never saw either one, but they say they were responsible for what happened to you. When they brought you into the station you were completely comatose."

"When *they* brought me in?" He blinked at her. "You didn't pick me up in the skimmer?"

"I looked but I couldn't find you. Even your emergency locator was down." She fumbled with her backpack, seeking the medikit. "You still haven't told me what happened. The Parramati say that you used the stones to travel down a bad road." She handed him a couple of energy tablets, which he promptly chewed up and swallowed.

"I was seen taking the second stone. They came after me, and I ran. I remember tripping and falling. The stones must have been thrown together when I fell, because I remember a light coming from my backpack. I remember . . ." His voice trailed away, his eyes unfocused, and he shook himself back to awareness.

"I'll tell you everything when we get back to the station. At least, I'll tell you as much of it as I can recall." A shudder passed through him.

"Cold?" she inquired solicitously. Within the longhouse, the temperature matched the humidity.

"Only spiritually. I saw—I saw some things I'm not sure I want to tell you about. Or try to remember. There are events I'd rather forget. That I'm going to have to work hard at forgetting."

"While the Parramati were using the healing stones on you, you made some—sounds. I'm not so sure I want to know what inspired them either."

"Healing stones. I didn't know . . ." He winced, his face contorting. His expression was drawn. "I don't feel so good."

"I'm not surprised. Can you stand?"

"One way to find out."

With her assistance he rose shakily to his feet, but he was able to stand and take steps without help.

"You can't walk all the way back to the station. Not in the shape you're in." She was unshakable in her opinion of his condition. "You haven't had anything to eat since the day before yesterday."

"Two days." He pondered this.

"I'm sure Ascela and the others will be willing to carry you back. Or I can go and return with the skimmer."

"You're right. I'd best not rush anything." He eyed the attendant Parramati. "Maybe I could get something to eat besides energy tablets and concentrate bars."

"Sure. Meanwhile you'd better take it easy or you're liable to keel over and hurt yourself."

He licked dry lips. "I don't feel like racing any of the village sprinters, if that's what's concerning you. But there doesn't seem to be anything wrong with my appetite." Again the gentle, familiar smile, which she appreciated now more than ever.

"Funny," he told her as she put the request for food to Ascela, "how in spite of whatever trauma the mind may suffer, the body responds with its own demands. Hunger, thirst, the need for warmth: some things are beyond shock. What have you got there?"

She held out her hand to him. "More concentrates." She urged him to take them. "Until real food arrives."

He nodded and took the thin, foil-wrapped bars. When his bare fingers touched her own she started slightly.

"You're cold, Pulickel."

"Too few calories and too much emotion."

Her fingers wrapped around his and he smiled as he squeezed back, but the usual wiry strength was absent.

They spent the night in the village. Pulickel ate everything that was placed before him and asked for more. Fearful of overloading his stressed system, Fawn rationed his food and drink accordingly.

It had been a long time—a very long time—since he'd been mothered, and while he had a hard time thinking of Fawn Seaforth as maternal, he found himself warmed by the attention nonetheless.

Not until midmorning of the following day, and not until after he'd demonstrated to her satisfaction that he was capable of sustained physical exertion, did they start the long hike back to base. He snacked on concentrated field rations all the way and ran half a dozen programs through the food processor as soon as they entered the station. Just when it seemed that his bulging belly was about to explode, he declared with great satisfaction that he was finally sated.

Retiring to the main lounge, he settled into the same couch on which he'd lain comatose the previous day and tried to give her some impression of his experiences.

She listened to it all. Initial disbelief gave way to gradual, awed acceptance. It was too fantastical for her prosaic associate to have imagined, too rich in detail for him to have invented. Outside the realm of logic and reason, it hewed consistently to a frenzied, crazed internal logic all its own. For more than an hour Pulickel played the caterpillar and she was Alice.

"They were some kind of traveling stones." In contrast to his desperate downing of liquids earlier that day, he sipped judiciously from the mug on the table in front of him.

She eyed him cautiously. "So what you're saying is that they transported you to another part of Senisran?"

He found that he was able to laugh. "No, not to another part of Senisran."

Her incredulity was boosted. "You're not saying that they sent you offworld?"

Leaning forward, he crossed his arms over his lap. "I'm not only saying that they took me offworld, I'm saying that they sent me to worlds that seemed to have no place in the normal scheme of existence." For a brief moment his eyes looked haunted. "And once, to a place that not only wasn't normal, it wasn't even a world."

Slowly she sat back in her chair and regarded him silently. "Even if the stones aren't stones," she said finally, "and are something more, they're not big enough to contain the power to do something like that."

"I agree. They must key or otherwise activate a larger device somewhere else. Buried beneath the village, perhaps, or on some other part of the island. It has to be the same for all the other stones. They only activate specific functions. The actual instigating mechanisms must be sited elsewhere. Maybe not even on Torrelau, or within the boundaries of the archipelago. There's an awful lot of Senisran that's yet to be explored, and I'm just thinking of islands and atolls. The extensive shallow submerged plains have hardly been touched." He shifted his position on the couch.

"Ophhlia and the other humanx bases are swarming with oceanographers, xenologists, geologists, and the like. Nobody's looking for relics of a vanished civilization any more because the initial survey teams insisted there was no evidence of any. Well, I think we have incontrovertible proof to the contrary. Functional proof, no less."

She crossed her legs, another kind of functional proof that he always delighted in observing. "I don't suppose that in spite of all the convincing detail to your story you could have just fallen, hit your head on a rock, and hallucinated the whole business?"

"Of course I could have. Don't you think the possibility's occurred to me?" He finished his drink. "But I don't think I did. There was a clarity to every moment of it, Fawn, a sureness, that reeked of reality. Even during those moments when I thought I was going crazy."

She was thoughtful for a while before responding. "All right. Deranged as it seems, let's assume for a moment that this all happened for real, just as you describe it. When combined, the stones you had in your possession serve as, or trigger, some kind of interstellar transport mechanism. We either need to find the device or ascribe the entire business to magic."

"Magic science, science magic." He shrugged. "This experience has moved me beyond semantics, Fawn. Long ago humans learned how to slap two stones together to strike sparks and make fire. Now we point the appropriate device, and fire goes where we want it. Somebody else has learned how to slap two stones together and cast themselves between the stars. It's all a matter of knowing what stones to use. Of knowing the right roads, as the Parramati would say."

"Find how the stones connect to the larger mechanism," she surmised, "and we'll find the mechanism itself. Wave-form contact."

"Maybe." He laughed sharply. "It certainly isn't being done by wire. Try explaining vit to an aboriginal. He'll gawk into space trying to locate the pictures that appear on the receiver. That's what we're doing here: staring into space trying to find something whose characteristics we don't have the knowledge to define. We've found the needle, but the haystack's gone missing."

"I wouldn't bet that it's elsewhere on Senisran," she told him. "No other native society that we know of uses anything like the stones."

"If there's some kind of large concealed device located in the archipelago, it must be heavily screened or the survey drones would have picked it up, just as they reported on the rare earth deposits all the commercial interests in Ophhlia are so anxious to have a go at."

"Then you and I sure aren't going to find it without Parramati help." She rose and began to pace back and forth in front of him.

"You talk to them." He stared out the line of windows. "I'm already considered a possible thief."

"It's not as bad as all that. You're not Parramati, so you're not held to the same standards they are." She smiled knowingly. "I've already explained to them your rationale for 'borrowing' the stones. They're not happy about it, but they're not ready to dismember you, either. You see, our kusum is different from theirs, and that's something they can understand. They consider you misguided and inept instead of depraved."

He sniffed. "I suppose I should be thankful."

"Of course," she added, "it also means they're not going to leave you alone with even the smallest, most insignificant sacred stone lest your misdirected kusum gets the better of you again. But your head should be safe in their company."

"That's a great relief. Keeping all my body parts in one place should facilitate my continued work here." Smiling thinly, he turned away from the window and back to his associate. "So where do we start? By questioning your friend Ascela? Jorana, perhaps, or this ancient Vounean Ijaju?"

She chewed reflectively on her lower lip. "With Jorana, I think. Of all the big people on Torrelau, he's always been the most patient and accommodating."

"We'll need some patience of our own if we're going to find an answer to all this." His voice dropped slightly. "The stones are the keys to the roads, which link individual 'spaces' in the Parramati mind. Combining the stones and handling them in specific ways make the stones work, and these ways are part of the oral tradition of kusum. It all fits together very well. If only it didn't smack so much of the incredible." He turned wistful.

"I wonder if the Parramati have used the stones to go traveling, if they've visited some of the places I visited." A cloud came over his expression. "Not all of them, I hope."

She shook her head. "I don't know. I've never heard them speak of such a thing."

"I can understand why." He gathered himself. "We must try to extract all the information we can, but if someone offers to 'send' us somewhere by way of demonstration, I think I will pass. I've had all the demonstration of these stones' capacity that I want."

"If you're right about what happened to you, Pulickel, then I still don't understand how they found you."

"It's simple. They know the roads, I don't. I imagine it's all a matter of knowing how to read the indicators along the way, the street signs. Not only couldn't I do that, I didn't even know I was on a road. Only that I was traveling, and lost." He stared hard at her, and there was something forever lost in his gaze.

"I very badly want to find out how all this works, but not at the risk of getting lost again."

CHAPTER

15

Fawn was right. Jorana was forthcoming and responsive when they questioned him about the transportation stones. As near as she could tell, the big person wasn't holding anything back or attempting to sidestep their queries. The Parramati could be evasive in conversation, and a big person like Jorana more so than most, but he made no attempt to circumvent their questions, answering everything in a direct and forthright manner.

"The stones have always been with the Parramati, the Parramati have always been with the stones. They are the foundation of kusum."

"Are there stones and stone masters on all the islands of the archipelago?" Fawn asked.

"Not all, but many. They have been here for as long as people can remember. They have been here for as long as people have been."

The three of them were seated on thick woven mats in Jorana's longhouse, deep bowls of fruit juice in front of them.

"So the stones were just lying around when the first Parramati came here?" Using both hands in the accepted manner, Pulickel sipped from his bowl, swallowing the pith suspended in the liquid and politely spitting the seeds into his closed palm.

"Yes. It is told that Kureo'o'oa, of the original Parramati, was the first person to understand the working of a stone. He found a stone that, when combined with another, brought all manner of good things to eat close to his boat, so that he might catch them. These were the first fishing stones. After that, other first people tried many different stones. Some did nothing, others led to different roads."

"Hundreds of years of trial and error," Fawn whispered. "Maybe thousands."

"Over time, more and more stones became known to us, and their workings a part of our kusum. Some of these original Parramati became the first stone masters. Some vanished, never to be seen again. Some died." Jorana's barks and yips rose and fell euphoniously in the still, humid air of the longhouse.

"Are all stone masters considered to be big persons?" Pulickel asked.

"Yes, but not all big persons are stone masters." Jorana's lips rippled along the sides of his long snout. "The stone master legacy is passed down within families, within clans. They are the ones who have charge of the stones, they are the ones who know the roads."

Feeling very self-conscious, Pulickel nonetheless asked the next question. "And no family or clan tries to take another's stones?"

"What good is a stone to one who does not know its road?" With the long middle finger of his right hand, the big person stirred patterns in his juice. "Besides, the stones are brought together for the good of all. One stone master helps another, just as big persons help small persons. When needed, stone masters from one island will assist those of another. Torrelau is a big island, with many villages and stone masters. We are always ready to help Parramati who live on smaller islands, even if it is only one family that lives by fishing from a sandbar."

Pulickel glanced significantly at Fawn before asking the question they had been leading up to all morning. "What about the transportation stones?" A group of youngsters outside was playing the elaborate Parramati version of leapfrog. Occasionally a deep *thump* would echo through the longhouse as one of them ricocheted off the exterior wall.

"Like the ones you borrowed to try to study?" It was difficult to tell when one was being teased by a Parramati. Formal sarcasm had no place in their conversation. "Sometimes the masters of such stones will use them to explore certain roads. From these travels they bring back fresh knowledge, new ways of seeing and thinking. It is only for big persons that they do this, for such learning is wasted on middle and small persons. If what they learn proves useful, it is made a part of kusum."

"That's all very interesting," Fawn agreed. "Do the masters of these stones use them to travel frequently?"

"No. It is difficult and can be dangerous." For the first time, Jorana showed reluctance to elaborate. "Such stones are for use only in great emergencies."

"And what would qualify as an appropriate emergency?" Pulickel leaned forward intently.

Jorana considered. "An incurable sickness. A war that the Parramati were losing. Anything that threatened kusum."

Was that an implied threat? the xenologist wondered. He didn't see how the transportation stones could be used against the Commonwealth presence. Apparently Jorana thought such a thing was possible. It was an unpleasant thought, one they could come back to later if the need arose.

"This Koreo'o'oa and the other first persons," Fawn was saying, "they must have been very brave people."

Holding up the outside finger of each hand in the accepted manner, Jorana sipped from his bowl. "They were. I wish I could have known them. Since I cannot, I honor their memories."

"The sacred stones." Fawn shifted nervously on her mat. "I don't mean to commit blasphemy. Please remember that there is much of Parramati kusum I am still ignorant of, but—has anyone ever tried to break one of them open, to study the inside?"

Jorana's pupils parted wide and his long dark lips drew back in horror. "No! It would be a violation of the stone. Why would anyone think of doing such a thing?"

Fawn hastened to reassure the big person. "I didn't mean to suggest that it *should* be done. I only wondered if it had happened. By accident, perhaps."

Jorana seemed mollified. "To my knowledge, no stone has ever been broken open. Either by design or by mischance." He looked sharply at Pulickel. "That was not what you were going to do, friend Pu'il?"

"Who, me?" The xenologist was being at least half truthful. Had he succeeded in bringing the two stones he'd taken back to the station, initial studies would have preserved their structural integrity so that they could have been returned to their owners intact.

Fawn hurriedly changed the subject. "Down through the centuries the Parramati have found hundreds of stones. Do you ever find any unmastered ones any more?"

"Not in several lifetimes," Jorana admitted. "Some think that the Parramati have identified all the sacred stones that there are to be found."

"Are there any transportation stones on Mallatyah?" Pulickel asked tersely, thinking of the AAnn.

The big person's reply was not reassuring. "Of course. Mallatyah is a large island, also, and home to the masters of as many stones as we of Torrelau."

They paused as one of Jorana's several wives brought food and filled their bowls. Pulickel recognized cured chierofa, a molluscan delicacy from the outer reef. When chewed, it released a taste that suggested a jalapeñoed snail. He popped a strip into his mouth, bit down, and tensed slightly as flavor exploded against his palate. Fawn's tolerance for hot and spicy being considerably less than his own, she chose something blander from among the offerings.

Maybe it was the stimulating food, but a half-forgotten question suddenly occurred to him. "Jorana, has anyone ever tried to bring together more than two stones at a time?"

Their host did not try to conceal his shock. "Of course not! There is no telling what would happen. Stones are always used in combination of twos."

Perhaps it was the delectable fire in his mouth, but Pulickel couldn't let the matter drop. "Well, then, has anyone ever tried to use more than two stones together in combinations of twos? Four at a time, say, or six?"

Jorana was staring at him out of gold-flecked eyes. "Why would anyone do such a thing? How much can a person eat? How healthy can they be made? How deeply in love can they fall? No, to my knowledge such a thing has never been tried. If it was, those who did so did not survive to speak to others of the consequences." Jorana did nothing to hide his discomfiture. Unashamed, he found the concept distasteful.

Ignoring their host's unease and Fawn's warning glare, Pulickel pressed on. "Four fishing stones might bring in better eating. Six healing stones might extend one's lifespan."

Despite his discomfort, Jorana found himself speculating. Impiety, Pulickel knew, is ever a subject of fascination to the faithful.

"It would violate kusum," the big person finally declared, as if that put an end to the matter. "We *know* how the stones are to be used, and they are to be used by twos."

"But how do you know that that's the only way they can be used?"

"Because that is what kusum tells us," the Parramati replied, closing the circle of logic. "In this manner the stones have served us well. We are not about to tempt fate by going against kusum in the fashion of the Eolurro or the Simisant." Pulickel expected the usual lecture on kusum violation to follow. Instead, Jorana looked frightened.

"No one could say what would happen if many stones were conjoined. No one would be responsible for the consequences."

"Are you so sure there would be consequences?" Pulickel watched the native unswervingly. Jorana looked up sharply but said nothing.

Fawn turned the conversation to more prosaic and less controversial matters, and soon had their host relaxed again. By the time the two humans were ready to leave, he was once more his usual composed, affable self.

They stood outside the entrance to the longhouse, squinting in the bright light of midday.

"We thank you for taking the time to answer our many questions." Fawn underlined her words with the appropriate gestures. "You have been a great help to us and we appreciate it."

Jorana's fingers fluttered complaisantly. "The sharing of knowledge is never a burden, always a pleasure. You are welcome anytime."

As they turned to depart, Pulickel switched to terranglo. "This isn't enough. Somehow we have to obtain a stone for examination."

Fawn's gaze narrowed as she shouldered her pack. "Didn't you learn your lesson last time? No stone master is going to willingly relinquish possession of his or her specimen, and because of your little escapade neither one of us is going to be allowed near one unsupervised. Forget it, Pu'il. We're going to have to study them from a distance and do the best we can."

He looked up at her as they made their way out of the village, heading for the trail that would take them over the barrier ridge and back to base. "You know that's inadequate, Fawn."

"Yeah, I know. But I'm damned if I can think of a way around it." As they entered the jungle she turned her shirt evaporator up a notch. "Watch that cluster of vines. Shelath stingers sometimes nest in those." At her urging, he gave the dense knot of yellow-brown foliage a wide berth. "I don't think even the ever-courteous, ever-understanding Parramati will be as forgiving if we're caught trying to steal stones a second time."

"Not stealing," he reminded her with that familiar fey smile. "Borrowing."

"I wouldn't count on that to save me again, either," she warned him. "The Parramati have fought plenty of wars with their neighbors, some of them in recent times. They're quite capable of violence."

He stepped over a narrow gully. Small spotted creatures peeped querulously in the shallow water below. "I don't see that we have any choice. The alternative is to call in a full-scale research team. If we can't bring the necessary equipment to a stone, we have to bring a stone to the equipment."

"I know, I know. Don't you think I'd love to run Ululiapa's earth stone through the station's geoscope?" She jumped over a fallen log that he ducked beneath. "I don't want a hundred specialists in here, crawling all over the archipelago."

"We've already discussed what would happen to the stones in that case," he reminded her. "The Parramati would take them to sea in their outriggers and dump them in the nearest oceanic trench. Our choices are limited."

"What choices?" she muttered. "All we can do is wait for them to use some of the stones, try to wangle an invitation to the relevant ceremony, and make what recordings we can."

"There has to be another way. Somehow we have to convince, bribe, or frighten a stone master into letting us borrow a stone. Surely there's one who's willing to bend kusum just a little. A young one, perhaps, not yet as steeped in tradition as senior big persons like Jorana and Ascela. What if we offered to let them participate in the process of analysis, brought them right into the station? That way their stone would never be out of their sight."

Fawn looked doubtful. "Won't work. Remember, stone utilization is a tandem process. No stone master does anything with a stone without consulting at least one colleague. Sure, we might tempt a young stone master. But they won't do anything without first seeking advice from another."

He pushed leaves aside. "How can you be so sure, if it's never been tried?"

She looked back at him. "You never give up on a line of reasoning, do you? When you find one you like, you worry it like a dog. Not only do you still think you can borrow a stone, now you want to borrow a stone master, too."

"I'm always glad when my aims are perceived so readily." He grinned up at her.

"You know this trail as well as I do by now. How come you always let me lead?"

"Because you're bigger, are more familiar with the potentially dangerous flora here than I am, and can push all the vegetation out of the way for me."

"Ah." She frowned uncertainly, then set the matter aside. He was being truthful, of course. She just wasn't sure he was enumerating all the truths.

CHAPTER

16

Essasu RRGVB looked around the meeting room. Piarai was present, along with the two ranking survivors of the ill-fated expedition to Torrelau. The memory of that failure still burned in his mind, as he knew it must in theirs.

Since returning, he'd immersed himself in everything the staff xenologists had been able to find about the sacred stones of the Parramati. Taken together, this constituted a singularly uninformative and inadequate body of work.

"You've all seen the latest report from our native contacts on Torrelau. What do you make of this talk of the male human using stones to take a journey to far-off places?"

The assembled underlings exchanged glances and gestures. It was Yaarinda who spoke. "We now know that certain so-called sacred stones, when manipulated by those Parramati trained in their use, can displace individuals in space. What the extent of this displacement may be we still do not know, but it is real." Her hands gestured second-degree importance colored with danger. "Several of us saw this happen."

Piarai continued. "It appears that at some unknown time in the past, historic Parramati acquired the use of advanced technology whose origins remain for us to discover. I admit that these stones do not look like much, but in this instance it clearly is dangerous to confuse appearance with function. Through the use of these 'stones,' two companions were significantly displaced. If this new information is true, then it appears that the human was similarly transported but was able to return."

"There is a greatness to be learned here," Essasu proclaimed. "We must find the truth of it. All our other work now becomes secondary. Energies must be redirected." He turned his gaze on each of them in turn. "Our first priority must be to acquire as many of these stones as possible for detailed study."

"According to our information from Torrelau, there are dangers involved in such acquisition." Requesting permission with a gesture, Vuikak settled into a resting lounge.

Essasu glanced at him. "According to the same information, only if certain stones are allowed to come in contact with one another. Apparently the human was careless. We are not careless. We will not repeat his mistake."

"The natives who have charge of the stones, these so-called stone masters, will not surrender their possessions freely," Piarai pointed out.

Essasu executed a curt gesture of indifference. "Then we will shoot a few. That should persuade the others. If we keep our distance from the stones that cause spatial displacement, they cannot harm us."

"What kind of stones do you wish us to obtain first?" Yaarinda leaned back in her lounge, her long tail tracing abstract patterns on the sand-carpeted floor.

"Anything that hints of real power. After these transportation stones, weather stones would be an excellent next choice. Now that we are aware of the stones' true nature, I would be interested to discover if there is any connection between the native weather stones and these fascinating and damnable mastorms."

Piarai blinked both eyelids. "You think the aboriginals may use the stones to control the weather?"

Essasu showed many teeth. "If certain stones can displace individuals in space, it is not so great a reach to imagine that others may displace clouds and rain. After what we witnessed on Torrelau, I believe nothing can be ruled out."

Yaarinda looked thoughtful. "I wonder where the human was displaced to. The report does not specify. It says only that he was unconscious when he was found."

"Even if it was from one side of a room to another, that is enough," Essasu observed impatiently. "It is the fact of the displacement that is important. The technology to accomplish such a feat has been a dream of imperial scientists since the dawn of modern physics."

Piarai rose. "With your consent then, Commander, I will organize a group to obtain several stones. With the natives' consent if possible, by other means if they prove recalcitrant. How many do you wish us acquire?"

"As many as possible, obviously. Half a dozen would make a nice beginning. We don't wish to leave the Mallatyahans stone-poor. Employ everyone who can be spared. This supersedes all other research, and a show of strength may make it easier to deal peacefully with the locals."

"We could request reinforcements from Chraara," Vuikak suggested.

"No. The humanx monitor all comings and goings from headquarters, just as we record their activities around Ophhlia. We do not want to give the impression that any unusual or extraordinary activity is taking place here. We will do this as quietly and quickly as possible."

Yaarinda contemplated the ceiling. "Perhaps the natives can be persuaded to cooperate and the need to employ less flexible means of persuasion will be obviated."

"It is to be hoped." Essasu added a gesture indicative of third-degree amusement. "We have one advantage already. We have not tried to 'borrow' any of the sacred stones, so the Mallatyahans do not regard us as potential thieves. For this moral preeminence, however temporary, we have the male human to thank."

"Assuming we are successful in obtaining several of the stones," Vuikak commented, "what do we do when the Mallatyahans come seeking their return?"

Essasu displayed indifference. "They cannot penetrate compound security. We will tell them that the stones are not being harmed and will be returned to them when we have concluded our tests. If they are unhappy with those conditions, that is unfortunate. What can they do? If they come bearing the stones that cause displacement, we will keep them at a distance with weapons. If they send bad weather against us, assuming they are capable of such a feat, this installation has survived the worst of many mastorms. Along with imperial power, we will teach them that futility leads to patience.

"When we have finished with the stones, they will be returned undamaged."

"Can we guarantee that?" Yaarinda wanted to know.

The station commander eyed her evenly. "I am Essasu RRGVB. I do not give guarantees to aboriginals." His attention returned to his second-in-command.

"Now then. What do we know of stone types, of their locations, and of the potential malleability of their masters?"

Piarai looked to Yaarinda, who responded. "We have some information, though evidently not as much as the humans. This can be increased."

"We do not need to know the location of every sacred stone on Mallatyah," Essasu declared. "Only sufficient for our purposes."

"We could make a few stone masters our 'guests,'" Vuikak suggested, "until they have told us all that they know about the workings of their stones."

"Only if necessary. I have more confidence in our own specialists." Essasu turned to gaze out a narrow ground-level window. "Besides, I grow tired of sly natives and their devious mannerisms. They delight in utilizing their kusum for obfuscation. I prefer the language and response of advanced instrumentation." He turned back to his subordinates.

"We will proceed with or without their cooperation, and expend no special efforts to secure the latter. I will brook no delay in revelation." His eyes flashed. "My fellow nye, I feel that we are on the brink of discoveries that could alter the balance of power between the Empire and the Commonwealth." Seeing the looks in their eyes, he realized that his explication was teetering on the grandiose, and moderated his ensuing rhetoric accordingly.

"Stones first, then speculation."

"Yes," Yaarinda agreed. "Let us embark with modest expectations."

The AAnn force was prepared to kill to acquire the requisite stones, but this proved unnecessary. Advanced search-and-detection technology allowed them to bypass occupied buildings and concentrate on those whose inhabitants were elsewhere.

From a nondescript house in a temporarily deserted village situated high up on the north flank of Mallatyah's tallest peak, they plucked a fine big weather stone. No one leaped out of the forest to challenge the camouflaged tech-soldiers. A storage hut on the edge of terraced fields lying fallow yielded a nice growing stone. Again they were not confronted.

By the time Essasu was satisfied, the sun had long since set. In addition to the weather and growing stone, they had accumulated a pair of healing stones, a fishing stone, and three transportation or traveling stones. Or so their information insisted. All were carefully packed in thickly padded individual containers and distributed among the members of the group. Essasu was taking no chances on having two stones come together accidentally.

"It was almost too easy." Vuikak shouldered his own pack effortlessly. "I think we could have seized half the stones on the island."

Essasu's mood was decidedly upbeat, all the more so because everything had gone so well compared to the earlier disaster at Torrelau. "Yes. I suspect that word of the human male's transgression has yet to reach here. Consequently, the locals cannot conceive of someone ignorant of the relevant roads helping themselves to a sacred stone. So they remain unguarded."

Yaarinda had three stones in her pack, a carefully chosen mix. In a further effort to avoid incidents of the kind that supposedly had befallen the human, no member of the group carried two stones of any one type. Her camouflage suit kept the pack from chafing against her scales. The stones were sizable and heavy, but she strode along uncomplainingly under the burden. Working in the field, she and her colleagues frequently returned to the station carrying prodigious loads of specimens.

"We must take care not to repeat the human's mistake," Piarai was reminding everyone for the tenth time.

"If what was told to us is true, he was clumsy—as is the nature of humans." Essasu was unconcerned. "Proper care will be used. If these primitives can make them work, surely their operation cannot be so difficult to divine."

"That is so," the base's second-in-command conceded.

"I think there may actually be less here than meets the eye," Essasu continued. "Operation may be no more than a matter of shoving two stones together and giving them room. Certainly they exhibit nothing in the way of visible switches, controls, or touch-sensitive contact points."

Near the rear of the column, Vuikak was considering many of the very same points. Once back at the station, the stones would be turned over to the base specialists for detailed study. As an administrator, he would be left out of the excitement. The stones must be simple to use. Why not try two of them out and be the one to receive the credit for discovering their function?

He would avoid the potentially dangerous transport stones in favor of something simple, domestic. Already he felt he'd been passed over twice for promotion. At his present rate of advancement, with eleven clan-family designates following his given name, he would die of old age long before achieving a five-designate level like Commander Essasu.

Unless he did something dramatic to merit exceptional notice.

He broached the idea to Prenkip, the lowest-ranking member of the expedition. The technician was hesitant.

"I do not know, Vuikak. The stones are dangerous. Better they be examined under controlled conditions."

"What controlled conditions?" Vuikak was not to be denied.

"The natives make use of them openly, with nothing in the way of visible safeguards."

"What about what is said to have happened to the human?"

Vuikak performed a gesture of first-degree dismissal coupled with overtones of disgust. "The human was stupid. We are not. Surely we can abort any reaction if it appears to be getting out of hand."

Prenkip's resistance weakened. Like Vuikak, he would not be counted among those charged with learning the stones' secrets, and he badly wanted to see a demonstration of these rumored powers.

His fellow tech pressed him. "What if the stones do nothing? What if they are no more than what they appear to be—the inert talismans of a primitive alien species? Suppose the tale of the transported human is only a fiction, designed to confuse and trouble us?"

"Two members of the commanders' expedition to Torrelau did not return," Prenkip mumbled. "Talk is that they were killed by stones."

Vuikak snorted in disgust. "No one believes that. The commander committed fatal errors. Blaming two deaths on the natives is a way of deflecting responsibility from himself. No doubt the missing ones drowned during the storm, or were struck by one of the many poisonous creatures that inhabit these islands.

"Consider! If this is all a clever ploy by the humans, they will even as we speak be readying themselves to benefit from our theft of these stones. If we can prove that they are incapable of anything save the reflection of green light, we will have performed a valuable service. If not, we will be the first nye to descry one of their true functions."

Prenkip pondered the possibilities. "You really think all this stone business may be nothing more than a human ruse to discredit us with the Mallatyahans?"

"It makes more sense to me than tales of green rocks disappearing troopers and humans," Vuikak replied with fervor. "Why should we not find out for ourselves?"

"Why not, indeed?"

Vuikak pushed the argument home. "What is the harm in placing, say, two of the designated 'growing' stones together? That if this is not all fiction we will be overwhelmed by a surfeit of fresh vegetables?"

Finally persuaded, Prenkip gestured consent. "We should do this here, away from the base." Already bringing up the rear of the column, they purposely let themselves fall farther behind. In the fading light of evening, no one took notice.

To further ensure that they would be able to carry out their experiment unimpeded, Vuikak unwrapped the first stone from Prenkip's pack as they walked. Falling behind his companion, the technician returned the favor. Shielding the stones from sight of their comrades with their bodies, the two AAnn examined the specimens.

"See? Lumps of green glass is all they are," Vuikak insisted. "Volcanic slag, static and harmless."

Prenkip had noted the labels on the respective wrappings. "You were right. These are growing stones. It will be fascinating to observe if they do anything and comparatively harmless if they do."

"The procedure is to bring them together carefully to see if they merge. At least, that is what is supposed to happen."

Prenkip turned the uneven olivine mass over in his scaly fingers. "None of the exposed faces appears shaped to fit into any other. I suppose we just push them against each other?"

"That is the rumor." Vuikak made eye contact with the technician. "If any kind of reaction ensues, we pull them apart. Agreed?" Prenkip gestured understanding and assent.

Out of sight of the rest of the group, they brought both masses together. A soft *click* ensued. That was all. No blinding flash of light, no aural implosion, no surreal distortion of reality—just an ordinary-sounding *click*. It was exactly what one would expect to hear from knocking two rocks together.

Vuikak was at once disappointed, angry, and relieved. "See?" he told his partner in experimentation. "I was right. This whole business of the sacred stones having mysterious powers is nonsense, a product of the perverse human imagination. They have deceived us." He lifted his gaze to the rest of the troop, marching stolidly along just ahead. "We must inform the commander."

"Perhaps we performed the procedure incorrectly." Having taken so long to be persuaded, Prenkip wasn't quite ready to give up. "Let us try once more."

A disgruntled Vuikak reluctantly agreed. "Very well. But it is evident that we have been wasting our time."

Turning the stones so that different sides faced each other, they brought them into contact a second time. The result was—another *click*.

"Rocks." A thoroughly disgusted Vuikak eyed the specimen he was holding. "Utilizing native mythology and a little imagination, the humans have fooled us badly. But you and I have discovered the subterfuge in time. We will tell the commander, and the stones can be returned to their holding places before any serious harm is done to our diplomatic efforts among the Parramati." He extended a hand to the technician. "Here—give me that useless thing!"

So saying, and before Prenkip thought to object, Vuikak took the second stone and whacked it angrily against the one he already held. The resulting noise sounded exactly like two lumps of volcanic glass striking one another: a *click* magnified. Disdainfully he dumped both of them by the side of the narrow trail, onto a patch of short grassy growth.

"I still think we may be doing something wrong." Having had promotion and glory waved wildly in front of him, Prenkip was now reluctant to surrender the vision.

"What? What could we possibly be doing wrong?" Vuikak was deeply disheartened. "Look at these things." He kicked one of the stones. It rolled up against the second and lay there, motionless and inert. "It is time to inform the commander." So saying, he raised his voice and hissed importantly.

"Perhaps the only stones that generate unexpected effects lie on Torrelau," Prenkip suggested.

Vuikak watched as those at the rear of the column turned. "If that is the case, then it is up to the commander to find a means of dealing with them. Regardless, it does not alter our situation here. These useless rocks must still be returned to their owners and our status among them preserved."

As the other members of the expedition gathered around the two unauthorized experimenters, Vuikak told them what had occurred. Essasu listened gravely, waiting until the technician had finished before commenting.

"I should have you downgraded in rank and transferred, but it seems you have saved all of us a great embarrassment." He nodded in the direction of the two stones lying by the side of the trail. "Show me."

Vuikak nodded. Bending, he picked up the two growing stones and brought them together. He did this repeatedly, without visible consequence.

"If among the Parramati only the stones of Torrelau have the kind of hidden power we witnessed firsthand," Piarai whispered to his superior, "then we will have to obtain specimens from that island."

Essasu nodded resignedly. "A far more difficult proposition, but not an impossible one. After we have returned these stones to their 'masters,' we will return to base. Tomorrow I will consider proposals for a surreptitious collecting expedition to Torrelau. Now I am tired, and greatly frustrated." Stepping forward, he put a clawed hand on Vuikak's shoulder.

"I will not downgrade or otherwise censor you." He glanced at Prenkip. "Either of you. But I cannot promote you for disobeying orders. The most I can offer is my personal gratitude." He withdrew the hand and turned to address the others.

"The stones in our possession must be taken back. We will claim they were stolen by agents of the humans—the agenting species needn't be identified. In gaining the gratefulness of the locals for their return, we may yet see some profit from this day's work."

Piarai was properly admiring. "An astute turning of a regretful situation, Commander."

"Thank you," Essasu hissed. "It may be that the events that unfolded before us that night on Torrelau had nothing to do with so-called sacred stones and were the result of some action or activity the source of which is still unknown to us. There is much we do not know about this world. From now on I will be most reluctant to jump to excitable conclusions about anything having to do with native mythology."

Piarai was dutifully supportive. "The history of imperial exploration among aboriginal cultures is fraught with research that yielded little that was useful at first but that proved highly salutary later."

Essasu made a casual gesture of agreement and turned away,

muttering to himself. "Why did I not see it earlier? Some other mechanism was responsible for the debacle outside the human station. The humans themselves may even have been involved. I can imagine them enjoying a diversion at our expense. Well, we will uncover the truth, and then will come the reckoning." Removing the weather stone he was carrying, he let it fall by his feet. It bounced once, struck the two growing stones, and rolled to a stop.

"Thanks to the enterprise of these two," he declared, indicating the attentive Prenkip and Vuikak, "we have learned something valuable and been spared much trouble."

Yaarinda considered the onset of night. "Could we not wait until tomorrow to return the stones, Commander?"

"I know that everyone is tired. I believe that I am more tired than most," Essasu replied. "But I wish to put an end to this. We have lights and adequate instrumentation to allow us to find our way and retrace our steps. I will sleep better knowing that relations between ourselves and the people of this island have been maintained."

Yaarinda bowed her head deferentially. "It shall be as you desire, Commander."

Essasu turned away. "Piarai, you and I will return to base. There is real work to be done. The others can take back the stones. Yaarinda, you will take charge of the returning. Remember our story: they were stolen by unknown agents of the humans on Torrelau and we, at some danger to ourselves, succeeded in recovering them for our friends the Mallatyahans. We can expect them to be grateful."

Removing the remaining two stones he carried from his pack, Essasu tossed them on the ground next to the three already there. The other members of the party could redistribute them as they saw fit. Piarai removed the pair of stones he carried and added them to the accumulated mass.

When the last stone made contact with the small pile, the agglomeration fused instantly. A rush of green radiance brighter than the noonday sun burst violently forth, shocking Essasu's pupils into temporary blindness.

When he was able to focus again he saw that the island had vanished, along with the evening sky of slate blue-black, jungle and trail, clouds and grass. All that remained of the familiar were his equally dazed subordinates—and the stones.

They had melted together into a single misshapen mass that pulsed with energy the hue of newfound emeralds. It had a faint brown tint to it and hovered an arm's length above the ground, rotating slowly like a miniature green sun. Like angular, deformed planets, the helpless and bewildered members of the expedition orbited the consequence of their own accidental creation.

Barely visible within the agglutinated mass was an incredibly dense network of interwoven black filaments and other . . . things. Some of them seemed to be alive, or at least conveyed the illusion of life.

"What happened?" That sounded like technician Vuikak, shouting but oddly muffled.

"The stones." Piarai rotated listlessly nearby. "The stones *do* work, do have power. Everything depends on how they are combined. Sequence may be as important as type."

"Roads," observed Yaarinda softly. "One needs to know the right roads."

"There is great significance in all this." Essasu felt light as a feather, free and alive. The last lingering effects of the light burst had faded and he found that he could see clearly all around him. He just wasn't sure what he was seeing.

They appeared to be drifting in a vast swirling void, a silent three-dimensional maelstrom of green and black cloud. In the distance, prickly flashes of light took on peculiar shapes, like sculpted lightning. It was not true weightlessness, but something else. Something *other*.

An obsidian coil showed itself and darted toward the lightning. One by one it enveloped and consumed the darting spikes, which gave every evidence of attempting to escape. When it was through, it gave the unmistakable impression of turning to face the bewildered travelers. Essasu's tongue caught in his throat.

The coil twisted fiercely in upon itself and vanished into a vortex of its own making.

They were not alone here, he thought to himself. Wherever *here* was. It did not feel friendly, and he was not comfortable.

"Where are we?" One of the other technicians had begun to moan. Within her slow precession, her posture was indicative of grave concern.

"We have to find our way back from this place, wherever it is." Essasu used his most commanding inflections, but in that place the words seemed lost and lonely. "We have made a mistake in judgment. It is clear that we have been transported by the stones. Therefore we must make use of the stones to find our way back."

"According to the information we received," Piarai put in, "the human twisted the conjoined stones to activate the transport function." He spoke with some assurance, but this was not reflected in his expression. After all, both he and Essasu knew that the human had not succeeded in returning through his own efforts, but that he had somehow been tracked down and assisted by the stone masters of Torrelau.

Nevertheless, according to the information they had acquired, exerting force on the melded stones had produced a reaction. But they had mingled many stones, Essasu knew. The human had employed only two. Might that complicate returning or recovery by anxious stone masters seeking the missing stones?

He was struck by a terrible thought. According to the report, the human had been seen taking one of the stones. No one had observed the careful AAnn at their work. Could questing stone masters track the stones by themselves, or did they have to know who had made off with them? And if they found out, would they exert the efforts necessary for recovery? Would the number of individuals as well as the number of stones involved make recovery and return easier—or more difficult?

How long were they doomed to drift impotently before the Parramati of Mallatyah decided to come looking for their missing stones? Planning to be gone from base for only a day, the AAnn had brought little in the way of food and drink. Certainly the prospects of scavenging any life support in this place were remote.

"We cannot float like helpless bubbles while waiting for the Parramati to find us, as they did the human," he announced. "We must try to extricate ourselves." He found that by kicking he could swim toward the green mass. The intense inner luminescence showed no signs of dimming. "Piarai, can you reach it? Everyone, try to make contact!"

"To what end?" Vuikak was disconsolate and made no effort to hide it.

"The human was able to alter his locale by putting pressure on the ends of the affecting mass." Reaching the stone, Essasu grabbed hold with both hands, trying to dig his fingers into its substance. Sharpened claws slid off the glassy sides, but strong hands succeeded in obtaining a firm grip. On the opposite side, Piarai did the same.

"Try to twist the ends," he instructed his second-in-command.

"Try to make them move." Canines sliding against one another, he strained against the unyielding material.

Something gave beneath his fingers. Green sparks overwhelmed his vision.

He was standing now, no longer floating free. Piarai stood nearby, the stone mass resting on the ground between them. The earlier feeling of well-being had been replaced by a growing lethargy. A consequence of stronger gravity, he told himself.

There was no sign of the other members of the expedition. Yaarinda, Vuikak—all gone.

He and Piarai stood on a flat, gravelly plain composed of sparkling black rock like crushed hematite. In every direction around them the horizon stretched to an unbroken infinity. There were no footprints, no vehicle tracks, no signs of civilization of any kind. Or for that matter, save for themselves, of life.

A sun seemed to be setting off to the west. Also off to the north, south, and east, twilight fading to pale in every direction. Above was a black sky devoid of cloud or any other redeeming feature, including stars. Of one thing a stunned Essasu was certain.

They were a long ways from anywhere.

What was responsible for the strange and unprecedented sunset? Were there four suns, each setting behind a different point of the compass? Or was natural law as they knew it simply foreign to this place?

It was getting cold. He did not want to be standing where they were when the light went away because he had a desperate, gut feeling it might never return. In that ultimate darkness things with senses better attuned to nothingness might arise and come seeking. The commander thanked every deity and ancestor he could think of that he was not completely alone.

"Physical contact with the mass must be necessary for

transport." Piarai turned a slow circle, inspecting a land that offered nothing to see. "The others must be . . . lost."

And if we are not careful, we, too, will be lost—in our minds, Essasu thought. Where moments ago there had been many there were now only two. The others were . . . elsewhere. Drifting free, screaming forlornly perhaps, two of their comrades and their green nexus gone forever. Eventually the black coil might come for them, do unspeakable things, and put an end to it.

He stood there on the hematite plain and shuddered, waiting for the pale to dim or brighten. "We have to try again. If we do not find the others, maybe we will find our way back to Senisran."

"Try again?" A dejected Piarai eyed the glowing green mass with little in the way of hope. "Travel from noplace to nowhere?"

"We must," Essasu urged him. "Wherever we end up, it cannot be worse than here."

The eyes of his second-in-command were haunted. "I wish I shared your certitude."

Essasu walked over and shook him. "Get a hold of yourself. You are an officer of the Empire! Your only release is death. Until then, we strive on, in the name of the Emperor."

"Yes, the Emperor," Piarai muttered. "How I wish he were here instead of I."

This was hardly the time or place to chide a fellow officer for sacrilege, Essasu knew. It was important not to give up hope, to keep thinking, to keep trying. He said as much.

"We have no idea how to steer this thing." Piarai indicated the enigmatic stone agglomeration that was simultaneously their source of hope and despair. "We do not even know for certain that there exists a means of directing it." His expression twisted, thick with sardonic humor. "We do not know the right roads."

"We can try," Essasu argued. "We can look." He put his hands back on the stone and waited for his companion to do likewise.

For a long moment Piarai did nothing. Then a deep, slow, resigned hiss emerged from between his clenched teeth. "I wonder how many possible destinations our stone here can access? One would hope that the number is finite."

Reaching down, he grasped the other side of the mass and exerted pressure. So did Essasu. Emerald shards flew, the continuum contorted, and they went from where they were to a place where they were not.

CHAPTER

17

Tomochelor and Seaforth tried to maintain the station's daily routine: collecting and cataloging specimens of the local flora and fauna, recording variants of the Parramati language, checking automatic instrumentation to ensure that the usual meteorological reports were relayed via satellite to Ophhlia, and doing their best to win over the inhabitants of Torrelau to the idea of a formal treaty with the Commonwealth. But throughout it all, their thoughts were never very far from the sacred stones: their origin, functions, design, and above all, purpose.

They were repeatedly frustrated by the problem that Pulickel had ineffectually attempted to solve, namely, that it's more than a little difficult to study something you haven't got. Interestingly, his unfortunate escapade seemed not to have swayed Torrelauan opinion concerning the proposed treaty one way or the other. The proportion of those favoring an agreement and those opposed remained the same as before.

Various attempts to study the stones were stymied, albeit politely, at every turn, and neither of them could come up with a more efficacious way to proceed.

Even so, they were in better shape than the frantic handful of AAnn who were all that remained of the staff of his imperial highness's research station on Mallatyah. Their colleagues, including base commander Essasu RRGVB, had vanished without word or trace. Attempts to reestablish contact with the sortie party had proven worse than futile, as first sealed and then open-beam lines of communication yielded nothing in the way of a response, not even static. It was as if the entire expedition had suddenly and without warning vanished into thin air.

In point of fact that was exactly what had happened—but not into thin air. Among the skeleton staff remaining at the installation, there was very little talk of stones and much of drafting a request for evacuation. Yet this could not be done unless they could provide hard evidence that something untoward had happened to the group. Since no one was in a hurry to visit the area where the expedition had disappeared, this placed the survivors in something of a quandary.

Perhaps the commander and the others had a reason for keeping silent. If so, stumbling out to "rescue" them would constitute a grave insult, not to mention complicating the expedition's situation. So those who had remained behind kept to themselves, maintained the base in an orderly fashion, waited anxiously for a response from those who were not responding, and hoped that someone in a position of authority would show up to tell them what to do next.

After all, it had only been a few days.

While the few surviving AAnn huddled inside their suddenly uncrowded installation and the two humans strove to maintain a semblance of a daily routine, the Parramati were not as indifferent as they seemed to the events that had taken place.

It was true, as the AAnn Essasu had once commented, that the Parramati could not communicate any faster than their boats could travel. But beneath favorable winds the highly specialized outriggers were exceptionally fast. So while the inhabitants of Mallatyah were being informed of Pulickel Tomochelor's actions on Torrelau, the citizens of that island were learning from their brethren on Mallatyah of the AAnn expedition's ill-fated attempt to abscond with a much larger number of stones. Meanwhile, humans and AAnn alike remained ignorant of this quiet exchange of information.

Subsequently, big persons from both major islands along with representatives from Tiniara, Omeuleek, Culicuanna, and more than thirty smaller islands stretching the length and breadth of the archipelago assembled in the village of Ataap. Located on a small hook-shape island situated midway between Torrelau and Mallatyah, the gathering imposed a significant burden on those serving as hosts. The Ataapans did not complain. They were honored by the presence of so many important big persons.

Ascela and Jorana were present, representing the Torrelauapa Parramati. From Mallatyah came Oresivi and the famous scholar Leuwaramau. Smaller islands sent one representative apiece, while even tinier islets that might be home to only a single village or even a few families combined to choose one delegate to speak for them. All told, some seventy big persons and their attendants crowded into the meeting house on Ataap. Some but by no means all were stone masters. It was a convocation the likes of which Parramat had not seen in some thirty years.

On that occasion the purpose of the get-together had been festive. This time an air of solemnity hung over the proceedings, as the matter they had gathered to discuss was of a far more serious nature.

This is not to say that the atmosphere within and outside the meeting house was funereal. Old acquaintances greeted one another warmly, and new friendships were forged. Between discussions there was much ceremonial drinking and feasting, and the younger big persons participated in bounding and leaping contests. Amorous assignations were encouraged, a few were formalized, and in this way relationships between the affiliated islands of Parramat were strengthened.

When other island groupings held similar conclaves, disagreement and fighting was common, and not thought of as unusual. The Parramati had long since dispensed with such familial altercations. It made no sense to fight with a neighbor who might control a stone you would need next month, or next year, to improve your crops or heal a sick relative. Mutual interest preserved the peace.

Besides, you could share another person's space but never steal it.

When the last of the representatives had arrived and all introductions and greetings had been exchanged, everyone assembled in Ataap's meeting house. It was crowded, but there was just enough room for all. None could be left out or overlooked, not even the delegate from the smallest island. One might come from a large village or a single family, but everyone was equal in the amount of space they shared.

Most squatted in positions of formal rest, their flexible tails barely reaching the floor. Those along the walls were compelled to stand in order to be able to see. Standing for long periods of time was no hardship for a seni; not with their huge feet and powerful leg muscles.

Those designated as speakers waited their turn, and none spoke longer than was fitting. Everyone listened politely even to those elders whose thoughts were less focused and who had a tendency to ramble. Such individuals were viewed with fond amusement rather than dismay.

The delegates from Torrelau and Mallatyah spoke last, not because they represented the two largest and most densely populated islands of the archipelago but because they were the ones most intimately and immediately affected by the events of the previous days. Yet what had happened concerned every Parramati, to the last shell gatherer on the farthest outlying islet.

Of most immediate concern was the apparent loss of seven stones from Mallatyah.

"Seven stones!" Old Leuwaramau turned slowly as she spoke. Her body was bent and her vision impaired, but her voice rang out youthful and strong. Her words reverberated the length of the longhouse. In the singsong language of the Parramati it sounded more like an aria than a speech.

"Can they not be traced?" called out a stone master from Yevaluu.

The renowned scholar turned toward the questioner's voice. "Seven stones have been used. Not two, as was the case on Torrelau." Squatting nearby, Ascela and Jorana gestured solemn accord. "The users of the seven have gone farther. Finding them and bringing them back may be impossible. It is certainly dangerous."

"They can take only the stones," someone commented from near the south wall. "Not the space they occupied." A murmur of assent rose from the assembly.

"But still." The representative big person from Ataap did not try to conceal his distress. "Seven stones!"

Leuwaramau blew through the end of her long snout. "Two stones open two roads and their permutations. Difficult but not impractical to follow. Seven stones weave a trail far more than seven times tangled. Impossible. Too many roads crossing too many intersections. We must face the fact that these stones are gone. So are those who foolishly made use of them."

Huril'ila of the island of Rerenik rose. "Stones will be shared. If any need be replaced, Rerenik will share." In response, the longhouse shook to shouted offers of assistance.

Leuwaramau gestured for silence. "Thanks be to our Rerenik brethren, but this is not necessary. The loss is of course irreplaceable, but we of Mallatyah are rich in stones. We will not suffer." She drew herself up.

"But this must not be allowed to happen again. If enough stones are taken from us, the links between some roads could be lost forever. We could lose control over our own space."

Angry voices echoed throughout the meeting place. For all their inner peace and melodious speech, it had not been so very long since the Parramati had fought with their neighbors. Because they chose not to war did not mean they were ignorant of its ways.

"What are we to do?" a big person from Tassai wondered aloud. She had a big belly and, for a seni, a booming voice.

"Kill them all," another delegate suggested. "Soft- and shiny-skinned ones alike. Feed them to the apapanu."

From the center of the room, Ascela rose to turn and disagree. "That will not work. We know both peoples well enough to know that if these die, more will come to take their place. They are like kikau weeds in the gardens. Better to deal with those who are here now, with those that we know."

"We are not afraid of the aliens," another insisted. "Let them come as many as will. We will use the war stones against them!" This proposal was greeted with cries of support—but not many. A larger number of delegates expressed reservations.

It had been generations since the war stones had been employed to repel a large and especially vicious invasion from another archipelago. If the histories were to be believed, the entire attacking force had been destroyed by means too terrible to relate—together with nearly all the defenders. The war stones were not like growing stones or fishing stones. Those charged with their care had a greater responsibility than nearly all other stone masters. Such stones were few in number, and as a precaution no more than one was kept on any single island. The old stories warned that bringing them together could pose as great a threat to the users as to the enemy.

"I do not think that is a good idea. There must be a better way."

"Then propose one!" shouted a representative from the far side of the longhouse. This suggestion met with considerably more support than its predecessor.

Ascela was not intimidated. "The humans are intensely curious. Not only about the stones, but about all aspects of Parramati life and of kusum. Kill them, and others will come, curious to learn what happened." A three-fingered hand gestured toward the longhouse ceiling. "They drop from the sky, and the sky is full of them."

"*Ah-weh,*" old Leuwaramau whispered. "Then our purpose should be to keep their numbers among us as few as possible."

"Can we convince them to go elsewhere?" Huril'ila wondered. "Persuade them somehow to leave us and study the Eolurro? Let them set their strange longhouses among our neighbors instead of here."

There was an outburst of barking laughter. "More interesting to study the dirt than the Eolurro," someone declared, provoking welcome amusement.

Ascela continued to hold the floor. "That is exactly why it will not work. Like that of many other seni, the kusum of the Eolurro has been debased by contact with both humans and AAnn. These humans are so interested in ours because it remains pure."

"Can we keep it so?" someone asked from near the west wall. "If these aliens are allowed to remain among us, will their influence not begin to dilute traditional kusum? The young in particular are always susceptible to new and interesting ideas."

Jorana rose to stand alongside Ascela. "There are no stones for seeing into the future. We cannot predict what may happen. But we can try to convince the humans that kusum should not be threatened and that the Parramati should be left alone. There are only two of them, and they insist that they want only what is best for us."

"The shiny-skinned ones say the same." Oresivi let his gaze rove through the crowd of attentive big persons. "Perhaps that is part of the problem. These humans and AAnn both want only what is best for us—provided they are the ones to determine what that is." A surge of universal approval rose from the assembled. "Let us decide what is best for Parramati kusum and tell *them*."

"How can we convince those who are so interested in us to leave us alone?" another wondered aloud.

"Kill them," exclaimed a small but persistent minority. It was a collective voice that was disturbingly persistent. Jorana chose not to acknowledge it.

"Perhaps we should consult the stones and let them show us the way. The most *important* stones." He surveyed the crowd. "We could have a Goggelai."

This astonishing and completely unexpected proposal provoked immediate and vehement discussion in every corner of the meeting place. It did not die out completely even when Leuwaramau staggered again to her feet.

"A Goggelai has not been held in living memory. It opens the road to the unknown. There are great dangers in the unknown."

"But also answers," Jorana argued. "Do not these visitors also bring unknowns full of dangers? These aliens are a big thing that has come among the Parramati. It requires a big thing to counter them." He spread his arms wide.

"We want no treaties with them, yet without an answer, they will not go away. We do not want war with them, because they will keep coming back. So I say, let us see what the stones show us. Let us see what roads the Goggelai opens and how the humans react to them. Perhaps among all the roads we will find one that leads to understanding."

General discussion ensued. Those who argued for the use of the war stones to kill the visitors made some headway and swayed a few opinions. But it wasn't nearly enough to convince the majority, who opted, albeit with reluctance, to convene the Goggelai.

Debate continued until the small hours of the morning, but in the end Jorana's proposal prevailed. There was undeniable excitement among the delegates as they filed out of the meeting house. After all, though they knew it well from legend and story, none of them had actually participated in a Goggelai.

It was decided to hold the ceremony as soon as possible, on the slopes of sacred Mt. Erirota on Torrelau. Without divulging the full significance of the ritual, Ascela and Jorana would invite the humans to attend at the last moment.

Discussion continued as the big persons drifted off to their assigned sleeping quarters, walking or hopping to huts and longhouses that had been prepared for them by their honored hosts. The ramifications of a Goggelai were many, and not all necessarily benign. But these were portentous times for Parramat. Radical problems required radical solutions.

Stones had been lost. The protection of those that remained, and of the roads they guarded, had to be ensured. The roads could not be damaged, of course, but access to them could be lost.

So they would see what paths the Goggelai opened. Perhaps even, as Leuwaramau pointed out, the road to enlightenment.

"A multistones ceremony?" Fawn turned to Pulickel, wondering if she'd heard correctly.

They were standing by the river just above where it poured over the cliff into the shallow inlet lagoon below the village. The noise of the waterfall just downstream was constant but not overwhelming. Nearby, middle and lesser female persons were washing household items and preparing food in the crystal-clear water.

Jorana had come up behind them and politely requested a moment of their time. That in itself was unusual. Normally it was the visiting humans who had to interject themselves into Parramati conversation.

Pulickel confirmed her translation. "This sounds like something we should see."

Jorana's slim fingers traced lithe patterns in the air. "Your presence will add to the significance of the Goggelai."

Fawn fluffed out her blond tresses. "I've made notes on quite a few Parramati ceremonies, but I don't remember writing down anything about a Goggelai."

Jorana looked up at her. "One has not been held for a long time. For quite a long time."

"So why now?" There was something odd in the big person's manner, Pulickel thought. He ran through his mental catalog of seni postures and expressions. Not discomfort, not anger or upset, not nervousness. He couldn't quite put a finger on it or a name to it.

At least he knew that Jorana was not displeased with them. Otherwise he would not be inviting them to attend this special ceremony.

"The decision to hold the Goggelai is bound up with your

coming among us." Pulickel continued to wonder at the big person's manner, which was at once deferential and demanding. "Important decisions will be made afterward."

"The treaty," Fawn hinted.

Jorana indicated agreement. "About the treaty, yes. And about other things. The Goggelai may tell us if your road and that of the Parramati coincide or diverge. It may tell us all manner of things. No one knows for certain because it has been such a long time since one was held."

"So if it develops that our roads converge," Pulickel pressed him, "then the Parramati will sign the treaty?"

"Perhaps." Jorana looked away. "I cannot speak to such matters now."

Fawn asked the inevitable follow-up. "And if they diverge?"

The big person studied her out of long, dark eyes. "Space is vast, F'an, and there are many spaces within it. Each holds different responses to different situations."

"But even if there are an infinite number of spaces, the number of roads is finite," Pulickel countered.

Jorana favored him with the seni equivalent of a smile. "You have not been long among us, friend Pu'il, but you have learned much. Everyone hopes that the road followed is the right one. You are so interested to learn about kusum. Now you will have the opportunity to contemplate one of its most sacred foundations.

"As to which road will be shown, I know no better than you. It is not like the bringing together of growing stones or weather stones. The Goggelai is the biggest thing there is." He turned to depart.

Both Pulickel and Fawn were reluctant to let him leave. "When you say that this is a multistone ceremony," she queried their visitor, "do you mean that stones from all over the island are brought together in one place?"

The long skull turned back to her. "Not only from all over Tor-relau, but from the length and breadth of the Parramat. I said this was a big thing." He turned apologetic. "Remember when you asked me, friend Pu'il, if more than two stones were ever brought together at one time and I said no? I lied. This is the one time when many are gathered. It is a great and important secret, one that you will now share with the Parramati."

"Sounds like it." Pulickel found himself wondering why the native had lied earlier. Perhaps the infrequency of this particular ceremony explained it. Jorana might have been saying that no more than two stones were brought together at any one time under normal conditions. Clearly this Goggelai was an exception to the usual rules. That made it only the more intriguing.

"Are all the stones from all the islands used?"

The big person eyed him as if perhaps he hadn't learned so very much after all. "Of course not. What would be the point of com-bining earth and weather stones, or healing and fishing stones? No, the Goggelai requires the bringing together of more stones than any other ceremony, but they are all of one kind. It will take awhile to assemble them because they are used for nothing else but the Goggelai and have not been used in such a long time."

Fawn hoped that a description of the stones under discussion might offer a clue as to their function. "If they're not healing stones or earth stones or any other kind of stone that we're familiar with, then what are they?"

Jorana's reply was evocative without being informative. "They are the howling stones."

"So you bring all these howling stones together from all over the islands," Pulickel noted, "and then what happens?"

"No one can be sure," the big person replied maddeningly, "except that roads are opened."

"How many of these howling stones are there?" Fawn noted that even though the busy villagers could easily overhear, all were studiously ignoring the conversation.

Pulickel deduced from Jorana's reply that this time the native was being honest with them. "I do not know." Delicate hands fluttered. "I do not think that anyone knows for certain, not even the senior big persons of the outer islands. The howling stones have been held and watched over and unused for many generations. Only when all have been assembled in one place can they be counted and the answer to your questions known."

"Well," Fawn told him, "we're flattered that you're doing this for us."

"We are not doing it for you," Jorana corrected her. "We are doing it with you. To try to show you the depth and importance of preserving our kusum untrammeled."

That didn't sound like someone anxious to sign a treaty of mutual aid and cooperation, Pulickel thought. But he did not comment. Perhaps he was misinterpreting.

"There could be some danger. Or nothing at all may happen." The big person was watching both of them closely.

"We'll take our chances." Fawn smiled down at him. "You know that Pu'il and I aren't afraid of a little danger. When is the ceremony to be held?"

"In five days time, on the western slope of Mt. Erirota."

That in itself was interesting, Fawn mused. Normally, the far side of Erirota was off-limits even to big persons. She hadn't been especially curious about it because reconnaissance vits showed nothing out of the ordinary, nothing but jungle and rocks. They revealed no crumbling temples, no ancient burial grounds. Obviously the region had great significance to the Torrelauans and to the Parramati in general, but it was not because it was rife with structural antiquities. Certainly it was an honor and a sign of confidence to be invited to attend a gathering there—especially after the incident involving Pulickel and the "borrowed" stones.

"May we bring our recording tools along?" she asked.

Jorana eyed her unblinkingly. "You may bring anything you wish, so long as you bring yourselves."

"And you can't give us an idea of what we might expect to see?" Pulickel was reluctant to let the big person go.

"I have never traveled the road of the howling stones," the native told him. "No one living has. Who knows? Perhaps you will tell me." His lips flowed in the equivalent of a grin. "It is told that through the Goggelai lies the road to wonders. Or there may be nothing. We will find out together."

Following Jorana's departure, the two xenologists spent the rest of the morning studying and recording native activities along the river. Their thoughts, however, were on the earlier meeting and not on cultural explication.

"What do you make of all this?" Fawn asked her colleague. "Of what Jorana said. Was he telling us everything, or was he being selective?"

"I'm sure he was being selective. Or evasive. That bit about not knowing anything about what happens during the ceremony? I don't think I buy that."

She made a face. "I guess we're going to find out. You don't think they're inviting us to a big gathering so they can get rid of us?"

"Why should they? If they wanted to dispose of me, why would they go to the trouble of bringing me back from the road the transportation stones took me down? They could have left me out there, wherever out there was, wandering around forever trying to get back on my own."

"Maybe that wouldn't have been in accordance with kusum."

She watched the females working on the riverbank, but her mind wasn't on it. "As you know, when it comes to collective decision making, the Parramati are more obtuse than anyone else on Senisran."

"Five days. We'll want dual backups on all systems, and we'll want to check them out at least a full day in advance."

She nodded without replying, knowing that he was talking more to himself now than to her. It was an aggravating habit, but one she found she was becoming comfortable with.

CHAPTER

18

The ceremonial locale on the far side of Mt. Erirota was more attractive than impressive, a pristine grassy clearing high up on the slopes of the extinct volcano. Beyond the clearing the native vegetation grew thickly, reflecting the high rainfall the area received. Either the grassy sward was carefully maintained, Pulickel decided, or else it lay in a slight but significant rain shadow.

It was early evening and Senisran's compassionate sun lingered on the distant horizon, pausing briefly before its daily disappearance to paint scattered clouds with streaks of gold and crimson. Sunset was the only time of day that could reduce sea and sky on this world to insignificance, he mused as he soaked in the spectacular panorama.

Irrespective of the incipient ceremony, the gathering itself was most impressive. It looked as if every big person in Parramat and not a few of their attendants had assembled in orderly fashion on the edge of the clearing. Recorders humming inconspicuously, he and

Fawn stayed where Ascela and Jorana had left them. They had an excellent view and felt no need to roam.

The assembled Parramati had dressed for the occasion in their finest regalia. Colorful woven skirts vied for attention with flamboyant headdresses and elaborate necklaces. Snouts, cheeks, eye sockets, and ears were decorated in vibrant facepaint while rings hung in profusion from long fingers and tails. Shoulder garlands of the rarest and most exotic flowers the archipelago had to offer filled the air with wild, confused perfume.

Yet the gaudy spectacle belied the attitude of those present, which was solemn rather than celebratory.

Having been made ready earlier, torches and standard-borne bone lanterns were brought forth and lit, their individual lights strengthening as that of the sun faded. Querying Ascela as to the ceremony's duration, Pulickel was told that it would take as long as it took, a response that grated on the xenologist's sense of the precise.

The Torrelauapan was not being cryptic. It was simply a fact that no one knew how long a Goggelai should last. The ceremony would define itself, the visiting humans were told. They would have to be satisfied with that. Ancient oral guidelines, Fawn pointed out, were inherently obscure.

As the last of the torches and lanterns were lit, the dusky peak of the volcano glowed bronze in the final light of the setting sun. Drinking in the sight both natural and synthetic spread out before her, Fawn Seaforth found that she didn't care if the Goggelai produced any profound revelations about Parramati culture or not. The spectacle was sufficient unto itself.

In addition to the unprecedented display of color and design, there was music in abundance. Flutes, stringed instruments, and an astonishing assortment of barbaric percussion filled the evening air with energetic melodies interspersed with eruptive bursts of jagged rhythm. Unable to resist the seductive ostinatos, many of the assembled dignitaries were soon chanting and dancing in place. While Fawn occasionally found her own body twisting and arching in time to the alien tempo, Pulickel was apparently immune to all such melodic blandishments. He remained stolidly in place, his recorder whirring, doing his best not to stare disapprovingly—or otherwise—in her direction.

As for the mysterious, revered howling stones themselves, their actual appearance was something of a letdown. Carried in woven bags or brought forth in intricately patterned baskets, they looked no different from any of the other stones the visitors had seen. Irregular lumps of green volcanic glass, some were larger than the growing stone whose use had been demonstrated to Fawn, while others were even smaller than the two stones so briefly borrowed by Pulickel. Several were so big they had to be carried in on hardwood litters supported by four Parramati apiece.

One by one, the stones were removed from their traveling containers and placed before a big person standing along the inner rim of the great circle that now enclosed the modest meadow, until the grass was ringed with a line of sacred stones. Each stone, Pulickel noted, rested no less than half a meter from its neighbor. None was allowed to touch.

Even when the ring was complete the procession continued, until two concentric stone circles and part of a third lay gleaming on the ground. The two humans were given free rein to wander in and among the stones and stone masters, musicians and attendants, recording whatever they wished. For the most part even those Parramati they knew, like Ascela and Jorana, ignored them. All were enraptured by the ceremony.

When Pulickel accidentally tripped over a particularly long stone, no one so much as twitched. As for the stone, it rocked back and forth a couple of times and lay utterly still, a big dark green rock that differed only in color from the igneous escarpment that backed onto the meadow. If it and the several hundred others that had been so laboriously brought together embodied any significant powers, Pulickel reflected, these were being held efficiently in check.

From Jorana's original description, he and Fawn had supposed there were no more than a few dozen of the howling stones. The presence of hundreds was therefore the biggest surprise of the evening so far. Judging from the expectant attitude of the assembled, there promised to be more.

By the time the last vestige of sunlight had fled from the horizon and the scene was lit entirely by torch and lantern light, the chanting and music-making had risen to such a pitch that he had to shout to make himself heard above the noise. The relentless Parramati percussion in particular gave new significance to that part of the ear known as the tympanum. While his recorder could adjust automatically to the rising din, he had to struggle to tolerate it.

The rolling artificial thunder boomed down the slopes and echoed through the valleys. Fortunate wildlife fled, but he and Fawn had no such option. With luck, he winced as an especially loud burst of music assailed his ears, it would all be over soon.

Fawn's thoughts were stumbling down the same discordant path. "I wonder if this is going to go on all night? If so, we could probably return in the morning for the big finish."

He checked his chronometer. "No one's said anything to me about time. We probably ought to inquire. For all we know now, the ceremony could take days."

"I suppose we should wait it out awhile before asking. Our presence here is something of an honor, and we don't want to insult anybody by making it look like we want to leave early." She smiled encouragingly at him and he nodded reluctantly.

It was well after midnight when he checked the time again. The music and chanting gave no sign of slackening, the assembled participants no indication that they were running out of steam. If anything, they sang and played louder than ever. Torches and lanterns burned as brightly as at sunset. Fawn's notion of leaving for a while and returning later was looking more and more attractive. The activity, as well as the hour, was exhausting.

Those stone masters who dropped out of the inner circle promptly had their positions assumed by others. No such reinforcements waited in the wings for the two tired xenologists. Pulickel found his thoughts drifting more and more often to his room back at the station. His quiet, soundproofed room.

Without any warning, signal, or fanfare, the music ceased. Chanting fell to a sustained murmur. Several big persons representing the outermost islands of the Parramat Archipelago stepped forward and raised three-fingered hands skyward. The music resumed, only this time it was pointed and brief.

Words were uttered that neither xenologist recognized, though from their inflection Fawn knew they were archaic. But though those who spoke them might be ignorant of their meaning, they enunciated each one carefully and with great respect.

Supplicating hands were lowered. Selecting them from the innermost circle, several big persons brought the first stones forward. The two speakers accepted the offerings, placed them on the ground, and pushed them together. Their fatigue now forgotten, Pulickel and Fawn double-checked their recorders and tensed.

Contact was achieved between stones. Green sparks flew from an emerald flash. Fused, the conjoined stones emitted a steady, soft green glow.

"What now?" Pulickel whispered aloud.

"I don't know. Remember, the Parramati haven't performed this ceremony in a very long time. They probably aren't too sure of the consequences themselves."

Two more stone masters removed their respective burdens from the circle and brought them forward. Others were preparing to do the same from the opposite side of the ring. One at a time, they added their stones to the lambent green mass in the center of the ceremonial encirclement. With each additional stone the irregular shape added to its size.

Pulickel watched as a stone as big as his head was placed against the near side of the burgeoning aggregation. Vibrating noticeably, it slid *up* the side of the mass and rotated several times before slipping neatly into a slot in the top of the heap. Other stones similarly maneuvered themselves into position, displaying an inner animation none of the sacred stones the Parramati used in everyday life had previously exhibited.

There was no formal organization, no apparent rhyme or reason to the process. The natives merely dumped the parts in a pile, Pulickel realized. Whatever the growing green mass might be, it was putting *itself* together. It was apparent that in addition to assorted helpful powers, certain stones were possessed of something very different but equally impressive.

Memory. Memory ancient and, so far, inscrutable.

By now the refulgent green lump was taller than an adult seni and had assumed a roughly rectangular shape. It sustained its baffling growth as more stones were brought forward and added to the enigmatic structure.

Fawn leaned close. Even above the excitement and noise, the sights and the pungent presence of hundreds of highly active Parramati, he could still smell the perfume of her.

"Somehow I don't think this is intended to make the pohoroh grow bigger or the river run clean," she whispered.

The ceremonial stone rings continued to shrink as more and more of the glassy green pieces were added to the growing puzzle. It was far taller than any seni now, but individual stones continued to maneuver themselves up the uneven flanks and fasten themselves to the top, steadily adding to the height of the luminescent mystery. The assembled Parramati were as entranced by their handiwork as were the visiting xenologists.

By this time the object was putting out so much light that it was impossible to look directly at it for long. In addition to the meadow and the softly chanting circle of natives, it illuminated the surrounding jungle as well as the looming flank of the mountain. Yet heat remained a by-product of the reaction notable only for its absence. The intense green radiance was entirely cool, allowing supplicating stone masters to touch the product of their efforts with impunity. From its apex, a meter-wide shaft of coherent green light suddenly shot skyward to pierce the night sky.

From the time the first two stones had been brought together, a distant hum had been audible. With the addition of each new stone, this had grown steadily in volume and intensity, until now it vibrated within teeth and bones. It was a whine, a single high mechanical note, an antediluvian call, the song of something endlessly dormant and only now slowly reawakening.

A howling.

Few stones remained, and these were piously added to the pile. Pulickel saw Fawn shielding her eyes as she tried to follow the activity. Meanwhile, except for suffusing the meadow with light and sound, the impressive green agglomeration had done nothing. The world hadn't shifted on its axis, the ground beneath his feet remained stable and the solid, grassy growth common to Senisran still cushioned his sandaled feet.

Even if whatever it was managed to complete itself, he realized, that didn't mean that anyone present would know what to do with the final result. He wondered if any of the orbiting surveillance and survey satellites put up by the Commonwealth and the AAnn were presently in position to detect the green beam and, if so, what they would make of it. Couldn't worry about that now, he knew.

The last stone was brought forward and reverently placed against the mass, which by this time was the size and approximate shape of a Parramati longhouse. The stone efficiently slid up and around the right side to settle itself into and fill one remaining gap. Pulickel and Fawn tensed, but nothing happened. Together with the Parramati they found themselves confronting a substantial structure that put out a vast intensity of green light, and it in turn confronted them.

But nothing happened.

A few uncertain mutterings began to be heard among the assembled. Pulickel found himself echoing them. Was there anything to be learned here, or was it all a colossal bust? Perhaps the device was designed simply to put out a shaft of green light, possibly as some kind of unknown navigational aid. Or maybe it was no more than an elaborate marker.

Frustrated, he walked up to it, shielding his eyes from the evanescent glare. No one stopped him.

Up close, he found that he was able to see into the mass to a surprising depth. A network of complex internal striations was clearly visible. They appeared to link slightly darker masses buried deep within the body of the construct. Reaching out with one hand, he lightly traced the lines nearest the surface. Like the light it put out, the object itself was pleasantly cool to the touch.

Behind him he heard Fawn call out sharply, "Watch yourself, Pulickel. There's something coming *out*."

As he stepped back, the construct began to exude something very like a large, transparent egg, as if the glowing green lump was giving birth. The voices of the assembled big persons rose in unison, chanting loudly.

Approaching this new and unexpected phenomenon with caution, he saw that in contrast to the rest of the mass, the protrusion had a faint reddish tinge, like an excited fiber optic. He was unable to gauge its thickness or even if it was hollow or solid. Already, three-quarters of it had emerged from the howling green lump. Indifferent to urging or chanting, suspicions or hopes, the remainder resolutely refused to ooze free of the construct. From a tactile standpoint it felt no different from the rest of the green mass.

Fawn joined him, along with Ascela and Jorana. As they inspected the faintly reddish ovoid, the curving, tapered end facing the circle suddenly opened. There was no door, no hatch. One moment the end of the object appeared solid; the next, it displayed an opening.

Together, Pulickel and Ascela peered inside. The interior of the ovoid was floored with what seemed to be a layer of dense fog. Ignoring Fawn's admonitions, he reached in and down. His fingers sank a centimeter or so into the frothy substance before encountering an unyielding surface.

He straightened. "Interesting stuff. It looks like you could brush it aside with one hand, but it doesn't move. There's initial give, and then it turns solid. What do you suppose this thing is?" His ears were filled with Parramati chanting and the high-pitched whine of the construct.

Hands on hips, she studied the mysterious protrusion. "Your guess is as good as mine. I'm inclined to think that anything that has a floor, walls, and an entrance is designed to be entered." Blue eyes speculated on the protrusion. "The big persons have been saying all along that the Goggelai is supposed to open a different sort of road. This could be some kind of transportation device."

He nodded contemplatively. "Uh-huh. Or an oversized alien food processor. Right now we are somewhat lacking in information."

She was studying the ovoid intently. "If it's a means of transport, it's odd that it didn't emerge completely from its surroundings."

"Is it? When did we become specialists in alien transportation systems?" Bending low, he put both hands on the exposed rim of the ovoid and leaned inward.

"And where the hell do you think you're going?" she challenged him sharply.

He glanced back with that fey, confident smile she'd come to know so well. "Not there, I pray. Hopefully just down another road, as the Parramati would say."

She was less than encouraging. "I'd think that after your last experience with the vagaries of stone-impelled transport you wouldn't want to try it again. The Parramati might not be able to bring you back a second time."

He tapped the ovoid's outer rim. It gave back no sound. "We're not dealing with a couple of loose stones here. If this is indeed some kind of device intended to transport individuals down a particular road, then it quite likely is designed to also transport them back. Otherwise why design and build something this elaborate? Why not just use a couple of the transportation stones? I don't think it's unreasonable to assume that the more intricate the device, the more complex and varied its function."

"You're assuming a lot," she insisted.

Again the smile, a little wider this time. "I certainly am, but I have a feeling it's the only way we are going to divine this object's intended function."

"It could take you someplace," she brooded, "and not bring you back."

"There is that possibility," he conceded. "But the liturgy of discovery is rife with explorers who never looked over the next cliff or climbed the next mountain because they were afraid they might fall off."

"Or run into something with a bad attitude and lots of teeth," she added dourly.

He nodded knowingly. "Either way, we can expect to get some answers."

"Before we go stumbling off in search of them," she countered, "let's see what the Parramati think."

He hesitated, then reluctantly deferred to common sense.

"Histories insist that the howling stones open new roads." Ascela exchanged a look with Jorana. "But they do not say what kind of roads, and I have never seen a road open like this." She indicated the beckoning, enigmatic ovoid.

"This is a new thing," Jorana agreed.

Fawn framed her question carefully, not wanting dialect to get in the way of meaning. "Do the histories of the Goggelai say anything about returning back along any roads that are opened?"

"No," the big person admitted, "but it is well known that the clearer the road, the easier the return. I believe we should go and find out." Pulickel was a little startled to find his position so readily supported.

"If it looks like anything," Jorana put in, "it looks like a boat." He was studying the ovoid's exterior. "It is covered to keep off the rain, but there are no outriggers."

Pulickel essayed a seni bark indicative of low-key humor. "If you are right and it is some kind of boat, Jorana, then I think it will have outriggers—but of a kind we cannot see and cannot imagine."

The senior big person indicated agreement. "No matter their kind, so long as they work. We will go together, friend Pu'il." He straightened on his powerful hind legs. "It is the responsibility of big persons to investigate any new roads."

Fawn's attention shifted from alien to fellow xenologist. "You're determined to go through with this, aren't you?"

Pulickel nodded. "Most assuredly." Peering into the device, he added off-handedly, "There is room enough for all of us."

A three-fingered hand gripped his shoulder. "It is good," Ascela told him. "Each of us may see things only another will understand. Knowledge can be shared." Slitted blue-black eyes gazed deeply back into his own, the bond of curiosity linking their two species more effectively than any words.

"Nothing may happen." Fawn eyed the ovoid uneasily. "Or it may collapse in on you."

"Or fill up with water, or toxic gas." Pulickel looked up. "Possibilities will remain nothing more than possibilities unless we do something. There's nothing for it but to try it. Either way, the results will be recorded. Despite all its claims to precision and exactitude, great science often boils down to a leap of faith."

"That's a fine sentiment for a book, not a life." The line of her mouth tightened and she took a couple of steps back. "So go ahead and leap." She raised the forearm to which her recorder was strapped.

Jorana touched his side and he turned. "Let us find out what the howling stones do, friend Pu'il. Let us learn together."

"Yes, together." Knowing that the memory of his recent transgression still burned hot in Parramati memory as well as his own, he was touched by the sentiment.

Ascela had conveyed their intentions to several other big persons. Now, as she entered the ovoid, they explained what was happening to the rest of the assembled. Everyone retreated to the edge of the meadow as every eye focused on the luminous green mass. Fawn found herself surrounded by warm-bodied, heavy-hipped alien forms.

Jorana followed his fellow villager into the device, moving toward the rear and making room for Pulickel. While the seni squatted, he was forced to assume a cross-legged position on the foglike floor. Arrayed in single file, they faced the opening, the emerald brilliance at their backs.

"Just a minute! Wait!" came a frantic shout. Breathing hard, Fawn crawled in next to him.

"Of course we'll wait," he told her. "We don't have any choice, since we don't know how to go." At that moment she was closer to him than she'd ever been before—and not just physically. "I thought you were going to stay behind?"

Scrunched up against the curving, transparent wall, she did not have enough room to cross her long legs but had to stretch them out in front of her. "I've always been an avid mountain climber, and I'm not afraid of heights."

"Good. I am."

They sat silent and motionless within the ovoid, listening to the howling whine of the device and the distant, submerged but still audible chant of the assembled big persons. After a while, Pulickel began to feel foolish.

"It's not responding to our presence. Maybe we're overlooking some means of activation. Look for a depression, a discoloration—any kind of imperfection in the structure of the inner surface."

Fawn translated for the two Parramati. Together the four of them commenced a section-by-section search of the ovoid's interior. Except for the fog floor, it proved to be as featureless as it looked.

"It has to be here," Pulickel muttered. "There has to be something."

"Does there?" Fawn was less assured. "We're dealing with the technology that made the stones. Stones that stimulate instant growth in plants, affect the weather, send a curious xenologist god knows where but lets local aborigines bring him back, and merge to form glowing green searchlights the size of a skimmer hangar. We don't have a clue how any of this works, what powers them, or why they're here. I have yet to recognize so much as an on-off switch on the least of them, so why should we expect to be able to find one in here? Face it, Pulickel: the Goggelai's a no-go."

"Thank you for those encouraging conclusions," he replied dryly.

"Hey, I say what I feel."

"Perhaps we must use the proper chant," Ascela suggested.

Pulickel didn't laugh. In the absence of any obvious method of physical activation, who was to say that an oral variety might not prove more effective? It certainly couldn't be less so.

As it turned out, the correct thing to do proved to be to do nothing at all, a dynamic in which they were at present actively engaged.

Before the Parramati could commence any new chants, the open end of the enclosure shut. As with its opening, this took place in utter silence and without warning. Again, no door or hatch appeared. One moment egress to the outside world was readily available, and the next a red-tinged barrier as transparent as the rest of the ovoid had silently taken its place.

Perhaps it had finally detected the presence of living creatures within and responded appropriately. Possibly it self-activated after an indeterminate but predetermined period of time. Perhaps a sniff, or an especially deep breath, or the exact intonation of a word had activated some hidden mechanism. It was impossible to tell what had done the trick, and quite likely they would never know.

Light, warmth, and a flow of fresh air emanated from the fog beneath. How the machine knew what of which the occupants required, Pulickel couldn't imagine, so he settled for being grateful instead. In finally sensing and reacting to their presence, the device had also sensed and reacted to their needs.

Perhaps something outside changed as well, because a number of big persons were hopping frantically toward the ovoid. Their mouths were open and they were gesturing emphatically. Within the transparent egg, however, all was composed and surprisingly quiet. They could no longer hear the Parramati chanting or the howling of the stones.

Leaning forward, Fawn pushed gently, then firmly, on the end of the new enclosure, on the place where they had entered. Unsurprisingly, it did not yield to her efforts. She sat back.

"Won't budge," she reported tensely. "Whatever happens next, we're sealed in tight."

"Something must be happening." Her colleague leaned close and pointed.

The Parramati who had leaped so anxiously toward the ovoid had halted abruptly. All were staring while a number had begun to retrace their steps as fast as they had advanced. It looked like they were conversing loudly among themselves—Pulickel could clearly see their mouths moving—but the two xenologists and two big persons within the device could hear nothing beyond the ovoid wall.

Ascela and Jorana were utterly calm, resigned to whatever might happen next. They were no less curious about this than their human companions—simply less concerned.

As the world outside began to vanish, it took a moment for Pulickel to realize what was happening. The ovoid was sinking, or retreating, or being absorbed back into the efflorescent green mass from which it had partially emerged. He kicked experimentally at the front of the egg. It yielded no more readily to his foot than it had to Fawn's hands.

Satisfied that they were safe—or trapped—he settled back to await whatever Fate and an ancient alien technology had in store for them.

CHAPTER

19

Though they were being sucked into the very heart of the emerald radiance itself, the light outside actually dimmed slightly. While the composition of the transparent material encasing them did not appear to have changed, the potent efflorescence no longer fully penetrated their sanctuary.

As the ovoid continued to be absorbed into the pulsating mass, their window on the outside world shrank proportionately. Soon only a small circle of visibility remained through the forward tip of their enclosure, and then that, too, was gone.

It was black outside the ovoid. Black, but not threatening in the manner of the darkness Pulickel had experienced previously. Unlike that abomination, the current absence of light did not carry with it the flavor of evil. Within the device, the lambent fog beneath their feet provided enough pink-hued illumination for them to see one another without straining.

There was also the slightest sensation of movement. Fawn

found this especially interesting, because if the original pace of absorption had been maintained, they should long since have come out the other side of the main green mass. That they had not yet done so suggested that they had either halted somewhere in its depths or else moved on—somewhere else.

The impression intensified. Nor was it restricted to the two humans, for Ascela and Jorana felt it equally. There was a definite sense of being impelled *forward*, though in what direction no one could say.

Something gave them a sharp jolt, the ovoid rocked, and Pulickel instinctively grabbed for a handhold. There were none available, unless one counted his companions. Sound once more began to reach them, steady and unvarying. Only mildly surprised, he recognized it.

The stones were howling afresh.

Just when he didn't think he was going to be able to take it any louder, the whine leveled off. Beneath his feet and posterior, the ovoid vibrated like a well-tuned violin string. It was impossible to escape the feeling that they were going *somewhere*.

Ascela confirmed it. "We are set upon a road—though by my grandmother's tail I cannot say what road that may be, or where it may lead." She rested back on her haunches in a position that would have painfully cramped any human but that the seni found most relaxing.

Jorana tried to lighten the atmosphere within the ovoid. "I know this road. It is the road to wherever."

"To wherever the howling stones lead," Ascela agreed.

With nothing to see, nothing to do, and no control over either, Pulickel saw no reason why he should not emulate the attitude of their nonhuman fellow travelers. Shifting his body, he put his hands behind his head and leaned back against the pale red transparent wall. This was now slightly warm to the touch. Fawn attempted to do likewise, but the length of her limbs made it difficult for her to find a comfortable position. She was expectant, but not particularly happy.

"So you have no idea where this 'road' leads?" she queried their companions.

"No," Jorana confirmed. "But I think we are going to find out."

"Look here." Pulickel held out his wrist. "My chronometer's stopped."

Fawn glanced down at herself and nodded. "Mine, also." She checked her other wrist. "Recorder's not working, either. Readout says the cell is drained, but I put in a fresh one before I joined the rest of you."

"Mine read half charged before I climbed in here." Removing the protective backplate, he slipped a fresh cell from his belt into the appropriate receptacle and snapped it shut. The readout did not change. "Dead, also. I have a feeling they've all been drained, or discharged, or Tesla knows what else."

She nodded confirmation after checking her own inventory. "Then we'll just have to rely on the only recorders left to us." She pointed two fingers at her eyes.

He nodded. "Let's hope nothing drains that power source."

Time passed without measure. They were still discussing the mystery of the depleted power cells when it happened—so suddenly no one had time to react or prepare. Subsequently, they were too overwhelmed to remember the exact moment when everything changed.

Gone was the all-pervasive darkness as the ovoid burst out into a gigantic tunnel composed of brilliant streaks of excited plasma. Yellow, red, and blue flares darkening to deepmost purple twisted and writhed around them, raw energy disciplined and held in check by immense unseen forces. It was an electric pipe, a piece of hollow lightning, down which they were being sucked at inconceivable speed. The ovoid was channeling an aurora.

It wasn't straight, their chosen course. It bent and looped, and, given the radical twists, they should by rights have been sick all over themselves. But while the universe outside went mad, something unseen maintained their internal equilibrium. No one upchucked, though Pulickel was about ready to throw out everything he'd ever learned about physics.

And as if the astonishing road down which they were flying wasn't wonder enough, beyond the flaring walls of the tunnel could be seen dozens, hundreds of others of equally impossible brilliance, coiling about each other like mating pythons or flaring off in a thousand different directions. Awed, they could only stare. Numbed, Pulickel could only wonder how many ovoids like their own were racing along those improbable lengths at impossible velocities to unknown destinations. Fawn speculated aloud on who or what might be riding in them.

Strands of a rope, threads of a weave, the tunnels were not inviolate. Occasionally a burst of sheer radiance would jump from one tunnel to another. The travelers looked in vain for signs of another voyaging ovoid similar to their own but saw none. It left them to wonder if they simply didn't know how to look, or if they were truly alone, the only ones abroad on the immense network.

Within the speeding ovoid the air stayed pleasant and fresh, the temperature agreeable. Hearts, however, raced.

"I wonder if we're traveling along some kind of natural structure," Fawn speculated, "or if someone actually built all this."

Pulickel stared at the web of plasma tunnels, thoroughly entranced. "If the latter, it would qualify as the most impressive piece of engineering in our part of the galaxy."

She laughed softly, a sound that always made him think of fired brandy. "What makes you think that we're still in 'our part of the galaxy'?"

He smiled back. "Figure of speech. Everyone needs a reference point to start from."

"Roads." Jorana was speaking. "There are an infinite number of roads leading to an infinite number of spaces."

"Yes," Ascela agreed. "This one chose us. We did not choose it. We are not the masters of the howling stones."

"Well, somebody must be." Fawn tried to stretch, had to settle for a half. "Roads have builders. And destinations."

Pulickel recalled the naked, overpowering, soul-crushing evil he had encountered. Did one of these roads lead to that? Did the one they were on? But if anything, they continued to suffer from a surfeit of light and not its absence.

Fawn was right. They had no idea where they were. Perhaps not even in the same galaxy or, for all he knew, in the same universe. What, after all, did roads of such magnitude and wonder connect? Different dimensions, parallel universes? He would have given a great deal to see just one star—one ordinary, everyday, spherical ball of thermonuclear fire. But there were none; there were only the roads.

The two transportation stones he had taken and inadvertently activated had sent him careening wildly from place to place, with no control over direction or destination. This was different. This was controlled travel down a designated route. To where, neither human nor seni could say. But Fawn was right: a route implied a destination. He wondered what would happen when they reached it.

If they reached it, he corrected himself. They knew nothing of the lifespan of the beings that had fabricated the network, nor of their tolerance for long-term travel. Perhaps a real-time journey of a century or more was like a week to them. In that event, when it finally slowed to a halt the ovoid would bring forth a load of desiccated corpses.

He felt of his field pack. They had a few concentrates with them, a little juice and water. It wouldn't last very long and, consequently, neither would they. If they didn't stop fairly soon, they would have to try to turn the ovoid around or find another way back.

He smiled sardonically to himself. Might as well try to reverse the spin of a pulsar. Which, though he did not know it, was an evaluation not far off the mark. Senisran, Earth, the whole Commonwealth seemed very far away. In that view he was completely correct.

Eventually the maze of fiery, flaring plasma tunnels began to thin out until less than a hundred remained, twisting and coiling like emancipated Aztec deities in the vastness of empty space. As the ovoid sped on, showing no signs of slowing, this number was reduced until only a handful remained, then less than a dozen. Finally there was only the one, a cascade of explosive red and lambent purple, coruscating yellow and throbbing blue. Their tunnel. Their road.

The notion of comparative velocity had long since lost any relevance. With nothing to measure themselves against, they had no way of estimating their speed. Faster than fast was the best description Fawn could come up with. No one was foolish enough to propose an actual number.

Without warning, the plasma tunnel began to constrict around them, until it was no wider than the ovoid itself. This must be how a corpuscle in a capillary feels, Pulickel imagined. And then, as the tunnel walls drew tight, so at last did the cosmos.

They were surrounded by stars. Ordinary, normal-looking, unremarkable stars. Sol-types and red giants, white dwarfs and binaries, they were clearly visible through the blazing walls of the tunnel. They swam in a sea of coruscating nebulae, and Pulickel wanted to reach out and kiss each and every one of them. Instant conflagration aside, it would have taken him quite a while.

More stars were visible than any of them had ever seen at any one time in a crystal-clear night sky or from an orbiting platform. So many stars that they crowded the nebulae for living space and threatened to eliminate the blackness of space in which they swam. Enough stars to make the middle of the Milky Way look empty and unpopulated. You could skip from star to star, hop from system to system, Fawn thought. Or such was the impression the sight created.

A new sensation rippled through them: one of progressive deceleration. Curving to their right, the attenuated plasma tunnel carried them toward a yellow sun surrounded by a ring of matter and energy that coexisted in a state foreign to either xenologist's experience. Out past this striking system they flew, curving sharply above another star that boasted an entourage of no less than twenty planets plus assorted moons and comets and asteroids. Half these worlds were linked by lesser versions of the energy tunnel through which they were traveling.

Still another system, arrayed around a black hole orbited by strange fan-shape objects whose mouths pointed toward the gravitational monster in their midst, drawing upon its energy, sucking up collapsed matter and feeding it to a world the size of Jupiter. There it was molded and shaped, energy bending energy into a bridge that spanned a galaxy. This galaxy.

Pulickel and Fawn had already decided that they had abandoned one in favor of another, but they didn't know the half of it.

Proceeding down the tunnel at speeds that had dwindled from the impossible to the merely incredible, they passed structures so immense and overawing as to leave them bereft of superlatives. How could they be expected to relate to an entirely artificial world built, as it were, from matter up?

There was one individual fabrication so grandiose in the conception, so breathtaking in its execution, that it was difficult to believe in its existence. As the tunnel passed through a portal the size of Io, they found themselves confronted by a star that had been entirely englobed by an artificial structure. On its inner surface lived unknown beings in their quadrillions, warmed and nurtured by their captive star. The ovoid passed quickly through its orbit and out an opening on the far side of the englobement.

New tunnels hove into view, passing close to a pulsar to boost their cargoes between the multitudinous stars at ever more incredible velocities. Here were suns enough, planets enough, for individuals who might desire it to have a whole world unto themselves. Desire company, and the plasma tunnels could bring it to you in less than a day.

Above one world someone or something was tracing abstract designs in the planet's upper atmosphere, using its ionosphere for a canvas. Elsewhere stellar winds were focused through hollow moons, resulting in true music of the spheres. It was a universe of wonders and enchantments.

It was also very far from home.

Once, a ship passed close. Or was it a planet, fitted out with engines and powered out of orbit, vacationing from one sun to the next? Pulickel couldn't be sure and size gave no clue. The scale of values and comparisons on which he relied for such things had long since crumbled to dust.

A smaller speeding artifact came near enough for astonished faces to be seen staring back at the occupants of the ovoid. Anything but godlike visages of authority and power, they conveyed a certain shyness rather than omnipotence. Black and gray wraiths, hairless and wide-eyed, they left in their wake a sense of startled surprise at the nature of the ovoid's passengers.

Fawn felt a wrenching dislocation, as if they had suddenly reversed direction and picked up speed. Sooner than they had left them behind, they were once again surrounded by hundreds of the dazzlingly effulgent tunnels. She fought to recover her internal equilibrium.

"What happened there? If felt like someone pulled the floor out from under us!"

Pulickel swallowed several times, working to clear the rising gorge from his throat. "Maybe somebody did."

"The gods saw us." Having long since resigned herself to what-ever fate had in store for them, Ascela wasn't overly concerned. Jorana gestured agreement.

"They didn't look much like gods to me," Pulickel countered. "They were small, and kind of skinny. Builders yes, engineers cer-tainly, perhaps miracle-workers even, but gods? I don't think so."

"I know what happened." Fawn squeezed her eyes shut, blinked once, and shook her head. "Somebody just pulled our superstring."

He summoned up his usual subdued smile. "I wouldn't doubt it. I wonder what they're going to do with us now that they've seen us?"

It didn't take long to find out. There was a renewed sense of slowing. Their tunnel took a sharp turn away from the mass of fiery filaments, which vanished rapidly behind them. This was followed by an interval of utter blackness.

Not long thereafter, the ovoid stopped. Light slowly returned to the interior. Not light from a million stars, or a thousand blazing plasma tunnels, but a softer illumination. Moonlight, supplemented by the flickering dance of torches and lanterns.

The ovoid was oozing its way out of the green mass. They were back.

Through the transparent walls they could see a joyous mob

of Parramati leaping and hopping toward them. And when the far end of the elliptical capsule evaporated, they could hear them, as well.

Behind him, Fawn Seaforth was speculating on their unexpected return. "They sent us back. Reprogrammed the egg, or threw us into reverse, or whatever was necessary. But they sent us back." Rolling onto hands and knees, she prepared to exit in Pulickel's wake. "I have a feeling we weren't supposed to be where we were, sort of like a kid who borrows the family transport and goes for a run without first asking permission."

"I disagree." Emerging from the ovoid, he fought to make sense of what they'd seen. "I think the process was automatic from beginning to end."

Pushing past him, the jubilant Parramati surrounded Ascela and Jorana, embracing them exuberantly. There was much clasping of hands and rubbing of snouts. Ears bent forward to catch the travelers' every bark while sensitive nostrils sniffed for signs of foreign roads. Swallowed by the howling stones, the two big persons had been given up for lost. Their return, alive and in apparent good health, was cause for more than ordinary celebration.

Congratulations were passed on to the humans, as well. Pulickel dimly heard Jorana explaining that they had visited the abode of the gods, seen many wonders, and traversed the preeminent road. It was a miraculous place, the Torrelauapan big person avowed, but not for Parramati. Torrelau, Mallatyah, and the rest of the islands were better. None disputed him, there being little merit in trying to remonstrate with an eyewiteness.

What it ultimately proved, of course, was that those who hewed to the ways of kusum would always have miracles and wonders at their beck and call, to enhance their lives and confound their enemies.

A hand clutched at Pulickel's shoulder, one with five familiar fingers instead of three long, double-jointed ones. Fawn was looking down at him and smiling.

"How did that compare to the trip you made with the transportation stones? At least this time nobody came back comatose."

"Completely different. This time I felt like something was in control, that it wasn't random jumping from place to place." He looked past her, to the glowing green bulk. Its radiance had not diminished. "These howling stones assemble themselves into some kind of station or terminus. It's one tiny part of the incredible transportation system we saw. Those hundreds of tunnels—many if not all of them must begin and end with terminals just like or similar to this." Excitement shone in his eyes.

She was nodding slowly. "Tunnels or highways, it's all the same. Thousands of them, all leading . . . where?"

"We can find out." His tone was urgent, eager. "Make a map, learn the routings."

Her eyes widened. "Whoa, let's back up a step. We still don't know for certain that someone built these."

"Of course we do. We even saw some of the builders."

"We saw aliens. We don't know that they were the originators of the tunnel system, or that the builders even still exist. You don't have to be an engineer to find your way around on public transport."

"No, but somebody keeps those tunnels functional. Somebody lives on that spherical artificial platform facing the enclosed sun, and somebody builds and operates starships the size of worlds. Or planiforms worlds into starships. If not the original builders, then who?"

She made a face. "Ask me another simple one."

"Leap of faith, remember? Sometimes you just have to accept, even in science." He was puzzled by her tentativeness. "These beings englobe stars and tap black holes for power. They string tubes of supercharged plasma between star systems, probably between galaxies, and maybe between adjoining universes. They're for real, and we have to make contact with them."

She smiled wanly. "Excuse me if I don't feel up to monkeying with anything like that. I'm a field xenologist; not a philosopher, metaphysician, or theoretical physicist."

"Same here," he retorted. "I just like to see what lies over the next mountain." He was looking past her now. "All those stars, all those systems! There could have been a thousand intelligent races out there."

"A million," she added somberly.

"Yes, a million—and we only saw the one. Don't tell me you didn't get the feeling that they reacted to our presence."

"Reacted to it," she murmured, "by turning us around and getting rid of us."

"The engineers." Pulickel was insistent. "The builders. I know they didn't look like much, but that doesn't mean anything."

"So I've been told."

He missed her sarcasm entirely. "But why a terminus here? And why abandon it who knows how long ago, along with the other stones? It's almost as if they wanted to break connections with this system, or this part of the galaxy, permanently."

Extracting a drink cylinder from her pack, Fawn snapped the tip open. It chilled immediately and she downed half the contents in a series of long swallows, then looked long and hard at her colleague. "A reasonable interpretation of the evidence. Think about it."

He turned away to eye the perfect, unpolluted night sky of Senisran. "But that still doesn't explain why this world?"

She brooded. "Maybe Senisran isn't the only one with connections. Maybe if you know where and how to look, howling stones can be found on other worlds within the Commonwealth."

He gestured sharply at the amorphous structure from which the cryptic emerald radiance continued to emanate powerfully. "Nobody's ever found anything like this."

"You mean nobody's ever reported finding anything like this," she corrected him. "That's not the same thing as knowing for a fact that nothing like it has ever been found." She waved at the star-speckled but uninformative heavens. "There could be howling stones scattered across half the Arm without humans or thranx or AAnn or any of the other sentient races knowing about them." After draining the drink cylinder, she tucked the empty container back in her pack.

"There are a lot of tribes and clans right here on Senisran, and of them all only the Parramati have access to and knowledge of the stones. And that probably by accident. Who knows? This may be the beginning of the discovery of sacred stones throughout the Commonwealth."

His voice fell. "You're mocking me."

"Nothing of the sort. Just being realistic." She looked back at the glowing green terminal, or whatever it was. "Maybe I'm just not ready to rethink everything I know about natural law."

Before he could respond, Ascela hopped in between them. The Torrelauapan big person regarded them both. "We have made a decision. All the big persons of all the islands, resolving together. Jorana and I have told them of what we have seen and experienced, and a conclusion has been reached."

Fawn brightened at this return to reality. "You mean you're going to accept the treaty?"

Ascela peered up at her. "You have already been told: we make no treaties with anyone. This is not about treaties. Our kusum has just proven its superiority to all other ways of knowing and of acting. Commanding such knowledge frees us from any need to concern ourselves with your technology or that of the shiny-skinned AAnn.

"There will be no treaties. No one will be allowed to come and dig in our islands. We readily forgo any benefits this might have brought to us." The seriousness of her pronouncement was confirmed by her careful inflection.

"You have seen how the stones are tied to our kusum and how kusum relies for support on the stones. There will be no more demonstrations. The howling stones will be removed and returned to their places of rest throughout the islands."

"No, you can't do that!" Seeing the look in the eyes of the two big persons and interpreting it correctly, an agitated Pulickel struggled to compose himself. "I mean, you need to think this through carefully. If the howling stones are disassembled, next time they may not fit together properly. Or the source of their energy could disappear."

"It does not matter." Ascela was unyielding. "The Goggelai is ended. We have seen the meaning of the howling stones, and that is enough. It opens the road that does not heal, or make the heart grow, or bring happiness. A road that gives questions but not answers holds nothing for us. Closing it will keep kusum pure." She put her face close to the xenologist's. "It was to try to show you the importance of this that the Goggelai was held."

At a gesture from Jorana, several big persons stepped forward. It was obvious to both visiting humans what the Parramati intended to do next. They had assembled the remarkable terminal stone by stone, and they were going to break it down by employing precisely the same procedure.

Ignoring Fawn's warning, Pulickel rushed to place himself between the advancing big persons and the green mass. His words were hurried and so his enunciation of the alien words and phrases not as polished as usual.

"Please, you cannot do this!" He indicated the edifice behind him, the protruding cone of the ovoid. "I cannot explain its importance unless you give me some time. There are concepts that are difficult to render in your language. But I can tell you, with every fiber of my being, that this is more important than mining rights, than any treaty, than my life, or yours, or the supposed sanctity of kusum.

"Your traditions will not be harmed by leaving this as it is, to be examined and studied. Indeed, I promise you that they will be enhanced by the knowledge that is to be gained."

Jorana had joined the gathering line of big persons. His reply was flat. "We will begin by removing the largest stone from the top. One by one, the stone masters will take their stones back home. This is the way of kusum."

Ascela was less brusque. "We have learned what the Goggelai had to teach us, friend Pu'il. You should have learned it, too."

Pulickel didn't move. "You can't just destroy something like this, just take it apart and throw away its promise!" Behind him, the front end of the ovoid still gaped temptingly, beckoning to long-vanished passengers.

Standing off to one side, Fawn spoke gently. "I think we ought to listen to them, Pulickel. This—this is almost too big."

He shot her a challenging look. "What are you talking about? Are you siding with these aborigines?"

She stiffened. "Put it that way if it makes you feel more comfortable. We have no conception of the possible ramifications of continuing to use this device. Neither do the Parramati. We're dealing with something more than mere science here. This is a door to a technology we can't begin to understand. Maybe, just maybe, we're not advanced enough, not mature enough to deal with it."

His gaze narrowed. "Don't be oblique with me, Fawn. You know I can't stand that. What are you trying to say?" The Parramati held their ground, watching the two humans, listening to their strange speech.

"You had a bad experience with the transportation stones. Just two stones." She nodded in the direction of the softly lambent terminal. "We were lucky this time. Next try might be different. A photo-trap is a wonderful piece of technology. They're placed all around the station to secure specimens for study. But the fauna they catch probably don't think they're such a wonderful piece of technology. They don't even know what's happened to them, or how. If we're not careful, we could find ourselves in a similar position."

He shook his head sadly. "This is a modus for travel, not a trap! I am sorry, Fawn, but your analogy fails me. I cannot believe what I am hearing—and from a fellow scientist, no less." He spared a quick glance for the terminal, as if to assure himself it was still there.

"This discovery may change our view of the entire cosmos. It's fundamental. The tunnels may give us access not to a few new worlds but to millions. It will alter humankind's entire future."

"Yes," she murmured, "but how? New physics are one thing. New ways of thinking are harder to cope with. We can't even keep a lasting peace with the AAnn or maintain psychological peace among our own kind. What makes you think that we're ready to deal with hundreds, maybe thousands of new sentient species, at least one of whom is not just more advanced than we are but inconceivably more advanced? Beings who push worlds around like cookie crumbs."

"There's nothing magical about this." He indicated the terminal. "Once the principles are understood, we can manufacture our own and access the tunnel network with them. I have yet to hear of a piece of engineering that dedicated research couldn't break down."

"As easy as that," she muttered.

"Yes," he replied defiantly, "as easy as that. We'll use the tunnels to travel wherever we wish. I'm not saying that the process will be simple, or immediate, but it will happen."

"I'm not so sure." She took a step toward him. "I really think maybe it would be better to let the Parramati take charge of these stones. They'll keep them safe, and someday the humanx will discover the secrets of the tunnels on its own. When we're ready."

"We stand on the threshold of the discovery of the ages and you stand there spouting Luddite clichés." He eyed her pityingly.

She was not to be moved. "I just believe in taking existence one universe at a time."

He backed up until he was standing next to the ovoid. "Come with me, Fawn."

"Come with you? Come with you where?" She watched him warily. "What are you thinking now?"

"We'll go back. Instead of racing about aimlessly we'll find some way to make contact. Draw attention to ourselves. It is the right thing to do. You'll see. I have so many questions . . ."

"Too many questions. I'm sorry, Pulickel, but you're wrong about this. Let the Parramati dismantle the terminal. Then we'll talk. I'm having enough trouble trying to deal with this one world without having to worry about thousands. Let's see if the humanx can get a proper handle on this one corner of this one galaxy before we expose it to a few thousand others we know nothing about and may not be able to handle. Somehow I don't think that we and the thranx are the only intelligent species with an agenda for advancement."

He stared at her in disbelief, tight-lipped and quivering with anger and frustration. Had she lost her mind or just gone troppo? She'd been too long alone in this place.

Finally he would get the recognition he deserved. Government-wide, society-wide recognition; not just piddling little promotions in the aftermath of each assignment successfully carried out. He would have anything he wanted. This would make him the most famous scientist in the Commonwealth, placing him on a level with Newton and Einstein and Kurita. And his colleague, his *friend*, wanted to consign it all to the care of a group of heavy-legged aboriginal aliens, who in their turn would reduce it to a pile of useless, inert green rocks.

Absurd, unthinkable, mad. He would *not* be denied.

He had only once used the pistol that was part of his field kit. It was intended for defense against Senisran's less benevolent species. But he'd carried similar devices on other worlds and was no stranger to their function. They were tools, nothing more. With careful deliberation he removed it from its holster.

". . . and that's why we—," Fawn was telling Ascela and Jorana when she saw the gun. She stopped in midsentence, her eyes widening. Pulickel had seen her surprised before, but never shocked. A first time for everything, he told himself.

"What . . . do you think you are doing?"

"You know, Fawn, a man waits all his life for one big chance, one real opportunity to rise above the crowd, to distinguish himself from the herd. To take it and fail is bad, but not to take it at all is a hundred times worse." It felt good to give voice to his feelings. He might not convince her, but he was certainly convincing himself.

"Most people never get that chance. I've spent a career toiling for the Department, doing good work but not great work, receiving commendations but not accolades. When the media want comments on the division's inner workings, I'm never the one they interview. When procedural decisions are made, I'm not the one consulted. I'm a valuable functionary, but nothing more. Well, I'm tired of being a cog."

She did her best to reassure him, but she wasn't smiling. "Take away one cog and the whole machine stops."

"Nice try. Please don't come any closer, Ascela." The big person had taken a short hop toward the diminutive xenologist. Now she retreated. Fawn had demonstrated the effectiveness of modern weapons for the Torrelauapans on several occasions. Ascela herself had seen a pistol cut a revavuaa in half. She passed a warning along to the increasingly restless big persons nearby.

Retreating slowly, Pulickel used his left hand to feel behind him for the entrance to the ovoid. "Please keep back. It would distress me greatly if I had to shoot anyone."

Fawn just stared at him. "Don't do this, Pulickel. You're not feeling well."

"On the contrary, I feel fine. Very much alive, thank you. Exhilarated, even. I'm going back, Fawn. By myself, it seems. I'm going to try to make contact, to learn as much as I can, and then I am returning. I will see that you receive due credit for your degree of participation in this seminal exploration."

Watching the weapon, she chanced a couple of steps in his direction. "You need to come back to the station with me, Pulickel. You need to rest. I'll take care of you." Striking a pose, she bestowed on him the most inviting, sexy smile in her considerable but infrequently unveiled arsenal. "Come with me, and we'll talk it over."

"Just stay back, Fawn." The pistol didn't waver. "Tell everyone to keep away." This wasn't as difficult as he feared. Unable to see over the heads and ears of their tightly packed brethren, most of the Parramati were unaware of what was going on.

Still pointing the gun, he climbed backward into the ovoid and sat down. It was easier now. They could only come at him from one direction. As he tried to watch Fawn and the nearest big persons simultaneously, it occurred to him that he was going to look very foolish if this time the device didn't react to his presence and nothing happened.

Her expression a mix of hurt and anger, Fawn moved to converse with Ascela. He couldn't hear what they were saying, but they glanced frequently in his direction. Let them look all they wanted, he thought grimly. He was snug and secure within the ovoid.

It was all bluff, of course. He couldn't shoot anyone. But the Parramati did not know that, and Fawn didn't know him well enough to count on it. Especially if she thought he'd gone off the deep end. By the time she reached the conclusion that he was incapable of harming another intelligent being, he would be long gone. Or so he hoped.

As he sat pondering, the pistol positioned loosely between his knees, the entrance sealed over. The sensation of movement returned and the outside world darkened as for the second time the ovoid slid backward into the terminal. Outside, he could see Fawn shouting at him and gesticulating. No sound penetrated his shelter.

He smiled to himself. Throughout his career, his official reports had been models of precision and organization. The one he intended to file from Torrelau would top them all. It had to, since it was destined to be filed alongside *On the Origin of Species*, *A General Theory of Relativity*, and *Proposals for a Special Gravitational Algorithm for Space-Plus Routing*.

For a second time that night blackness enveloped the ovoid. Vibration increased.

He was on his way.

CHAPTER

20

It seemed to take a little longer than the first time until the capsule burst out into the realm of fiery plasma tunnels and rampant rivers of channeled energy. Having some idea of what to expect, he was able to devote more time to studious observation and less to slack-jawed amazement.

After a while the tunnels began to fall from view, exactly as before, until only the one down which he was racing remained. Arching sharply to the left, it punched back into the star-rich region that had so entranced him and his fellow travelers previously.

Somewhat to his own surprise, he recognized several systems and structures in passing. But then, he'd always been good at recording details for future analysis, and when some of those "details" were the size of entire worlds, they tended to remain firmly in memory.

He saw new megastructures, as well, and marveled afresh at the skills of those who had fashioned them. Whoever these beings were, they had mastered the art of materials science, for art it had to be called. They had bent matter to their needs. He made notes using the old-fashioned stylus and paper he always carried in his pack, and sketched as best he could. *That* human technology, at least, seemed to function without difficulty in this place.

Unexpectedly, the incredible starfield began to shift less rapidly around him. He was slowing, much sooner than on the previous journey. Putting up his writing materials, he turned within the ovoid. No immediate changes were visible, but then, the smooth interior offered little that was subject to alteration.

External motion ceased. All about him, channeled plasma roared silently. The capsule came to, as near as he could tell in the absence of suitable reference points, a complete stop.

While he did not panic, his curiosity was underscored by a growing tension. What if something had gone wrong? As ancient as the system was, it was not unreasonable to expect that individual components would break down from time to time. It was a dazzling, resplendent place to be marooned, but he could die here as readily as in total darkness. As alone as it was possible for a human being to be, he sat and meditated and waited for something to happen.

Only the sharp curve of the tunnel allowed him to see the object as it approached. Though a long way off, he was able to determine that it was definitely moving toward him. Immense beyond imagining, the star-treading torus was fringed with an exotic and unrecognizable assortment of protrusions and bulges. It was accompanied by a flotilla of other craft that darted and drifted about it like worker ants attending to their queen. The least of these vessels was far larger than the biggest KK-drive ship ever built.

The plasma tunnel down which he had been racing was rapidly vanishing into the exact center of the toroidal wanderer. It did not reemerge on the other side. One did not have to be an alien megaengineer to understand what was happening.

The road-builders were taking up the pavement.

Where the tunnel disappeared there flared an aurora the size of the Earth. Energy was not consumed so much as it was shifted. Unable in any way to affect his own destiny, he stared, enthralled, as the torus maintained its methodical advance. If it did not stop before it reached him, both he and the ovoid would vanish in an insignificant puff of ruptured particles.

Then he was no longer alone. Vehicles too small to be seen at a distance, which had been dwarfed by the torus and its support craft, were suddenly hovering close by, just outside the raging tunnel wall. As the conduit collapsed around him, he was able to make out more of the big-eyed, smooth-skinned creatures he and his companions had glimpsed so briefly on their previous visit. His earlier impressions were confirmed. Physically, at least, these creatures were decidedly unprepossessing. Slight of stature, they were small beings with big machines, and they were closing down the Parramati tunnel. All because of him?

Their aversion to uninvited guests could no longer be denied.

While several of the small superfast craft remained nearby, allowing their occupants to study him, others vanished, presumably returning to the vicinity of the advancing torus. He found that he was starting to sweat. Though he'd faced death on more than one world, it remained a confrontation he did not relish.

A jolt sharp enough to knock him backward rattled the ovoid. Acceleration resumed. Gathering himself, he saw that the torus had begun to recede. Or more likely, he from it. His sanctuary had been thrust into reverse. At the whim of alien engineers, he was going to live a little while longer.

Several of the small craft tracked his withdrawal, paralleling the ovoid as it retraced its path back up the tunnel. Though he felt he was moving more slowly than before, he soon lost sight of the plasma-consuming torus. When eventually the starfield vanished to be replaced by the Gordian knot of intertwined tunnels, so did his escort.

For all their inconceivable physical accomplishments, the engineers had struck him as a timid species. It was an impression, a sensation, that ran deeper than a few brief visual contacts ought to have been able to convey, but no less tangible for that. As tangible as the feeling that they didn't want anything to do with him or with his kind.

Though he couldn't be certain from what he'd seen, it seemed that they were in the process of closing down the tunnel permanently. Privacy and isolation were one thing, paranoia was another. Had the entire gigantic apparatus required to shut down the tunnel been brought into use only since his prior journey in the ovoid? Had that visit set off some kind of alarm? Certainly these cosmos-spanning beings couldn't be that frightened of him.

The corollaries were unsettling. They implied that there was something else to be afraid of. Something that on the basis of a tiny, insignificant intrusion would drive beings like these not just to close off but to break down a construct as complex as the plasma tunnel, to eliminate it from the fabric of existence. From within the safety of the ovoid he had seen many wonders. What was out there that he had not seen?

What was out there that so terrified these masters of matter?

The rationale for the terminal's original dissipation was clear enough. Its makers no longer had need of it and did not want it used. Its components had been taken apart and scattered, perhaps in haste. Evolving subsequently, primitive Parramati had learned that when combined, certain stones had useful consequences. By far the most complex of these combinations resulted in the auto-reconstitution of the Senisran terminal. No doubt the engineers hadn't counted on anyone discovering the component stones, much less their inherent recombinant capabilities.

Among other things, it suggested that they had left in haste. That, too, was not a pleasant thought.

The blackness returned, blotting out his view of other tunnels and rampaging energies. In contrast to previous journeying, the ride became bumpy and uneven. Once, a violent wrenching to the right slammed him against the opposite wall of the ovoid. Dazed, he lay on the floor, trying to focus on the rose-hued ceiling. How far behind him the consuming torus lay he did not know, but clearly its operation was affecting the entire length of the tunnel.

He found himself wondering if it would collapse completely before he made it back to Senisran.

The ovoid began to slow and he relaxed. Any moment now, he knew, it would start to emerge from the terminal, the end would open, and he would step out to rejoin Fawn and the waiting big persons. Feeling suddenly ashamed, he knew he owed all of them a general apology. Blinded by the light of potential discovery, he had acted in haste and, not to put too fine a point on it, rather badly. He determined to make things right with the Parramati as well as with his dismayed associate.

The capsule came to a halt. Outside the transparent walls, darkness continued to reign supreme. No soft moonlight, no welcoming lanterns illuminated his anxious expression. He could see outside, but only into varying degrees of blackness. A feeling of dread crept over him.

He had been here before.

On the fringes, on the edge, on the half-safe periphery only, he sensed. This time penetration was different, deeper, darker. He had traveled to the place where thrived the worst nightmares of childhood, the threat of oblivion, purgatory, and damnation.

They had sent him here, he realized as he tried to shrink back inside himself. The alien engineers had put him on course to this place, perhaps shunting the ovoid onto another tunnel. He'd been wondering what made them so uneasy, so apprehensive of visitation.

Beware what questions you formulate, he thought feebly, for you may get answers.

Bringing up his knees, he drew himself into a tight fetal ball with his soul in the center. Only the faint pink glow that emanated from the capsule walls kept him sane, gave him something to focus on. Though the tunnel that had brought him to this place remained intact, even the burning plasma of its substance was overwhelmed and subdued by the monstrous, invasive darkness that seemed to be everywhere and everything. While his senses fed him perceptions he didn't want, his mind conjured images he was unable to banish.

Something was out there. A formless form, it was growing curious about the microscopic intrusion in its midst. He wanted to scream but feared provoking more intimate attention. He was also afraid that when he opened his mouth nothing would emerge. While the composition of the Presence remained unknown to him, he had no doubt as to its active nature.

It was Evil.

His mind shrank from confrontation, from contemplation. Once there might have been stars in this place. Suns, planets, people not unlike humans or seni or even alien mega-engineers. All gone now, all vanished; beaten down, overwhelmed, smothered by the darkness that occupied this space. There was only one of it, he sensed, and it was everywhere.

It wanted more. It wanted totality, and was relentless in its search for pathways and conduits to other places. Tunnels, Pulickel told himself. It possessed no directing intelligence, no mindful purpose. It was a disease, a cosmotic pathogen, aimless and blind as a bacterium, and it had to be isolated. Vaster than imagination, it relentlessly consumed galaxies, whole universes, engulfing them like trophies, snuffing out the light of stars and intelligence, leaving behind not so much as a breath of interstellar hydrogen to begin the life-reaction anew.

This, Pulickel knew, was what the engineers were so afraid of. They had used the tunnels to flee. He understood.

Perhaps his understanding triggered some mental-mechanical subset of a kind he could not understand, or possibly it had all been carefully timed. The engineers could not only build: they were also capable of compassion. They would show him this thing, but they would not leave even one intelligent being to it. To do so would have been to violate their own rationale for existence.

Besides which, the dead could not lead by example.

A mindless gibbering Something reached out to flay his soul, but he was already beyond its reach. The ovoid was moving again, carrying him away from that place of aversion and loathing, picking up speed as it fled. The doors of his mind, which had shut tight in self-defense, began to reopen. Cold sweat plastered shirt and shorts to his skin.

He'd been exposed to only an insignificant portion of It, he knew, for a minuscule length of time, and that was too much.

It felt as if days had passed, but in reality it had been only minutes. He'd returned full of questions to the universe of the engineers, and had received one answer too many. Now he wanted only to get away, to go home. Home was Earth, but Senisran would do. Anyplace there was light and life would do.

Did universes bicker? he wondered. Oblivious and indifferent to what he thought of as life, did light do battle with the darkness? He'd always thought of the cosmos as a fractious place, but never before as a sinister one. The physical revelations and technological enlightenment for which he had embarked on his present journey seemed suddenly inconsequential. *Everything* seemed suddenly inconsequential.

Careful, he told himself. That way lies the lassitude that leads to madness.

Not long after he determined that he was likely to survive the experience, he found himself returned. Plainly visible through the transparent walls, agitated Parramati rushed the emerging ovoid. Many were armed. Towering above them, Fawn was borne along in their midst.

Moving, the capsule stopped. Sealed, it opened. Trying to rise, he found that he couldn't move. So tightly had he balled himself up that his legs had cramped in position.

"Help me," he heard himself say. It was a pale shadow of his normal voice, but his voice it was. He was astonished at how relieved he was to hear it.

Several big persons squeezed into the ovoid. Their arms and hands were not strong enough to lift him, but they used their powerful hind legs to gently push him out the aperture.

"Pulickel? You can get up now." Fawn was there, staring down at him with a mixture of mistrust and concern. When she saw that he couldn't move, her misgivings vanished. "He's alive but there's something wrong with him," she said to Ascela, who stood close at hand. As the Parramati bent to assist her colleague, she carefully removed his pistol from its holster.

They carried him away from the terminal and over to the edge of the meadow. With her support and that of the attendant natives, the errant xenologist slowly regained the use of his limbs.

Behind and around them, the chanting had resumed. Not quite a dirge, it rode on a cadence that was noticeably slower than what had gone before. Boosted by his fellows, a big person from Mallatyah stood atop the glowing green terminal. As the others looked on, he removed a large center stone from the summit and passed it down to waiting hands.

The piercing shaft of emerald light winked out. Near the base, the glassy ovoid sank back into the interior. One by one, the howling stones were detached from the remarkable structure they had formed and were distributed among the gathering, like a sugar cube being dissembled by ants. The resonant whine that had filled the meadow and reverberated through the surrounding trees faded to silence.

The Goggelai was over.

Clouds masked the moon, enhancing the importance of lanterns and torches. Fawn eyed her colleague reproachfully. "Think you can walk?"

Bending, he massaged his thighs. "I hope so. I'd like to walk. How do I look?"

She squinted in the intermittent light. "Like you've been through hell."

"Something like that." He looked behind him. "I see that they're taking the terminal apart. Good."

"Good?" She frowned in confusion. "That's not what you were saying a little while ago. What made you change your mind?"

Haunted eyes gazed back at her. "Being through hell. I will explain later, as best I can. There's a lot to explain. I got answers to questions, but they weren't the ones I wanted to ask." Turning, he started purposefully toward the shrinking mound that had been the terminal. "This is taking too long. Let's help them."

She hesitated. "That may not be such a good idea. A number of them want to kill you. A few would like to kill me, as well."

He nodded understandingly. "They can't hurt me. I've already died. If they don't do anything to me, I am certain they will not harm you."

She moved to join him. "You're very sure of yourself. What happened to you in there?"

"A minor epiphany. I'm pretty sure I'm the same person I was when I left, but I believe that the basic model has suffered some improvements."

They were not allowed to join in the dismantling. Before they could reach the remnants of the terminal, they were surrounded by a cluster of excited big persons.

"Do not try to talk to us again. We do not wish an alliance, a treaty, with either you or the AAnn," the leader of the group declared loudly.

Pulickel's response was an apologetic smile. "I know. We won't try to force one on you anymore." Fawn looked at him sharply but he ignored her. "You must do as kusum dictates, and we will abide by that."

Clearly his response was not the one they had been expecting. Gradually weapons were put up and much soft barking ensued. It was Jorana who finally spoke.

"Be warned. *You* know the stones, but if any others of your kind come to study them, we will throw them into the deep sea."

The stones, Pulickel wondered, or any newcomers? He hoped to avoid either eventuality. It was evident that the stones could be studied only with the aid and acquiescence of the Parramati. Any further attempts to push the issue would result in the loss to science of the stones and all they represented. He wanted very much to learn more about them. He just didn't want to use them to go traveling.

He'd done enough of that.

The cluster of armed Parramati wavered. Pulickel jumped on

their indecision. "I promise that if you let us go, neither I nor F'an will speak of this night to *our* big persons. No others will come—at least, not for a long time. Let us stay and learn the ways of kusum. Isn't that what you want?"

"We never tried to prevent it," Jorana responded. "It was only that you and the shiny-skinned ones thought you knew better, that your ways were superior." Flashing, slitted eyes came close to examine the xenologist's face. "I see that you now know otherwise."

"I'm not sure about that," Pulickel replied, "but I do know that certain roads are meant to be avoided. F'an and I must follow our own kusum, but that does not mean we cannot learn from yours.

"We will report that the Parramat Archipelago is not ready for development. Requests for mining concessions will be denied and actively discouraged. We will help you maintain your kusum."

The Parramati discussed the xenologist's words. Though Pulickel listened intently, he was unable to decipher their overlapping dialogue. But their posture was no longer threatening, and he allowed himself to feel hopeful.

Conversation ceased and Jorana turned to face the two humans. "We will accept this if F'an will guarantee it." The senior big person looked pointedly at Pulickel. "*She* has never broken her word to us."

"Of course I guarantee it." She put a hand on Pulickel's shoulder and squeezed firmly. "I'll keep him in line."

Now that the tension had been released, he couldn't repress a grin. "I believe I would like that."

Jorana's lips curled approvingly. "It is good that you finally recognize the truth of kusum." A three-fingered hand reached for his own. "Now we can be friends again."

The xenologist accepted the proffered fingers in the traditional entwined manner, having to strain his less flexible joints to accommodate those of the far more limber seni. "I am sorry for what happened and for what I did. Sometimes if you want something badly enough, it can make you blind and dumb."

Fatigue and the lateness of the hour led to the gradual breakup of the great gathering. Carrying their respective stones, individual big persons retired to their assigned longhouses and huts. Tomorrow, Fawn knew, the impressive armada of outriggers lined up on the beach below would once more put out to sea, swallowed up in ones and twos by the blue horizon on their way back to outlying alien islands replete with unknown mysteries and exotic names.

They slept in Torrelauapa that night. By midmorning, Pulickel avowed as how he thought he could manage the hike back to the station. Taking no chances, she monitored his vital signs at regular intervals. A couple of times he stumbled, but without injury. By the time they topped the last ridge he was near exhaustion.

"I wonder," she hypothesized as they started down, "if the Parramati have the only correct view of existence and every other sentient species is wrong. Maybe we should all adopt their belief system."

"Not if it means having to live by the rules of the sacred stones." Pulickel spoke with feeling. "Learning their properties is one thing, letting them govern your existence is another." He shook his head. "Too many surprises there."

"If we don't report an occasional revelation, we'll be replaced here," she warned him.

He wasn't worried. "We'll handle it. If we do things right, eventually Ophhlia authority will tire of reading pleasant nothings about the Parramat Archipelago and focus on more fertile and accommodating island groups. We'll bore them with mildly entertaining but commercially unviable discoveries. Meanwhile we'll learn what we can about the stones."

"And then?" she prompted him.

He stepped carefully over a slippery spot. "I don't know, but I'm sure we'll find out." He smiled. "Kusum will tell us how to proceed."

She frowned at him. "You sound like a convert. What happened in there? Did you have some kind of religious experience?"

To her surprise, he took his time replying. "I don't know. I haven't decided yet if it's quantifiable. But I will let you know if and when I figure it all out."

He wasn't joking, she saw. A ready quip sprang to mind, and then she remembered the expression that had been frozen on his face when they'd hauled him out of the ovoid. She decided, for now at least, to swallow the joke.

She watched him carefully all the rest of that day and into the morning of the next. By breakfast time he was nearly his usual imperturbable, infuriating self.

"How do you feel?" She picked at her reconstituted omelet.

"Worn out, dizzy, utterly drained." He sipped at his juice. "Thoroughly ashamed of myself."

"Forget it. The Parramati forgave you. I guess I can, too." She waved a utensil at him. "I understand temptation. I gave in to it once. It wasn't profession-related, but it did cost me a piece of myself."

"Want to tell me about it?" he inquired solicitously.

"No. Let's just say it had to do with the male need to triumph and conquer over all odds." She didn't look up at him.

"Don't gender-generalize me."

"Why not?" Now she did look up. "It's one of those psychological components of human society that we'll never be able to rid ourselves of entirely. Deal with it. I've had to."

"I think we should start with a growing stone," he said calmly, changing the subject. "A small one. From its study we can hopefully extrapolate and infer a great deal."

"I'll speak to Ascela about it." Her comment was noncommittal. "When the time is right." They ate for a while in silence before he spoke again.

"I don't think it's going to matter if the howling stones are ever used to reassemble the terminal again or not. Because they were shutting down the tunnel behind me. The engineers."

"Shutting it down?" She eyed him uncertainly. "How do you 'shut down' something like what we experienced? It's too big, it's—"

"Small," he told her. "Very small. In the scheme of things. On the scale of mega-engineering. While they were doing it they sent me someplace else." The dark spot in his mind that wouldn't go away flared like burning oil. "They wanted to show me something."

"Is that what you meant before, when you spoke about being through hell?" Her tone was gentle.

"It was the worst thing you can imagine. Universal evil. Or maybe a universe of evil, I don't know. All I do know is that I am glad no one will ever be able to access it from Senisran. The engineers are hiding from it. At least, that's the impression I received."

"I'm not sure I understand."

"I am not certain I do, either." He finished the last of his juice.

"Why put a terminal on Senisran?" she wondered after a pause. "Why this world?"

"Why not Senisran? Maybe you were right, Fawn, and there are disassembled terminals on other worlds. Now that we know what to look for, we might be able to find them." His voice fell. "I'm just not so sure that would be such a good idea. We might accidentally open a tunnel to the wrong place. To *that* place. Only when we know more about the stones, about how they function and on what levels, will humanxkind be able to think seriously about collecting howling stones and accessing tunnels."

She nodded understandingly. "Other worlds will have to be searched, of course. It's the way we're made."

"I know. But there are all kinds of searches. Vigilant and circumspect is best. To be safe, the knowledge must be restricted and access controlled."

"I'm certainly not sorry I missed what you went through," she told him.

"Yes. Be glad that you did. Try as I may, and believe me, I intend to, it's something that will never leave me. Each time I relive it, I will die a little. But there is something I will always wonder about."

Leaning back in her chair, she deliberately put her amazing legs up on the table for him to enjoy. "What's that?"

"If the race we've been calling the engineers, with their sun-girdling artificial worlds and plasma tunnels and black-hole energy vents, moved from here to there—and why. Or if this galaxy, this universe, was just another way point in their travels. In their search."

With effortless and unsurpassing grace, she crossed her legs. "Search? What kind of search?"

Reluctantly he shifted his eyes away from the expanse of exposed flesh. "For a safe place."

Swinging her feet to the floor and rising from her seat, she walked around the table until she was standing behind him. With great deliberation, she put one hand on his forehead and eased him back against her. She could not see him close his eyes, but she could hear him sigh.

"The Parramati are right about one thing, Pulickel Tomochelor. Each of us picks his or her own road. Me, I choose not to worry about whether one universe is battling for dominance over another, or over several." She stroked his brow, enjoying the slight but solid weight of him against her. "For a long time I wasn't sure that I liked you. Then I wasn't sure what was going to happen to this installation, or to us. Now I'm not entirely sure what I want to do next."

His voice was easy now, relaxed. "You're not sure of very much, are you?"

"What do you expect? I'm human." He sensed rather than saw her smile. "It's my kusum."

EPILOGUE

In another space, in another place unimaginably far away and incalculably difficult to reach, the Xunca considered what had happened. They would not interfere, of course. They had fled for reasons that could not be compromised and in the quiet interval that resulted had raised their civilization to heights greater than even they had once thought possible.

Others were not so fortunate. The Xunca monitored them, and so knew. But they never interfered, limiting their concern to their own safety and well-being. They could do nothing for others lest they pique the interest of the thing. If that happened, they would be forced to move again, and that was no longer such a simple matter. Besides, they had grown fond of their current cosmos.

They were confident but frightened, assured but afraid. Perhaps some day their science would reach a level that would enable them to deal finally with the ancient nemesis. Until then they could only live, and strive, and hide. Lesser civilizations would have to fend for themselves.

In their observations they had made note of one exception. Unpretentious and easy to overlook, it was so extravagantly different even they failed to understand it. Whether it could affect the thing they did not know. It seemed unlikely, but it was such an anomaly that nothing could be ruled out. Or ruled in.

So they continued to watch and monitor and observe. Not out of concern for the survival of the anomaly's species, or out of any elevated sense of altruism, but because despite their grand and unparalleled accomplishments, they had not lost the curiosity that had raised them to their present lofty level of accomplishment.

Also, they were lonely.

ABOUT THE AUTHOR

Born in New York City in 1946, ALAN DEAN FOSTER was raised in Los Angeles, California. After receiving a bachelor's degree in political science and a Master of Fine Arts in motion pictures from UCLA in 1968–1969, he worked for two years as a public relations copywriter in a small Studio City, California, firm.

His writing career began in 1968 when August Derleth bought a long letter of Foster's and published it as a short story in his biannual *Arkham Collector Magazine*. Sales of short fiction to other magazines followed. His first try at a novel, *The Tar-Aiym Krang*, was published by Ballantine Books in 1972.

Foster has toured extensively around the world. Besides traveling, he enjoys classical and rock music, old films, basketball, body surfing, scuba driving, and weight lifting. He has taught screenwriting, literature, and film history at UCLA and Los Angeles City College.

Currently, he lives in Arizona.